Ex Libris

Edward E. Koonce, MD.

Animal Treasure

Animal Treasure

IVAN T. SANDERSON

WITH THIRTY-TWO ILLUSTRATIONS BY THE AUTHOR

THE VIKING PRESS · NEW YORK

1937

To our Auntie May
in fulfilment of a promise made when I was six,
and
to my Mother for many other reasons

Contents

Illustrations

9

Introductory

THE animals that crowd their little faces into the following pages lived, or are still living, in the deep virgin forests of West Africa, around a place called Mamfe, a place known to but a handful of the earth's inhabitants. It is some two hundred and fifty miles north-north-east of Calabar, which town is in the extreme south-east corner of the Protectorate of Nigeria. There is probably some doubt in most people's minds as to where those places are. There was in mine before I went to Africa, so if it is of interest to you or seems to matter, I must ask you to open an atlas as I did.

Calabar will probably be marked as Old Calabar, a statement which cannot well be refuted. If the map is exceptionally good or German, Mamfe may be indicated, but it will certainly be called Ossedinge, for what reason nobody knows, least of all the local inhabitants.

Running north from Calabar is a river known as the Cross River— a logical name for a river that one has to cross continually because of sandbars. This river suddenly turns right, out of Nigeria, into the adjacent territory mandated to Great Britain, where it loses itself in a network of waterways and the primeval forests. All the country to the west or left of this river is intersected by roads and railways; to the east is untouched, unspoiled Africa as it was before Europeans began crawling about it.

But before I go any further perhaps I had better explain why I went to Mamfe at all.

In the beginning I was a child—a very small child with very big childlike fancies. It so happened that the first light of day that I saw was in Edinburgh, which is synonymous with saying that it was grey and cold and damp. Thereafter I craved the sun from pure cussedness. Then some compassionate elder gave me a book filled with pictures of palm trees and people sleeping in the sun. My course was set.

I had a beloved nurse—I have her still—who showed me animals, who chased butterflies in the sunlight with me, and taught me to blare out the names of strange beasts as she turned over the pages of the book with palm trees in it. Somehow the ideas of sunlight, beasts, and palm trees got all mixed up in my childish fancies like a hybrid seed planted in a fertile soil.

I suppose all of us can fathom the beginnings of ourselves if we choose to think back to our childhood, yet in all our little personal histories there comes a blank. After the seeds have been planted, things go on underground until one goes to school and learns to correlate one's fancies with realities. At school I learnt that sunlight and palm trees encircled the earth's tummy like a girdle. The word "tropics" appeared on the horizon. It loomed larger and larger. I almost aggressively gave up orthodox studies for an avid compilation of a list of the antelopes of Africa, so that I had to be coerced and cajoled through essential examinations. However, through the sweat and exertions of others I found myself one day in the happy position of choosing between another year at school, before going to a university to learn more about my beloved animals, or doing something else. I chose the something else and bolted from Europe, like a shot rabbit, at the tender, impressionable, and exciting age of seventeen, my boxes filled with traps, butterfly nets, skinning implements, and all the other recognized stock-in-trade of the collector.

By a series of monotonous floating suburbias I eventually deposited myself in the land of my dreams. Palm trees sulked in the sun all around me, brown people slept, white people sweated and grumbled. It was all so exactly what I had pictured that nothing fell short of my wildest childhood fancies. I made my way across the violet waters of the East Indies to the goal of all my dreams—Macassar. Could any name be more romantic? From there I went far inland with my traps and nets and other paraphernalia, fully convinced that the work of the great Alfred Russel Wallace was about to be completed at last.

Then came the first great shock to my youthful enthusiasm. I worked and laboured by night and by day setting traps, stalking animals, skinning animals, stuffing animals, packing animals. Difficulties were surmounted with enthusiasm, but the net results when all was said and done, when all those thousands of miles back home had been accomplished, and when all the animals so painstakingly accumulated had been looked at in the cold light of a museum, amounted to what? Just nothing more than a repetition of some of the great Alfred Russel Wallace's looser moments.

There was obviously something wrong.

Slowly it dawned upon me. Scientific methods of collecting animals were out of date.

I went off to Cambridge a wiser but no less enthusiastic person. What I saw and learnt there only confirmed my half-formed theories. One professor actually put them into words. He said that zoology had been divided into three stages—*what, how,* and *why.* He explained that through the activities of countless collectors we had almost reached the end of asking *what.* All the animals of the world were more or less known and classified, though there were still little gaps to be filled in and some new forms to be found. Zoology was now in the *how* stage. Research workers were all asking *how* nature worked, and that was why the universities were encouraging experimental biology and physiology rather than what is called "systematics." The more advanced students were now beginning to ask not only *how* nature works on the lines that it does, but *why.* I now knew why I could add nothing to the work Wallace did in the year 1860. I understood why one expensive expedition after another was returning, having done little more than spend its money. I also realized why nothing seemed to be known or recorded about the actual behaviour in life of any animals except those seen or kept alive in Europe and America, and little enough about those. I even saw a reason for the endless repetition of false statements about the majority of animals.

The truth seemed to be this: Nobody knew anything about the *how* and *why* of animal behaviour other than from studying those few animals kept in institutions. Only the bold differences that can be observed through a comparison of dried and pickled remains in museums seemed to have been recorded.

My troubles in Malaya showed me how this might be rectified— only somebody had to be persuaded that this new idea was practical, necessary, and comparatively inexpensive. The game had begun in real earnest.

The task of organizing an expedition is, if you come to think of it, somewhat bewildering. Fearful problems beset one: where to go, what to collect, for whom to collect, where to get money, what to buy by way of equipment and where to buy it. These problems are not easily solved even if one is a millionaire. For a mere scientist they appeared at first to be insurmountable. I soon saw that business methods had to be employed if a real portable research station was to be taken to the jungle, and therefore the question of capital should be tackled first.

Just at that time a circular fell into my hands stating that a famous scientist required internal organs of some particular animals. Curiously enough, these animals were to be found only in the place that I had had in the back of my mind as being a promising spot for operations. I had chosen it because it had the worst climate and medical reputation in the world, and therefore a place likely to have been neglected. Even scientists have a strange habit of leaving the nastiest localities until last. I visited this famous scientist and fell completely under the spell of his quiet and wonderful personality.

Then, again by chance, I was introduced to another great man of learning who wanted definite evidence of a whale in the rivers of the same country. From him I returned to the leading scientists at Cambridge and informed them of my project; I found that they required the exotic giant water shrew from the same place, and also a general collection of the animals inhabiting the country.

While all this was going on I had been holding conversations with those friends at the British Museum who had been so kind to me since the days when I had feverishly collected the names of African antelopes. It turned out that they also wanted many things from the same country, in particular the queer tick-like *Podogona*, only a half-dozen of which had ever been collected. One and all, moreover, offered to assist me in making application for financial backing from scientific societies.

All at once half the problems were solved—where to go, what to collect, for whom, and how to cover expenses. What to buy and where to buy it didn't worry me in the least. I had thought all that out in detail, though if the scientists who backed the project had seen what I was spending money on by way of equipment, they would have had several and collective fits.

The next problem then arose: Whom should I take with me? If you ask anybody: "Whom can I get to come on an expedition with me?" the answer is invariably: "Oh, good Lord, there are thousands of young fellows who would give their souls for the opportunity!" But, believe me, there is more in it than that. When you announce that you are going to West Africa, forty per cent of the enthusiasts fall away at once; to explain that one intends to work and not shoot big game quickly disposes of another thirty per cent. Of the remainder, half will probably be zoologists. These must be eradicated without delay because there is nobody with less imagination or more hide-bound notions of procedure than the average young zoologist.

Having winnowed the applicants down thus far, the question of suitable physique must be considered. Upon this subject I hold views diametrically opposed to everybody else's, the medical world and people who have lived in the tropics not excluded. My methods have, however, worked three times to date, so this is my story and I am sticking to it.

For the tropics and hard work weed out all the athletes, sportsmen, and anybody who is large, beefy, or tough. From the remainder select all those who are at least used to and at ease in smoky bars, airless cabarets, and crowded subway trains. From these "worms," probably numbering less than half a dozen, one must take a chance upon selecting one who will not carry with him some illness that will flower in the tropics. The chance is not such a long one, because a man who can live in real smoky cabarets can live anywhere unless he is already starting to die! Last come questions of compatibility of temperament and similarity of tastes.

When I had finally despaired of finding anybody to go with me, I remembered a conversation I had had over a pot of tea in a kitchen at four o'clock in the morning some years before. By an amazing coincidence, within three days my companion of the tea-pot turned up from Paris, where he lived, and literally bumped into me.

George Russell and I got together, but instead of talking vaguely, as on the previous occasion, about tropic lands over a pot of tea, we completed the actual organization of the expedition.

George fulfilled all the conditions and yet strangely enough happened to be on the quiet a better athlete in many respects than the beefy gentlemen, and certainly a greater sportsman than anybody else I could have selected.

And so we sailed for Africa one August and went together to work out our great scheme hundreds of miles in the jungle behind Calabar. When George got persistent low fever and was told that he was dying of consumption, I rushed him down to the coast, meantime wiring frantically for somebody to be sent out to me to take his place. No sooner had George got to the coast, seen another doctor, been told that he had not the slightest trouble with his lungs or anything else, and decided to return to me, than I learnt that the substitute had already left. George waited at the coast for this substitute and brought him up to me. We had a great meeting and I soon perceived that by some fluke another amazing human being had been sent to me by the fates.

I can think of nobody but the Duke who would have fitted in with us or done such splendid work so painstakingly, despite the fact that he was half-way through an engineering course at Cambridge when he left England at three days' notice to join us. There was only one trouble. He was slightly beefy and suffered from it in characteristic fashion until he got thin. First he had an extremely violent attack of fever, went yellow, and scared us all out of our wits. Then he got his legs covered with tropical ulcers and had to return to the base camp while we were away in the northern mountains. Eventually, after a second attack of fever, he got thin like us, and was positively bouncing by the end of the trip.

The arrival of the Duke was the only major adventure of the expedition. This is the principal reason why I am going to try my hardest not to write a travelogue. There have been and are so many little histories of expeditions; so many charging rhinoceroses, humorous cooks, highest mountains to be climbed, wicked chiefs, and naughty "boys." Please let me get away from the little domestic incidents that amused and irritated us, and tell you if possible of the country and the life as we saw it through the eyes of zoologists going and living there with a definite purpose. We went not to shoot, nor merely to collect, but actually to study the animals in life and record their differences of appearance, behaviour, and habits as they really are in nature. Further, we intended to do this by the methods that are customary in museums and offices, not those that had already been tried by the few travelling or floating laboratories that had previously been in the field. I intended to do just what the museum expert does, but to do it from fresh specimens instead of from dried ones and the writings and drawings of others.

I kept a very detailed diary in Africa, and I could reproduce that in the form of a continuous story, but it would be full of bad cooks, angry chiefs, shipping offices, and all the rest. The animals would appear at odd and irregular intervals in an incomprehensible muddle—monkeys, ticks, hippopotamuses, and fleas. That is not the way we saw the country. As the animals appeared they fell into their places as in nature, so that one met first one assemblage and then another as one got deeper and deeper into the real vitals of the country.

The first thing a collector encounters in a new country is the vermin, which, as you will see shortly, is a somewhat broad term. Then, after he has been there a little time, his curiosity will lead him into the forests around. Here he will meet with an entirely different life, which in its turn will resolve itself into several more or less watertight compartments. Above there is a flying continent, and along the great rivers a completely different assemblage of animals; upon the floor of the forest another, and beneath its surface yet another. Or again, from the point of view of the animals, he will find that the frogs all behave in one way, the monkeys in another, the rats in another. On the high grassy mountains, and in the dense dripping forest patches dotted about their faces, are other entirely different animal worlds. Lastly he will meet those poor creatures who do not seem to belong to any place in particular, and are being displaced and buffeted about by the encroachment of man or the changes of nature.

I want to try and bring all these vividly before you in their exact order and place in nature, as seen through the eyes of one who is studying both the true genealogical classification of animals and the natural (or ecological) classification. Zoologists have overlooked the fact that these two classifications are not at one, though they are both important. We went to Africa to get certain specific animals and to test out the theory that any increase in our knowledge of animals must be made in the field.

Let the animals tell their own story, and answer for you the questions that I hope you will want to ask.

Part One

UNUSUAL VERMIN

1

Birds, Shrews and Snakes in the Grass

FROM our little house at Mamfe the view was ordinary
enough, provided one looked west, south-west, or south;
fields of grass, a little stream, a tennis court, some small sheds
with corrugated iron roofs, and a second-class metal road winding
among them all. Even the trees seemed familiar. A horse grazed
quietly, it drizzled from a grey sky, and a white man wearing grey
flannel trousers and smoking a pipe passed along the road on a bi-
cycle.

All of a sudden incongruity appeared in the form of a dazzlingly
white bird with awkward black legs and a long beak which fell
rather than flew into sight and attempted to land on the horse. It
missed its objective, as egrets always do. Hurtling against a fence,
it closed its wings before finding its feet and remained wobbling
drunkenly back and forth, giving vent to shrill cries and staring
wildly about, as if this were not its own fault.

These birds are vermin, or rather, Africa is verminous with them,
for nothing so beautiful or artistically satisfying as an egret could
ever really be classed with rats and the body louse. Previously they
were much sought after for their plumes, which stick out from under the wings like a tiny snow cloud. Now that better and cheaper
plumes can be made out of cellophane, this lovely bird is spared to
play the part of the London pigeon around the houses of West African settlements.

On this particular morning, when the whole world as viewed
from the Mamfe rest house seemed grey and dark green, the egrets
stood out like lights in their dazzling whiteness. On one side of the

21

house a long string was stretched between two poles. Along this at intervals little cheesecloth bags were tied, containing the skulls of animals that had been skinned. The skull is about the most precious part of an animal from a zoologist's point of view and receives special attention. It is cleaned of as much flesh as possible, soaked in running water, rolled in sawdust, and finally hung out to dry in little bags to which a label is attached. The bags are to prevent the loss of teeth that may become loosened through drying or decomposition of the flesh.

The flies, however, soon found out what was in the little bags and proceeded to lay their eggs in them. The egrets found the flies, which buzzed incessantly, multiplying among the offal almost while one watched. Egrets are presumably waders, if judged by their legs and feet, which are long and slender. The process of chasing fly grubs suspended about three inches below a swaying string becomes for them, therefore, about as great a problem as eating an apple tied below a rope would be to a rather inexpert tight-rope walker. Each bird fell off once every few minutes; sometimes all would topple over together in a cloud of flies.

The string of little bags was removed at sundown and taken indoors as a precaution against the undue attentions of the many nocturnal marauders. One egret, a rather seedy-looking bird, discovered where they went to, a small shed at the back of the house. Unhappily, the bird got wedged between the wall and the eaves of the roof in trying to gain an entrance, though how it got so far I could never make out. Here it remained, squawking like a child, while we searched for the focus of the commotion. I found it not particularly frightened but obviously rather angry, like Walt Disney's duck, its eyes filled with that expression of surprised wonderment that an egret always assumes when committing its daily folly or error in judgment. As I grappled with its feathery posterior in an endeavour to squeeze it through the eaves, it gave a hiccup, opened its beak, and let fall three balls of fly maggots each as large as an apple. The egret looked more surprised than ever and slipped through the eaves without further difficulty.

The egrets of Mamfe had enemies, one of whom met his end suddenly on this particular gloomy day. The seedy-looking egret, after its miscalculation at the back of the house, had assumed an impertinent attitude towards its kith and kin. Scorning the swaying skull-string, he took to intruding upon our privacy at the skinning tables and had to be constantly ordered off the field for rough-housing with the skinners. On this occasion he was shooed off the veranda at the moment when his brethren were beating a hasty retreat to the safety of the bushes behind the kitchen.

Swaying and chattering with anger, he stood among the stuffed animals pinned on boards that had been carried out to dry in the sun, now making its first appearance in several weeks. So taken up was he with his indignation, that he failed to notice the hurried departure of the other birds or the silent cruciform shadow that glided mysteriously over the hard-beaten earth around him. Gong-gong, the youngest member of the staff, who was posted at the corner of the veranda throughout the day to watch for the hawks and kites which swooped out of the sky to snatch up our stuffed rats, thinking them to be alive, gave the warning.

The hawk, a particularly big one which would probably be called an eagle in England, was, however, after our little friend the egret. Gong-gong's call to arms was the signal for a wild scramble for loaded shotguns, always kept to hand. We dashed for the open only to see the shadow of the marauder flash across the ground as the great bird nose-dived for his prey. The little egret, suddenly realizing his peril, struggled to gain the air.

Two barrels gave tongue with a deafening report at the very instant the hawk was stalling to bring his talons into position for the death grip. With a burst of feathers, the interloper swerved, somersaulted, and crashed with wings outspread. The excited staff rushed eagerly to the kill but the fierce bird was by no means done for. Hissing, yellow eyes blazing, he hurled himself at the men's legs. He was quickly dispatched with a shot from an automatic.

In the excitement of victory the egret was forgotten. He had escaped and apparently benefited from his experience, for he never returned again, though we saw him later on the sandbanks in the river with his drooping left wing and incredulous expression.

For a whole year we waged ceaseless warfare against the hawks, and on only one occasion did we obtain the same species of bird twice. There are countless varieties scanning the forests by day, where they take the place of vultures. They are dreaded and hated by animals and man alike. Silently they swoop down to carry off a chicken from a native's compound, an unsuspecting monkey from a forest tree, or a bird from the sandbanks. If you go to the zoo, you may notice the smaller monkeys are for ever glancing furtively at the tops of their cages. This action is almost automatic, the result of countless generations of their ancestors always on the look-out for their enemies, the hawks, gliding silently above them.

Their only use to us was as targets for shooting practice, and fine sport they provide for this. On one occasion, when trekking back to Mamfe from down river in a great hurry, we came to a native village nestled at the foot of a hill. As I was travelling fast to cover some forty miles in one day, my dozen-odd carriers had pushed on far ahead. I was following with Ben, my head skinner, carrying the 12-bore shotgun. Passing through the village, which was silent as a grave with all the houses tightly closed, I had the impression that many eyes were watching me—uncertain, slightly resentful eyes. The sensation was unpleasant, and we hurried on up the hill to where stood a small ju-ju house containing a symmetrical mound of baked earth surmounted by an earthenware pot. Here I paused to look back at the mysterious and vaguely malignant cluster of houses.

At that moment an immense hawk wheeled out of the forest and commenced soaring above the village in ever-widening circles. Ben passed me the gun.

Now this gun was an exceptional weapon, having been constructed with specially long barrels, of which the left was unusually well "choked" at the orifice. Its carrying power was prodigious, which fact endeared the weapon to me greatly. I always feel safer with this gun than with any rifle.

As the hawk came nearer in its circular flight, I decided to take a chance shot at it though I thought it almost certainly out of range. As the smoke cleared away (and there is a lot in damp, hot climates), I saw the bird wobble, then turn over in the air and fall like a thunderbolt in the middle of the main and only "street" of the village.

Before I had recovered from my surprise, a tumult arose below.

Crowds of wildly yelling Africans brandishing small spears and huge bush-knives burst from the houses and charged up the hill, headed by a terrifying old gentleman who had snatched up the dead bird and stuck it on a grinning ju-ju mast. My exaltation quickly left me and so did Ben. Gruesome and probably quite untrue stories of the horrible deaths meted out to white men who had killed sacred animals or interfered with other African ju-jus crowded into my mind. Being above all a coward, like everybody else, I had half a mind to bolt after Ben; but thoughts work quickly in an emergency and I decided a fish-spear in the chest was preferable to several in the backside. Anyhow, I had little time to do else than stand my ground.

The multitude swarmed about my sheepishly grinning person. Drums began to beat and the assembled company broke into a sort of African "For He's a Jolly Good Fellow" while the old gentleman ceremoniously handed me the feathered corpse. Apparently I had rid the community of its Public Enemy Number I, the local G-men having been unable to throw stones far enough to hit it or to find its hide-out. My relief was so great I became slightly stupid and, pulling out the tail feathers, I placed them on the ju-ju mound. Again I had, quite by accident, done the right thing. The assembled company burst with excitement, the drums fell into a quick reverberating rhythm, and everybody began to dance. A youth donned the ju-ju mask and executed a dance before me with a young girl. My eyes nearly popped out of my head as it proceeded, for not only in movement and rhythm, but even in phrasing, it was the *béguine*, the dance of the French Negroes of Martinique in the West Indies, well known to me from happy evenings spent in the super-sophisticated cabarets of Paris.

I dallied a long time among my friends at this village. The chief and I held long discussions upon all the local "beef," that is, animals. He implored me to stay or return to his village, saying that my placing the feathers on the ju-ju would rid the vicinity of hawks and there would be plenty of chickens and fresh eggs for me to eat. Unhappily, I could not accept his offer, which I have always regretted, but I did visit him several months later and could not find one solitary hawk. The chief assured me there was none, and seemed to regard this as a matter of course.

"Master, man bring beef."

There was always excitement at that announcement, which was made to me at all times of the day and night as I sat before the catalogues measuring rats' feet and frogs' bellies, pickling lice and worms, and doing the other multitudinous odd jobs that a scientific collecting trip entails.

A grinning black face appeared above the veranda, level with my feet.

"Well, what is it?" I inquired.

"Beef," replied the face. "Master go take 'em two shilling," and he fumbled in his cloth. With a scream he withdrew his hand and started sucking his finger, cursing loudly and roundly in Baiyangi. Willing helpers came forward, searched him, and produced two minute black clots of glossy fur each about two inches long. These were placed on the veranda, where they instantly rose on their hind legs like pugilists and, screaming in almost inaudibly high-pitched voices, proceeded to wrestle and box with each other. I say wrestle and box, but there certainly weren't any rules.

Of all the mean, unpleasant, evil-smelling, vicious things that live, the West African shrew (*Crocidura*) is the meanest, most unsavoury, and irascible. These screeching little horrors were bought for a penny each, placed in a tiny cage, and supplied with a haunch of strong-smelling anteater meat. They fought and screamed for the rest of the day and most of the night. Next morning all the meat, larger than both of them put together, had vanished, and only one

SHREW (Crocidura occidentalis)

shrew remained alive. The other lay in a corner of the cage, eviscerated and with most of its head eaten by its companion.

These shrews will attack anything, man and large bush-cats included. Their tiny jaws are armed with a phalanx of needle-sharp teeth and their pungent smell protects them from predatory birds and mammals alike. They are classed as insectivores, but they are more omnivorous than man himself. I have seen them eat each other, insects, shellfish, corn, putrefied flesh, and even a dead snake. They inhabit the long grass of forest clearings, where they are often caught, as in the case of these two, when natives are clearing the ground.

As the day wore on, our friend who had been bitten returned several times with more shrews as well as a variety of other local vermin, until the whole house began to stink. This smell is unbelievable until it is encountered. In the British Museum I have merely touched a large bottle of alcohol in which some shrews had been sealed for more than three years, and I had to wash my hands twice to avoid being sick. Nothing drowns the smell; it gets everywhere. Yet by a simple process the natives transmute it into the most delicious, delicate, and lasting scent I have ever encountered, smelling somewhere between sandalwood and tangerines. The shrews are stewed whole with certain leaves and palm-oil to bind the brew. The oil rises to the surface and is skimmed off, carrying with it the wonderful aroma that is so unlike the beastly little animal.

Among other prizes brought by the man who left us the battling shrews was a variety of snakes. After lunch, during that peculiarly silent hour when beasts take their siesta and only man toils on, a sudden shout rent the sultry air. The grass cutters were seen running together towards an old tree stump. We raced out of the house and down the newly cut grassy slope towards the river.

Here we found a most puzzling sight. Some twenty husky Africans armed with long bush-knives—a Birmingham product about eighteen inches long by three inches wide, with a wooden grip handle—stood silently round a tree stump. Now silence among a group of excited Negroes is in itself unusual and alarming; in fact it invariably presages really grave danger of one kind or another, and one must beware. Besides, they kept at a respectable distance and did not move. I attempted to advance into the circle but the headman, an ugly-looking fellow with shoulders wide enough for one to dance upon, pulled me back. I addressed my queries from outside the circle.

For answer I was knocked flat and three natives came tumbling on top of me. Madly I scrambled out to the air expecting to be confronted by at least a snarling leopard. There was nothing to show for the treatment I had received. Everybody now began to talk and I addressed the assembled company emphatically.

From the babble of pidgin-English and strange tongues, we eventually learnt that somewhere in the tree stump was a snake who was watching us. Now this snake not only bites but defends itself by spitting poison. His range of fire is about ten feet, but he is not certain whether you are animate or merely another tree if you keep still. The man who had been clearing grass near the tree stump had been shot at but the snake had missed. Others heard his shout and came too close in their ignorance. They were waiting for the snake to show his hand (or head) when we arrived, and the movement of the headman to check my onrush had given the snake his mark. He had fired at me, and those in the know had jumped. Nobody suffered, but some of the brown liquid fell on my flannel trousers. I did not notice it at the time but a few days later there were tiny holes where it had been, as if acid had been spilt on the material. Imagine the effect of such a substance if it finds its mark—the eyes.

Once the snake had wasted its ammunition, the natives fell on the tree stump and, poking their sticks into the holes beneath, soon drove out a snake, but not the one they had expected. Instead of a long slim dark-brown form emerging, as everyone had anticipated, an evil, flat, chartreuse-green head appeared, its nose surmounted by two small horns. With much hissing, the short fat body was dragged out. It proved to be a fine puff adder, the most deadly of all African snakes. This reptile is a beautiful creature, conventionally marked with beige, dark brown, and green in a pattern often seen on handbags; further north in the desert country, its colouring is much less vivid. Its tail is only about an eighth of the diameter of the body and absurdly short, so that it hardly reaches the ground but sticks out behind when the animal is in motion.

Pleased and excited with this unexpected addition to our collections, we did not notice that the other snake had also been found and by the time this had dawned upon us, it had been hacked to pieces by the natives, who would rather see it thus than sold to us for what was to them a handsome sum. Perhaps they, like a Malay tribe among whom I once lived in the Celebes, thought I brought the animals that we preserved in alcohol back to life when I got home, and considered it more circumspect to render this at least difficult in the case of such a dangerous beast.

The grass of Mamfe station, even when cut short, as it was every few weeks, could be of considerable danger in so far as snakes were concerned. The worst of the vermin that inhabited the station was a species of snake, small and brown with a purple and white collar, known as the night adder (*Causus rhombeatus*). It is well named, for it lives in small holes and emerges at night to prey on its only food—the common toad of these regions (*Bufo regularis*). This combination is peculiar; both the snake and the toad are found only on the open clearings in the forest, never in the forest, which may surround the clearings in an unbroken wall of virgin greenery. Both must get there somehow, probably by migration in swarms when young. Nothing except this toad has ever been found in the stomach of the night adder, and it is one of the commonest of African snakes.

At Mamfe, both the toad and the snake swarmed everywhere. We caught nine night adders in one evening around the house, and why we didn't step on one I don't know, as they are perfectly camouflaged. I met one at midday at the foot of the veranda. It tried to make its escape but I spotted its hole and pushed a small butterfly net over it. The snake lost its temper and made a jab at me. I was ready for it and bounced out of the way. A snake is a fool and not so quick in attack as one is led to believe; provided you don't lose your nerve, there is no snake except a hamadryad which should get the better of you, that is, if he doesn't take you unawares. This adder got frightfully excited, hissed and rushed about. At length it gave a sort of backfire and vomited up one whole toad and another one partly digested. After this it was so exhausted I scooped it up in the net and ran into the house where it was drowned in a bottle of alcohol.

This story, when recounted to a certain gentleman who was passing through Mamfe, had a curious sequel. The man considered the snake's death an enviable one for obvious reasons. That night all the white inhabitants of Mamfe were assembled at the house of a certain German trader. There were ten all told, including ourselves and two visiting missionaries. After dinner, when the servant brought drinks, the man again referred to the snake's death in a jocular way. He was sitting with his back to an open window overlooking a sheer precipice. I was at the opposite side of the circle.

Suddenly I saw a sleek black head appear between the man's

rather fat cheek and his collar. It waved malignantly to and fro, its beady eyes flashing fire in the lamplight. Remembering my experience at the tree stump, I leant forward and said quietly: "There is a snake going down your neck." The man moved as none of us suspected he could, and the snake which was inexplicably coiled round the lintel seemed to leap to the floor. We fell on it with sticks. When captured it proved to be a harmless variety, but the good gentleman never again referred to death by drowning in alcohol.

2

Crabs; Their Foes; Mongoose; Frogs and Toads; Rats; Lizards

PROBABLY all people are struck at one time or another during the course of their lives by something that appears to them individually as not only strange but almost unbelievable. Such phenomena are as often as not quite ordinary matters to those who know about them. I have encountered many.

To me the most outstanding of all is the land crab. I cannot explain, even to myself, the sensations I feel when I see one. I have always known that there are such things as land crabs and yet, having been born and having lived in a country where crabs are confined to the seashore or the dinner table, the sight of these rather evil-looking, wildly staring, and excitable creatures meandering about beneath mimosa bushes, scuttling down holes in my kitchen, or ascending palm trees, never fails to unnerve me.

The Cameroons swarms with them, from the muddy seashores to the tops of the highest mountains. The rivers and streams are full of them. They excavate holes among the roots of dry grass in clearings; they ascend trees and scuttle about the floor of the damp and the dry forest alike. Some are small, rotund, and rosy, others are large, damp, and purple. Others again are brown and green and flat. They ogle at you wherever you go.

On the Mamfe clearing they abound among the tangled vegetation that springs up as soon as one forgets to cut the grass. They also go backwards into holes underneath the houses; drains are a scraping, scratching mass of them that scramble away as soon as one looks down their retreat. They are vermin indeed, but like all other vermin they are more useful to man than the harmless decorative beasts.

As I was returning from the near-by forest one night, the beams of my powerful torch disclosed an eerie and really quite revolting sight at the edge of the grassy clearing. A giant rat (*Cricetomys*), larger than a rabbit, which frequents the low bush and raises an awful racket at night, had been caught in a snare set at random by our native trapper. It must have met its death about sundown, only an hour before. As I came upon it suddenly, a sea of staring, ghost-like forms scuttled around it. I cannot help the constant use of the word scuttled; there is nothing else that so aptly describes the furtive, hurried, and crooked progress of a crab. A nearer approach to a nightmare of wildest fiction I have never seen, and I still shudder when I think of it. The very evilness of those loathsome brutes was terrifying, as they scrambled like vultures over the corpse, clanking their armoured bellies and limbs, tearing the flesh with their paw-like pincers, and then darting out of the ring to squat, stuffing the glistening morsels into their mouths like starving children. The fact that they themselves were silent, unlike other carrion feeders, somehow made it all the more ghastly; the superfluity of legs and the eyes on pedestals removed the whole from reality to the realm of fevered imagination.

I could not bring myself to go near the scene of operations, so I threw a large clot of earth. It fell among them, crushing a few of the smaller ones, and went bouncing away into the long grass. The crabs scooted backward in a wide circle and sat glaring menacingly with their pincers held wide apart and all those disgusting appendages round their mouths twitching and fluttering as if they were licking their chops. Then, slowly they began creeping forward again in little jerky rushes until the corpse once more became a seething mass of shiny shells and clambering legs. But first their squashed and wounded mates were torn apart and devoured before they settled down to the serious matter of the rat.

These crabs are the scavengers of the countryside. Rats, shrews, and ants are others. Half the animal population seems to be likewise employed. The crabs appear to prefer their meat fresh; ants set to work before it is actually meat, that is, while it is still alive. Shrews prefer theirs high.

Like every other animal except the elephant, however, the crabs have their enemies; in fact they seem to have many. Later, when I take you into the silent forests, onto the windy mountain tops, and down among the reeds by the great rivers, I will introduce you to a few more. On the clearing of Mamfe station, the crabs fell prey to two animals in particular.

One, a strange little creature, is known as the cusimanse, or *Crossarchus obscurus* to the zoologists. Its "Christian" or specific name is well chosen, for, both in habits and in appearance, it is indeed obscure. Being a kind of mongoose, it falls into the great class of carnivora or flesh-eating animals, which contains such well-known forms as the lion, cat, dog, wolf, bear, fox, skunk, weasel, and racoon. The cusimanse defies description, however, by being, except perhaps for its rather long slender snout, so utterly ordinary. It has four short legs, a tapering tail, is covered with coarse nondescript hair, and has small ears. Its face is sharp and its expression eager. Its life is concerned primarily with scratching up crabs and bolting them as fast as possible with much crackling of hard shells and pig-like grunts on its own part. We often watched these eager little fellows scratching about on the open grass between the houses on moonlight nights. They look like rabbits, which they resemble in size and shape. We kept one, which had been brought to us alive by a native hunter, for some time. It spent all night trying to scratch up the bottom of its wooden cage.

It has a near relation, another mongoose (*Atilax paludinosus*), which is also obscure both in habits and in appearance, though its back is elegantly cross-striped. This animal also relishes crabs and will come close to human habitations in search of them.

The crab's other enemy in open localities is a frog known as *Rana occipitalis*, which devours young crabs by the thousands.

I have referred to this frog by its scientific name, for the good reason that it has no popular one. I think I had better digress here for a moment to settle this problem of nomenclature now, so that I need not refer to it again.

During our expedition to these regions, we collected some seven thousand odd animals comprising about 450 species. This is only an approximation, as several of the groups have not yet been completely identified and named. There proved to be 92 species of mammals, 64 different reptiles, including snakes, 46 different frogs, and about 250 different spiders, centipedes, parasitic worms, ticks, crabs, lobsters, snails, scorpions, and others. Only a handful of the whole lot are sufficiently well known to have popular names, and quite a number, being entirely new even to science, are only now receiving Latin names. The result is that I have no choice but to label the creatures to whom I introduce you by their fabulous scientific names.

This may, however, serve a double purpose. First, it may answer a question that is constantly asked: Why do scientists persist in allotting such stupendous titles to such obscure animals? Second, it may act as a kind of confirmation for the mere facts that I have perforce to include in my tales.

Facts about lions and rhinoceroses are open to verification or speculation as the case may be, whereas facts about a frog with hairs are open to neither, unless some peg is provided upon which that frog may be securely hung. The scientific name does this, as it gives a guide to the purely zoological and gruesomely intricate literature upon the subject.

This practice of giving animals their true and complete names springs from the necessity of labelling the wild life of the world and not merely that of some small region. There are more than twenty thousand different beetles in the British Isles alone; when investigating a place like the Cameroons, one finds the varieties almost infinite. In England we have but three frogs; in Mamfe there are at least fifty different kinds. Try to think of fifty different names for frogs without becoming idiotic or grammatically absurd! I hope also that the accompanying illustrations will serve to counteract bewilderment, though it is by the very obscurity of these creatures that I hope to entertain.

To return to *Rana occipitalis*, this frog's name means literally "the back-of-the-heady one who makes noises." The word *rana* was used by the Romans for "frog," but it comes from the more ancient Sanskrit or Aryan stem *ru* or *rau*, meaning "one who makes a sound," hence the inference. The *occipitalis* signifies the great width of the head, which really is prodigious, so the Latin name is quite justified.

These frogs are very numerous in all cleared spaces of the jungle. They are aquatic, spending most of their time floating on the surface of the water with their eyes sticking out like periscopes. They grow to a length of about six inches and are very voracious, swallowing insects, spiders, crabs, smaller frogs, and almost everything else that comes their way. Without them and their allies which inhabit the same waters, man would be in an even sorrier plight than he is in at present in these lugubrious climes. They devour countless myriads of mosquito larvæ per year, and without them these carriers of the mortal yellow fever and malaria would become so numerous that man would be driven from the country altogether.

Rana occipitalis is smartly spotted below with black on his otherwise pure white belly. He was a sore subject to our native staff of skinners and trappers. Several large specimens were brought to us alive and placed in a large bowl with a lid weighted with stones. They all jumped in unison, knocked off the lid, and made their escape while we were occupied elsewhere. They scattered far and wide before we discovered our loss. Some "made for bush," as the West African term is for going home to the vegetation; others behaved in a peculiar and decidedly questionable manner. They apparently found their way into the bedroom (or, rather, the space where we slept) and concealed themselves in a certain unmentionable article of bedroom furniture.

As I was lying under my mosquito net shivering and aching with an attack of malaria, strange metallic sounds were wafted up to me.

I could not imagine where they were coming from or what they were. Time passed and the light began to fail. All of a sudden I forgot my fever as a raucous sing-song clamour broke out beneath my ear. "Car-r-r-ach, car-r-r-ach," it went, reverberating through the room and the stanchions of the mosquito net quivered in unison. I leapt out of bed convinced that my temperature had risen to the point of delirium. The noise ceased abruptly. I yelled for the household staff (No, I won't call them "boys"!), and hurrying feet came out of the rapidly descending dusk.

"Am I talking gibberish," I inquired, "or is there a peculiar whirring noise going on in here?"

Gong-gong listened intently, but his face belied his concern for my mental condition. He didn't hear anything, he assured me; I began to retire below the mosquito net. No sooner had I done so than it burst out afresh. Gong-gong dived under the bed.

"Master, the beef!" he shouted, pushing out an article of enamelled furniture, from which sprang half a dozen eager amphibians.

The whole household turned out and a great pursuit began. All the frogs were eventually caught and drowned in the all-absorbing alcohol. I burst into a profuse sweat more from laughter than surprise, and another attack of malaria was satisfactorily overcome.

Such vermin as I have mentioned are common features of the inhabited parts of the land, but there are others more numerous and more essentially "verminous." In speaking of the deadly night adder, brief reference was made to the common toad (*Bufo regularis*) which is its only source of food. This frog—for all toads are frogs, just as all gnats are mosquitoes and all dromedaries are camels, despite what your nurse or your schoolmaster may have told you when young—is an interesting animal notwithstanding its commonness and reputation. Toads are not evil, are quite harmless to handle, and in fact make intelligent though rather unconventional pets. *Bufo regularis* is not unlike our common toad, but its behaviour is very different in many respects.

When we arrived in Africa in September, the misty, though often rainy, nights were filled with strange noises. Predominant among these was a terrific, colossal, stupendous babel created by our friend *Bufo regularis*. I eventually tracked down the nearest colony to a well-head by the house which was crowded with individuals gathered together to mate and to "sing," which functions appear to be intimately linked in amphibian ethics.

The males were small and yellow, the females large and dark brown. Only the former "sing," but the power of their lungs, or rather of the special pouches in their throats, compensated for their mates' inabilities. Colonies of toads are dotted about the countryside within hearing of one another. For a time all is silence and only the whirring of the myriad nocturnal insects can be heard, a noise that is itself akin to silence by reason of its incessant stridence. Suddenly one toad, acting as a sort of precentor, will begin: "quir-rrr-rrr-whirr, quir-rrr-rrr-whirr," the others of his colony joining in perfect rhythm. Other colonies take it up until the whole countryside is deafened with the racket, which is as precise as a machine.

All at once it ceases, as if every toad had been struck dead at the same instant by an electric current. Occasionally one choir far off will fail to stop and will carry on for a few seconds like an echo. The effect is very remarkable and remains as unexpected as it is irritating throughout the night.

This behaviour, concerned as it is with mating, was in full swing when we arrived in Africa. As the weeks passed, the rains ceased and the toads got done with their spawning. They then left their damp abodes and scattered over the drier country. They also quit their strident community singing and adopted a sort of "cluck-quack" which they uttered incessantly but at irregular intervals throughout the night, and individually.

Still later in the year, when we were in the big river living on a sort of glorified punt, these busy little beasts were congregating on the sandbanks, apparently waiting for the rains to come down and swell the rivers making them thirty feet deeper and enabling the toads to gauge the safe limits of their spawning grounds. They seem

to know that if the eggs are laid too close to the swiftly running
stream they will be washed away and perish.

On one particular night we tied up alongside a narrow sandbar at
the bottom of a deep gulley clothed in virgin forest. When the
paddlers had put away their gear and gone off to a near-by village,
night descended on us, engulfing us in that world of ephemeral
loveliness known only in the deep tropics where the whole air is
filled with lascivious smells and sounds. Gradually a roaring rose
above the gentle swirl of the oily waters. Louder it grew, and still
louder, like a gigantic turbine, though muffled and apparently coming from all directions at once. Shining the torch onto the sandbar,
for it was now quite dark, a myriad pairs of tiny rubies leapt into
being, and there, crowded in thousands together, we saw the little
toads all squatting with their eager little faces directed upstream.
There must have been hundreds of thousands of them stretching as
far as the eye could see, all pale-fawn in colour, all with their little
throats pumping in and out like tiny bellows as they called incessantly for the rains to fall and wash them up over the banks into
the flooded forests beyond. We stepped out among them, and
although scores leapt into the dark waters, thousands remained hopping around our feet, blinking their ruby-red eyes in the torchlight.

Here were the same toads we had seen yellow and black in
Calabar, deep reddish-brown on the grassy slopes of Mamfe station, mottled brown at other places, and now all light fawn in
colour. Protracted research eventually elucidated the puzzle, and
here is the answer. The colour of toads' skins is produced by minute granules of colour known as chromatophores. These congregate in tubular cells situated in the deeper layers of the skin. When
the toads are in the water to breed, their skins are moist and transparent and the colours show through. Not only this, the changes
of colour produced by alteration of heat and light, or by anger or
fright, as in ourselves when we blush, may also be seen, and frogs
have an ability in this respect far surpassing even the chameleon.
Later, when they leave the water, the outer layers of their skin dry

up and become opaque, their colours become duller and more static. By the end of the year the skin is hardened and dead, so that practically all colour except that of contained dust particles is gone, making them appear dusty and greyish-brown like a dirty white handkerchief.

A toad we kept alive reached the limit of its patience while in my hands. It squatted down on its legs, gulped down mouthfuls of air until it was inflated like a miniature football, and then literally burst. The skin split from its chin to its belly and from one knee to the other through its groin. Slowly and deliberately it enlarged the rent, scraping the old skin off with its hind feet then stuffing it into its mouth with its hands and eating it. After half an hour it emerged a slightly greenish saffron-yellow and able to change its colour to a variety of browns when angered, whereas before it had been a dull fawn-coloured animal incapable of showing its feelings at all.

Any space that is not taken up by crabs and toads and snakes seems to be filled with rats and lizards around Mamfe. We caught twenty-one different species of rats, and ten of these were denizens of the clearings only.

Now when I speak of rats I am being a bit misleading. A rat in England is either a brown animal (*Rattus norvegicus*) or a black one (*Rattus rattus*). All smaller varieties are spoken of as mice. In Africa, as in most other countries for that matter, this simple distinction breaks down utterly. Rats include animals smaller than our house mouse and others a great deal larger than a hare. There is a beast with the delightful name of *Thyronomys swinderianus*, or, more colloquially, the "cutting grass," which is even bigger still. It is a lumbersome rat without a tail, nearly as big as a beaver, which makes loud clucks and bangs as it literally eats away the grass stems behind the African homestead.

There is another rat which has already been mentioned, *Cricetomys*, which with its prodigious tail measures more than two feet in length. This genus of rats is very common in West Africa, where there are a great number of species, some beautifully coloured terracotta above and saffron-yellow beneath, others coarsely haired with six-inch whiskers. We had many alive at different times and I received several nasty gashes in my hands, inflicted through thick leather gloves, while handling them. They are dirty, mangy creatures infested with parasites, in particular a strange insect known as *Hemmimerus*, as large as and not unlike an earwig. More than a hundred of these can conceal themselves in the sleek short hair of a single rat, where they slip about almost as fast as the eye can move.

Cricetomys makes a noise which is highly exasperating but which is put to a very practical use. Being a single "clock, clock," uttered at irregular intervals in batches of any number from one to ten, it provides an excellent gamble. I must admit that we followed the example of our staff when off duty at night and often had a bet on *Cricetomys's* next utterance. The jungle lays better odds than the pari mutuel.

I once told a white man who had been in charge of a strip of African territory the size of Wales for many years that I had trapped in his garden a rat with a spiral tail and another with yellow spots. He looked sympathetic and put away the whisky. For the rest of the evening he watched me closely, presumably expecting me to announce that I saw pink rats running a relay race round the walls of his bungalow. It was he who had been under the influence of alcohol, not I, for he had been in the country most of his life and run into thousands of whisky bottles but never the harmless little *Lemniscomys*.

This little rat that swarmed around the township of Mamfe certainly does administer a shock to the eye when first encountered. Down the middle of its back is a black stripe bordered by a row of yellow spots; the whole of the remainder of its back and flanks is crossed by longitudinal lines of similar yellow spots. Further north and to the west of Mamfe, this little rat is replaced by an allied species in which the spots merge forming stripes and the colour changes to black and white.

We spent hours trying to photograph this animal, but at the slightest sound it would leap perpendicularly into the air as if on

a powerful spring, and be off like a streak of electricity. The nervous sensitivity of these creatures must be beyond our wildest conception. Their responses to stimuli are more than instantaneous, if
such is possible. In fact, they invariably leap even before one has
made a move. They made runs among the grass and in these we
placed our traps, but they are so wary that two rats from three
hundred traps was considered a good night's catch.

The other rats of the clearing displayed an almost infinite variety
of shapes, sizes, and colours. The brown rat and the black rat,
which have followed men all over the earth since leaving their
original homes in Central Asia and the trees of the East Indies respectively, have hitherto not been thought to have yet reached
Mamfe. To my surprise, however, the native bluish-black rat turned
out to be *Rattus rattus rattus*, our own black rat. There is also an
indigenous light-brown species.

At one period a dreadful and ever-increasing stench pervaded the
house. At first we merely looked at each other, but as time went on
and it got steadily worse we tacitly came to the conclusion that
"such things could not possibly be"; and besides, the consumption
of soap was increasing, if anything. Eventually I decided to conduct
a thorough search and discovered that the bluish-black rats had
taken to committing suicide in great numbers amongst the rafters
of our house, through, I believe, nibbling our skins and skeletons
preserved with arsenic.

Rats, though so numerous, are seldom if ever seen by day, with
the exception of the one diurnal species which I sometimes met
gambolling about in the grass with its vivid green and rufous fur
flashing in the sunlight as if it were lacquered metal and trying to
rival the butterflies. By day the rat runs are occupied by several
varieties of startlingly lovely reptiles.

The agama lizards rival the paint pots of the Chinese Sung
dynasty and the ultra-modern Parisians put together, at least the
males do. The female is merely olive-green with brick-red spots on
her flanks, but the male is decked out in vivid reds, blues, greens,
and yellows which fade or intensify with the degree of sunlight.

YELLOW-SPOTTED RAT (Lemniscomys)

These lizards frequent the house, dashing after insects on their long
legs or squatting on vantage points, bobbing their heads as if agree-
ing with everything the world around them was saying.

I wanted a number of these lizards for study and offered a small
reward to that member of the staff who should catch one first from
a given start. I would stand on the veranda, spot a lizard bobbing
its head in the sunlight, and give the waiting racers the signal. A
mass of brown bodies would dart forward. The lizard instantly
spotted his pursuers and then the fun began, because his home was
invariably somewhere in the house, probably among the eaves. The
lizard would bolt one way and the more eager racers dashed after
him, but a few schemers like Gong-gong and Faugi, our second
skinner, would deploy, knowing the animal's tactics. Sure enough,
finding its progress barred, the lizard would suddenly swerve back

the other way. Faugi, thinking his moment had come, prostrated himself in its path, tripping up the others who had wheeled about in their mad rush. The lizard, of course, always escaped, and Gong-gong came into the play. Being only about twelve years old and very agile, he often gave the agama a serious fright; twice he caught the flying streak of blue and got well bitten. Once he caught it by falling on it and biting it himself, but he never held it. We eventually did procure some, but the only chase of this kind that ended in a kill was terminated by the imperturbable George, who remained placidly in his chair on the veranda drinking tea out of a glass, and put his foot on the lizard as it paused to gain breath before darting up the wall to its retreat.

No record of the "vermin" of Mamfe should exclude man's greatest little tropical friend, the gecko, though it is an outrage to place his name even at the foot of the list. This little lizard, universal to hot countries in his manifold forms, appears mysteriously in any house as soon as it is inhabited. Running about the walls, or stalking insects across the ceiling in his world that is upside down or tilted to an angle of ninety degrees or more, and uttering his shrill little chatters, this animal has been a friend to many a lonely man far away in the wilds. Night after night the little geckos will appear as the lights are lit, until each one becomes familiar, this with his recently broken tail, that with his all but new tail.

Geckos have been known to get so tame that they would come onto the table every night at dinner time for tit-bits. After months, even years of absence, the resident in the tropics may return to his former quarters and on the second or third night there will be the little gecko standing eagerly by his plate, his great lustrous black eyes keenly watching, his precarious tail wagging like a tiny dog's.

We had one such that lived in the drawer where we kept our skinning implements. Every morning he was disturbed when we got out our tools, but he persisted even after he lost his tail through getting entangled with a pair of compasses. He just shed his tail from the roots as if it were a useless umbrella and left it wriggling and squirming like another animal in the drawer. He soon grew another, but his affliction didn't deter him from his nightly labours as self-appointed watch dog to us. Prowling about the ceiling he would wait for some insect to settle, attracted by the lamplight. Then, whatever its size—and there were many as large as himself— he would stalk it just as a cat would a mouse. Nearer he came, and nearer, until, forgetting his feline tactics, he would rush in like a terrier. Sometimes he missed, sometimes the beetle, moth, or praying mantis would fly off just as he was preparing to pounce, but if he caught it a great to-do commenced. The powerful insects fought to get free, but the little gecko worried and shook them until one would have thought the sucker-like pads on his feet must lose their grip on the ceiling to which they clung, in opposition to all the laws of gravity.

Only once did he fall, and that time he did it properly. When he seized a praying mantis a little more than three inches long, a strenuous fight ensued. So great was the noise that we put down our pens to watch. The mantis is a truly terrifying creature, apparently always willing to engage in a battle, even with man. If one alights on the table before you, it will stand up on four legs, turn its beastly head on its narrow neck and stare you straight in the face with its evil protuberant eyes, at the same time presenting its two forearms crooked like a pugilist's and bristling with rows of slender tooth-like spines, with which it not only seizes its prey but also its mate, from both of which it sucks the life blood. In fact the love-life of the mantis consists of this gruesome performance alone, for without it the male is unable to impregnate the female. Only in its writhing death-agonies can it conclude the act of copulation.

Such was the antagonist our little friend had assaulted. The struggle was protracted and the mantis was strong. Suddenly the combatants fell with a crash, squarely into my cup of tea, sending it showering all over me and my work. The gecko was none the worse but somewhat dazed and utterly amazed. Had I not fished him out

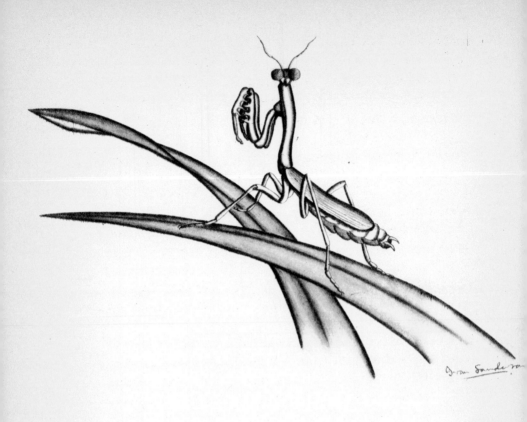

PRAYING MANTIS

he would assuredly have drowned. I placed him under the lamp to dry, which he did at his leisure while I dispatched the mantis, for I dislike these vampires.

When the gecko had recovered, I proffered the still writhing torso of the insect, but he would have none of it. He allowed me to handle him without attempting to bite, a thing he had never done before; perhaps he knew I was a willing accomplice. Presently he trotted away to regain his exalted topsy-turvy world.

The body of the mantis remained on the table in two completely separate parts. Next morning at 11:30 it was still wriggling. I wonder if it was a male?

Part Two

THE GREAT FOREST

3

First Encounter of the Wild (Drills);
The Second Encounter (Scorpions);
Porcupines in Holes; Meeting Leopards;
The Other Large Cat (Profelis)

WE temporarily usurped a bit of land, rightfully the free-hold property of the chief and villagers of a place named Eshobi which borders the Great North Road leading out of Mamfe into the wildernesses of the great forests and then beyond to the grass-covered mountains and orchard-like plains of the north. Upon this piece of land we built our camp, around and among the giant pillar-like trunks of the trees.

This main road, the only artery for commerce in the whole district, would be something of a revelation to the average pedestrian and a surprise even to the hardened globe-trotter. It was only a few feet wide and consisted solely of hairpin bends. The gradient varied between one in four and one in one, the descents all being arranged so that one lost in about four minutes the exact altitude to which one had laboriously clambered in the previous four. This continued for about eighty miles northward until one entered a region where one gained in two minutes roughly three times the altitude that one had lost in the previous eight. This portion of the road culminated in a stretch where one didn't lose at all, the gradient being about five in one. Here nature had thoughtfully provided three-foot steps like a giant staircase to assist the tired traveller.

The road surface also added greatly to the joys of travel. Upon the crests of the knife-edged ridges, at the angle of each hairpin bend, and at the bottom of the gulleys, the surface consisted of a large open-work mesh of roots exposed by the erosion of the soil which lay flat and smooth some eighteen inches to two feet below. On the gradients the roots gave way to a jumble of broken boulders of varying sizes, moss-covered, bare or slime-besmeared. Every few hundred yards a little diversion was provided in the form of a slippery, rotten, cylindrical log, about eighteen inches in diameter and anything up to thirty feet long, spanning a deep gulley filled with rocks and gurgling water.

I mention all this lest an impression be gained that the presence of a road near the camp indicated unnatural conditions or the advent of civilization. It did not; even local hunters sometimes proved themselves incapable of distinguishing the road from any other gap between the trees. Besides, trees grow very fast and Africans don't travel much.

We camped near the road because, while it lasted, it served as a useful method of getting about the otherwise almost impenetrable forest and also because it was useful to know whether it was cloudy or fine and whether the wind was blowing or not, which was discernible only through this narrow cleft in the roof of the forest.

Along it we wandered with shotguns and field glasses, in the heat of the evening—at least so we judged by our watches, for the light was always somewhat crepuscular.

I was thus lazily employed on the third day after our arrival in the forest, when all our gear had been stored in a ship-shape manner and mysterious little bush-stick and green-leaf houses had finished sprouting up around the domains occupied by the communal cooking fire. I carried my shotgun gingerly while I moved from root to root and boulder to boulder, my mind filled with reminiscences of cleaning four hundred traps, and forebodings of the collapse of the tent, which appeared to be only a matter of time.

All at once I was arrested by a sound that I could have sworn was an organized revolt on the part of my own stomach against the unnamed muddle that had been forced into it at lunch time. A little confused with that unreasoning but inbred bashfulness born of civilized ethics, I paused, prepared for the indignity to repeat itself. Sure enough, it did, but from somewhere among the foliage to the left of the path.

Such a phenomenon when encountered for the first time is arresting, to say the least; yet it very soon became the second time, then the third, then the fourth, until I began to feel quite used to it. I have dined with a most illustrious Chinese family, also with the inmates of a Balinese seminary, who both showed their appreciation of the ample fare provided for them with great gusto in this unmistakable though, to the European mind, somewhat unconventional and rude manner. But the little chorus that went on around me as I waited silently in the African jungle surpassed the wildest fancies of the Orient.

When I moved, the babble (or gurgle) mysteriously died away. This was repeated several times. I took to wondering whether after all it was not a trick of the forest with its unaccountable echoings and ghost-like sighings, that I had begun to appreciate so well. Pausing again at the bottom of the gulley, however, the local intestinal disturbances became almost deafening, and I felt a strong desire to see the perpetrators of this outstanding performance. Every time I moved to try to peer among the undergrowth, the noise ceased abruptly, only to commence again more loudly than ever. Annoyed and mystified, I crouched in the path among the roots, waiting for my tormentors to show their hands, or any other portions of their anatomies.

As they did not do so, but were getting uncomfortably close on both sides of the path, I conceived a plan. By a method learnt at school and employed with marked success around the coffee-pot in the less accessible parts of the Orient, I joined the chorus, weakly at first, but with ever-increasing volume—if I may put it that way. The results were beyond my fondest hopes, and, for that matter, fears. The accompaniment of my jungle acquaintances came closer around me, though I had thought that they were already as close as they could be without showing themselves.

This was very awkward, for it now appeared that they were of considerable size and, if judged by the only sounds they uttered in comparison with the same sort produced by man, they would have been about twice the size of an elephant. I indulged in a hurried zoological stocktaking of all the inhabitants of the West African tropical forests that I knew of. Nothing seemed to fit the case except chimpanzees and bush pigs, yet the former should be away up in the trees and the latter would certainly have given other fair warning of their identity. I consequently gained in inquisitiveness though also in uneasiness.

A few moments later, I had dropped positively all inquisitiveness, unbefitting as this may be for a zoologist to admit. Suddenly before me sat a most menacing figure, apparently wrapped in a grey shawl, and scrutinizing me with a pair of unpleasant-looking eyes from beneath a scowling brow. He (or she) and I both ceased our visceral mutterings promptly and uttered a surprised "uh" so precisely in unison that I got an overpowering desire to giggle. This was, however, as quickly wafted away also, when my zoological reasoning came to an abrupt halt. I had not suspected that drills (*Cynocephalus leucophæus*), though baboons of a sort, went about in large, belching parties.

Now I had met baboons before and although I took a great interest in their behaviour and would have liked to have returned to camp with a fine specimen such as now sat complacently before me, I remembered that discretion was always the better part of valour when in their presence. I therefore stood up to go, trying to be as unhurried as I imagined I would be at a vicarage tea party, though I have never attended one. This simple movement, however, was heralded by unmistakable complaints from all sides in the form of the most unpleasant grunts. The old lady (or gentleman) before me also rose, but on all fours so that his or her posterior came into view. It happened to be bright pink at this time of the year, and I thought

DRILLS (Cynocephalus leucophæus)

absurdly of the homeric description of the dawn as "rosy-fingered."

This display had remarkable effects. The bushes parted on all sides and a surprising array of sub-humanity presented itself, ranging from one obvious male of quite alarming proportions, to the merest toddlers with pale, flat faces quite unlike their dog-nosed, black-visaged elders and betters. Their movements were leisurely, as if they were taking their places for a boxing match; they chattered and grunted exactly like any crowd of pleasure-seeking human beings preparing for an entertaining display.

While all this taking of seats was going on, I was retreating gingerly backwards up the path, while trying to learn the rules of monkey ethics in the raw. The outsize gentleman seemed to have been appointed as doorman. He trotted into the path behind me and stood squarely upon three boulders, one for each back foot and one for his gnarled hands. This was all very unpleasant and I found myself waiting with some trepidation to see what was the next item on the agenda. As they continued to sit and grunt to each other, it appeared to be up to me.

I don't expect you have ever been surrounded by a troup of expectant baboons, but if you have, you will probably agree that it becomes extremely difficult to think up any suitable parlour tricks. My mind was a blank, especially as each part of the circle to which my back was turned in succession seemed to think its chance had come to grab a ringside seat, and since one can't face all ways at once, the ring began to diminish rapidly. I remember thinking stoically and hopefully that drills are vegetable feeders and that I was not a vegetable although I doubtless looked like one. When the old gentleman yawned, and I had a glimpse of his three-inch fangs, I began to doubt the words of wisdom uttered by the worthy professor of my late and, at that moment, greatly lamented university.

I did remember that almost any animal, even a surprised tiger, will shy away if one stoops to pick up a stone and makes pretence of throwing it. This I instantly put to the test, but in my excitement I accidentally did pick up a stone and hurled it at the big yawning male with a force of which I did not believe myself capable. We were all greatly surprised when it found its mark in a glancing blow. This, combined with my sudden action, made the spectators jump backwards with some emphasis so that I was given quite a lot of room to move about in. My target seemed quite angry, as might be expected, and as I stooped to gather more missiles, he waltzed about and returned the compliment with some vigour, scraping the ground with his hind feet, gathering up a small boulder in the process, and projecting it straight at me with considerable accuracy.

This heralded a great commotion. Apparently the show had begun. I hurled more stones in all directions, and although the admiring onlookers retreated each time, those on the opposite side advanced, the gentleman who had yawned so indulgently most of all. He was now very angry indeed, projecting stones and big blobs of spittle at me alternately as he waltzed about, presenting first his revolting, dog-like visage and then his still more revolting and quite uncanine other end.

These tactics, combined with more stones and the fast-descending dusk, made me not only definitely frightened, but inexplicably angry too. Once I nearly put a charge of lead into him, but luckily checked myself, realizing that this trump-card would be even more useful later on when the difference of opinion became general. Matters appeared to be rapidly drifting in that direction.

During one of the periodic lulls between these diplomatic interchanges, now carried on in a more or less tense silence, one of the smallest and most youthful of my audience uttered a peevish squeal and bowled a small lump of earth at me, just as an underhanded lob-bowler in a juvenile cricket match would do. The action was so ludicrous that in my decidedly agitated frame of mind I burst into roars of laughter. Why it seemed so screamingly funny I don't know; perhaps it wasn't really so at all. But my action proved a most fortunate one.

The brat's mother made a dive at her now cowering and shivering prodigy, gathered it to her bosom, and bolted, followed by several other mothers and their offspring. The remaining "stag party," numbering some dozen, began running to and fro looking surprised and angry. I continued laughing and shouting as if I were at a football match, and soon became quite incoherent from sheer nerves. I advanced on the old male, shouting: "They've made a goal; run, run, you old idiot; bonjour, mademoiselle cochon; nunca café con leche," at the same time executing a spine-rocking rumba combined with all the other outlandish dances in my repertoire. He stopped dead in his tracks. His eyes opened wide and his whole face took on a quite ludicrously human expression. He muttered to himself. "Standing aghast" is the only way to describe his poise, as if he was just as much shocked at my behaviour as he was bewildered and frightened at what he saw. A few seconds he stood his ground, amazement written all over his face; then his nerve gave way and he shied like a dog. His final rout was accompanied by a flood of the choicest swearing from my Cockney vocabulary. He fled.

With his hurried retreat "to bush," my way home was open before me; I wasted no time in taking it, swearing and bellowing with full conviction. Once on the crest of the incline, I sent a couple of shots below in an ecstasy of human bravado and with a feeling of swaggering superiority towards the mere beasts of the field over whom the power of speech had been proved to cast such a spell.

The night following my encounter with the street urchins of the wilds also had its unpleasant surprises, though on this occasion I took the offensive at the outset.

A camp in the forest is not, or ought not to be, a haphazard affair. Into its planning should go a great deal of careful thought, despite the scoffing of the veterans and the simulated mystification of one's native satellites. A man who plants his tent haphazardly may survive to regret it bitterly. The fact that I frowned on "ribbon development" need not, however, be gone into here. Suffice it to say that the tent was backed by a fifteen-foot pile of dense vegetation cleared from the square in front and augmented by the tons of matted head-foliage cut from the trees far above to allow a little light to penetrate to our abode. Around the square on other sides were bush-houses covering skinners' tables and tunnels leading to the kitchen, the "forecastle," and the outside world.

In the centre of the square stood a quite crazy structure consisting of a framework of long slender bush-sticks (young saplings that have to grow up and up in the forest to attain the light, two hundred feet above) lashed together with creeper cords and covered with mosquito netting. I always carry one of these mosquito rooms made in one piece with a canvas floor hemmed all round, so that one may sit in the open free from mosquito boots, silk scarfs, Sketofax, Flit, and all the rest of the paraphernalia said to counteract insect pests. This room is large enough to contain the table, two chairs, the gramophone, ourselves, and a slim African who winds the gramophone, blots catalogues, cleans microscope slides, mops up spilt drinks, brews more tea, measures rats, and generally makes up for one's own bodily shortcomings.

This evening I gave orders to dig up the roots of the mosquito room and move it across the square, as the trees above dripped a viscous greenish fluid all day and all night, which collected on the linen roof of the contraption and subsequently seeped through to drop on us in still more oleaginous, though slightly lighter greenish blobs, about an egg-cupful at a time.

Now the earth beneath the mosquito room was, as you can imagine, well beaten down with the constant coming and going above the canvas floor. What was our surprise then, when, upon raising the whole off the ground like a giant lump of sugar, a scrambling mass of black, evil-looking things was revealed. The lifting had been accomplished by half a dozen stalwart Africans, as the uprights were sunk in the sticky ground. They all caught sight of what lay concealed beneath at the first warning shout. They dropped their load and jumped hard, for they were, naturally, barefooted.

The canvas floor did not quite reach the ground all over, since the anchor poles held it up, and there was much heaving below. While we dashed for nets and long wooden forceps, the exodus began. The black, evil things left their disturbed abode not in ones and twos, but in tens and twenties, and they ran very fast, straight for the tent, into which they vanished like black ghosts swallowed by the shadows.

Now I must explain that the tent was also of a special variety. I had had the floor sewn to the walls all round, a procedure that I should have thought would have been obvious to the second, if not the very first, tent-maker of all time, as it is the only obvious deterrent to seepage and other forms of dampness. Also the "flies" of the outer tent (ours was a "squatter," which is really two tents, one beneath the other) were forced out on horizontal poles to allow the spaces each side to be converted into tunnel-like passages under which stores and other equipment could be safely kept dry. On this occasion, these spaces under the flies were well stocked with boxes of food, sacks of traps, guns, and other necessities.

Under, into, and among these, the beastly creatures went before we could organize an attack upon them. The reason for this is that a scorpion is a remarkably one-sided affair, meaning that it is flat from the top to the bottom. There is only one creature I know that is flatter, and this I shall refer to later. It seems to have no depth at all, being only length and breadth in opposition to all known laws of physics and geometry.

We scotched a few scorpions in nets and the Africans picked up a few more by their tails so that the deadly stings were harmless and the formidable pincers could not be brought into play, owing to their own dangling weight. These dangerous flatnesses had been happily meandering about under the mosquito-room floor where we were constantly walking about and now they were placidly taking up their quarters beneath our beds, in our food boxes, and goodness knows where else, ready to be trodden on by our barefooted staff.

It was late, very dark, beginning to rain, and we were without one of our powerful paraffin pressure lamps because the jet had got choked. Lastly, we were surrounded by potentially deadly scorpions.

A great hunt began. Boxes and bales were moved with care and their contents examined in the near-by bush-houses with the aid of hurricane lamps. Scorpions were found everywhere. The floor of the tent was raised and people dived after scuttling dark forms. A scream rent the forest.

"Master, bad beef done chop me."

A mad rush ensued in the direction of Eméré, who was hopping on one foot. I examined his great toe, which he woefully tendered to me. No blood oozed out, not a sign of a wound.

"Where did it happen?" I asked.

"Here," the excited Eméré answered, pointing to a canvas bag lying among the equipment. I looked. Then I looked again carefully, for there was the wet imprint of Eméré's flat, muddy foot and under the great toe, a flattened cigarette butt, still warm and dry, nestled in an aura of singed canvas.

Almost every little incident brought its reward in Africa. In the deep forest this was doubly so. One thing leads to another if only one can read the book of wild life.

As an example, I will cite the case of a Munchi, E'twong, who reported the discovery of large termites' nests in a belt of secondary forest bordering an area of natural grass, such as is encountered here and there in the forest where the soil is too meagre to support giant trees.

I was interested in the monumental dwellings of these strange communal insects—often spoken of as "white ants," though they are not ants at all—for a variety of reasons. I therefore ordered a cavalcade to form up, headed by the now all-important E'twong and followed by people with spades, bundles of dry grass, traps, and guns, and tailed by ourselves carrying cameras and a strange instrument called a "trapper's friend," devised by a most enlightened person in Devonshire whose acquaintance I have never had the pleasure of making but who ought to be knighted or elevated to the peerage at once for the invention he has placed in the hands of the collector.

The procession headed off into the forest, cutting its way through the tangled creepers.

Termites' nests are almost beyond comprehension to a person brought up to the reality of things. Later I will take you into the depths of their mysteries, but on this occasion, our interests were merely external.

The nests were numerous, averaging about nine feet in height— colossal edifices raised by the combined efforts of countless tiny insects, chewing wood-pulp and spitting it up to bind tiny packets of puddled clay. Each had its full quota of large tunnels leading down into the base of the cone. Deploying, we tackled one nest at a time. Each tunnel-like entrance was cleared and by it was placed either a gin trap or a net or a man with a stick. Two holes on opposite sides were left free. By one of these we waited with cameras, while down the other, bundles of smouldering grass were pushed with long poles.

At the first nest we had a surprise. Almost before the smoking bundle of grass got down the hole, out from the other side came a slender green snake, twisting and wriggling in its haste to get away from the smoke. He was soon scooped up in a small butterfly net, though about two feet of tail hung out, and strangled through the mesh, the perpetrator wearing a pair of thick leather gloves. The next mound rendered nothing; it appeared to be deserted for some reason.

The third, however, proved to be our goal and the undoing of Faugi. A lot of clearing had to be done, as the undergrowth was thick and tangled. The entrance holes had to be enlarged to allow of the laying of traps and nets. Both these were accomplished with the trapper's friends, which are, amongst other things, axe, spade, sickle, and hammer combined. When all was ready and our cameras set facing the exit, I gave the word to plunge in the smoking bundles.

Faugi stepped forward to do so, but instead set up a dreadful racket, leaping about from one foot to another. Blood dripped from both his legs, but everybody stood around laughing.

He had axed away some of the hard mortar-like ant-hill in order to enlarge the hole down which he must drive the grass. On this exposed portion, he had placed his bare foot.

As soon as a termites' nest is "wounded," the insects get busy. The soldiers—the size of small wasps, with great square red heads—swarm out of the internal chambers and take up positions at all vantage points, turning their open razor-sharp pincers this way and that. Meanwhile, the workers get down to the laborious business of repairing the damage. As much as twenty-seven cubic feet of material can be replaced during a night by the efforts of only a part of one colony, so great is their activity and well organized their industry.

Faugi's feet were a living memorial to their powers, gashed in a score of places as if stabbed with a scalpel. The wounds were not mere nips or pricks, but clean slits about an eighth to a quarter of an inch long, penetrating the thickened "hide" on his tough feet.

In the confusion, everybody left his post, during which time things happened rapidly in the large, cave-like chamber below the ant-hill. Something shot out of a hole, became entangled in a net, and rolled back into the bowels of the earth again, net and all. We dived for our stations and in went the smoking grass. Bedlam broke loose below and we focused our cameras and waited.

Smack, bang. E'twong's bush-knife descended into a hole followed by himself, only to appear again with soldier termites clinging to his lips and ears.

"What was it?" everybody shouted.

"Chook-chook," spluttered the excited Munchi between mouthfuls of earth and white ants.

Then out they came, like bullets from a rifle barrel, Papa, Baby, and then Mamma. Cameras clicked, guns went off, and bush-knives whizzed past my ears. There were two rings of people to be passed and the animals dodged back and forth. I got my hat over Baby and a pile of excited people fell on Papa, but Mamma cantered off into the bush squealing like a pig. I got scratched by the baby, and the cook, who had come to join in the fun, got badly bitten by the old father. Lots of people were "chooked," but we were well satisfied, since I had badly needed live specimens of this interesting animal to study and from which to collect the parasites that infest its skin by day and those others that appear apparently from nowhere to take their places at night.

The chook-chook or brush-tailed porcupine (*Atherura africana*) is a most remarkable animal in several respects. It gets its African name from its stout, straight spines which pierce a human skin almost as easily as the doctor's "chook" (hypodermic), well known to Africans as the only cure for sleeping sickness, yaws, craw-craw, and their other maladies. It is a rodent and, like its relations, very partial to an insect diet. This, combined with the difficulty of burrowing in the forests—despite their chisel teeth for cutting through roots—leads these animals to take up their quarters in the holes beneath ant-hills. They are very plump creatures with short fat legs and a fairly long, scaly tail terminated by a bunch of quite remarkable white quills. These consist of a stiff chain of hollow, blister-

BUSH-TAILED PORCUPINE (Atherura africana)

like swellings with solid, constricted portions between them. The whole bunch has the appearance and texture of a dried sheaf of corn, and when shaken, which is done in anger or fright, makes much the same noise, only louder. I have seen a mother porcupine call her offspring to her from considerable distances by this method, the tail being vibrated faster than the eye can follow.

The chook-chook, for all its fatness and prickles, is a swift-running animal with great staying powers. In certain parts of Africa where there are clumps of bush in open grass-fields, it takes the place of the fox in the chase. Hearty British sportsmen, having perhaps only the slightest acquaintance with the shires, mounted on tsetse-fly-blown mountain ponies, ride to a pack of hounds (including staghound, dachshund, and other, unnameable members of that family) with loud whoops and tallyhos among the thorn bushes and a cloud of perspiration. The chook-chook, like his distant brush-tailed relation, often goes to ground after a long parabolic run, out of which he is also sometimes dug by laconic local peasantry. It is a fine sport, having the added attractions of a complete absence of barbed wire, countless brooks in which mountain ponies will insist upon bathing, and, perhaps most important, the edibility, nay, the fine succulence of the quarry. There is also a periodic hunt-ball at which one's servants do all the dancing, while the gallant sportsmen are free to gossip in the open-air bar.

Porcupines are not the only things that come out of holes, as I subsequently learnt.

We had a rowdy and not altogether bright fellow about the place for some time; he was known by the name of Dele. He had determined to work for us and had walked about one hundred miles with that end in view, arriving at a time when we were short-handed and far from anywhere. Also, he was a Munchi, to which tribe I had learnt to be particularly attached. He therefore stayed as trapper until I found some adequate reason to get rid of him. During this time he became most enthusiastic, and as he seemed to have a considerable bush-craft as well as a capacity to keep quiet, I often went grubbing about with him in the more inaccessible regions of the forest. We dammed rivers, climbed trees, wriggled among masses of creepers, and generally felt the pulse of the jungle. The results of our labours were varied and now lie in the bottles and boxes of quiet museums.

One afternoon we came upon a cliff some forty feet high but, of course, entirely buried and hidden by the blanket of forest. Patches of sunlight penetrated the gloom, and where they fell clots of dense herbage had sprung up. Diving beneath one such clump of vegetation we instantly saw the openings of a number of large burrows. Into these we pushed our faces, sniffing like dogs and listening for any sounds. Sure enough, there were slight movements within.

We began clearing away herbage around us until we had a sort of cavern beneath the matted bushes and all the entrances were clearly visible. Next, we began digging and probing with trapper's friends. After a time I saw something heave among the cut leaves behind Dele, at which I promptly took a swat with my t.f., as I called it.

The result was appalling. The whole ground seemed to heave, earth and sticks flew about, and Dele scrambled off on all fours to a distant hole which he proceeded to belabour smartly. I was left more or less vacantly kneeling on the heaving soil, which gradually subsided until I felt it time to move. Reaching Dele's side, I inquired what he thought it could be.

His English was sketchy and somewhat throaty at the best of times, but now it was incomprehensible and all I could make out was "bad beef." Slowly the commotion beneath us subsided and Dele let up on his energetic battle-axing. Still mystified, I watched him cut away the soil and probe about below. After some time of feverish activity in which I co-operated heartily, he seized what appeared to be a bloody clot of earth and began to pull. We both pulled for some minutes until at last ten feet six and a half inches of *Python regius*, king of African snakes, came out, slowly twisting, undulating, and quivering here and there like a horse's haunches when a fly tickles it. When I say six and a half inches, I am not strictly accurate, as the head was a mere meaty slush, hacked to pieces.

This was an odd capture indeed, but more surprising things were to follow, for there were still mutterings and movements below in the network of subterranean galleries. We dug and dug until the perspiration streamed off us, and nearer and nearer we came to the centre of the disturbance.

At last we unearthed them—three great tortoises (*Trionyx triunguis*)—huddled nervously together, blinking out from under their shells with their soft black eyes as though they knew they were at our mercy. I have never seen any animals look quite so sad and pleading, though all animals so helpless make me almost die with compassion. Dele wanted to take them back for the pot, but I put up a stubborn defence for my protégés, more particularly because they were susceptible to being tickled on the back of their shells, which gave us another bond of understanding and sympathy. Of course, I won, though not altogether by mere authority, for Dele, being an African, quite appreciated my emotions; besides, he was not hungry and I intimated that tortoise-killing was bad ju-ju in my country.

I feel that it is necessary to mention leopards, not because the doings of these are white as well as black man's ju-ju, but because they are extremely plentiful in these particular forests.

The first occasion upon which my attention was definitely drawn to the actual presence of leopards (*Panthera pardus leopardus*) around us occurred only a few days after we had moved from the confines of Mamfe station, where we had been studying the wild life that exists among the unnatural surroundings of cultivation. Our camp was then pitched in a patch of scrub and smallish trees in the middle of an area of tall grass in the depth of the primary forest. This grass-field was one of many that occur in the depths of the high forest because of the almost total absence of soil. The forest ends around them like a tall green wall, and small islands of tall growth are dotted about where depressions allow soil to gather. To reach our camp, we followed the Great North Road from the "ferry" (an old canoe) below Mamfe up over the brow of the hill beyond. This road here passes through alternate patches of forest and grass. In the last arm of the grass that the road traversed, we had cut a track leading off to the left which meandered across the grass-fields, taking always the line of least resistance, until it entered our shady domain.

I had been back to Mamfe collecting certain equipment from our base camp there, also a pet monkey which I carried on my shoulder. With me was Faugi. Our work kept us late and it was dusk before we paddled across the river. On this account we borrowed the old leper canoeman's lantern and set off into the forest. For some reason best known to the fates or the powers of African ju-ju, I did not carry my pet shotgun, but only a rough stick and the monkey who balanced herself on my head or my shoulder.

Faugi walked ahead carrying the dim hurricane lamp which cast dancing amber beams among the great boles of the trees. The night was quiet, yet strident with countless myriads of chirruping, whirring insects, and the air heavy as an anæsthetic. Our progress was silent as death, for the ground was loamy and I wore rubber shoes, while Faugi padded along on his own bare, horny, naked soles. Only the rhythmic squeak of the lantern handle betrayed our passage.

On entering the last and longest stretch of high forest before reaching the grass, the monkey began to shiver and chatter. She descended from my shoulder and gained an entrance to my shirt with some dexterity. This I thought odd at the time, but it was not until we reached the next bend that I called an abrupt halt and looked back. My eyesight is bad, which is probably the reason for my almost uncanny sense of hearing—a constant source of surprise to all Africans, whose ears, as sense organs, leave a great deal to be desired when compared to the white man's. I had heard something unusual and I was greatly interested.

The sounds recurred as soon as we continued our march. Their faint rippling followed us in the undergrowth. Faugi sensed nothing and kept walking ahead, for which I was subsequently grateful because, had he seen what I saw, he would doubtless have dropped the lantern and bolted, leaving me in a dark and most uncomfortable position. As it was, an uncanny sensation overcame me—an uncontrollable shudder that was cold. It seemed to claw at my spine so that I kept looking round.

I have always laughed inwardly at people who contend they have quaked for no apparent reason; I now know better. I have met a tiger (a small one, I will admit) face to face, with a butterfly net as sole protection, and I have seen leopards wild and very free, but neither actually did more than frighten me in the way that an angry bull in a field might do. This sensation was altogether different; it seemed to come to me from without, not from myself at all.

Then I turned and saw something that made me quite cold.

Right across the path stretched a long, sinuous form, apparently nowhere more than about a foot tall. Its head was small for its great length and, strangest of all, it seemed to be quite white all over. For a second only it paused, then the front part slewed round and the after portion followed like a train navigating a bend. The confounded thing was deliberately stalking us in broad lamplight. Its eyes were orange in colour, not green as one is always told, and yet there was no doubt about its being a leopard, indeed a most healthily active one.

It advanced to within thirty yards of me. As Faugi was rapidly gaining the same distance in the other direction, being unaware that I had stopped, the light was getting decidedly dim and I decided it was high time to quit.

At my first movement to do so, the leopard gathered up its back portion in a heap and left the field of vision in one bound, landing in the pile of dense undergrowth without a sound. I hurried after Faugi and we presently emerged on the grass-fields, just as a tremendous crashing and grunting broke out at the edge of the forest. Faugi attributed this to the flight of a duiker antelope. I kept my counsel, though I believed I knew better.

After this informal introduction, we saw only pieces of leopards for several months. These tantalizing morsels consisted chiefly of skins and skulls without lower jaws, treasured by village chiefs or even more highly valued and reverenced in ju-ju houses. The leopard enters into a great number of ritual ceremonies, as well as being itself intrinsically valuable for more than one reason. Every part of it, therefore, is carefully preserved and well guarded. Later we got in touch with a very powerful affiliation of the Leopard Society and, after passing through certain initiation rites, were allowed to make specific contributions to a particular ju-ju faculty which permitted us to gain a much closer contact with leopards generally, as well as giving us the valuable right to purchase and possess remains of the animals when dead. Without this, it is practically impossible to hold possession of such trophies for any length of time in this country; mysterious and unaccountable accidents occur to them, or they simply vanish and nobody seems to know how or why. It is only pure sportsmen surrounded by "foreign" natives (that is, natives from another part of Africa), or a political officer accompanied by native police and orderlies, who may obtain leopards by shooting them themselves. We, as doctors in the African sense of the word, had very little chance, if any at all, of even meeting a leopard.

On three other occasions, nevertheless, during the period between being stalked and joining the African Leopard Society, when out hunting with torch and gun in the deep forest, I felt that uncanny sensation of creeping coldness. Once when more than a hundred feet from the ground, following Dele along a branch of a tree as wide as a footpath, I suddenly flashed the powerful torch in the direction from which I felt the sensations were emanating, and there, sure enough, glowed a pair of monstrous orange fires. As I had had to leave my gun at ground level, I could do nothing but stare back, which was not pleasant, since the eyes were exactly level with my own in the centre of a dense clot of creepers and ferns which enveloped the next-door tree. Dele saw them too, and, breathing out the word "tiger," slid down the swinging creepers to the ground.

I followed as best, or rather better than, I could, since my creeper ended some eight feet from the ground, and suddenly finding myself clinging to nothing tangible, I let go the torch and fell squarely on the naked African, whom I mistook for the leopard! In total darkness in an African jungle one is apt to make the silliest mistakes! We eventually found the shotgun—not that it was of much use in any case—and then cautiously ascended the tree in which the eyes had been glowing.

This proved very difficult to climb, especially with a gun, and we took a long time reaching the level where I had seen the prize we so much wanted. Of course there was nothing there, and although we searched the tree from end to end and roamed about the surrounding bush for hours, nothing showed up. Every other animal had cleared out of the neighbourhood, doubtless wisely. When I look back on our behaviour that night, I am amazed and aghast at the idiocy of what we did. It was obvious that the "tiger" would have gone by the time we climbed aloft and if it hadn't, I imagine a lot of interesting and uncomfortable things would have occurred.

Leopards were among the animals of which we were especially desirous of obtaining specimens and information. We therefore made full use of our privilege of being affiliated with the Leopard Society, and offered to purchase anything the natives offered. This brought a full-grown leopard, while still warm, into the hands of my colleague, Seaton. Seaton, to whom I shall in future refer as "the Duke"—a mysterious title which he acquired for no apparent reason on the day of his arrival in Africa to join George and myself —was working alone at the time near a place named Bachuntai. When he received the leopard it was intact in every detail.

He set to work and skinned it with his own hands and finished the job before dark. With him were Omezi, his own skinner, and, as always, a crowd of onlookers. By the time the skin was off, all the whiskers had disappeared. They had not been cut off, but pulled out by the roots.

The Duke reported this to me when we all joined forces again some weeks later. I was interested but not sufficiently annoyed at the small loss to think twice about it. A few days later, however, unrest broke out among the entire staff, an entirely novel departure in our household and one which was never repeated. I eventually unearthed the cause. Omezi was accused of being in possession of the leopard's whiskers, his father being a ju-ju official, and it was suspected that he *might* have been or be about to start poisoning his fellows. Omezi and I then had a ju-ju contest at which I triumphed with the aid of a magnet and some other ordinary gadgets.

During the proceedings I learnt a great deal about this vexed question of poisoning by the use of the chopped-up whiskers of large cats such as leopards, tigers, and jaguars. The stories have been heard in many countries widely separated, and nobody seems to have been able to confirm them or dispute them.

With this new knowledge, I prepared some leopard's whiskers, obtained from another skin, according to the prescribed rules. These I tasted without swallowing, as the process entailed a very thorough sterilization. There appeared to be no poisonous extract. Later I offered some, well disguised among garry-corn and banana mash, to a chimpanzee. It sensed something amiss at once and, after picking carefully through the food with its forefinger, it spat out what it had tasted and vigorously trampled the rest underfoot. Another portion of the mash, but without the chopped whiskers, was greedily devoured. I subsequently persuaded a monkey (*Cercopithecus nictitans*) to eat some and when it died some weeks later, I carried out a careful post-mortem.

At first I found nothing and supposed that all the whiskers had passed right through the intestinal tract. A closer examination, however, revealed a great number of small cyst-like inflammations deeply buried in the lining of the stomach wall. Upon opening these, I was most astounded to find a single chip of the leopard whisker (never two or more), quite unaltered, as on the day it was swallowed. The monkey had, however, died of bronchial pneumonia and, as is the way with wild animals, had preserved a hearty appetite until the morning of its death.

Are leopard whiskers, then, lethal when eaten? I should imagine they are, since any increase in the size of the tubercles in the stomach wall would doubtless lead to ruptures and, subsequently, peritonitis. People said to have been killed by this method are reputed to have died in great agony some time after the poisoning, and the Africans say of these victims that they had "tiger-for-belly."

Leopards in Africa are in some weird but none the less definite manner connected with the supernatural. The "tiger," as he is called by the Africans, is a lurker in dark places and unique in his habits generally. This seems to impress the European as well, who never fails to mention his comings and goings. The leopard stalks through the pages of every book on Africa, like a watermark in the paper, rasping like a saw or jumping in and out of compounds, in the limelight only here and there but ever present somewhere in the background.

For us, however, who went to Africa *expecting* such a back-

GOLDEN CAT (Profelis aurata)

ground, there arose before long another and still more baffling lurker in dark places.

The great cat tribe is headed by a group of proud beasts well known to all—the lion, tiger, leopard, jaguar, puma, ounce (snow leopard), etc. There are also the long-legged cheetahs, servals, and caracals, and then a tail of animals of ever-diminishing size—civets, palm-civets, genets, and fossas. In addition, between the first and second groups mentioned above, comes a large group of smaller typical cats. These are little known to any but specialists and are rare even in large museums. Every continent harbours a few and Africa is no exception. There is always much discussion as to exactly how many kinds there are in any particular place and every large area of virgin forest is reputed to contain at least one species that has never been actually killed or preserved, in addition to those definitely known. They are, in fact, obscure beasts rarely encountered.

There is one such in West Africa, the golden cat, (*Profelis aurata*) by name. This animal assumed a most peculiar significance for us. Whenever we asked hunters for information about it, they declared they had never heard of it. Later I found portions of a golden cat's skin in a chief's ceremonial coat and when I pointed it out, I was told that it came from a "far, far country." We bribed and cajoled everybody and hunted high and low for it ourselves, but nothing came of it all.

Not until we were initiated into the mysteries of the local religious and social customs regarding the leopard did I realize that this animal is of equal, if not even greater, importance. Through the influence of certain old gentlemen connected with leopards, we eventually obtained two skins, but skulls we never saw, nor any other part of the beast. One was killed not more than three miles from our camp, but the hunters skinned the animal on the spot and disappeared into the forest for four days before returning to us. I went in search of the scene of the kill, but never found it for a variety of very good reasons, not least among them the determination of everybody to lead me to any place but the right one.

There are several skins of this animal in museums, but only a handful of skulls, and ju-ju is again the reason.

4

Encounter with River Hogs;
The Green Mamba; Ants;
Other Biting Things (Horse Flies)

THE world of the great forests is a veritable paradise for those who will take the trouble to read its mysteries. Enveloped by towering walls of greenery, like a microbe in a pile carpet, I found never-ending restfulness and comfort in this safe retreat from the glare of the world. Perhaps these unconventional reactions to an environment hated and feared by the majority who penetrate them were in some respects connected with my upbringing as a town-dweller. Life in great cities is not unlike that in the primeval forests. One passes from one burrow to another along canyons that are only a little lighter, and breadth of vision is everywhere excluded by towering battlements palpitating with the lives hidden behind them. Always there is life around one, but it is hardly visible; imagination must work overtime to formulate its progress, lest one pass for ever through the dense crowds utterly alone.

When the sun shines upon the roof of the forest, vistas of indescribable beauty spring into existence below. Golden lights fall upon shady tunnels of riotous greenery backed by sombre halflights. We used to sit by little crystal-clear streams, where pools of sunlight fell upon the moss-covered rocks like spotlights on a stage, and bask in the silent stillness of the day, awed and made reverent by the very beauty of the scene. Here would rise a feathery palm, its roots in the dim recesses of the forest, its fronds extended motionless into the shimmering sunlight with countless slender fingers of delicate jade; there would pass a dancing sapphire insect, while beyond and below and above rose billowing waves of foliage, chartreuse-green and delicate, bottle-green and shimmering, or blending here and there in colours and textures indefinable.

The sleeping silence of the days and the strident stillness of the nights may be ruffled by the storms and the thunderings of the clouds, but nothing is mighty enough to ruffle the eternity of the forests. Rain falls and the winds blow but soon they pass, and the trees, stirring no more, stand motionless to drip away their discomfort in eternal immobility.

To dwell amidst this endless foliage is akin to life amongst the gods of old. Past, present, and future have no meaning; the eternity of nature becomes something real. To sit alone in the midday silence of the jungle and try to visualize the machinations of civilized life is an impossibility. All the acts and histories of men become so futile and ephemeral before the grandiose stature of eternal nature, that it seems somehow unaccountable and altogether crazy to imagine little humans believing that their comic and futile efforts count for anything at all. The whole human race becomes just a phase of natural history that will pass like the great dinosaurs of old, leaving not a trace of their worries and their cares. How strongly one feels that, when this and many other self-important herds of striving beings are gone, the forests will remain basking in the sunlight, lords of the earth, unconquerable, perhaps divine.

People have lived in the forests for days, weeks, months, even years, without seeing anything living except an occasional monkey or squirrel. Intelligent men whose lives have been spent in the jungle of West Africa have told me with what interest and surprise they viewed the endless stream of life we extracted from the apparently dead world around them. Gradually one learns the sociology of the forest; slowly, day by day, one becomes more attuned to the organization of the life around; piece by piece the camouflage that conceals everything is lifted. There is revealed a world of endless variety, of never-ending beauty and interest.

One of the first laws revealed to us was the unsuspected fact that the life of the jungle is like that of the ocean floor. This has never been observed or remarked upon before. Everything drifts slowly hither and thither as if wafted forward by currents and cross-currents. To stand still is to arouse suspicion, just as a diver, who can actually handle fish and other sea creatures provided he drifts with them across the bed of the sea, becomes an object to be feared and shunned as soon as he remains immobile and anchored.

When hunting, we adopted two entirely different methods. George concealed himself at some vantage point and waited for the waves of forest life to drift by him; I drifted and eddied with the animals themselves. Doing this, I learnt many things and so did he. The speed at which I drifted, I found, must vary with the weather. Bright fine days brought life almost to a standstill. In a hurricane I had to run to keep pace with things. Sometimes terrestrial animals would be drifting one way while all arboreal creatures above me would be passing in quite another direction.

Then we perceived that certain animals and types of animals followed quite definite roads through the trees and upon the ground, and, further, that they had times at which they passed to and fro as regularly as machines. Some animals betrayed the presence of others, certain fruits drove animals away when they should have attracted them, and so on; the laws and rules were never ending in their variety.

Drifting thus across the floor of the forest, I once approached a little dell into which flowed a small stream. The ground was boggy and covered with lush vegetation, so that the waters spread far and wide, forming a small marsh. As I slid noiselessly along following the tracks of a small squirrel, a murmuring and rumbling came to my ears, dim and faint at first, a mere ghost of a sound. Gradually it gained in volume until, when I stood in the marsh, it seemed to be all around me. I moved forward slowly, as I had learnt I must do to gain a glimpse of the animals that were causing all this "talk."

Abruptly I came upon them, a veritable herd of the weirdest animals I have ever seen. Rich orange in colour, with monstrous heads, they formed a vivid contrast to the sombre greens of the water weeds. It seemed, in fact, as if they were more than half head, since their short legs were sunk deep in the morass that they were busily creating in the soft earth. On their heads they bore tall crests of spotless white which passed backward into a long white mane falling this way or that over their shoulders. Their ears were long and pointed, terminated by a long white plume, which they constantly flicked and twitched as they ploughed up the ground in long, even furrows. All the while they grunted and grumbled contentedly.

A herd of river hogs (*Potamochœrus porcus*) is an unusual sight. They seem as contented and lazy as ordinary farmyard pigs, yet their vivid coloration and grotesque form make one pause to consider whether one's sight is playing a trick. In the wilds they don't look like pigs at all. They are, in fact, unlike any other animal with their big heads, long, tapering, plumed ears, and tall narrow bodies.

Having drifted right in among them and been scrutinized by a large, dangerous-looking hog and apparently found quite welcome, I allowed myself to move gently forward. I had read of people in East Africa approaching to within a few feet of perfectly wild lions at the midday siesta—in fact, my own father was one of the first to show that this was possible provided one moved slowly enough—but I never suspected that these tactics were applicable to such sly and arrogant animals as the red river hog of the forests. Nevertheless, I soon found myself right in the centre of the herd, noticed but unfeared by them. Perhaps the fact that I carried nothing smelling strange like a gun or camera or other oily metal instrument reassured them. Gently they moved around me, as we were all drifting in the same direction; sometimes four would be in view at once, sometimes all would vanish amid the foliage so that I knew of their presence only by their ceaseless, moaning grunts.

For ages, it seemed, this unique contact went on undisturbed, during which time I was favoured with the priceless opportunity of watching these rare and obscure animals carrying on their everyday existence in perfect harmony with their surroundings. They are in-

RED RIVER HOGS (*Potamochœrus porcus*)

deed peculiar hunters. I had always supposed them to be herbivorous, yet I saw one large sow unearth a cluster of huge snails and set to work cracking the shells and munching up the juicy contents. In this she was assisted by three small hogs who tussled and bit each other in an effort to get at the morsels. The tactics consisted of flying tackles in which they threw their whole weight into their shoulders and banged their opponents, one of whom was sent sprawling into the muddy bog. The sight of a wild animal floundering on its back was really most remarkable and gave me the impression of watching a group of school children at play.

One old hog who kept looking at me as if realizing that I might be potentially dangerous made a most comical misjudgment. He was rooting along the edge of the marsh, stopping now and then with his long snout several inches in the mud to crunch up some hidden root, when he inadvertently pushed under a particularly tough root extending from a large tree on the solid ground near by.

It appeared that he had small tushes (as I saw later) and these must have got locked under the root, for he suddenly set up the most terrific racket, dancing about with his back legs and giving little hops like a ballet dancer, heaving, pulling, and squealing as if caught by the nose. At first I thought he was fighting something on the ground, since his nose was out of view behind a small plant, and I stupidly moved to see what it was all about.

This worried the others, who began to move off hurriedly, but I got a good view of the hog as he writhed in fury, tugging at the root. Then my attention was drawn to one of the loveliest sights I have ever seen. As the herd moved past me with increasing speed, out trotted some individuals I had not seen before. Among them was a swarm of tiny piglets, each immaculately striped with gold on its little, otherwise unmarked body. They trotted along in line uttering high-pitched grunts and herded from behind by an agitated mother who kept prodding their delicate little hind legs as if to say: "Go on, hurry up, or the bogyman will get you." The whole scene was so perfect that I stood spellbound at the sight of it.

Just then a young animal, whether male or female I know not, trotted by and I instantly determined to try to capture it. It came so close that I saw a vision of this amazingly colourful creature in the zoo, the centre of surprised and wondering crowds of holiday makers, and I made a dive for it. Although I moved with lightning speed, and actually touched its hard, bristly haunches, it leapt aside and plunged off into the undergrowth yelling like a human. The old hog must have made a super-porcine effort at that moment and got free, for I heard him crash off at high speed into the distance.

Dusk was falling as I waded back across the swamp, now churned up like a ploughed field by the sharp snouts of the hogs. The way in which they can overturn a plot of ground is really unbelievable.

It often became necessary to leave our camp in the forest and set out on the weary trek back to our base at Mamfe to collect items of equipment or stores. Upon the particular day of which I now write, N'gwa, who was temporarily in charge of the commissariat, accompanied me, as the most pressing matter to be attended to happened to be groceries.

Hard by our camp were some grass-fields in which were open patches of bare rock. While awaiting N'gwa's arrival to make the trip, I lay down to take a sun bath. George lay beside me, his topee tilted over his eyes, and we discussed, I remember, the comparative heights of African mountains. Having completed the roasting of my breast and "wings," I rolled over to cook up my back and legs, basting myself well with a cloth to protect my spine and neck from the sun's evil rays.

What, then, was my consternation upon opening my eyes to be confronted by a slender brown snake swaying to and fro above me.

With a yell, we both scrambled away and a flood of excited Negroes dashed out of the path leading from our camp. A great chase over the bare rock ensued; nets were brought and people danced about, taking random shots at the enemy who retired into an island clump of grass struggling for existence in a crack of the rock surface. From this retreat he was driven with long sticks and dispatched in a most novel and practical way.

As the snake raised its head and forebody to strike, one of the Africans administered a sharp cut with a fine, thin switch. This seemed to have broken the creature's spine, for it collapsed in a heap and hardly moved again.

The commotion over, N'gwa and I set out for Mamfe, but, foolishly deciding to dispense with the track, we cut across the grass to join the main path further down the hill. The grass was waist-high, though every here and there flattened like corn after a storm. Through this we ploughed in silence.

Suddenly N'gwa let out a yell, rose perpendicularly off the ground, and crashed headlong sideways, disappearing into the long grass. I peered over to see what it was all about and there, glaring angrily, was a huge green mamba (*Dendraspis jamesoni*), one of the most deadly of all snakes. As I dived for N'gwa, thinking he had been bitten, the mamba disappeared below the mass of bent grass stems.

N'gwa was still writhing about in the grass and since he had been carrying lots of miscellaneous objects, he was in something of a huddle. Having ascertained that he was not wounded, I tried to extricate him, but as soon as I got him on his feet, he stepped on the cold polished handle of a butterfly net and, imagining he had really landed on the snake this time, he uttered another yell, turned a sort of cheese-colour under his shiny brown skin, and bolted forthwith for the neighbouring bush, discarding valuable equipment as he went.

I had a most unpleasant quarter of an hour gathering up the various objects strewn far and wide, conscious all the time of the fact that somewhere around and beneath me was a large, deadly, and very angry snake. I was wearing thin india-rubber-soled shoes, no socks, and thin trousers.

However, I reached the near-by bush unscathed but festooned like a Christmas tree with all sorts of nets and boxes. I eventually located N'gwa in a small paw-paw tree and rated him soundly for being a coward, expanding on the theme that Negroes, if they wished to rule the world, as they assert they one day will, must cultivate the calm and stoicism of the phlegmatic Nordics. This proved to be a particularly stupid admonition, quite apart from the fact that N'gwa's action was by far the most logical and practical.

Having accomplished our errands in Mamfe, we dallied on the way back to camp, collecting tree frogs. While N'gwa repeated his performance of the paw-paw tree, I pottered about at ground level.

Without warning, I felt the most excruciating pain on my hip. Something pierced my skin like a searing dart. I clenched my flesh as one possessed, only to leap in the air when I was pierced again on the left thigh. In an instant I was writhing in indescribable agony as a result of an unceasing battery of stings inflicted on every part of my body.

Tearing off his clothes, a dejected example of the stoic European race thus found himself yelling for his Negro companion like a soul in purgatory, crying for succour from an angel. Help came in the form of N'gwa, who beat me unmercifully with his horny hands and then fell to picking off with his nails the swarms of vicious ants still clinging to my now more or less livid flesh. What a pathetic sight a scrawny white body must have been, smarting in the sunlight like a great, bloodless slug unexpectedly turned over by a spade.

Ants in the forests are an ever-present plague. There are countless varieties, from minute red ones to immense black creatures the size of a wasp with luminous, iridescent, old-gold abdomens. All can bite ferociously and several of the larger species in addition sting like hornets. Hardly a day passed but that we came to rest with one foot in an ants' nest, when our eyes were intent on the trees above us. All of a sudden you feel a bite, and then it is all over. You flee in disorder, discarding your clothes and swatting at your tormentors. Silently they creep over you, sometimes as far north as your chest. I have even had them in my hair, so swift is their onslaught. Hours we spent picking them from the inside of our clothes. Later I will tell you of our most terrifying experience at their hands, by far the worst moment of our whole trip.

On one occasion we were lost in the forest for two days. Tired and hungry, we wandered on through the night, colliding with trees, wading through swamps, and scrambling up precipitous cliffs. Despairing of ever getting out of our leafy grave, we sent the same N'gwa aloft to try to spy out from a tall tree any landmarks to guide us.

Quickly he swarmed upwards out of sight among the foliage while we waited hopefully below. Minutes passed during which time he might as well have vanished into heaven. Suddenly, with a scream, he came down, slithering, slipping, tumbling down the trunk, clawing wildly at passing branches. He arrived with a resounding bump but, to our amazement, leapt up and started tearing off his native cloth. He had sat on a tree-ants' nest, though to look at his face one would have thought he had been bitten by an angry leopard.

These tree ants were big and black, but there were others, very small and brown. Our tent was pitched in a small clearing in the forest; our mosquito-netted beds extended out into the open. It appears that while I slept peacefully one morning, George was awakened by a persistent dripping noise. This proved to be a steady stream of small ants, ant larvæ, and ant eggs landing on the top of his mosquito net. Scrambling out of bed, he yelled for assistance, at the same time searching for the centre of dispersal which he instantly saw was a dead tree overhanging the camp. One hollow branch of this tree reached over the tent, and from this was pouring a ceaseless stream of ants and their offspring—in fact, the whole colony seemed to be bent on taking its departure. Amazed at this effrontery, George had the tree pulled down, but not before the entire ground was carpeted with ants.

What, he inquired of the excited staff, was to be done?

Somebody, however, was equal to the occasion. Several fowls were instantly fetched; small logs were attached to their legs by long pieces of string, and by the time I awoke, they had cleared away the last trace of an ant and were clucking expectantly around for more food, in the vacant way fowls have.

Many people tell me that they would never go to the tropics because they hate insects. It is just as well that they realize this, lest they go mad in their innocence. Ants are a torment that can be avoided, but there are other horrors that cannot.

In the deep forests, the usual pests—mosquitoes, tsetse, chrysops, and other flies—are present, but are not the main cause of discomfort as they are elsewhere. There is present a tribe of winged devils that can cause even greater pain though less lasting woe.

In temperate climes we have a sombre brown individual spoken of loosely as a horse fly. Occasionally this insect alights on one of our happy swimmers and administers a smart sting with its dart. This is regarded by the undressed bather as an unwarranted presumption but is soon forgotten. In the African jungles the horse fly's relatives are legion. Every now and then the record for sheer bulk in our camp was surpassed by a new arrival that suddenly appeared on the sunny tent flap or the sleeve of one's shirt.

The positive holder of the title for unsurpassable bulk eventually made itself felt in the following manner. Bassi came running into camp one evening, at the hour when we were absorbing weak tea from glasses, to announce that he had seen two small lemurs (*Galago demidovii*) entering some isolated low trees near the camp. These lemurs were our chief reason for going to Africa, so we grabbed guns and darted off, full of hope. Since these lemurs are agile animals about the size of a small rat, and the trees in question were very dense, we took up positions some yards apart and waited in complete silence for the quarry to betray their whereabouts by agitating the foliage. We held our guns pointing towards the trees with their butts on our hips and our hands ready to bring them to the firing position with the greatest possible address.

After many minutes of intense vigilance, I diverted my gaze in order to rest my eyes and saw that George was silently beckoning to me. I advanced towards him cautiously. When I was still a few paces from him, something about two inches long suddenly appeared on the seat of his trousers, as if by magic created out of nothingness.

Before I had time to investigate the nature of the beast and before I could warn George, the latter literally went up in smoke. Both barrels, the gun, and that usually imperturbable person himself all went off at once. The two charges entered the foliage above; the gun described a neat parabolic course and landed upright in the soft earth with several inches of barrel out of sight; and my deeply respected colleague was projected forward and upward to the extent of several feet. When he landed, both his hands were clutching "the afflicted parts," as a druggist's label would state.

When he was eventually persuaded to release his hold, the remains of the aggressor were examined and proved to be those of a monstrous horse fly armed with a veritable lance. This was subsequently discovered to have pierced poor George's epidermis and a great deal beyond, with an adroitness and instantaneity that neither of us had previously believed possible.

5

Rats and Frogs of the Forest

IT is an interesting and in some ways an incomprehensible fact
that all the human beings in the world, if gathered together
shoulder to shoulder and packed chest to back, could stand
on half the Isle of Wight. As lords of the earth, we consider ourselves of paramount importance, both in quality and quantity.
Nevertheless, among us, around, between, and often below us, is
hidden an army of another, though in some respects not very unlike, kind that far exceeds us both in numbers and aggregate bulk. It
is also a mammalian army, like ourselves.

This hidden populace consists of the countless hordes of rats
which infest and inhabit every part of the globe. Wherever man is
and wherever he is not, there rats live and multiply. Neither the
arctic wastes of the north nor the waterless deserts of the tropics are
immune from their scratchings and their burrowings. After working out the number of rats that go to an average human being,
allowing for the fact that a rat extends horizontally whereas we are
projected vertically, and discovering the numbers of rats in popu-
lated areas of the earth's surface and the numbers in the unpopulated
—figures which become positively astronomical—it appears that if
all these neighbours of ours were gathered together on the remaining half of the Isle of Wight, they would overflow onto the main-
land and extend many miles beyond.—Where are all these rats?

The answer is simple—everywhere. Gas and bombs will kill rats,
but not nearly so easily as they will kill men; and on the death of
men, rats thrive. Abandon a location and in come the rats to in-

habit the land. Destroy a farmer with your gas-bomb and he and his single yearly offspring will vanish from the scheme of things; but in his stead will appear some rat with his monthly quota of a dozen healthy progeny, all of which are ready to repeat their parents' multiplications in a few weeks.

Perhaps one day we will awaken to find ourselves in the enigmatical plight of the inhabitants of the Laccadive Islands who once, in the bombastically complacent way of our species, lorded it over all their little archipelago in the Indian Ocean. Nowadays every male inhabitant of the islands must turn out twice a week, to the detriment of all other occupations, and join in a rat-hunt lest the rapidly diminishing food supply, already threatened by the rats, be completely swept away. And still the rats increase.

Through forest and plain, field and swamp, they run, countless millions of them, eating, multiplying, and being eaten. At least so the world went on until the advent of this organizing animal called man—man, who thinks his powers equal to nature, cutting and hewing the forests, draining the swamps, planting the fields.

I have mentioned the results of his advent in the lands cleared of forests: Mamfe station with its hordes of yellow-spotted inmates, its black denizens dying among the rafters, its countless four-legged inhabitants roving the plantations, clucking, banging, and squeaking about their business. To give an insight into the undisturbed rat life of the forests, in comparison, is a task of far greater difficulty.

The great jungle of unmolested forests is like a limitless cathedral, its arching roof supported on a myriad towering pillars. Between the smooth barrels of the tree trunks grows an orchard-like canopy of broad-leafed vegetation casting a double gloom on the bare carpet of dead leaves and tangled creeper stems. The moist air and the blazing sun are for ever sucking the buds, the flowers, and the fruits from the undulating roof of greenery above. The fruits fall down into the depths of the gloom, an unending cascade of succulence and fragrance. Some part of the forest floor is for ever strewn with a mat of juicy sweet-smelling fruits, like manna from the heavens, bewildering in its abundance and variety.

Every night it is cleared away by a swarm of hungry little mouths. From the tangled undergrowth, from the trees above, from the swamps and out of burrows deep and shallow, they pour—huge fat rats, long slender rats hopping on prodigious legs like kangaroos, plain ordinary rats, and tiny fragile rats. Night after night one may set traps baited with odoriferous tit-bits in their runs, amid the fallen fruits, by their burrows or their piles of droppings, but only every now and then will a fool among rats stop to investigate your carefully prepared bait and leave his dead body in your trap to be found in the morning. The horde passes by to the piles of food provided by nature as its forebears have done for countless æons.

Slowly we pieced together evidence of this. Sometimes one rat a night, sometimes more, and very often none at all would fall victim to temptation and nibble the bait. Often the corpse would be almost devoured by his companions, more often by the ants, but slowly we gathered material as proof of what we saw around us.

Lying silently among a tangled mass of foliage brought down from above by a fallen tree, I waited in the eerie light of evening to see for myself the life of this mysterious hidden world. Before it became too dark to see, I was rewarded by a sight that finally shattered all my beliefs in the balance of life.

I had selected a vantage point from which I could watch unobserved and unsmelt a long vista of bare forest floor leading from a stream choked with lush herbage and a clay bank beyond to a patch of ground covered with newly fallen fruits. I had settled into my hide-out shortly after three-thirty in the afternoon, fully expecting some two hours' wait during which time I should get used to the bites of ants and other insects and perhaps have the opportunity of witnessing the passing of some monkeys, bush-cats, or other larger animals. I was very much mistaken, however, since streaks of brown and red began flashing among the leaves and tree roots as soon as I fell quiet.

Within half an hour the life of the forest had returned to normality and I was completely forgotten. From everywhere nervous little brown forms appeared, darting hither and thither, investigating crevices that caught their fancy, sitting up sniffing the air and rubbing their noses with little clenched fists, or playing with each other like immature wrestlers.

As I lay motionless in my now ant-infested bower, I prayed, a thing I had never before understood, and which I have never since been able to recapture. I prayed to I know not what. One more orthodox would doubtless have identified his Christian, Buddhist, or Islamic God of omnipotence, beauty, and holiness, but I am, rightly or wrongly, happily or unhappily, differently constituted. I prayed to all the people and causes that had made it possible for me to see what I saw, to all the everlasting forces and conjunctions that had combined to produce the indescribable beauty of the present that moved before my eyes. I gave thanks to the fact that I was granted the opportunity of witnessing such perfection before the sordid squabbling beastliness of our kind sweeps it away to allow more room for its organized squalor and unhappiness.

There before me emerged a world so perfect, so eternal, so dainty, that the inner lining of my body seemed to grip me as if prepared to rack me with tears, with pain, with gay laughter all at once. You alone know how you feel when you see some little fragile thing, so sweet and gentle and pathetic that you want to seize it to you, caress it and squeeze it into your very self—it is the secret of Walt Disney's cartoons, the basis of mother love, the very essence of sympathy and compassion.

Above me rose the immensity of the primeval forest, filtering the golden sunlight, as it has done since the dawn of terrestrial life. Below stretched the tangled world of roots and leaves and the strand-like arteries of the creepers. In the bowels of this woody giant scampered the trembling feet of little rats, furry squirrels, countless birds, and scaly lizards. Free, living untrammelled in the superfluity of their tiny lives.

So much I saw lying there. *Deomys*, a lanky rat with hind legs like springs, came bounding past in pairs, their sleek orange fur glistening in the half-light, their white bellies immaculate as snow. Bundles of purplish fur bobbed up and down amongst the water

LONG-LEGGED MARSH-RAT (Malacomys)

weeds, every now and then appearing on open patches of mud and sand, balanced on their pale stilt-like supports and long, naked tails. A marsh-rat (*Malacomys*) has much to do as darkness falls, searching out likely feeding grounds, cleaning his dense woolly coat, preening his immense whiskers, and apparently fraternizing with his kind.

Never, until I watched this kaleidoscope of little life, did I realize how much rats co-operate and gossip. Members of each species met their kind, exchanged countless sniffs, chased each other, gambolled in play, and dug among the roots in consort. Individuals of different species, on meeting, would either pass each other by or rise on their haunches with their tiny forepaws clenched like a pugilist's and sniff the air while peering at the stranger through a

maze of quivering whiskers. Sometimes each would fall forward
onto its splayed forepaws and glance ahead like an old solicitor's
clerk over his spectacles. Nobody seemed to molest anybody else in
this miniature world.

Four *Hylomyschus stella* (a small reddish-brown rat) gathered
around an apparently bare patch of leaf mould almost directly in
front of my hide-out. Two had been playing about for some time
around this neighbourhood and it was getting very dark before they
were joined first by one and then by another of their kind. I cautiously moved my field glasses into position, which brought the
whole scene almost within reach. Their behaviour was typical of
that of all the rats in the vicinity.

At first they gambolled about, rolling over and over, peering under leaves, suddenly scuttling away only to sit up twitching their
ears and vigorously rubbing their noses. Then, after what appeared
to be a sort of conference, they commenced systematically scratching and delving among the leaves at the base of a huge flange-like
root. They worked almost methodically, clearing away the leaves
and bringing to light a most unsuspected number of beetles and
other insects, which they greedily devoured. Big struggling beetles,
about the size of the common cockchafer, can put up a considerable
struggle with their powerful prickly legs, and the rats had learnt a
very practical method of dealing with them. Sitting up on their hind
legs, they fumbled with them between their forepaws like a stage
comedian trying to hold a fragile object that he wishes to give the
impression he is going to drop at every second. Thus the insects
never got a chance of gripping their enemies and in the meantime
the rats kept nibbling bits off them.

So it was that we discovered the origin of the little piles of insect
wing-cases, legs, and other fragments so often encountered in the
forest.

When it became too dark to see my little friends clearly, I
crawled out, stiff and covered with bites, but well repaid by the
most perfect nature film that I could ever have witnessed.

Africa is so very different from Europe or North America, the whole tropics so utterly unlike the temperate regions of the earth, that even in these days of rapid transport, travellers must be excused for drawing endless comparisons. Perhaps there would appear to be less excuse for constantly repeating the dissimilarity between the cosmos locked away by nature in the deep forests and the rest of the tropical world in general. Nevertheless, a few general observations seem necessary as a medium in which to scatter the isolated incidents that occur in searching out these wild creatures, just as a thick sauce is added to bind a stew.

If you bear in mind the complete dissimilarity of the life of which I speak from anything to be encountered in other parts of the world, you will be able to share the thrill that a shout such as was heard in our camp one night, gave to us.

Torrential rain had been falling since midday and we were crowded into the nine foot by seven foot tent with our large table, two camp beds, boxes, lamps, catalogues, and a thousand and one other items. Since sundown (and our frugal meal) we had been busily employed measuring, examining, and cataloguing the day's catches. The incessant beating of the rain upon the taut canvas above was only fitfully dispelled by blasts of stentorian jazz produced by the gramophone. We were hot, busy, and silent.

Putting down my pen, I lay back and stretched my legs. Then I sat bolt upright and fairly goggled at my right knee. On it sat a green and orange frog surmounted by a pair of enormous pearl orbs and blowing pale-blue bubbles at me. We continued to stare fixedly at each other until I had almost regained my composure, when this startling intruder began creeping slowly forward, blowing sky-blue bubbles ever more vigorously.

I made a grab at the frog but, although my hand closed over it, all its four feet remained fully spread out on my trouser leg. A slight jerk was required to release them and as soon as I showed our welcome guest to George, its long bony fingers fastened on his hand. Each finger was terminated by a circular pad, its surface crossed by innumerable tiny ridges which made the whole strongly adhesive.

Further examination of this unusual tree frog (*Cheiromantis ru-fescens*) disclosed the fact that all its bones, as well as the lining of its stomach and mouth, were bright peacock-blue, as if stained with indelible ink. This colouring showed plainly through the thin white skin of its underside and accounted for the tint reflected in the bubbles that it was blowing in the lamplight.

We forthwith called for a receptacle in which to house our catch. No sooner had the echoes died away than a positive menagerie of other frogs of all sizes, shapes, and colours broke cover. Instead of the usual answering shout from the "forecastle" (the domains of our staff), a real, good African bawl disturbed the night. Feet were heard pattering outside and Faugi appeared with a bush lamp.

"Master, master, it is all frogs out here!"

And so it began. The rain had stopped and the whole earth seemed alive with frogs. Great painted fellows had come down from the trees, fat sluggish ones up from the ground, and droves of tiny hopping ones from goodness knows where. Everybody set to work catching as many as he could. Over ninety were collected, of an incredible number of different varieties.

Frogs were found everywhere in the forest. Some lived among the topmost foliage of the giant trees, never coming down to the earth but laying their eggs in artificial pools made by sticking leaves together to catch the rain. Others, we found, inhabited the low trees and trekked great distances to breed each year. There were species that lived for ever below the ground and others that were aquatic. The greatest number, however, roamed about the floor of the forest, hiding among the dead leaves and appearing in swarms after rain. Their shapes were of endless variety.

Searching through the undergrowth beside a stream, I came upon a beautiful ruby-red frog. It was clinging to a slender stick no fatter than itself, with all four legs folded closely to its sides. I took hold of it with all the fingers of my left hand and lifted, but it remained immobile as if dead. First one leg and then another stuck to the stick. It was not until I had pulled each limb off separately with my

right hand that the animal showed any signs of life. Then it kicked
furiously and I had some difficulty in getting it into a glass jar.
Once in, it clung to the perpendicular side all neatly folded up, but
with such tenacity that I could not shake it off. On the back edge
of each thigh it had a pad-like gland which appeared to act as an
adhesive anchor. This frog has no popular name and is in fact very
rare. It is known as *Petropedetes newtoni*.

Only a few feet further on I became firmly entangled in a mass
of slender creepers. While hacking myself clear, a small leafy bough
fell over me. Squatting on a leaf which came to rest just at the tip
of my nose was a most beautiful little frog of the vividest green colour imaginable. Its whole body glistened like finely glazed porcelain,
only its monstrous eyes stood out—a pair of pearly hemispheres.
Wherever my fingers touched this animal's skin during its transfer-
ence to the collecting jar, the delicate green colour was scarred, as
if the skin had been rubbed off.

It appears that all the colour in this frog (*Leptopelis brevirostris*)
is due to a mere refraction of the light reflected back through its
slimy epidermis by the deeper layers of its skin. When the skin is
squeezed and handled, the refractive index is altered and ugly brown
patches appear. Placed in a large cage with other members of its
species collected elsewhere in the jungle, it retrieved its immaculate
porcelain-like green covering, in which guise it was so perfectly
camouflaged among the green leaves provided for its comfort that
it became quite impossible to detect its presence. When we came to
search the cage, we spent more than a quarter of an hour locating
the half-dozen individuals, although there were only eight cubic feet
of space in which they could conceal themselves.

This second type of frog clung to the swaying leaves with sucker-
like pads on the tips of its fingers, but the next specimen, a *Rana
albolabris* caught only a yard or so away, belonged to quite another
group. It retained its precarious hold on a slender stick by strange,
T-shaped terminations to its toes. It was also green, but darker in
tone and iridescent in quality, so that in different lights it was shot
with blue and yellow. This amazing frog always hung upside down

DWARF LEAF-TOAD OR "INCREDIBLE FROG" (Nectophryne afra)

when at rest, its head thrown back with the nose pointed to the ground.

On the way back to camp that day, I encountered still another method by which a frog can retain its hold in precarious places. On the very summit of a broad-leafed sapling I caught sight of some small thing stirring, which I mistook at first for a beetle. On closer inspection it proved to be a very small green frog standing helplessly in what appeared to be four small pools of viscous orange jelly. As it seemed unable to free itself, I detached the whole leaf from the plant and descended to the ground to make a closer inspection. As I did so, the frog, together with its four dots of orange jelly, left by a series of jerky runs which carried it over the edge of the leaf, along its underside to my hand, and thence up my arm.

Never have I seen anything quite so incongruous as a frog clad in monstrous orange boots running like an insect. Its tiny size, less than an inch in length, and the dim light prevented me from discovering how this was performed, so I bottled my catch and hurried home.

Everybody in camp that evening was treated to a side-splitting little show. We released this tiny frog under the powerful lamplight and watched its movements beneath a large magnifying glass. Everything it did looked ridiculous in the extreme. First it continually winked one eye, making its expression even more comically like that of a slightly tiddly old roué. Then its walk was precise, staggering, and laborious, as though its orange boots were loaded with lead, which made its small head bob back and forth like a broody hen's. Its legs were as slender as pins and it was quite incapable of hopping. The feet were altogether remarkable, being edged with a fringe of jelly-like skin and soled with half a dozen cross-pads of swollen flesh having the general outline of minute sausages. Each boot was larger than the animal's head.

This frog is known by the name of *Nectophryne batesi* and is actually an arboreal toad. Its discoverer, the well-known collector Mr. G. L. Bates, who has been responsible for unearthing most of the greatest mysteries of nature in Africa, found a male sitting on a brood of eggs laid in a little cup made by neatly sewing together two pendent leaves.

It has a near relative—*Nectophryne afra*—which we found among some tall water weeds in one inaccessible part of the forest only. It is a vivid black and white, but also has orange-coloured feet and hands surrounded by "jelly." Its behaviour was equally ridiculous, which led to its being christened the "this 'ere frog" by ourselves and our collectors.

In one day we thus collected four frogs, each having an entirely different method of retaining its foothold among trees. We found hundreds of others that had developed as many other ways of clinging to life in the most utterly diverse abodes.

In England all the frogs are confined to ponds and ditches. The world of the African forest is something very different in so many ways.

6

Game Animals (Buffalo and Buck);
Queer Beasts beneath Logs;
The Lesser Members of the Cat Tribe

CAN you take a three-ton tank through a larch wood? Could you take any tank through any wood without making a noise or breaking a single twig? I think it may safely be said that neither could be accomplished in any circumstances; but you all know an animal that can do both. That animal is the elephant and he often weighs a great deal more than three tons.

How this is accomplished nobody really knows, but it must be by some special means, because the commotion set up by an elephant when he is charging or running away has to be heard to be believed. On the hunting grounds of a village called Bakebe I came across the track of a number of elephants. They had trampled down and torn up by the roots most of the trees in a small native plantation and must have moved off just as we entered the clearing, for water was still trickling into the great circular depressions left by their feet. We never heard a sound, though we ran into the near-by forest in the direction they had evidently followed.

Elephants are usually shown in photographs standing among tall grass, by rivers, or among more or less open scrub. These pictures come from East Africa and are most misleading. Elephants are seldom seen in such country in West Africa; in fact they are hardly ever seen at all though there are considerable numbers of them, particularly in the Mamfe area and immediately to the south of it. These huge animals in these parts dwell in the depths of the high deciduous and dense rain forests. To look at either of these growths one would never suspect that they concealed elephants; most of the leaves are well beyond the reach even of an elephant and the whole ground is one tangled mass of creepers of all sizes from the thickness of string to the girth of a man's body.

There are many other animals besides, both great and small, concealed in the forest. I have so far only mentioned those creatures that we more or less bumped into during the course of our daily life, but there were others for which we had to search. One of these was the buffalo.

I allowed myself to be persuaded by a grim old hunter to go in search of these wily, dangerous animals. I was not at all keen, for a variety of reasons besides the unpleasant habits of these beasts. In the first place I am not in the least interested in anything that may be described as big game. I lived to regret my weak-mindedness, however, but for quite other reasons.

We left the village at dawn, the hunter—Eantdudu by name, as far as I could make out—carrying an immense Dane-gun which would have been quite useless against a charging buffalo, and myself a rifle, which is an instrument that I dislike and have no confidence in, chiefly on account of my uncertainty in using it. We set off to the north at a steady four miles per hour through low tangled growth. By midday we were still going, now towards the west, and I began to suspect that I was being put through one of those common African jokes that delight the heart of the Negro. Knowing the average Englishman's fetish for walking and sport, they announce that they will take him to game, then lead him off all day just to see how far he can walk, and never go near any place where game might be.

At about two o'clock, however, we ran right in among a lot of big game. Old Eantdudu became frightfully excited, bobbed up and down, smelt the air, the ground, and the bushes, discovered piles of dung and a network of spoors, wriggled around on his belly, and ran about. I followed.

Suddenly there was a great crashing ahead and a number of heavy bodies could be heard drawing away. There was then a lull until all at once something came crashing past. We fell on our knees to peer under the small trees but saw nothing. All at once a shot rang out just behind us, and Eantdudu leapt into the air so that I thought he had been hit. We ran forward.

In a small clearing we came upon four completely nude hunters standing round a tiny dead duiker antelope. This was too much for my friend. His curses shook the forest and, apparently, the other hunters because—surprisingly for Africans—they remained more or less mute. I eventually discovered that they were trespassing on the hunting grounds of Eantdudu's village and I expect they are still litigating over it now.

This only made matters worse, since the old diehard was not to be put off. He announced that we would try another ground, but this proved to be about as far to the south-east as we were to the north-west of the village. This I unfortunately discovered only later, so that by the time we got back to the village, without buffalo of course, I didn't really care much about anything. I was nearly a week recovering from this outing, during which time we got our buffalo. At least I suppose one can call it a buffalo.

After dinner a few days later we were sitting quietly at work when a most appalling racket arose somewhere at the back of the house. This bellowing and crashing advanced towards the house with extraordinary speed. Before we could get outside to investigate, the entire staff came dashing into the house. We were living in a big native mud-and-wattle hut raised on a slight earth platform and behind it there was a row of small cubicles which served as kitchen and staff quarters. Then with a terrific yell Ayuk, our cook, was projected into the room covered from head to foot in patches of boiled rice and curried chicken.

"Help, help, master," he screamed. "Bush-cow [forest buffalo] done come through wall of kitchen backwards, do walker for fire and spoilt dinner all."

"That's obvious," I yelled. "Make you get gun, go on. . . ."

Guns and torches were brought and we advanced cautiously round the house. The turmoil had drifted away from the kitchen down a gently sloping valley at this point cleared and planted with small pepper bushes. At the limit of the torch's beam we could see two big animals with their heads down heaving back and forth.

"Ahr! The beef do fight; 'em beef strong plenty."

I handed the rifle to George.

"For God's sake, shoot to kill," I said, "before they back into our domains."

With shaking hand I held the torch while George took careful aim and fired. There was a terrific bellow and both animals disappeared from sight. In the following silence we heard something in headlong flight through the neighbouring bush.

"Ah, master shoot good too much."

"Master shoot fine," in fact; it was master this and master that from everybody! True enough, there was nothing wrong with George's marksmanship at any time.

We gathered up our courage, torches, and a varied assortment of weapons, because the bush-cow when wounded is the most dangerous of animals, and cautiously advanced down the slope. There was no sign of a corpse and everybody began looking nervously about, expecting an onslaught from every direction. Then we came to the brink of a deep ditch into which we shone our torches.

What was it that met our eyes? There lay a fat little domestic cow with its four stumpy legs raised to heaven, straight and rigid like a stuffed animal ripped from a glass case.

The wilful slaughter of the local villagers' pet cows might have led to endless complications, because a cow in Africa is to its owner equivalent to a Rolls-Royce car to us. Very little was said about the matter, however, because its owner belonged to a different village from that upon whose land we were residing, and he therefore had no valid reason to offer in explanation of his beef's presence in the locality. I made it quite clear before the chiefs of both villages that if a man allowed his cows to trample down his neighbours' pepper crops and ruin their guests' dinners and whole kitchen premises, he must take the consequences.

This did not quite let us out, nevertheless. Both chiefs parried with the observation that if we were so proficient at driving off night marauders we might offer a little assistance in protecting their other crops. A considerable quota of these, it appeared, were devoured nightly by some large voracious beasts. The chiefs put the question in such a way that there was only one course left open to us, and we accordingly agreed to lend our help. We promised to go into hiding before dark on the next evening at a point where these unwelcome guests were known to issue from the near-by forest.

Nothing appeared except a great number of ravenous mosquitoes and, as I suspected the villagers of having arranged our hide-out for this very purpose, we rather let the matter slide after that. Yet, feeling that perhaps after all there might be something in it, I made a point of wandering every evening with a gun into the forest along the edge of the farmland, and about three days later I came upon something very tangible.

There was a small native house right at the edge of the farmed land. The roof had fallen in; tall grass grew as profusely within as without. As I came upon this, something dashed out of the door. I stood completely still and waited. As nothing happened and yet I was sure the animal had not gone far, I made small clicking noises with my tongue and in a few seconds the tall grass began to move in half a dozen different places. Suddenly I realized that I was staring not at a patch of grass, but at a whole herd of bush-buck (*Tragelaphus scriptus*).

These beautiful, graceful little animals were so perfectly camouflaged in the striped lights and shades of the grass stems that they had simply melted into obscurity; but now that they were on the move I could see them plainly. There was one fine buck with exquisitely twisted horns bearing little white tips. His coat was literally painted a golden orange and crossed and recrossed with delicate white lines like giant writing, just as the scientific name implies.

There were a young buck, three does, and several immature specimens in sight.

I began advancing cautiously upon them, drifting as far as was
possible in the same general direction that they were taking. They
were very suspicious, however, and kept steadily on towards the
forest. When I stumbled over a dead branch, they all leapt into the
air with one accord like a lot of great springs, and the next instant
were all gone.

I followed as quickly as I could into the gloom of the deep jungle,
but they were out of earshot in a few seconds. I was left to wander
on into the undisturbed depths. There was practically no undergrowth in this part of the forest and I could walk on without hin-
drance as one would on the pavement of any city, my rubber shoes
eradicating all noise except the occasional crackle of a breaking
twig.

After some time I came to a little dell where the trees grew so
very close together that the opposite bank was almost completely
obliterated by the continuous rank of their trunks. As I descended
I heard a slight noise below, but took little note of it until all of a
sudden some large animal began lazily walking forward in front of
me. Quickly I got behind a tree trunk and began creeping forward.
When I eventually peered round the flange at the base of an immense tree, I could see the opposite bank. On it stood a most amazing antelope.

It was about the size of a donkey, which gave me quite a shock
at first sight. Its head was ridiculously small, its rump very large.
The general colour was a vaguely purplish maroon and grey beneath, but by way of vivid contrast a bright-orange crown surmounted the head and extended backwards along the ridge of the
back. There was a pair of straight, short, smooth horns directed almost directly backwards.

Every time that I made a small noise or stirred at all, this strange
beast gave a little jump with its hind legs but remained otherwise
quite stationary. As it was a little too far off to be killed with the
only weapon I had with me, a shotgun, I decided to try getting

closer, in order to observe its habits. When I did so, I was more than surprised to see that a constant stream of small things was falling from its belly and haunches to the ground. I was so intrigued at this phenomenon that I must have made a hasty movement, because the animal suddenly took to flight. In my excitement I stupidly and cruelly fired a shot at it which of course did not kill it. The action was more or less involuntary. No sooner had I done it, than I regretted it bitterly and decided that the animal must be followed.

I paused to examine the ground where the antelope had been standing and found that there were a great number of huge bloated ticks lying among the leaves. These must have been the small things that I had clearly seen falling from the animal. While I bottled these I thought over the situation and decided it would be wiser to call in an experienced native hunter to track down the wounded animal, as he would be much more likely to produce the desired result. I therefore hurried back to the village and hunted up old Eantdudu, who willingly undertook the job.

Next morning he appeared before breakfast with the dead animal. It was an old male yellow-necked duiker (*Cephalophus sylvicultrix*) with shotgun pellets in its rump and multitudes of ticks in its fur.

"Well, what have you got, Faugi?"

"Only some very small millepedes, master."

"Good heavens, is that the best you can do after you have been out all day?"

"T'ick-ehn, um'er, I no . . . I find a very funny place, master."

"Oh, what sort of place?"

"There're plenty big tree all fall for ground. They lie so." (He crossed his arms.) "It is very peculiar."

"Is it far?" I inquired.

"No, it is just here," and he pointed to a small valley behind the camp.

"All right, we go look 'em," I said. "Call the others."

Soon a whole crowd of us were on our way through the forest, led by Faugi, who still looked extremely puzzled. After only a few minutes we came upon a place that was indeed most odd. There were a number of gigantic tree trunks lying at all angles, each terminated by a monstrous disk of roots clogged with earth. These formed a natural arena which was comparatively clear, but all around great piles of dead branches cut off the view. The strange thing was that there were plenty of trees still standing roofing over the whole area so that it seemed that there could have been absolutely no room for the trees that had fallen ever to have stood there. Many of the trunks lying on the ground were hollow, and great burrows descended into and under them.

Into these we peered and poked long sticks. Nearly all of them, moreover, seemed to house some form of life, as all kinds of strange grumblings and other noises were wafted out to us. After some effort we drove out two "chook-chooks" and a giant rat (*Cricetomys*), but one large log proved a task of such magnitude that all possible hands were mustered to tackle it. It was very old and extremely rotten, so that one could dig away its interior with trapper's friends and bush-knives. To this labour we applied ourselves assiduously in relays because of the commotion that was going on at the other end of the big central hole.

After a few minutes' labour it became obvious that the hole turned downwards, left the tree, and entered the ground. We therefore decided that the tree must be rolled aside if possible. Long, stout saplings were therefore cut as levers, and logs rolled into position to act as fulcrums for them. After a few abortive attempts we managed to turn the log over. Great sheets of decayed bark were left behind, filling the depression where the tree had lain, and upon them crawled a host of weird-looking creatures, shiny black in colour and about six inches to almost a foot long.

These were giant millepedes, larger than Frankfurt sausages. They are harmless, timid, and friendly animals, filled mostly with air and completely devoid of any sense. If one of these millepedes be placed on a table, it will set out in great style with all its hundreds of legs working overtime and its antennæ waving hopefully. When it reaches the edge of the table, it completely fails to notice the fact

SCALY ANTEATERS (Manis tricuspis)

and the forepart of the body continues walking straight ahead into thin air with all the legs functioning as if on terra firma. When the weight of the forebody has bent it down, the stupid creature realizes that something is amiss and comes to a halt suspended over the edge. Then slowly the legs—starting with the extreme back pair—begin reversing until little waves are passing forward instead of backward, as when the animal is going full steam ahead, and it slowly regains the level surface of the table.

The most ridiculous part of the whole animal is the last pair of legs. If one gets down to the animal's level and concentrates one's gaze on this pair only, they will be seen to gallop like a skittish foal, the tips being flung out backwards and upwards with a motion that is altogether absurd and most amusing to watch.

When the layers of crumbling bark had been removed, a number of chambers and sunken passages were laid bare. Coiled up in them were two very remarkable animals about the size of a football and covered with large, brown, horny scales.

I always remember coming across a picture of one of these animals—the pangolin or scaly anteater—in a book on wild life in my
earlier youth and receiving a great shock. Being unable to make
much of the accompanying text, which took for granted some
knowledge of zoology on the part of the reader, I remained for
years in a quandary concerning the place in the scheme of life of
these creatures that amounted in the end to serious doubt of their
very existence. Scaly things with tails seemed to imply something of
the reptile orders, and the tubular mouth, small beady black eyes,
and heavily clawed feet as shown in the first illustration I saw of a
pangolin only augmented the impression. In addition, it was almost
impossible to unearth any lucid account of the brutes and their
habits.

Finding specimens in the wild was therefore a great thrill, although by now I had come to some definite conclusions as to their
relationships to other animals. They were carefully lifted out of
their snug burrows and proved to be warm balls of a heaviness quite
disproportionate to their size. Nothing was to be seen of the essential parts of the animal, the head, legs, and forepart of the body
being doubled up and wrapped around by the long scaly tail which
was securely hooked onto some scales of the back by a naked
thumb-like pad on the underside of its tip. Any attempt to unroll
them was countered by vigorous and completely successful muscular contractions on the part of the animal.

We carried our animated footballs back to camp. They were
placed on the floor of the tent, where they remained inert. It was
only after more than half an hour that one began tentatively and
jerkily to unroll, but at the slightest movement on our part it would
at once snap together again. Towards the end of dinner one suddenly came undone like a bud bursting. Its long tail flipped over,
leaving the animal on its back for a second so that the naked white
underside was exposed, and then it righted itself and set off out of
the tent as fast as it could go with a most pathetically eager expression on its funny little face.

"Shut up!" I yelled at it, and it complied with incredible adroitness, remaining tightly rolled up for a further half-hour. I then saw why the Hausas call this animal "the modest one."

The predacious animals, that is to say, the cats and other carnivores, are denizens of the forests that have definitely to be hunted. One seldom if ever encounters them in one's daily meanderings because their own habits make them wily, suspicious creatures. Besides the leopard and that phantom creature, the golden cat, there were several interesting and little-known animals of this type brought to us. Native hunters brought us two servals, a species of long-legged cat with black spots on a yellowish fur, that they had shot in the deep, high forest. This is very remarkable, for these animals have always been regarded as inhabitants of the open savannas.

Most furriers will show you beautifully spotted pelts and coats and will assure you that they are real genet. This you may treat with the usual suspicion that discriminating women customarily adopt in such circumstances. There are, nevertheless, such animals and they are beautifully spotted, though their pelts, like most tropical skins, are exceedingly difficult to dress satisfactorily. These genets were common inmates of our little private zoo. They are short-legged and have exquisitely ringed tails, black and white or black and yellow in colour. They are active creatures yet, strangely enough, readily tamable. [*See title page illustration.*]

We became very interested in these animals and made repeated attempts to get to grips with them in their wild haunts, but they were so very wary that we did not meet with much success. The Duke, however, seemed to have a way with *Nandinia*, an allied form, and was constantly meeting them. These false-palm-civets, as they are called, are covered with dense chestnut-brown fur dimly spotted with chocolate and bearing two cream spots between the shoulder blades. Why these two spots should always be present is more than science can at present say. This animal has a neat little pink muzzle and pads on its feet.

There were two other animals belonging to the group called carnivora. These were large mongooses, both types with long legs. One, black in colour, with sparse, coarse hair, is named *Herpestes naso*. It appears to be very rare. The other is of startling appearance and first came to our notice in a rather remarkable manner.

Besides the squirrels that inhabit the trees of the forest there are others that live exclusively on the ground. These are quite different in appearance and, being more difficult to obtain, are of more importance for study. We managed to collect a few in traps set for rats, but when a live example was brought to the camp by a small African boy, I felt that our chance had come. These animals (*Funisciurus leucostygma*) make a peculiar ticking-clocking sound as if the tongue were being flicked down between the lower teeth, and from this fact I inferred that they could call each other together to partake of the food they unearthed, or for other reasons.

We therefore took this little squirrel and placed him in a cage that had previously been freed of all human smell by being buried in the leaf mould of the forest floor. This was transported to a remote part of the forest without being touched, and suspended on a crooked stick. We concealed ourselves near the decoy and awaited developments.

The sun was shining brightly when we "went to earth" but after half an hour or so, during which the little animal kept up an excited "clocking," it clouded over. A stiflingly hot wind like a blast from a furnace flue blew up and the sky got darker and darker. The few tiny patches of sky that could be seen through the leafy roof turned to an ominous purplish grey like the night sky above a great city, and the trees began to sigh and murmur. It got darker every minute and all the sounds of the jungle ceased except the plaintive call of the little squirrel.

All at once a noise like that of an express train started far away to the east. The effect was most peculiar and eerie, because down below in the gloom of the jungle only its echo could be heard, the main volume of the sound passing by overhead, above the foliage. The trees began to sway with increasing violence until even the giants were bending towards the east, a tearing, roaring hurricane blasting through their summits. We remained in a terrible, ominous

WHITE MONGOOSE (Galeriscus nigripes)

calm, the daylight faded to a portentous pinkish half-light, while above us the whole world seemed filled with a host of screaming, demented devils, so that the jungle, usually so solid and stable, was bent at a frightening angle. The roaring came swiftly onwards, mounting in volume every second until we had to shout with all our might to hear each other.

Then suddenly it came. The hot wind came to a halt, the trees quivered at the shock of it, and without warning the whole floor of the forest rose up with one accord and was blasted upwards into the upper branches of the trees. Leaves, branches, clods of mould, and even logs swirled past us, ripping away our camouflage and hurrying across the turbulent forest floor like live things, then suddenly and unaccountably leaving the solid earth and soaring into the air with increasing speed only to be whisked out of sight above. Blinding flares of lightning shot and flickered through the bedlam. Huge branches and a cascade of heavy things crashed all about us only to be caught up in the general headlong flight as soon as they reached the ground and again be projected into the upper air.

Even buried as we were at the bottom of the dense jungle, we had to cling to roots and gasp for breath in the swirling tornado of dust and leaves. Choking and buffeted, we saw an awe-inspiring change. The flying rubbish of this primeval world suddenly paused, quivering in the electric air, and then, as if at a given word, reversed, screaming in the direction from which it had so recently bolted. Things tore past us again, colliding with tree trunks and exploding with reports like pistol shots. A new wind, icy cold and cruel, dived into the forest, the giant trees bowed groaningly away from the terror, and amid vivid electrical discharges solid water came spewing down to earth with the force of miniature bombs.

In two seconds we were drenched to the skin; water poured off us as if we were in a shower bath. I struggled to my feet and staggered forward through the blinding cascade towards the cage that housed our precious squirrel. The water was falling so compactly that I could see very little, but I soon discovered that the cage had gone. We then began a search and eventually stumbled across the string that had held it. Ben and I advanced again towards an immense tree base formed of towering flanges.

As we entered one of the cubicles made by these flanges, a most incredible sight met our eyes. Right in the angle at the junction of the flanges with the base of the tree and the ground, a silvery white animal with a long bushy tail and tall slim black legs was worrying the cage containing a now terrified and screaming squirrel, just as a terrier would worry a rat. At our approach, this amazing animal jumped round, dropped the cage, and barked at us.

We took up our stand at the mouth of this natural pen and began a cautious advance. The animal growled menacingly like a dog and then made a rush at Ben's naked legs. Thoroughly surprised, he countered the attack, but the agile animal leapt back again. We continued to advance upon our quarry, who, instead of attempting flight, crouched menacingly behind the cage and bared his fangs at us. I told Ben to take off his singlet and try to put this over the animal's head so that he could effect a capture. I meanwhile stood back ready to dive at it, should Ben miss.

This he did completely because at that moment a large rotten log that must have been lodged up among the branches far above for many months was released by the tornado and crashed down between us. It landed with a sickening thud not two feet away from us and burst into a thousand small pieces. The nimble mongoose leapt aside, circumnavigated the startled Ben, and bounded past my equally unnerved self. I raised my gun to fire. A stream of water poured out of the barrels, but I let go both charges in quick succession at the fleeing animal. It fell dead after a few paces.

This was the first white mongoose (*Galeriscus nigripes*) we obtained. Later on we managed to film one of these obscure animals in the act of stalking its evening meal.

Part Three

THE FLYING
CONTINENT

7

The Frogs of "Up Top"; Monkeys;
The Flying Squirrel; The Galago;
Another Galago Hunt

YOU have met the strange vermin that dwell with man around the homesteads of Africa, replacing in this strange land the pigeons, sparrows, rats, and mice of our own countries. You have had a glimpse of the teeming and varied life that moves upon the floor of the primeval jungle, a brief vision of a world peopled with many queer animals having no counterparts elsewhere. Yet there are stranger creatures still that live in more remarkable circumstances. I will now tell you something of these.

The world of the great forests is divided into a number of layers one upon the other, like a chocolate cake. First there is a subterranean stratum in which an assemblage of animals, mostly of small size, spend their entire lives, seldom if ever appearing in the light of day or even the darkness of the night. Then, second, there comes that layer in which we have just been roaming—the floor of the forest.

Above this, life leaves the ground altogether and soars into the air, first into the low, broad-leafed trees, no taller than an orchard, that spread everywhere in the mysterious half-light, and then to another layer still higher up among the head-foliage of the giant trees which forms a continuous roof, supported by endless pillar-like trunks, covering the whole countryside. With us, I want you to climb up into this flying continent and see for yourselves an animal civilization that has endured since the days before man appeared in the world.

Standing and looking upwards in our camp buried in the hunting grounds of Eshobi village—or, indeed, at any other place where we set up our temporary abode over an area about the size of Wales—the same thing met our eyes. Over all this great area extended an almost unbroken canopy of green, sometimes dappled with little points of distant light, but for the most part only suffused with a reflection of the blazing sunlight above.

From above, this dense sea of foliage has the general appearance of a continuous pile blanket, undulating softly away in all directions as far as the eye can see. Its colour changes constantly as the seasons come round. The rains bring a pale-green stain; the dry season—the autumn of the tropics—a great red blush, when a thousand exotic fruits great and small fall ripe and colourful into the gloom below. Light rains and the hot sun bring a blaze of flowers, pink, blue, green, yellow, purple, brown, and red. Sometimes I have seen the whole forest roof a patch-work of golden mimosa and screaming red "flame of the forest."

A vast host of small animals pass their entire lives, as their ancestors have done before them for countless centuries and æons, hidden in this mysterious flying continent and never descending to the ground. Only a few forms—some monkeys, frogs, and rats—descend occasionally in search of water. To reach these animals and learn their ways one must climb up into their own exalted world.

"Make you sew 'em strong," I said as I stood over two Africans holding strips of white sheet with their teeth and their great toes while they pleated the edges with their left hands and stitched with their right. Slowly the pile of ripped bed-linen sorted itself out into an immense ribbon, stretching away out of the camp to the washtub where Gong-gong and Eméré scrubbed and lathered, and beyond to the taciturn Chukula, who smoothed and straightened it out before rolling it onto a pole. When all was stitched, washed, and rolled away, a little party set off for the nearest patch of open grass.

When we arrived, it was still early and the sun was only just gathering its strength for the day's roasting. The great ribbon was unfurled and spread over the grass tops, and the near-by forest resounded to the echoes of axing and chopping.

Soon a pile of wood had been collected, and the large solid table from the camp had arrived upside down on the head of a staggering African. While we waited for the white linen to dry in the sun, fires were lighted and Gong-gong put the flat-irons to heat. I sat down and collected two dozen long, thin, straight sticks, which I had notched. Then an enormous butterfly net made from rough buttermuslin was stitched onto a sixteen-foot-creeper stick bent into a giant loop thus $\mathcal{G}$. By this time, the linen was dry, the irons were hot. We were soon passing the former over the table to be rendered smooth by the latter. This done, the linen was again rolled up and everything taken back to camp.

Here I selected a heavy stone and fastened it to a four-hundred-foot cord, which bifurcated at the other extremity and was attached to each end of a five-foot pole. Onto this pole, one end of the huge linen ribbon was rolled and securely tacked. This completed our preparations. We then returned to our other business until sundown.

After dinner, when the forest had come to life with its whirring and buzzing, solitary calls and eerie whistles, the whole camp turned out to experiment. Just behind the camp the floor of the forest was comparatively clear and here I whirled the stone round and round on the end of its string and sent it rocketing far up into the high canopy of foliage. After three attempts, I succeeded in getting it over some unseen branch and as I paid out the cord, the stone came slowly down to earth. It kept catching, but at last we had it within reach and could begin pulling the long white strip upwards into the darkness above. When we felt the cross-pole jam at the top, we made all fast below so that the linen was stretched taut like a great white knife-blade extending perpendicularly up into the night.

Next, a powerful torch was focused on the top part of the linen and left blazing, while we joined together all the long notched

sticks and slowly raised them, surmounted by the great butterfly
net, until they drew level with the illuminated portion of the linen.
Then we waited, while moths, beetles, and other winged denizens
of the night air gathered in clouds on the illuminated white patch
that had so suddenly and unaccountably appeared in their unattain-
able dominions.

Nor did we have long to wait. All at once there appeared a dark
object where before there had been only immaculate whiteness,
though to us, watching below, it seemed a mere dot. The great un-
wieldy net was moved forward and the tree frog scooped into it.

We were so delighted at the quick success of our enterprise, that
we delayed too long in dropping the net. Also we had not got the
technique perfected or learnt that the holders of the long stick must
run away at top speed as soon as a catch was made, so the net might
descend near the torch. The tree frog therefore leapt out of the net
again, back onto the illuminated linen band, doubtless in search of
some more of the insects now settling there by the hundred.

Ben and Faugi, who were in charge of the net, made an eager
swipe at the fugitive, after which I am rather hazy as to what did
actually occur. I remember a shrill whistling sound, then the torch
going out and everything getting dark and frightfully involved. I
believe I got knocked out—I certainly had a most painful lump on
my head next day—but I soon found myself wrestling with innumerable moving things, some warm and moist, others cold and dry,
all as tough as steel and apparently bent on entangling me. Everybody was shouting and something was uttering threatening growls.
Ben, who seemed to be near me, was shouting only a little less loudly
than myself for the torch to be relighted. In the darkness we all
fought like beings possessed; I was bruised, buffeted, and quite sure
that a whole troop of chimpanzees was among us.

At last the torch flamed forth again, lighting up a most amazing
scene. A huge pile of foliage containing half a dozen human beings
heaved about the floor of the forest, wrapped round and round with
endless coils of white linen. From it protruded black legs and long
creeper stems like wriggling worms from a giant puff-ball. I was

only partly in its clutches, and Gong-gong alone, who had the torch, was entirely free. By pulling and cutting away the tough branches we freed first one man and then another until only the formidable growls were left issuing from beneath the tangled mass.

Certain that some rare specimen lurked there, I called for assistance in overturning the whole pile, but when we had done so, I could hardly believe my eyes. There lay Chukula, his back hunched up like a porcupine's and his face buried in the leaf mould, growling and snorting with all his might. A guffaw of laughter brought him up for air, covered with dry leaves.

He assured us that his queer behaviour was a common practice in his own country (which was so far away as to render his statement irrefutable) when large snakes fell on men out of the blue. It seems he was praying—or at least invoking the spirits or the snake goddess. I thought his behaviour was more reminiscent of that singularly impractical bird, the ostrich, which is said to bury its head in the sand at times of great stress.

Our first arboreal frog-hunt had ended in disaster, caused, as it turned out, by suspending our linen to a particularly rotten branch; but subsequent attempts bore fruit. By this and many other experiences, we slowly learned our technique, resulting in the capture of many remarkable frogs.

As I strolled silently along the floor of the jungle scanning the lattice-work of leaves and branches silhouetted against the evening sky like a veil of jet and twine, a nasty problem revolved in my mind. We had set off in the headlong way of the novice, and particularly the youthful novice, promising to get a river dolphin, the giant water-shrew, the eggs of worm-like newts, *Podogona*, and specimens of a lemur and a flying squirrel while yet unborn. Assistance in preparing an expedition had been generously offered in return for an attempt to obtain this particular material and if one came to regard this bargain as an ordinary business deal—in which light I, for one, consider scientific work should be conducted—the attempt must be one that should not fail. In military or commercial duty there is no excuse for failure, even if there be a good reason. In addition, I felt an overwhelming debt of gratitude to the scientists whose trust in the enterprise, and whose efforts to create financial backing for it, had made it possible for me to be meandering thus through the jungle.

George had left camp that morning and returned to the base for a rest, because persistent low fever made him feel, as he put it, "like a dish of scrambled eggs." I was shivering myself and hourly expecting another malarial attack. This problem, therefore, assumed monstrous proportions and an awry outline. It seemed that the malarial "bugs" were actively allying themselves with their larger co-inhabitants of the wilds to combat our attack upon them. After three months, the fevers had taken the offensive and seriously depleted our forces, while the animals remained concealed in deep green obscurity. We had seen almost every conceivable animal except those two from which we could obtain the priceless pieces of embryological currency that alone would repay our debt to our sponsors.

With aggravating persistence, troops of monkeys crossed my path, swinging and crashing through the trees, sending a cascade of shimmering leaves billowing away as they passed. Uttering little conversational croaks, they ran along monstrous branches, their tails looped behind them—animated jugs of exotic design with fantastic handles.

At one time I was standing immediately beneath a troop of green monkeys with white noses (*Cercopithecus nictitans*). I watched them stripping the thin bark off young shoots, which they gobbled greedily although bunches of succulent fruit were within reach all about them. The ways of animals are always unpredictable.

I started wondering then, and have continued to wonder ever since, whether people understand the real use of the monkey's tail. Only in South America do monkeys use their tails as prehensile organs with which to grasp branches when all their hands (and feet) are otherwise occupied. The walls of a room in a certain great London hotel are decorated with lanky forest trees and a host of monkeys. The artist, with commendable care, has depicted the commonest African monkey (*Cercopithecus æthiops*). The species is easily recognizable with its white face fringe and horn-like ear tufts. We can disregard the fact that this species doesn't live in straggling forest trees—a misconception forgivable under the plea of artistic licence—but how excuse the portrayal of thirty per cent of these mural monkeys as hanging by their tails, like Christmas turkeys in a shop window, a thing that they could never do under any circumstance whatever?

That is, nevertheless, probably the average conception of the monkey's tail as a mechanical organ. Zoologists, I find, though more enlightened, are compensatingly vague. They say the tail of the African monkeys is an organ of balance.

I watched this troop of putty-nosed guenons feeding and saw them moving about their daily business. The trees stood side by side in serried ranks, their foliage sometimes intertwined. Nevertheless, great chasms constantly lay across the animals' paths, which they crossed in prodigious flying leaps. To accomplish this, the animals take a short run, jump upwards with their arms outspread as in a "swallow-dive," and sail headlong through the air. But this is the point at which the tail comes into play. By its long, trailing weight, it soon alters the monkey's position from a nose-dive to a perpendicular position analogous to our upright stance. The monkey then lands, not on top of a branch, as is popularly supposed, but on the side of a mass of leaves and smaller twigs, with its arms and legs spread-eagle fashion. It grasps the foliage in an all-embracing hug and then scrambles to safety.

This evening was the first occasion upon which I saw a monkey fall. A small female took a flying leap and landed well, but the leaves she grasped with her hands came away from the twigs, and her body curved over backwards. She remained for a few seconds suspended upside down, clinging with her feet, her tail-tip touching the back of her neck, until with a little squeal she came away all at once and fell with a sickening thud on the soft earth below. When I reached her, she was not dead, but I saw her plight to be hopeless. After administering the only humane treatment possible, I carried out a post-mortem and discovered the fact that both legs and the base of the spine were completely shattered. Her tail had done its work for the last time.

The only other monkey that I have seen lose its footing fell into a river. The incident was very comical, proving that there is the light side to nature as well as the humdrum and the terrible.

I was in a canoe awaiting the arrival of a troop of mona monkeys (*Cercopithecus mona*) at their customary evening rendezvous. An ever-growing wave of crashes heralded their approach, but just as they reached the creek, an appalling racket arose. I do not know if you have ever heard one of the London Tube or Metropolitan trains emerge out of the ground at Baron's Court. Its wheels make a roaring, rustling crash and it gives vent to a blast intermediate between a whistle, a car horn, and a liner's siren. This combination of sounds is a common feature of the West African jungles and is the invariable result of disturbing a troop (or covey, or flight, or what not) of hornbills.

The mona monkeys invaded a tree occupied by these ungainly birds, who rose flapping their great wings and uttering long-drawn-out "phonks" that echoed away among the trees. As the monkeys reached the waterside foliage, the birds returned, phonking louder than ever, and the monkeys scrambled for cover, presumably mistaking them for hawks in their surprise. One individual, however, was attacked with a fit of nerves and started bouncing about on a dead branch, screaming with all its might.

Apparently the hornbill had a nest sealed up in the dead tree somewhere, as he alighted with a bang on the monkey's branch. At that moment the animal was in mid-air completing one of his hysterical leaps. The branch had been set in motion by the bird, but it vibrated horizontally while the monkey was going up and down, and the two wave-motions failed to coincide. The monkey passed neatly by the branch on his down-stroke and whizzed earthwards to meet the still waters of the creek with a resounding report, sending a column of water upwards.

I paddled off to try to pick him up, but after a lengthy submersion, during which time I thought a crocodile might have got him, he bobbed up some distance off, spluttering and coughing and staring wildly about in his distress. He struck out for shore manfully, bobbing up and down, his little head now sleek and shrunken. He reached the bank screaming with rage and indignation, only to be met by the hornbill, who had descended to a low tree to jeer and phonk at him.

Here are two examples of arboreal animals falling from their lofty dominions, encountered during a year in a very limited part of the forest. It seems the percentage of road accidents under natural conditions must be quite as high as in civilized life.

The troop of putty-nosed monkeys took fright at the fall of one of their number and moved off with much crashing and screaming. I dashed after them along the floor of the forest in the vain and stupid belief that I could keep pace with them and obtain a shot. All that I got for my trouble was that I suddenly found myself lost in the maze of woody pillars and monstrous, mould-covered ditches, with the trees now silent as death all around me.

For once I forgot my mental problem as I prowled about, pretending I recognized one tree from another and generally trying to get my bearings. It was rapidly getting dark; the branches stood out black and depthless. Coming to a natural window in the trees caused by a sudden decline, I eagerly scanned the skies for signs of a rising moon to guide me.

Then suddenly something like a huge caterpillar appeared silhouetted on the smooth perpendicular side of a giant tree trunk. From which direction it came, I know not; all at once it was there. Aiming quickly, I fired. The phantom disappeared and I waited listening. Something fell with a crash into the gully below and at the same instant a loud grunt sounded at my elbow, making me leap to one side in surprise.

There stood Ben, a black patch in the general blackness, grinning excitedly.

"Where in the devil did you come from?" I asked.

"I follow master."

"How and for how long have you been after me?" I implored, for it seemed uncanny that he should have tracked me so far.

But Ben just remained silent and grinned. The African had little ways of his own of indicating when he felt it useless or unwise to disclose something to someone whom he regarded in some degree as a fussy and rather stupid intruder in his country.

"Well, since you're here," I inquired, "did you see the beef and if so what was it?"

"Eh-m-m-m, I think . . ." he began as the West African does when he is not sure.

"Well, go look 'em one time, two times, or even sooner," I said, indicating the gulley.

Ben did so, with the aid of a torch which he had thoughtfully brought along with him. Minutes passed while he searched about below. It was quite dark before he called me and I set out through the tangled undergrowth to join him.

I found him excited, grinning, and uttering a series of those peculiar little sighing falsetto grunts which are typical African exclamations of pleasure, surprise, and uncertainty. Between his hands he held outstretched an almost completely square object. With hands that not only trembled but positively shook with excitement, I took over the prize. Here, possibly, was the first of my problems solved.

This animal, *Anomalurus fraseri*, is called a flying squirrel. Apart from the fact that it neither flies nor is a squirrel, it bears perhaps the least misleading of names. Any title that tried to describe it would be hopeless as its scientific name implies—Fraser's anomalous one! Its body is long and thin like a war canoe, its legs and arms crooked like those of a roast chicken and entirely enclosed in a thin, very soft "sail." Rather than describe the animal as a long, narrow squirrel with a parachute, it is better to depict a square kite, supported by a mid-rib (head, body, and tail) and four diagonal rods ending in a row of sharp curved claws (the limbs). The tail is almost as long as the body, practically naked at its base but otherwise bushy like

AFRICAN FLYING SQUIRREL (Anomalurus fraseri)

that of a cat. Where it joins the parachute and body on the under-side is a series of scales capped by sharp, hard spikes.

The flying squirrel lives high among the trees and appears only at night to move about in quest of food. As I stood in the darkness that night, this was just about the limit of my knowledge concerning these strange animals. I subsequently learned a great deal more, both of the details with which I should already have been familiar, and of other facts never previously recorded.

Ben and I returned to camp in triumph. At long last I could ex-amine the animal under a good light and carry out a dissection to determine whether it was pregnant. We required the uterus of the female flying squirrel in this condition for embryological study, and unless the contained fœtus is in an advanced state of development, it is impossible to detect its presence by fingering the animal. Only dissection will answer the question.

The degree of excitement that I underwent when parting the fur, which is softer and even more fine than mole-skin, and making the initial slit in the skin, is naturally incomprehensible to any but the most ardent zoologist. So also would be the depths of disappointment to which I sank upon laying bare the uterus and finding it to be quite unpregnant.

The following evening we descended a deep gully flanking one of the forest grass-fields. The forest was here characterized by a number of immense trees of various species, with very small leaves. The whole foliage was exceptionally sparse in comparison to the other vegetation and each tree stood at a distance of about its own diameter of head foliage from its nearest neighbours. The leaves on the uppermost branches looked like mere pinhead dots from the ground below.

The sun had just set. We were on our way to the deeper recesses of the forest with guns and torches, but on entering the jungle one instinctively scans the foliage above while the sky is still light enough to silhouette the branches. Besides, it was only the night before that I had thus spotted the first *Anomalurus*, and where there is one there are more in zoology. It is interesting to note in passing that it is extremely doubtful whether there is such a thing as a rare animal in the world. Certain species are "rare," but only in collections. Provided one finds the right place, they will be found to be really quite plentiful, though the area which they inhabit may be very limited and specialized.

I remember clearly that I was pondering this very question as I scanned the immensities of these openwork trees, half expecting to see an object like a small kite sail into view every second. However, just as on the previous evening, both my reason and my eyesight were caught completely unawares—an only too common occurrence in Africa.

Some small thing suddenly and miraculously made its appearance at the very summit of one of the trees. It was far beyond gun-shot,

but we were not beyond its sense of hearing, as I well knew. I
could not, therefore, hail George or the Africans and point it out
to them, since they were some distance ahead; I had to wait and
watch it moving slowly along a huge branch until it came near the
end. Then all at once it backed away, paused, and started a headlong
rush to the very tip of the branch. I paused, holding my breath, as
it momentarily disappeared from view.

Then, as I stared upwards, motionless with suspense, its tiny form
was projected out of the tree into mid-air and shot, like a miniature
rocket, quite one hundred and fifty feet across a window of clear
sky and into another almost leafless tree immediately above me. It
landed without a sound, apparently without disturbing a single twig,
and promptly disappeared.

I was so surprised at this incredible performance that I missed the
take-off of the second animal and only caught sight of it as it also
shot through the air and landed, it seemed, exactly where the other
had done. This second animal, however, did not vanish in a ghost-
like and altogether unaccountable manner, but instantly appeared
running down a perpendicular branch in the same manner as a dog
runs across a horizontal plank, except that its long tail—now plainly
visible—hung down over its back almost reaching its head.

I lost no time in taking a long and very sporting shot at its hurrying form. It vanished, as far as I could make out, along with the
small branch down which it had been climbing. Something could be
heard falling into the trees below an appreciable number of seconds
later.

Tremendously excited at my good fortune, and more than curious
to know what the animal could be, I called directions to Faugi, Ben,
and Bassi, who had immediately set off into the undergrowth on
hearing the falling body. They were far below me at the bottom of
the gulley. By shining their torch directly upwards among the trees,
I was able to guide them to a position directly below the branch
upon which I had sighted the animal. After a protracted search they
called out that they could find nothing. I scrambled down to join
them.

NEEDLE-CLAWED LEMUR (Euoticus elegantulus)

Searching the ground of the forest at night is a very trying business, as there are endless piles of dead leaves, roots, herbs, bushes, and dead branches everywhere and of every imaginable shade, colour, and shape that might or might not resemble any arboreal animal. Probing among these, one slowly wanders yards away from the only possible area where one's kill might have fallen. After some time, therefore, we all had to reassemble to determine the exact spot that was below the branch. To do this, we shone the powerful torch upwards. There, caught up among some slender creepers, we saw a round fluffy ball.

A few shakes and the animal fell into our hands, where it instantly came to life and fastened two rows of needle-sharp teeth on the fleshy part of my right thumb. This proved painful and extremely bloody, as revealed by the torch when relighted after I had so quickly dropped it. Clinging to my hand was an altogether terrifying apparition. A pair of perfectly monstrous orange eyes with minute slit-like pupils stared widely and directly at my face. The whole head seemed to be composed of the eyes; immediately above them was a flat, low crown and a pair of huge ears which curled, wrinkled, unfurled, and turned this way and that quite independently of each other so that at one moment they were upright and smooth and the next instant laid back and crinkled up like a concertina. What was most uncanny of all was a tiny pink hand perfect in every detail, with opposable thumb and neatly manicured nails that shone in the torchlight disclosing miniature half-moons. The hand protruded from a cuff of neatly fashioned grey fur.

The half-human, half-catlike appearance of this animal, combined with the fact that it was so very alive and that it was the first occasion upon which I had ever encountered anything like it or even expected to do so, reduced me to a state of utter incapability. In my excitement and interest, I forgot all pain and simply stared at the beast, yet, quite unlike any other animal I have ever seen, it never took its eyes off me, nor even so much as blinked. As I moved my head, it followed my gaze, turning this way and that, until it had to let go of my flesh and bend its neck right back to keep its wild eyes upon my face. Its little hands were cold and clammy and possessed of a vice-like grip.

There it sat on my hand, glaring at me and hissing like a cat, until a collecting bag was emptied for its reception.

Just at that moment the torch went out by mistake and I thought our catch would leap away into the night. Instead, it altered the position of its hands and I felt a hot rubbing on my thumb. When the torch came on again, the animal was eagerly licking up the blood running all over my hand. I imagine it relished the salt taste, for it is an herbivorous animal only occasionally eating insects.

Back at camp, I examined the animal carefully and found that it had only been hit by one pellet in the right ear. The shot must have knocked it off the branch, the force of the fall rendering it temporarily insensible. It proved to be a lemur, one of the long-tailed group known as galagos (or *Galaginæ*). It was a rare form known only by its scientific name, *Euoticus elegantulus*, and distinguished from the other galagos by a median ridge on all its nails. These ridges result in the free tips of the nails being produced into needle-fine points.

This animal was a female, though once again not exactly what we required. We needed pregnant female flying squirrels and galagos, but the latter must be of the species *Galago demidovii*—Demidorff's dwarf lemur—an animal less than half the size of the one we had now received into our midst.

The lemur lived with us for a long time and proved an unending source of interest. Although it never became in any way tame, always glaring, snarling, and hissing at one, I was able to handle it several times in a circumspect manner. Its fur, orange-brown above and grey below, is extremely thick and woolly, though soft. The texture is comparable to that of the cropped sheep-skin of which motoring gloves are sometimes manufactured. This lemur's chief pastime was a combination of acrobatics and trapeze, performed in and about the camp. On the ground it would leap up and down on its hind legs like a kangaroo, then suddenly it would sail upwards onto the perpendicular wall of the tent, from which it rebounded like a rubber ball onto the other wall and thence back to the central pole to which it would cling upside down.

This animal has a relative of about equal proportions. It is known as Allen's galago (*Galago alleni*) and is also plentiful in the Cameroons forests, though we did not encounter it until later on. This animal's hind legs are really very remarkable; by elongation of the bones of the ankle to the length of the thigh and calf, there is formed a third angle to the limb, as with a bird. All the *Galaginæ* show this peculiarity, but the development in this species is the greatest of all.

By its aid, Allen's galago can leap prodigious distances and perform like a kangaroo when on the ground. We had several of these animals alive when we were occupying a native house near a large village, and we decided to make a film of their movements and general behaviour. This proved to be a most unhappy decision.

Operations commenced before an audience of some two hundred nude and interested members of the Akunakuna tribe. As "extras"—

though unpaid—they were even more aggressive than their European and American counterparts. They did not wait patiently for their turn, but crowded onto the "lot" to the total exclusion not only of all background but also of most of the light. They would not respond to reason, and the Chief was reported to be in a "far, far country," as always happens in West African political circles when interference is not desired. The fact that his grinning visage, sandwiched between his slaves and menials, appears clearly in some of the film taken that day need not be enlarged upon here. We had to take the law and petty authority into our own hands.

Now I kept a dozen good-natured, broad-shouldered, muscular Munchis for this particular purpose, whose police methods were simple and effective, if a little harsh. These men were therefore summoned into the house by the back entrance, provided with long sticks, and mustered at the two doors and the only window. At a given word they burst out in all directions. As they were in the centre of the Akunakunas, the situation resulted in a two-dimensional rout. The house stood in a large grassy arena and the locals fled in all directions, followed by the Munchis in a widening circle.

This was the cause of much mirth on all sides. I was heartily joining in, when I noticed a number of small grey forms streaking across the greensward in hot pursuit of the Munchis. My hilarity instantly gave way to the most awful emotions as I stood there watching both our "stars" and all our "principals" disappearing into the oblivion of four hundred scampering African feet. What prompted these timid, nervous little galagos to behave in such a flippant manner I was quite unable to surmise; I simply stood there gaping. This also proved to be a serious miscalculation because the entire staff, seeing what was afoot, burst out of the house in full war cry.

All at once I came to my senses. Shouting my plan of campaign to George and the Duke, I grabbed up nets. Then we shot out onto the plaza, each taking a different direction. We had not gone a dozen paces before the limit came with guillotine-like suddenness; close in our wake followed two screaming chimpanzees and a very frightened squirrel.

The whole animate world seemed to have gone crazy. Here were six concentric rings, all, with the exception of the one miserable squirrel, members of the exalted order of Primates, disintegrating with ever-increasing velocity like Professor Einstein's cosmos. Strangely enough, every other ring, i.e., the Akunakunas, the galagos, and ourselves, was pursued, while the intervening contingents were furiously pursuing.

We realized that most of the live animals had got loose in some way or other, and it gradually dawned on me that it was best to leave the lemurs to the tender mercy of the staff and concentrate our own efforts on the chimps and the squirrel. I therefore called a halt and we rounded on our eager and excited pursuers; unfortunately my orders carried to the staff, who also halted, and even further to the Munchis. The Akunakunas, who were running only half-heartedly anyway, were quick to spot this. They paused. The diameter of their circle was by then about a quarter of a mile.

Horror of horrors!

We chased the chimps, who ran for the cover of their cages, the staff dashed to our rescue, the Munchis reversed, and the Akunakunas began to close in again. Believe it or not, this petty animate cosmos expanded and contracted two and a half times before its concentricity gave way. When it did so, it collapsed with a crash and pandemonium was let loose.

It was that damned squirrel that finished it. Getting bored with pounding back and forth, it decided to go straight on. It passed us with ease—there were so few of us—and it didn't really meet with serious opposition from the staff, but the jumble of galagos and Munchis was its undoing. Darting here and there among eager hands, it eventually broke through and dived in among the Akunakunas. The result was horrible. A pile of naked humanity fell upon it, which I calculated would be the end of our squirrel as a zoological specimen, yet by some miracle it passed right through entirely unscathed and made for the near-by forest never to be seen again.

Pandemonium now reigned supreme. The local populace proved its worth in the inimitable African manner by rendering very active co-operation with the best will in the world. Everybody dashed and darted about, so that the entire village green became a moving human kaleidoscope. The molecules in a gas are, we are informed, in a constant state of agitation, colliding with each other some billions of times a second; I wish the physicists could have witnessed our little performance. Everybody screamed, the chimps loudest of all, and some of the younger set in the village, imagining this to be a sort of European ju-ju dance, commenced an agitated beating of drums.

But the galagos held their ground. These essentially arboreal animals seemed to be just as much at home on the ground, darting about by methods commonly attributed only to frogs or kangaroos. If only all the humans had stood still, they would all have come to rest after a few yards, but the more one chased them the faster they went. Several even passed right through the house, one choosing the table as a suitable route, scattering papers and tea in all directions.

Slowly, and one by one, they were captured until all were safely housed. Apparently the front of their compound cage had come loose, though how they all managed to escape at once remained a mystery. It was only some hours later that I discovered that the Duke, with the most commendable presence of mind, had been placidly seated behind a small bush near the door to the house, busily filming each galago that flashed past. The film proved to be excellent and disclosed every detail that we could have desired.

8

The Life of Hollow Trees

THE camp was deserted. For once I lay sipping weak tea out of a glass at midday and contemplated the infinite. It was a memorable occasion, about the only time during our busy life in Africa that I had the opportunity to do so. Everybody else was out of camp. The catering staff under the guidance of George—Commissar for Food and Public Welfare—had departed for the base camp, Dele was laying a new line of traps far away, the skinners were distributed about the floor of the forest on their stomachs ostensibly collecting spiders and centipedes though doubtless indulging in a midday siesta, and, lastly, the water carrier had gone to bury a grandmother, which in Africa means keeping a date with one's girlfriend. The livestock had settled down to await the dusk with what patience it could muster; wild life might have been non-existent for all the noise that it made.

The steady, glutinous sunlight poured into our little clearing. The great trees stood around absolutely motionless and still. In the silence one could almost believe one heard them breathing. I was as utterly contented with the world as it is humanly possible to be—basking in the sensuous warmth, beauty, and solitude of it all.

For more than an hour I lay thus motionless, every possible fraction of my body stretched in the full sunlight, my mind a blank except for an occasional mental nod of agreement with all tropical humanity for choosing to dwell where it does and more especially for refusing to do any but the bare minimum of work. When one's whole soul is approaching an earthly nirvana, one's senses must be considerably deadened, and for this reason it only slowly penetrated my brain that there was a peculiar muffled noise apparently distributed more or less evenly through the heavy atmosphere. Every time I raised my head it ceased; in fact it was its absence more than its presence that betrayed its very existence.

I was most mystified by its quality, once I had definitely made up my mind that it was a noise at all. Lazily I turned the puzzle over in my mind, attempting to fit first this and then that cause to the general effect. Nothing that I struck upon seemed in the least plausible in a tropical jungle. Now it faintly resembled distant drumming, but its very irregularity precluded this, then it fell to a mere grumbling as if a giant political meeting were taking place deep down in the ground.

Ah! That was it, underground. I pressed my ear to the soft earth; the noise seemed somewhat more muffled. I became intensely eager to discover the true nature of this phenomenon. Cupping my hands behind my ears, I revolved this way and that like a sound detector. There was no amplification, and yet the disturbance seemed to come from all directions. I even got up and prowled around, all to no avail.

Can you picture to yourself the irritable dismay that this caused me? There are so many strange sounds in the jungle, but one can always assign to them some cause—doubtless wrong in most cases, but nevertheless sufficient for the day. This was insistent, faint, irregular, and apparently impossible of location. Exasperated, I flopped back onto the ground sheet to continue my ultra-violet-ray treatment and composed myself with my head pillowed on a large flat root that bulged up out of the soil.

Instantly the sounds swelled up into a volume of great diversity. Instead of a gentle murmuring I discerned scratchings, rustlings, very, very small cracklings, and an unaccountable sound like that of soot falling in a chimney. It was all so very unexpected and irregular that I sat bolt upright as if I had been severely bitten. Had anybody been watching me during the following few minutes, I am quite sure that, convinced I was in a really dangerous condition, he would

have run for the nearest doctor, despite the fact that the latter was
several hundred miles away.

I grovelled on the ground, caressing the root with fingers, nostrils,
and ears, for one can often feel or smell a sound better than one can
hear it, such are the properties of one's sense organs. Once assured
that I had located a faithful transmitter of the sound, I crawled
about trying to trace the tree from which it originated, which is not
nearly so simple as one might suppose. Two-hundred-foot trees that
grow in a land of tornadoes must have extensive anchorage, and
where the soil is shallow their roots may spread great distances
around their bases. This particular root plunged straight down into
the earth. I had half an hour's hard digging before I came upon an
angle and could judge in which direction it set off. This determined,
I still had some thirty woody giants from which to choose and therefore decided that a systematic search with a trapper's friend was the
best course to adopt.

I then began stalking trees. Approaching each with the utmost
care and the minimum of noise, I listened in by pressing my ear to
the trunk. When I was satisfied that there was no sound, I cut a
small mark in the bark and proceeded to the next. I had marked
eighteen trees when it suddenly struck me that the sounds might
have been coming from some subterranean channels through which
the root passed. I hesitated just behind the tent, full of doubt, irri-
tation, and mystification.

Without warning there came a "plump" at my side. As I wheeled
round, a little puff of rust-coloured powder rose from the base of
an enormous tree. I dived in among the foliage and discovered a
large hole at its base. Peering into the darkness within, I heard all
manner of squeaks, shufflings, and movements, and a continuous
cascade of rotten wood and dust kept falling from above and rolling
out of the hole. All these strange noises were instantly explained.
There must be animals moving about, scratching and grumbling in
the recesses of this great hollow tree. Their activities above were
causing an endless stream of dust, chips of rotten wood, lumps of
fungus, and small logs to fall down into the base, making there a

neat conical mound of considerable proportions. The noise in its cumulative effect was exactly like that of tons of soot falling in a colossal chimney. Close at hand I detected little chirps and squeaks.

Excitement at my discovery quite outdid my gratification upon having my intuition vindicated, but the explanation of one mystery only ushered in another. What were the animals causing all this disturbance?

At this moment Faugi appeared in camp, having filled all his collecting tubes with spiders and other small creatures. I confided my secret to him and sent him off into the jungle to call in the rest by that wonderful telegraph devised by hunters. The forest is so dense, or the tree trunks are so arranged, that one can see a man between them and call with all one's might but he won't hear a sound. The only way in which the human voice can be made to carry is to employ a high, long-drawn-out falsetto wail. This now rose above the trees, to be answered from several quarters. After a few minutes we were seven strong and I explained the nature of my discovery to the assembled company.

Faugi and Bassi were dispatched to a neighbouring grass-field to collect bundles of dry hay while the rest of us set to work clearing away not only the undergrowth but many of the trees around the hollow giant from which the noises issued. This entailed the most colossal labour, because we were equipped only with bush-knives and trapper's friends and many of the trees that required felling before we could obtain an uninterrupted view of the head-foliage of the big tree were as large in girth as the average tree in London parks. Added to this was the danger that any we felled might choose our camp as a resting place, and their fall was no mean event. Moreover, the foliage above was so tangled and dense that we had to send small people aloft to cut away the creepers before the trees would fall at all. Sometimes, though cut clean through, they still stood upright supported by the creepers above.

By the time Faugi and Bassi returned from the outside world carrying great bundles of grass, we had a wide arena cleared with the mammoth of the forest standing desolately in the midst.

"Bring plenty green leaf," I shouted, and all departed to cut arm-fuls, which they piled at the base of the tree. Meanwhile I got out the shotguns, ammunition, tins of kerosene, and nets.

In the middle of this activity George happily appeared at the tail of a little line of men bearing all manner of groceries, squawking fowls, and other edibles. Excitedly I recounted to him what I had discovered, all the preparation we had made, and what we proposed to do. George set to work with his customary promptness and in no time we were hard at work upon the base of the tree.

Before I proceed any further with the details of this day's happenings I wish to make a certain point quite clear. I have in the past found myself severely censured for cruelty, though as is customary none of my accusers has put his case directly to me. I fully see, moreover, how animal lovers have fallen into this mistake, being accustomed (or unaccustomed) to European trees and woods. That is one reason why I have stressed the dissimilarity of the jungle. This tree in which animals were hiding was so tall and surmounted by such a monstrous head of foliage that quite a third of it was completely out of gunshot range, and a very large part of the trunk and branches even out of sight. Its trunk formed a smooth unblemished pillar some two hundred feet high, all the holes and gashes permitting exit from the hollow chimney-like interior being either at the base or at the junctions of the big branches high above. Besides, we had only two guns and must of necessity stand right under the tree. The animals therefore really had a very sporting chance, anyhow more than a pheasant has in England.

The bases of trees in tropical forests are often produced into a star of enormous flanges, seldom thicker than a cheap brick wall and often as much as twenty feet high where they join the trunk, from which they fall away to the ground many yards distant. These structures act in an exactly similar manner to buttresses on a cathedral or the centre piece of a T-girder. The bases of the largest trees are nothing else but a series of these flanges radiating in all directions. In the angles between them a large car could be parked. Most of these trees are hollowed to such an extent that they become mere shells—more empty than a factory chimney.

This particular tree, however, only betrayed its emptiness by one small hole at ground level, two feet in diameter. To perform an operation upon it, we were therefore compelled to enlarge this opening —no small matter, in view of the fact that its wood was just about as hard as aluminum. What is a thin shell to a giant tree can yet be a battlement to a puny chopping human being, and so this wood proved. When we had eventually made a large enough opening, a neat pile of dry sticks was placed within on the top of the pyramidal heap of dusty rotten wood that had fallen from the great chimney above. This was saturated with kerosene and a blanket of damp green leaves arranged on top. We then gave the word to stand back. All took up their positions, forming a circle round the tree at a distance so that we could see as much as possible of the foliage above without being entirely hidden by the greenery of the surrounding jungle.

Kerosene was poured on the dry sticks and a light applied. The pathetic struggling flame went out almost before the first smoke appeared, so difficult is it to burn the forest wood, but soon a real fire was kindled and volumes of smoke began to pour upwards from the green leaves. Things began to happen at once.

I am not quite certain what I expected to come out of that tree. I knew there were live things within it, but their nature was a complete mystery. The whole procedure was rather on a par with opening a tomb of one of the sacred Egyptian Pharaohs. One felt all the time that one was treading on hallowed ground, disturbing the peace of the exalted, and slightly fearful of the results, though consumed with an intense curiosity.

As the column of hot air rose up the giant chimney, the billowing smoke crept upwards and we waited tensely with our thumbs on the safety catches of our guns. Ben alone, who was stoker-in-chief, moved about, struggling with a piece of wire netting that had to be held above the fire for a reason which will become apparent very shortly. During those few minutes of silence, broken only by the crackling of the fire, I believe all of us felt the same sensations. No-body moved; I could hear them breathing. The minutes ticked by. Little wraiths of pale-blue smoke began to curl out of the top of the tree, first here then there. We waited.

Instantaneously it began at both ends of the tree. A great shower of dust and dry wood poured out of the hole and I had a fleeting glimpse of Ben diving into the rising smoke column. At the same time somebody yelled out from the other side of the tree that there was a "beef" aloft. I scooted about here and there stumbling over tree stumps, trying to catch a glimpse of it, but the enormous height, the dense foliage, and my bad eyesight defeated me. Then George's gun rang out.

This was the signal for a general exodus. Something appeared on my side, running about the great tree as if it were a football field. I blazed away, but it was out of range and the animal flew back into a near-by hole. Next came three animals all at once and all different. Again I fired. This time one of them took to the air and went soar-ing away into the jungle in a headlong swoop. I fired blindly and, as usual, missed completely. By now a veritable rain of animals of every kind was falling all around. George's gun blazed away with-out ceasing; Bassi, Faugi, and all the rest of them were darting about, picking up animals that came running down the trunk and leaping for the ground. Ben worked overtime plunging into the smoke, snatching animals that fell on the wire netting and popping them into a bag.

Then something small and grey appeared from a hole on my side and began zigzagging about. I landed him with a clean shot and he fell at my feet. I hadn't time to verify the nature of this specimen before a cloud of flying things appeared whirling round and round the top of the tree. The smoke had reached the summit and dis-lodged a colony of bats. At these we fired incessantly but only a few came close enough. And still the tree disgorged its mysteries, al-though the fire had died down through lack of green leaves and fuel.

An *Anomalurus* appeared quite low down. It peered round the tree trunk, then advanced to my side. As it was well within range, I waited to see what it would do and I was well rewarded. First it scuttled up the tree in the most remarkable manner, for instead of using its legs in 1–2 : 3–4 rhythm as all other animals do, it hunched both hind legs up together so that its back was arched like a loop-caterpillar's and then released both forefeet at once and moved them forward. The back legs were then moved up again in unison, and so on.

At last I had struck upon an explanation of those amazing tooth-like spines at the base of the tail. Without planting them firmly into the bark at the same time that the claws of the hind feet are dug in, the animal would be unable to prevent itself from falling over backwards when it released both front feet at once. The tail and the two hind feet form a triangle, a perfect bracket by which the animal clings rigidly to a perpendicular surface. This it must be able to do, as the furry membranes stretched from its neck to its wrists, thence to its ankles and finally to the base of its tail, are so taut that should it endeavour to walk like other animals this valuable though fragile structure would soon be rent into shreds.

Having gained several yards' altitude by this looping method, it suddenly waltzed about so that its head hung down. As it hunched up its back legs I thought that it was about to start down again, but instead it left the tree altogether and soared across the space we had cleared, straight at another large tree. Curved like an umbrella, it hurtled through the air directly at the solid wood. I gasped, assured that I was about to witness a natural suicide. However, at the very last instant, when its head was definitely below the level of its tail, the whole animal suddenly stalled upwards, landed gently on all fours on the perpendicular face of the tree trunk, and commenced climbing rapidly again like a giant caterpillar.

After this the stream of "beef" ceased more or less suddenly and we had time to rekindle the fire. The lull in the conflagration, unintentional on this first occasion, was subsequently adopted as a regular manœuvre in the proceedings, because during this time a quite different set of creatures came out. These, we subsequently learnt, were the lesser forms of life that live in the ever-dark, blind ends of

WHIP-SCORPION (Amblypygi)

the rotten hollow branches which have no other exit to the outside world except that leading into the main chimney of the trunk. If the fire had been kept up, these poor creatures, unlike their furry compatriots, would have been driven further and further up their culs-de-sac and eventually would have perished. It appeared that all it required was to fill the tree with smoke once and then wait for all the animals to vacate it under the impression that it was on fire. Trees that fell down promptly as a result of our cutting and burning their shell-like base were always absolutely scoured of life unless the smoke had failed to penetrate.

These lesser creatures came crawling down the inside of the trunk and walked straight out among us. There were snakes, huge snails, a number of gecko lizards boldly banded with black and dark grey divided by thin cream-coloured lines, and a number of the most un-earthly of all animals, named by scientists the *Amblypygi*, or whip-scorpions.

It has been mentioned above that of all the unpleasant, evil-smelling, vicious things in West Africa, the shrew is the meanest, most unsavoury, and irascible. All the remaining loathsome, horrid,

GIANT DORMOUSE (Claviglis hueti)

lurid, gruesome epithets that remain are similarly applicable to this scurrying nightmare. Those who have a personal dislike or abhorrence of spiders should never be allowed so much as to look at one of these amblypygi. They are completely flat, with a body about the size of a quarter, all in one compact piece. There are four pairs of legs, bent permanently forward, which in large specimens cover approximately the area of a tea plate. In addition to the true legs there is a pair of immensely long palpi or jaw-legs. These are armed with a double row of sharp spines and teeth along their entire front (or inner) edge and, being permanently crooked, act as a pair of immense scissor mandibles. The first pair of true legs, moreover, are formed into slender whips more than twice the length of the other appendages. These creatures prowl about in the dark, waving their whips before them, and as soon as they locate any unfortunate insect they rush upon it with lightning speed and seize it with their vice-like palpi. Nor does the unfortunate captive ever get free until all its life blood has been sucked from it. These brutes were an easy prey as they wandered out into the unaccustomed bright light dazed by the smoke.

When the fire was eventually relighted there were no more animals left to be driven out, and after waiting some time we foolishly gathered up everything preparatory to a display in the camp clearing. This would have made any zoologist's mouth water. First there were a score of the loathsome amblypygi, one a mother swollen with eggs, another surrounded by her brood—little fellows hardly big enough to cover a dime. Then there were two snakes, both new to our collections, half a dozen giant snails shaped like winkles, and a bottle full of the banded geckos. Next came four bats and a whole set of small grey animals about the size of a brown rat, which they much resembled except for their wide heads and long bushy tails. These proved to be two species of giant arboreal dormice (*Æthoglis*).

Our English dormice are very misleading. First, they are not mice at all; secondly, they are the most unusual type of the group to which they really belong. This group comes somewhere between the squirrels and the rats. Most of its members live in trees in tropical forests, are very much larger in size, and have bushy tails. The two species we had before us were an even grey all over, the former being a little larger and somewhat blue in tint, while the latter was shot with a mauvish sheen. They are exceedingly beautiful little animals and always immaculately clean.

Alongside the graphiurids on the table lay a large squirrel which we instantly named "the painted one." Its face and underside were vivid orange, its back a scintillating lustrous green. The plume-like hairs of its bushy tail were spread out horizontally like a feather and were orange for that half of their length nearer the flesh and brown for the distal half. We afterwards learnt that this squirrel (*Funisciurus auriculatus*) is nocturnal and always hides in hollow trees by day.

Lastly there were three *Anomalurus fraseri* and the animal that I had seen fly away from the tree. It was a flying squirrel too, but of quite another variety and painted in colours almost identical with those of the squirrel. This animal—Beecroft's anomalure (*A. beecrofti*)—proved to be the only diurnal flying squirrel. Its silky fur was a vivid green above and the most intense golden colour below that it is possible to imagine. Some time later we kept one of these alive and were rewarded by discovering the remarkable and inexplicable fact that every night, as soon as darkness falls, the vivid green of its coat turns to brindled grey and the gold to a reddish orange. At first we thought this was due to an optical illusion produced by the lamplight, and later still to the presence of two different species each coloured differently. It was only when a green and gold animal was killed at night and proved to be grey and orange in the daylight next morning that we elucidated the problem.

In addition to the display of dead prizes on the camp table, there remained the livestock captured. These proved to contain not only all the animals enumerated above with the exception of the bats, but also two other species of squirrel, one more than two feet long, of a brindled brown colour and almost naked below, and the other smaller, greyish green-brown above and yellow-grey below (*Protoxerus stangeri* and *Heliosciurus gambianus*).

We were so excited and interested reviewing our catches that we did not notice until it was too late that a serious danger was close at hand. In our hurry and our ignorance we had left the fire burning in the base of the tree.

Warned by a terrific roaring, we raced back to see what was up. We found that the entire tree was alight within, and, owing to the natural draught formed by its towering chimney-like structure, flames were pouring from its summit. Hastily we estimated the range of its fall, and decided it was prudent to move the vulnerable portions of the camp.

For two days and nights it roared, although it seemed as thin as a shell in the first place. When the end did come at dead of night, we were saved only by the grace of God. As it crashed, it felled a line of other trees like ninepins. Had it chosen to topple over our way, we would have been utterly obliterated.

Once we had discovered that trees housed the most valuable specimens, we set to work to search the forest systematically. The trapper had instructions to mark any hollow tree that he came across during the course of his daily rounds; all the collectors who roamed far and wide in quest of the lesser animals were supplied with knives with which to cut crosses in the bark. All these were marked out on a rough topographical map of the area so that we could tackle one at a time. Each tree stands in a separate compartment of my memory, each presenting a new problem, each an adventure in itself.

Many of the trees that we smoked were completely uninhabited, others produced only a single squirrel. At every one, nevertheless, we spent hours of valuable time hewing down the surrounding growth.

One tree stands out more clearly in my memory than any other and was, like all our other most profitable undertakings, quite near the camp.

It was a busy morning, and as I had been kept up till three-thirty the night before, attending to a large haul from the traps, I was in no mood for African jokes. Ever since dawn I had been working under the mosquito room. The usual household duties had been performed around me, but by ten o'clock I was beginning to wonder why Gong-gong persisted in hanging about. In my ill temper I drove him mercilessly away and resumed my grovelling among papers. A few minutes later he was back again.

"What the devil do you want?" I growled at him.

"I find tree, master," came the unexpected retort.

Now Gong-gong could not have been more than twelve years old. I had found him in our kitchen a few weeks before and we had not yet learned that he was a born leader and guardian-angel of the

household, to which exalted position he soon wormed his way. I
considered him at that time merely as a useful makeshift and therefore dismissed his piece of information with a brief: "All right, we
go look 'em later," and there the matter ended.

Lunch, however, failed to appear at its appointed hour. When I
inquired the reason, I was informed that Gong-gong was nowhere
to be seen and that the cook found it impossible to leave the omelette
unattended for a very great variety of African reasons. I must explain that Gong-gong, for reasons of his own, had had the privilege
of serving at table bestowed upon him. After a minor reactionary
revolution which resulted in the prompt arrival of the desired (and
already cooked) victuals, I sent our small army far and wide to locate the renegade. Almost the first call was answered from close at
hand. Its tone, moreover, made me extremely angry. The young
imp's piping voice calmly demanded through the trees that we should
come to him at once. My opinion upon the whole matter was quite
the converse, so I sent Faugi off to bring in the recalcitrant youth.
As this lordly gentleman himself failed to show up although I
bawled at him, I decided to investigate for myself and set out filled
with the most unprintable emotions.

I found them arguing at the base of a very large tree that grew
out over a little valley at an angle of forty-five degrees.

"Why in the blank hell can't you come when I call?" I shouted
at them.

"Master," whimpered Gong-gong in a flood of tears, "my tree!"
I must admit that his tender age, combined with the abject misery
written all over his face, made me relent a bit.

"Are there beef for in?" I inquired of Faugi.

"Tic n'ah; I no hear anything." Faugi was beginning to squeak
as a West African will when he is a bit mystified. He pushed his
head into a small hole at the base of the tree and listened. No, he assured me, he heard nothing.

I rounded on Gong-gong, but he pleaded between hiccups, as-
suring me that there were beef inside. Eventually I made a bargain
with him that we should smoke the tree and if there were no beef

he would be sacked, whereas if there were valuable animals, he should be allowed to stay but not receive the customary "dash" (tip) that was awarded to any of the staff who marked down a "winner." The effect of this was remarkable. Gong-gong nearly burst with excitement and himself mustered a party to go and cut dry grass.

As we stood round this tree waiting for the smoke to rise, I was more than doubtful whether anything would come out at all. I don't think any of the others were decided in their minds either. But we were all very much mistaken except Gong-gong, who at least pretended he had known it all the time.

As the smoke reached the holes at the summit of the tree a swarm of tiny forms emerged from everywhere in serried ranks. At first I thought they were mice or some small arboreal rats as they skimmed about the tree trunk and the larger branches. In and out of holes they popped. Then all at once as if by some given signal they all began to leave the tree. A pile of them fell onto the wire netting above the fire and the rest took to the air.

If you have ever stood in a street and watched a chimney on fire you will have some idea of what we witnessed. Columns of smoke rose from the top of the tree and from this kept appearing little black things that floated leisurely away just as if they were flakes of soot or ash from paper. There was nothing about their departure in any way reminiscent of the hurried headlong leap of the anomalure. They simply soared out into the air and glided away into the near-by trees.

In a flash I realized that we were witnessing something probably never before seen by any but Africans, and doubtless precious few of them. Before our very eyes a colony of *Idiurus*, one of the rarest of animals, was enacting in broad daylight all the manœuvres that it had so far carried out at dead of night since the beginning of time; a method of effacement so perfect as to have kept its very existence a secret until only a few years ago.

These tiny rodents are placed near the anomalures in the scheme of life, but they have no near relatives. They are no larger than a house mouse, and clothed in a short silky down. Between the fore

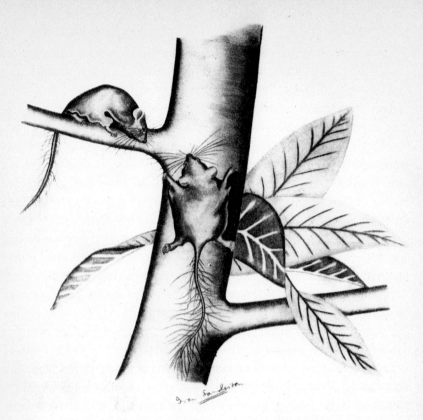

FLYING MOUSE-SQUIRREL (Idiurus zenkeri)

and hind legs and thence to the base of the tail is stretched a thin membrane, as in the flying squirrels, and from the elbow a thin cartilaginous rod, the length of the forearm, extends to the edge of this. When the animal is on terra firma—or rather terra infirma, as the trees often are—this support to the parachute is folded against the hind edge of the arm; when in the air, it is extended slightly backwards.

Idiurus's tail is perhaps one of the most wonderful structures found in mammals, and even among all animal life. It is long and rat-like but on the underside there are two parallel lines of very short stiff hairs extending from the base to the very tip. These are separated by a narrow naked portion and therefore lie a little bit to either side like the "rolling chocks" on a ship. The rest of the tail throughout its length—that is to say, the top and sides—bears, scattered here and there, extravagantly long and very slender wavy hairs. The function of this device is twofold and has not, I believe, ever before been elucidated.

The stiff lines of short hairs below point slightly backwards and act in exactly the same manner as the spine-scales at the base of the tail of *Anomalurus*. The long hairs above act as a rudder during flight. This explained why we saw these animals not only glide away from the smoking tree but turn and twist this way and that in the air with the greatest ease, as if they were in true flight like a bird. It also explained how they managed to alight on tree trunks with their heads pointing downwards, a thing that the flying squirrel never could do. I am not at all certain that the whiskers are not brought into play also for guiding the course of the flight.

From this tree we secured examples of two quite distinct species (*Idiurus macrotis* and *Idiurus zenkeri*) which seem to have been living communally in perfect concord. One is a little larger than the other. Unlike the big flying squirrel, which is as bulky as a small cat, the *Idiurus* runs with alternate feet, as was disclosed by a film that we took later on.

That day was fortunate; it gave us one of our greatest prizes and the irreplaceable Gong-gong.

9

Going Aloft; The Potto and the Angwantibo; Demidorff's Galago; The Colour of the Animals Aloft

MIRACLES apparently do occur. On one cold, misty morning I actually awoke under my own power! Turning over, I peered out through the mosquito netting and the open end of the tent and perceived that the day was still struggling for mastery over the night. Feeling rather sick and very surprised at myself, I crawled out into the morning like a bloodless invertebrate emerging from beneath a log. George slumbered noiselessly behind his nimbus of netting.

The world was all very different when seen emerging grey and dripping from the fleeting mists. At this hour there was a great silence comparable to the midday lull. Everything lay motionless; each tiny sound echoed in a muffled way that was more than eerie. Taking the shotgun and a few cartridges, I drifted out into the general dimness and groped my way through the half-hidden trees.

Small things stirred all around. Presently I almost stumbled upon a heavier body that went crashing away into the recesses of the undergrowth, breathing heavily. Then from far above a great gong boomed out.

The Balinese priests ring a huge bronze gong in the solitude of the morning, to disturb the bats in a holy cave. It is some sort of gentle reminder to the spirits of their ancestors who reside in these flapping draculas that they must not compose themselves to sleep before their descendants have had an opportunity of displaying their undying devotion. I wondered whose ancestors were calling whom among the tops of the jungle trees, but it turned out to be a calling to the quick and not the dead, because other still louder gongs resounded all around.

I commenced stalking the nearest of these sounds. Since the mist was rapidly evaporating, I scanned the trees above. The noise was most elusive, but after some minutes of bewilderment, shaking foliage betrayed the movements of an animal. Then far above me what appeared to be a dachshund trotted out onto a big branch. As I took aim it vanished round to the other side and I had to await its reappearance.

When it did appear again, it was completely altered in outline. Though the animal was still long and low, there had grown from somewhere a thick bushy tail which was carried bent forwards over its back. All at once it rose on its hind legs and boomed with an echoing resonance. I fired and the body fell with a thud among the dead leaves. I was taken aback on retrieving my kill to find that it was a large squirrel (*Protoxerus stangeri*). Even less expected was a large frog lying beside it in a mangled condition. It seemed to be impossible to solve one mystery without ushering in another.

So squirrels boomed like gongs! Though we have not discovered to this day how the sound is produced, I felt that I had learnt something worth knowing. But what about this frog? Had the two any connexion?

I at once opened up and examined the stomach of the squirrel and found, as I had expected, only a handful of undigested nuts and fruits and no signs of frogs. The only possible conclusion, therefore, seemed to be that the amphibian was a chance additional present from on high. This set me wondering and wishing. Could one possibly get up among these exalted animals and see exactly how they carry on their daily lives?

The desire to reach the animals that dwell in the tops of the trees obsessed us from that day onwards, but it was only after a great

GIANT BOOMING SQUIRREL (Protoxerus stangeri)

deal of inane scheming and attempting to put into practice several
even more ridiculous suggestions that we succeeded. As is customary
in every enterprise, the method eventually adopted was absurdly
simple and prompted by an accident—at least I shall call it that!

There is a law in England's African colonies and protectorates
that native hunters and other persons may possess guns of certain
prescribed types only. These are referred to locally as "shoot-
machines"—not a bad title, considering the number of these infernal
engines that turn on their owners. An efficient modern shotgun or
rifle is considered highly dangerous in the hands of the experienced
native hunter, though whether for political or merely physical reasons we never found out. Doubtless the authorities are best able to
judge; the British have a particular gift for this despite the criticisms
of the great "unofficial." The guns allowed to the natives are old
flintlock, muzzle-loading Dane-guns of monstrous length, antiquated
design, and other doubtful qualities.

That they are dangerous to life and limb but seldom to animals
is undeniable. These intrinsic factors are augmented by a number
of practices connected with their use. First, believe it or not, the

method of cleaning these infernal machines is as follows. At night they are stood on their butts, hot water is poured into the four-foot barrel, and a cork firmly rammed into the muzzle. This goes on for years, so the mere fact of their survival might be considered a miracle.

Secondly, as they are muzzle-loaders, any amount of powder that takes the fancy of the sportsman may be poured in and tightly pounded down with any kind of wad. To this may be added any kind and any quantity of shot. Buckshot and other grades of pellets being expensive and gravel and bits of old nails plentiful and moderately common, the thrifty and logical African naturally tends to follow the narrow rocky path.

The result is that after some time a charge has five or possibly six ways open to it—north, south, east, west, or either direction at right angles to these! Some portion of the owner's anatomy fore-closes three of them, and of the remainder one may possibly include the firer's left arm and another the target. When a gun explodes, therefore, there is apt to be an accident.

One which was brought to us had resulted in an unwarranted cicatrization of a much venerated hunter's right arm, chest, face, and both hands. The wounds were three inches long, swollen like miniature volcanoes, and clogged with unexploded black gunpowder. We did our best and saved an eye by a miracle (or a lack of medical knowledge) but were unable to prevent a permanent scarring and tattooing.

Consequent upon some further research into the anatomy, physiology, and life-habits of these Dane-guns, I promulgated a strict law that they were to be kept at a three-hundred-yard limit from our camp.

As time wore on, however, and we began to learn more about the ways of the animals around us and got to know our native staff more intimately, I perceived that we were missing a great opportunity in not pressing the services of the local Africans of all classes into our collecting operations. The help and co-operation of the chiefs and sundry minor secret societies had brought forth results beyond our personal reach, yet even these were limited because their sphere of operations was for the most part the villages and surrounding hunting grounds. Purchase of the lesser forms of life from the more adolescent members of African society likewise had its limitations. We therefore urged the hunters armed with Dane-guns to make regular trips around on our behalf, promising to buy all they killed at a high price either for food or for the collections.

This was satisfactory only to a point, because, when a hunter has got a good price for a good catch, he has no conceivable reason in Africa for taking another long walk until the money is spent; and as it may even be spent on a wife who produces all further requirements by a process of super-compound interest, this unhappy juncture may never be attained at all. Furthermore, you cannot permanently employ a hunter; he is far too important a person and knows that he is economically independent.

As in the days of ancient Egypt, therefore, trusted slaves appeared to be the only possible solution, but that implied having Dane-guns around the place, because the powers that be, even if one is hundreds of miles away in the heart of the jungle, would not like six-foot African "little boys" to be running around with modern shotguns at intervals of seven miles throughout the forest. After prolonged meditation and profound soul-searching, we decided that perhaps the authorities would not mind just this once if we lent our guns to Bassi and Ben, especially if they managed *not* to shoot themselves.

The Grand Council was forthwith convened. Mounting an improvised rostrum in my pyjamas, I announced that our unswerving intention was to follow up the provocative retreat of the hosts surrounding us with all possible adjuncts of modern warfare at our command. Furthermore, I announced that recruits to the voluntary militia would be rewarded with a cash bonus for their prowess and valour and also for the number and condition of their victims. The rally of the camp party at once broke up amid tumultuous cheers and took up arms to carry forward the mission of civilization in the dark continent!

That evening we were busily occupied completing catalogues and other written work. The camp was very still and Ben and Bassi had long since departed into the blackness of the night with the shotguns and the torch.

A shot rang out some distance away, followed almost immediately by a quick left and right. After a short pause there came further firing. This went on intermittently until a time came when I was viewing my mosquito-netted bed with considerable longing, but the barrage continued. As we all developed a keen desire to see the valuable spoils that our new idea seemed to be producing, I decided to slip out of camp and join the successful hunt.

Taking the spare torch, I crept away unobserved and was soon weaving my way among the trees and creepers in the direction from which the occasional shots still rang out. In order to avoid colliding with tree trunks I kept flashing the torch. Here and there I was arrested by a pair of eyes or a single gleaming one. These small, cold, and apparently single eyes are most deceptive. Sometimes they prove to be little drops of water or tree sap reflecting the light, or they may be spiders or insects. The huge compound eyes of these small creatures can reflect as much light as the eye of a large animal, and some of them are luminous in addition.

When I was still some distance from the position of the last shot fired, I entered an area where a considerable number of animals were noisily moving through the trees above me, apparently shifting from the centre of danger. I shone the beam of the torch upwards in the hope of catching a glimpse of them.

When I did so, my whole inside gave a clutch with excitement and delight as I gazed upward, for suspended from a branch almost directly above me was an animal of the most curious though unaccountably lovable appearance. This statement may sound mad, but to those whose childhood was spent among Teddy bears it may perhaps be intelligible. It was upside down, with an eager little round face peering down over its back at me. So low down was it indeed, that I could only watch fascinated while it licked its pink nose with a tiny pink tongue to match. The rest of the body was compact, brown and woolly. It blinked at me in the glaring light and then began laboriously clambering forward in the direction of the tree trunk still suspended upside down like a sloth. A presumably natural urge prompted me to attempt a climb so that I could get to closer quarters with this adorable little toy of the forest and perhaps even capture it, as I stupidly thought.

The climb was not an easy one, though it was a miracle that there were any branches at all to allow of an ascent. This was difficult, because I had to keep the torch beam on the animal all the time so that it would not disappear among the tangled foliage, and the whole procedure resolved itself into a race between myself and the potto (for that was what it undoubtedly was) to reach the angle between the branch and the trunk. Most unfortunately I got there first.

As I arrived astride the branch, the little animal realized the folly of its manœuvre and appeared on the upper side, where it stood on all fours just like any ordinary animal. Here it looked more awkward and not nearly so lovable. Its large feet and hands were turned outward like those of a very old rheumatic human, and its head hung down in exactly the attitude adopted by a ferocious bear. Being only a few feet distant, I could see plainly the parting in the hairs on its back and the row of spines projecting from its neck. These I knew to be the bony processes of its neck vertebræ which protrude right through the flesh and appear as a row of naked bony spines. What I did not know until that moment was that the animal could control the fur around them, opening or shutting it so that the spines could be revealed or hidden at will. Nor had I ever suspected the animal to be capable of what I subsequently witnessed.

The potto stood up on its hind legs with its forepaws clenched as if in prayer and then all at once doubled up so that its head disappeared between its crouching hind legs. If an attacker had been advancing to seize its throat at that instant, he would have been rent and pinned to the branch by the formidable row of spines. Is this the explanation of this weird provision of nature? I decided then and there to put the question to all the zoologists I know!

After this remarkable performance had been repeated two or three times, during which I had been cautiously advancing, the wise little animal turned about, swung onto the underside of the branch, and retreated towards outer space with a rapidity which I had not believed possible for him. The interesting fact was that, although only about the size of a small cat, he was able to cling from underneath to a branch considerably thicker than a man's torso, and hasten along without any apparent difficulty.

Holding the torch in my mouth I went after him. I was soon lost in a maze of giant branches and discovered that I could pass from one tree to another just as the animals do. I nearly lost the torch on several occasions and had a number of other singularly unpleasant moments when the only possible handhold was considerably out of range. The small potto disappeared among the foliage. I found myself unable to descend because the tree below, which connected with the branch that I was on, had no side shoots at all and I was now well over a hundred feet above the ground. For a time I struggled on in a more or less vain effort to reach a near-by mass of creepers by which I could descend to earth with the dignity befitting the uncrowned king of animal life!

Before I got near my goal, however, I found that I was suspended precariously among a number of branches that seemed by their feel to be far too slender. The time for succour appeared to be at hand. I let out a piercing and as nearly falsetto yell as I could muster without projecting myself into the outer darkness. I had hoped that Ben or Bassi would hear me, since they were, I imagined, near at hand, although I had not realized that no shots had been fired recently. There being no answer, I repeated the performance in an even higher key.

In reply a prodigious cackling, chirruping, and crashing arose all about me. Hooking my arms over some branches, I fumbled in my pocket for the torch and presently illuminated my surroundings. My predicament was worse than I had suspected. This occupied my attention for a time, but I soon saw shapes moving around me and discovered that I was in the midst of a sleeping or very sleepy troop of monkeys. Of all the amazing and unexpected things to encounter, a troop of agile monkeys in their own environment is perhaps the most surprising. Nearly every day we had seen these animals passing by like ghosts, scampering along their elevated roads, for ever out of reach and completely immune from the attacks of all landlubbers. Yet here they were quite dumb and hopeless, blinking in the torchlight, apparently less susceptible to being awakened than a club-man suffering from a surfeit of port.

These animals were quite helpless in the dark. They fell about, whimpered and whined; mothers clutched babies and the larger males crashed around as if they knew the troop should move, but they were completely devoid of any sense of direction. Many of them bounced about on the branches, suddenly lowering their heads to their forepaws, chattering at me, and pulling their scalp and ears backward so that their faces took on a most frightening though ridiculous expression. They were putty-nosed guenons (*Cercopithecus nictitans*). Though I was deeply interested in their habits, our association was not of long duration, because things began to give way beneath me. I had to put the torch back into my mouth and look to myself.

A very nasty few minutes ensued. One whole branch gave way with both my hands upon it, but by some freak I arrived upside down, suspended by my legs with a strong creeper wrapped round my chest. This creeper was my salvation; I was so long getting unravelled from it that my eyes became accustomed to the dim light (the torch had fallen to the ground) and I eventually swarmed along it until I reached other woody ropes that descended directly to the ground.

I arrived below covered with irritating scratches, with my clothes torn, and quite devoid of any sense of balance, so that I staggered about in the hope of finding the torch. By some miracle again, and with the help of matches, I did so and set out for the camp, which I completely missed. I eventually struck the narrow forest path and followed it back to our front door. On entering the vivid light of the paraffin lamps, I beheld Ben and Bassi.

"Hey there!" I shouted, forgetting all my troubles. "What did you get?"

There was a dull silence. George held up a small object.

At first I could not make out what it was at all, but a closer inspection showed that it was the head, arms, and foreparts of a small animal; from the waist downwards there was nothing.

"What," I inquired, "was the purpose of half a beef?" and everybody began laughing.

Apparently Ben had seen a pair of eyes among the trees and, after taking careful aim, had fired. Bassi, who was watching, saw the eyes go out and then come on again slightly lower down. He therefore fired both barrels. The eyes, however, remained in evidence, and the gallant hunters, convinced that they had either stumbled upon an unaccountably tough animal or disturbed a spook, continued to blaze away. When they were eventually persuaded that they had projected more shot than any self-respecting ancestral ghost could digest, and when the eyes still glowed above them, they decided to climb aloft. This must have been just about the time that I came to the same decision in another part of the forest.

Whereas I encountered a live potto, they found to their amazement the forepart of a small angwantibo lemur (*Arctocebus aureus*) clinging tenaciously to a small branch. Having released its dead, though vice-like, grip, they descended to earth and made for camp, sure that the game was not worth the candle.

This dreary conclusion to an exciting night gave us our clue. We now knew it was possible actually to go up among the arboreal animals of the flying continent.

After that we climbed and as a result obtained, I believe, the first photographs of the wild and rare lemurs in their natural haunts. We saw fashion furs prowling happily about, squirrels playing leapfrog, and countless other unforgettable sights.

We never again had to waste twenty-two cartridges on an angwantibo, but of course I never got so close to any of the animals after that—probably because I always carried a gun.

We learnt that these animals have recognized roads through the trees which they traverse every day in the same direction and at the same time. So precise is their passing that a watch could be set by it. One squirrel had its home in a small hole at the top of a tree and George had discovered that it returned to "roost" just before sundown every night. He soon learnt exactly by which branches it travelled.

I caught sight of a large, beautifully spotted genet (*Genetta tigrina*)—a kind of civet-cat common in these parts—disappearing late one evening into a large hole half-way up a stout tree. Every evening it returned for a few minutes before departing to hunt its nightly meal. I could not imagine why it visited this tree so regularly until I managed to climb up, and found that a small pool of clear water lay placidly in the fork of the tree. The animal came to drink every day by exactly the same route.

With traps, snares, nets, birdlime, and various other devices we collected these animals as soon as we had located their runs. When captured they were kept around the camp partly as pets and partly as living experiments so that we could study their habits, their food, their mannerisms, and their dispositions.

This little private menagerie would have made any zoologist green with envy. There were snakes and lizards, tree frogs, toads, and giant centipedes. Two baby chimpanzees were housed alongside three cages containing water-chevrotains (*Hyemoschus aquaticus*), one of the rare pygmy antelopes, mona monkeys, puttynosed and red-nosed monkeys. The latter are a rare species (*Cercopithecus erythrotis*) with a bright orange-red nose and a tail of the same colour.

Next to these were other cages with tortoises, large squirrels (*Protoxerus*), the perpetrators of the early morning gonging, giant dormice, and several genets. On collars attached to tent-poles and stakes driven into the ground were galagos, false-palm-civets (*Nandinia binotata*), pottos, and the priceless angwantibo. Cages, buck-

ANGWANTIBO (Arctocebus calabarensis)

ets, pots, and all sorts of other odd containers were filled with rats and other small fry.

Most interesting of all to the student of African wild life would probably be the live examples of the short-tailed lemurs, i.e., the potto and the *Arctocebus*. The former is a most puzzling beast, by reason of its obscure ways and, to no less an extent, on account of the variety of misleading names which it has acquired.

It is a lemur of a group which represents in Africa that tribe of slow-moving, ghost-like, nocturnal animals found in the East Indies and known as the lorises. It may be actually related to them or merely a case of parallel evolution, in the same relation as that of the galagos to the tarsier of the Orient. This animal is popularly known as the potto, presumably from the local Efik name in the Calabar province where it was first seen and collected by one Bosman, whose name is often added to the native one. In addition to its being called the potto or Bosman's potto or Bosman's lemur, zoologists have christened it *Periodicticus potto;* and to make matters worse, European residents in other parts call it the bush-bear, native bear, or bush-baby. To complete the picture, the pidgin-English designation for it is now "the half a tail." Nearly all these terms are misleading for the following reasons. Bosman's specimens prove to be a variety of the main stock; the Latin name means little to any but those with a close knowledge of the animal; it is not the bush-bear, because that is the name given to the koala in Australia (in fact, it is not a bear at all); and perhaps most misleading is its name of bush-baby, because that title ought to be exclusively reserved for the smaller galagos. I am inclined to think that the pidgin-English name is the best for everyday purposes as it has only half a tail.

The angwantibo has also been dragged into the muddle, though it is perhaps one of the least known of all mammals. We could not discover any native name for this funny little fellow and, being so seldom seen, it has acquired no pidgin-English title. We called it the tailless lemur. When it was first discovered, the natives were reported to call it the angwantibo and its scientific name is *Arctocebus.* Local residents have characteristically christened it the bush-baby, tree-fox, and little native bear.

Actually it is none of these things, but a small, woolly, reddish-coloured lemur, somewhat distantly related to the potto, with a sharp nose, large eyes, very small, close ears of intensely human appearance, and hands and feet of an even more extreme type than those of its larger cousin. Like the potto also, it spends most of its time suspended below the branches, sloth fashion; unlike it, it sleeps thus upside down. The pottos, and to a far greater extent the angwantibos, are able to retain their footing by reason of two unique pieces of mechanism. These are their limbs and their hands and feet.

The limbs are not only supplied with great belts of muscle far out of proportion to the size of the animal, but they are governed by a semi-automatic nervous control so that neither sleep nor death causes them to release their hold. This is the explanation of Ben's and Bassi's half animal, and incidentally the origin of a very prevalent legend concerning the potto. It is also the method by which the angwantibo manages to sleep suspended by its grip alone.

The story told is that monkeys have been shot, to the back of whose necks have been found attached the dried and shrivelled hands and stumps of limbs of a potto. The current explanation is that once the potto has taken hold he will not let go, and even when the entangled monkey has managed to kill his adversary by crushing him against a tree or by other means, the terrible little tenacious hands hold on with a death grip so lasting that even after the whole corpse has rotted away they still remain, a grim testimony to the character of their former owners. This does not seem to be strictly accurate. First, the potto does not attack monkeys, being too clumsy to catch one even if he bumped into it in the night; secondly, I have ascertained for myself that as soon as the necessary ligaments are severed higher up the arm, the vice-like grip which does, sure enough, continue after death, is released just as in any other animal.

The grip of the angwantibo is, however, something rather different, to which I can find no reference in any literature either purely scientific or popular. Like the potto it has both its thumbs and great toes enlarged to a prodigious degree and directed backwards, that is to say, in exactly the opposite direction to that of the other fingers and toes. In addition, both animals have the first or index finger so much reduced in size that in the potto it forms merely a small round lump and in the angwantibo an accessory pad to the palm of the hand. The wrist and ankle joints have been twisted until both feet and hands are set at right angles to the lower leg and forearm respectively. Here the likeness ends.

The angwantibo has much shorter fingers than the potto, and its hip joint is constructed on a looser plan with a prominent sphere on the end of the thigh-bone. This can revolve completely in a cup in the hip joint so that the little animal may be advancing along the underside of a branch and, if it decides to retrace its steps, can (and does) walk back over its own chest and belly, emerging between its back legs with its nose pointing down to the ground. It then seizes the branch above its back by putting its hands behind its head and proceeds until the body slung between the hip joint has turned completely over. One hind leg after the other is then released and flies back like a spring to be reattached to the branch as the animal turns itself over onto its back once more with its forepaws. The whole performance is uncanny and quite extraordinary.

The angwantibo's limbs, though muscular, are very slender, but the feet and hands are prodigiously strong. We found that, like the feet of the chameleon, they are practically insensible until the palm or sole is brought into contact with the object to be gripped. The animal was incapable of gripping the end of a matchbox because, although the fingers were in contact with one side and the thumb with the other, there was nothing pressing on the palm. Now the angle between the thumb and the fingers contains two big, fleshy pads which splay out as soon as they touch the branch and provide a solid hold. Most strange of all, touching the limbs and even sticking a pin into them below the elbow or knee joint when the animal was suspended asleep failed to wake it.

It appears that the limbs are fixed and the "power" automatically cut off before the animal composes itself to sleep.

The angwantibo is a flesh eater of no mean propensities. In captivity it seemed to prefer finely chopped bird flesh to other meat, but it must vary this diet with fruit and probably leaves in its natural state, because it could subsist for quite long periods on mashed banana. Every evening as soon as the sun had set, the animal commenced a thorough combing of its whole coat with its lower front teeth, first licking the fur with its long, rasping tongue. This toilet over, it would scramble about, uttering little whimpering wails and throaty cries.

One day Dele appeared in a great flurry at a most inopportune moment. I had just jabbed a sharp scalpel into my thumb and was running about cursing myself and looking for the iodine, and as I had already entered that phase where I disliked Dele's face more every time I saw it, I was in no mood to receive him. To make matters worse, he made the ostensibly fatuous statement that he had seen two galagos (the whole household had picked up the name from us) sleeping in a paw-paw tree.

A more obviously untrue statement I could not at the moment conceive. I was convinced that it was only an attempt on Dele's part to ward off the day that he knew was rapidly approaching when I should find a satisfactory reason in my own mind for dispensing with, among other things, the services of his face. First, galagos would not be asleep where you could see them; secondly, paw-paw trees don't grow in the virgin forest; and lastly, if they did, there wouldn't be room for two galagos to sleep together in one.

Yet the fellow was so persistent that by the time I had a dressing on my thumb and had somewhat regained my temper, I was seriously considering going to investigate. I must admit, nevertheless, that tea intervened; that is something that no possible number of sleeping galagos would make me forgo. After tea a "comedian" arrived with a common animal for which he demanded a fabulous sum, and by the time I had finished laughing at the bargain that ensued and eventually terminated in his leaving the animal outside the kitchen free of any charge whatever, another half-hour had passed. During all this time Dele hovered around, scowling menacingly, a habit of his that I disliked more than any other. Finally, still somewhat against my will, I took a gun and left camp.

Dele forged ahead along a trail that he had previously marked by bending and breaking saplings. Half an hour later we came to an unexpected little clearing on the brink of a steep bank leading down to a silently flowing river, whose presence in the vicinity I had not even suspected. To my surprise, there stood a solitary paw-paw tree. This plant is like an immense overgrown cabbage on a long slender stalk. It is a product of cultivation—or rather met with only where man is or has been resident—and provides the well-known melon-like fruit of the same name that customarily adorns the tropical breakfast table. This spot must have been the site of a small native settlement in former times, probably of people migrating up the river.

DEMIDORFF'S DWARF LEMUR (Galago demidovii)

The sight of this tree upset my calculations, but as soon as we were below it Dele announced that he saw the lemurs. These he endeavoured to point out to me. For at least ten minutes I could not locate them, though the foliage of the whole tree was not much larger than a rose-bush. Eventually, thoroughly exasperated, I decided to pretend that I had spotted them and just fire at the tree in general. I retreated to allow the shot to scatter, and blazed away.

Like a streak of lightning a tiny galago shot out of the tree, sailed over my head, and entered the low trees adjoining the forest. Here it galloped as a horse does, with both fore feet and both hind feet together, straight through the trees. I have never seen anything to compare with it. This was no leaping from branch to branch, followed by a rapid climb and then another leap. It was a continuous headlong gallop in a straight line as if there were a taut rope stretched directly along its path. I ran as fast as I could across the floor of the forest, which was here as clear as a ballroom, and arrived just in time to see the little animal disappear into an isolat d clump of ferns growing on a slender leafless creeper festooned t ween two tall trees. I carefully took aim. Though the range was extreme, the shot severed the delicate stem of the fern so that the whole clump fell to pieces and rained down to earth. The creeper was also cut through, and before I knew where I was, one half of it swished downward and bowled me over.

I scrambled to my feet and was at the spot where most of the fern lay before all its leaves reached the ground. The animal was nowhere to be seen. Dele had not followed me. I called to him. He answered that he was looking for the other galago which he seemed to think had fallen at the first shot. We searched in silence for nearly half an hour over an area of only a few square yards of more or less clear ground before either of us located our animal. I was firmly convinced that my animal had escaped and that Dele's had never existed at all, but the African was adamant.

It was Dele's great day. He seemed infallible.

We retrieved both animals and they proved to be an adult male and female *Galago demidovii*—our greatest prize. What was more, the female was pregnant. The acquisition of these two tiny green animals, with bright saffron bellies and hind legs, was a landmark in our trip.

Demidorff's lemurs are seldom encountered in the forest, partly because of their small size—about that of a rat—and partly because they live in the highest trees and are perhaps the swiftest moving animals that inhabit such places. There is another possible contributory cause. This is as yet only a supposition, but I give it merely as the conclusion that we came to in our own minds through seeing these animals in their natural surroundings.

I believe that Demidorff's lemur, unlike other galagos, is diurnal and not nocturnal.

Our reasons for coming to this conclusion are, of course, speculative, but are none the less worthy of serious consideration. In the first place, native hunters say they seldom see them; when they do, it is always in the day time and never by the light of the hunting lamp. Certainly on the very few occasions when we saw them, the sun was shining brightly. The second and, to my mind, most convincing reason is the coloration of this lemur.

We captured six diurnal animals in Africa that belonged to groups all the other members of which are exclusively nocturnal. All six animals—a snake (*Gastropyxis senaragdina*), a squirrel (*Funisciurus poensis*), a monkey (*Cercopithecus pogonias*), a rat (*Œnomys hypoxanthus*), a flying squirrel (*Anomalurus beecrofti*), and, finally, a lemur (*Galago demidovii*)—were bright green above and yellow beneath, whereas their near-related and nocturnal species were all of other colours. It may sound a rather radical thing to say, but this type of colouring has some connexion with bright sunlight. All animals showing these colours except the rat, which inhabits open parts of sunny clearings, are to be found at the very tops of the forest trees in the bright sunlight. If the numbers of these five animals we obtained in comparison to the numbers of their relatives be taken as the criterion, they would all appear to be rare; but the real reason, I believe, rests in the fact that we met these green and yellow species only when we encountered the rare natural clearings in the true virgin forest. At other times they were hidden out of range above the trees.

One of our later camps in the high virgin forest was situated among the foothills of the northern escarpment. Here the forest is never even visited by native hunters and conditions remain as they presumably were almost before man made his appearance in Africa.

Strolling through the jungle one sunny, breathlessly hot day, frankly in the hope of finding a small patch of unfiltered sunlight in which to bask, I came upon a natural arena. The towering trees ended abruptly, their billowing head-foliage cascading down to

earth as steeply as a waterfall. Despite the remoteness of the place
from any village, had I found stumps of big trees in the clearing I
would have been convinced that it was a man-made place. As there
were none, and as natives cannot fell and uproot the big trees—even
a European with dynamite finds it well nigh impossible—there was
no doubt that some natural explanation must be sought. The only
one that presented itself was the fact that the ground was boggy and
a thin scum of miscible multicoloured sheens covering the water
showed the presence of oil.

I lay down in the sun and was soon fast asleep. How long I dozed
I do not know. I awoke, bathed in perspiration, to find that the sun
had moved far enough behind the trees to leave me in deep shade.
I was stretched on a perfectly bare piece of hard earth singularly
free from ants. All around was tufted grass, a few small shrubs, and
some giant hemlock.

As I sat up I received a great surprise. All over the clearing were
monkeys busily scratching and searching among the herbage.

Loading my gun, I began wriggling forward on my belly until I
reached a vantage point behind a little knoll. From here I could see
most of the troop. They were in search of insects, particularly grasshoppers, the caviare of the monkey world. Presently another troop
arrived far above, on the edge of the flying continent's surface.
After great chirruping and talk between the two troops, two large
males descended and went into rowdy conference with their equals
among the first occupants of the territory. It was apparently agreed
that there was room for all, and the females and young descended
with much crashing and shaking of branches.

As soon as they were all down, I advanced round the knoll and
had a good look at the animals. What I saw at closer quarters quite
took my breath away. They were all bright green in colour with
vivid orange throats, chests, and bellies. The males' crowns were
surmounted by a tall central conical crest. We had never even suspected the existence of such a monkey in the neighbourhood, nor
heard of it from any native hunters elsewhere.

Selecting a large male, I took careful though not sufficiently accurate aim. I am sorry to say I missed him completely. The shot was so sudden that all the monkeys remained stock-still. I leapt up and made a dash for the nearest one. This was the signal for a wild flight to the trees. The mothers leapt for the hanging branches with their young on their backs or clinging round their necks. In a few seconds they had vanished over the brink of the high trees.

For several days afterwards I returned to the clearing. Although a scout appeared alone on one occasion while the rest crashed around the trees at a respectable distance, they never dared descend again. We eventually obtained two of these monkeys (*Cercopithecus pogonias*), one from a native hunter in the next village and another by means of George's rifle not far from the clearing.

On the last evening that I visited the spot Ben and I were, however, rewarded with the other two high-tree forms that I have named, i.e., the squirrel and the snake. Four months previously I had obtained the first specimen of the squirrel (*Funisciurus poensis*) at a camp situated some sixty miles distant. During the whole intervening time I had never seen a trace of this species, though we had been working on the high trees all the time.

Ben and I climbed as high as we could up a natural ladder of creepers that hung down from a giant acacia tree into the clearing. From here we managed to cross to a near-by kapok tree, among whose uppermost branches we ensconced ourselves, with an uninterrupted view of a considerable segment of the forest surface. This was the only time that I actually got above the forest by climbing from within. It was a unique experience.

The sun shone down with a glaring intensity that was magnified by the shiny reflection of the leaves. Myriads of brilliantly coloured butterflies flitted about, making calls at the clusters of waxy, exotic flowers. Vast congregations of bees buzzed and hummed like a duststorm round trees that were particularly to their liking. Flies great and small hovered and darted about everywhere—helicopters of such efficiency that their bodies could remain absolutely motionless for minutes together or be projected through the air with such speed that they became invisible. Birds of all colours and sizes fluttered about and bobbed in and out of exits and entrances plain to them but invisible to us.

This was a world of its own, green and flat and entirely remote from the rest of the earth. Ben and I were as complete strangers as Eskimos would have been. Even more strongly than in the cathedral-like solitude below did I feel cut off from the intolerable world of man. Ben, being an African, felt this in his own way and became quite communicative as a result; he gave little gasps of surprise at each new thing he saw.

His excitement proved very nearly disastrous when a flight of plantain-eaters came soaring over the tree tops and passed right between us, uttering ear-splitting shrieks and squawks. These gawky birds with their scraggy necks, staring eyes, and great fan tails are for ever breaking out into a positive sweat of excitement and turmoil, after which they flap their way out of the foliage and soar away to repeat their idiotic performance elsewhere. Their passing nearly dethroned my trusted follower.

Above us soared and wheeled all manner of hawks and eagles which descended every now and then in rocket-like nose-dives into the greenery.

After more than an hour of waiting, during which time we were never for a moment at a loss for entertainment, Ben spotted a movement among the leaves of a near-by tree. With the aid of field glasses we soon picked out the small squirrel. Since it was out of range, we could only follow its movements in perfect silence, hoping that it would drift towards us. Its behaviour was most erratic, as is the way with squirrels. First it would run back and forth along a branch half a dozen times before deciding to nibble a leaf; then it would pass to another perch and lie flat as if simulating a piece of wood. Every hole must be peered into, every nook and cranny must be investigated from all angles. It ran away up to the very summit of a bare tree, only to spot a large hawk at too close a range and bolt screaming below again. By all these endless hustlings hither and thither it eventually approached close enough for me to see that it was a green and yellow animal. I at once decided that, although a happy, pretty little fellow, he must become a piece of cold convincing scientific fact. Wrapping my legs round branches, with Ben steadying me from behind, I fired. The animal fell straight through to the ground below.

Ben was dispatched to pick him up, leaving me with the field glasses, a collecting bag, the gun, and other paraphernalia. We had arranged not to call to each other in order not to disturb other animals, a thing that the human voice can do but a single shot will not.

As Ben had disappeared below for some time, I decided to try to locate him by altering my position. This proved to be an extremely ticklish job, since I was loaded with accoutrements like a pack-mule. To climb a tree is always easier than to descend one, but to move across one is the limit. At last I attained a position where I could see Ben's back far below, and was groping round for a firm hold when the worst five minutes of my life began.

As I clutched a thin leafless branch, my fingers closed on something cool and slippery on the other side. At the same time a coil of vivid emerald-green sagged from the branch over my forearm. I let go with lightning speed, partly lost my balance, and let out an indescribable noise—at least, Ben couldn't describe it later. I then found myself staring directly into Ben's face turned upwards far below. The collecting bag was slipping round my neck; the shotgun, which was loaded and had the safety catch off, was entangled above and behind me. By some sort of superhuman effort I got back to the upright position to meet face to face with a sleek, green and yellow head in which were set the most enormous pair of lustrous jet-black eyes I have ever seen in a snake. A "snake film star" flashed through my mind, as stupid things will on such occasions.

The reptile and I then swayed about in rhythm while I got the gun free, the safety catch on, the breech opened, and the barrel pushed through my belt so that I had two hands free. I then grappled with the collapsible butterfly net, while the snake constantly flicked its little black tongue at me.

At last I had the net free and open and made a swipe at the

gleaming head, which flicked back out of range with incredible speed. Then began a game something like touch-last during which I nearly lost my balance again. Eventually, after what seemed hours of play, I managed to scoop the head and forepart of the snake into the net, but there appeared to be yards of the animal, all of which began a furious wriggling. In one last supreme effort I scraped the net down the branch and threw the whole lot, snake and all, away from me. As the net fell, the rest of the reptile came loose and fell down among the leafy branches below, where it lodged partly out of view.

Scrambling to a safe position, I drew the gun out of my belt, a difficult job on account of its extra-long barrel, loaded up, and blazed away at the net. This disappeared by degrees and with a crash something heavy fell almost at Ben's feet.

It was not until more than a year after our return to England, when we came to study our collection of snakes, that I learnt that this handsome green and yellow brute (*Gastropyxis senaragdina*) was as harmless as a chicken. All the same, one can never be certain of one's zoological knowledge in a tree top, and it is always unwise to take a chance with a snake.

Part Four

MISTY MOUNTAINS

10

Gorillas and Chimpanzees

A-go'i a-go'i ago-oma
Eanagbo,
A-go'i a-go'i etinko
Eanagbo,
A-goi, a-goi—MBU.

THE interior of the jungle echoed as if it were a cave and the trees carven in stone. Anongo's yelling voice rang out far ahead "a-go'i" again and again and a long thin trail of falsetto and bass "eanagbos" answered from above our heads and below our feet. We all roared "A-goi, a-goi—MBU" together. Then the world became quiet for a few moments and only the incessant drip of great blobs of water spattering on broad leaves and an occasional cough from a sweating carrier broke the deathly silence.

Slowly but surely all our possessions, the whole of our little cosmos, crept skyward as tiny insects must do when they fight their way up to the air and the light of day from the depths of the soil. The path was a giant's stairway of huge boulders piled one upon another, moss-covered, cold and quiet in the perpetual gloom—the turbulent floor of an ageless, changeless canopy of steaming greenery. A few paces forward and a man's naked heels appeared on a level with one's eyes. Then came a long pause while some heavy load was hoisted over an obstacle further up the line and at last one moved forward again. Would the top, like the mountain of Mohammed, never come? Would we, like the insects, never reach the summit and the fresh air?

175

Then all at once we came to it. The rocky stairway gave place to sticky red clay; the trees rolled back, festooned with waxy, crimson blooms, and we slid blinking out into the blazing sun.

There before us lay a tremendous valley stretching as far as the eye could see. To the right and left rose tier upon tier of softly moulded mountains basking placidly in the still clear air, bathed in sunlight and clad in tall waving grass, with the wind eddying silently across their face in endless parallel billows. Far up near the powdered sky, little ravines upholstered in dark-green forest clung to the face of the grassy mountains or filled in the interstices between the monstrous natural pyramids. The forest ended like a wall to left and right of us, and from our feet the ground dropped right away down to an immense amphitheatre. The air was crystal clear and paradisiacally still. The tiniest sounds—a tinkling bell-like drum, the bark of a dog, the call of some strange bird—came clear and undiluted from the utmost limits of vision.

The sun poured down, the tall grass waved and sighed in the gentle breeze, and little blue bees buzzed about the damp clay at our feet. Stupefied by the beauty into which we had stepped, we began to descend towards the village of Tinta, which we saw lying far below us.

When we were still some distance from the cluster of circular houses, we met a deputation headed by Chief Ekumaw surrounded by the other notables of this wonderful little tribe of unknown mountain people. With them we entered the little compound which was to be our future home, and after a great deal of palaver, exchange of greetings, and our respective renderings of jazz music, they departed, leaving us to set up house.

When all was straight, we sat down to a hard-earned dinner. Just as the "palm-oil chop" was being reverently placed before us, we heard a loud report somewhere far up among the mountains in the direction from which we had come that afternoon from the world beyond. We remarked upon its loudness and its lonesomeness, but soon forgot all about it amid the fragrant aroma of well-peppered palm-oil. We sat in silence until neither the food nor our

stomachs could hold out any longer, and then we fell to smoking in silence. As soon as it was physically possible to move, we reached out for books and sank into that radiant glow of contentment that comes only from hard labour combined with hard eating. The Africans in their half of the house had lapsed into a similar condition. A great hush fell over the world.

Then out of the night and the cries of animals came a burble that grew louder and louder. Through a hole in the mud wall of the house I could see tiny lanterns approaching. The chimpanzees—Mary and "The Oaf"—began whimpering and complaining from the darkness of their cage on the mud platform behind the house; people stirred around the cook's domains; but the burble passed by to the village below, where a still greater commotion began. Soon a small army was advancing towards the house from that direction.

"Ben, Faugi," I bawled. "Bring 'trong men for lift masters," for we could not possibly lift ourselves after a palm-oil chop. It was not that the food was so heavy in itself, but that we had eaten so much of it—shame on us!

So we were lifted bodily in our chairs, to the great amusement of the staff, who were nearly as moribund as ourselves, and planted down in a neat little row facing the door and the compound, into which the advancing army soon began to pour. I was surprised to see among them the princely Chief Ekumaw surrounded by many tall wiry men clad only in leather loin-cloths and bearing immense, long Dane-guns. I had not noticed such persons among the tribe before and I dislike Dane-guns, as I have already stated. Ety'i, that preposterous official court messenger who had been kindly lent to us by the political officer as interpreter for this particular trip, was also with the company. There were others too, in strange masks.

"Do they bring medicine?" I asked, which means music, a dance, or magic, as all these three together with medicine proper are part of one and the same thing in the mind of the African.

"No, masters," replied Ety'i with a positively pyrotechnic display of gestures. Then everybody began to talk at once, until we became equally excited.

"Ben, what the devil is it all about?"

"T'ick-ehn, I no savvy how they talk, master."

"Well, ask Ety'i then."

"He say they bring story of a great beef."

"Well, which man fit tell story, make you find out one time."

"Master, this old man he speak English better than Ety'i."

"Let this man talk then," I commanded, and he talked thus:

"This man"—the old fellow began pointing to a tall muscular African with a savage, insolent face—"do walker-walker for bush high for up"—pointing to the hills behind the house. "He hear much animal talk. He be great hunter for these parts"—loud grunts of assent from all quarters—"so he walker softly-softly-softly for side of small banana farm and, whough! there for him very eye he see huge beef."

At this juncture the old gentleman, who we subsequently learnt was a great-great-grandfather, became so excited that he leapt off the floor in an endeavour to reach the top of the animal's stature in his mind's eye. As he continued, he leapt about, groaned, burbled, grimaced, and acted out every detail and endless extemporizations on the whole story.

"Which kind of beef this be?" I asked by way of encouragement, but there was no need. After staring at me wild-eyed for a second, the old chap was off again.

"He no be beef, he be so-so man but he no be man, he be big too much," and he flung out his arms. "He black all, he 'trong like plenty-plenty man." Then he fell to a literal demonstration of the appearance and behaviour of this fantastic beast.

"Yes, but what the hunter make?" I urged.

"Ah-haaaa . . ." everybody agreed.

"Arrrr!" shouted the centenarian, rushing to the far corner of the compound. "The beef, he holler, he holler too much—bluooer-bluooer—he COME, so!" and he rushed bellowing towards us, sweeping everything within his reach into his arms. "The hunter he shoot BANG, then he run, he run, he run come for tell chief." At this our raconteur fell exhausted.

We held a hurried conference. Could it be a gorilla? We looked at each other and then commenced questioning the local inhabitants. Yes, they knew the "man-beef"; there were many of them about. This animal was indeed one. I sent for a picture of a gorilla and showed it to the chief. The place was filled with "ah-hurrs" of assent.

Was the beef dead? we inquired. The hunter didn't know. He had not waited to find out, the "wise guy"! If it was not dead, would it still be there? Were there others? Could we go and see? How far away did it happen? A hundred other questions we asked. Eventually it was decided that it was probably wounded and, as it was the father, the family would doubtless hang about; therefore it would be best to start before dawn in search of it. After some further talk they all went away.

We made great preparations, since we wanted photographs of gorillas. This we explained to the whole staff at great length. We were each to take a camera and each to have two Africans to carry spare films, other equipment, a gun or rifle, and a spare weapon of some sort—either a revolver or another gun—just in case the great ape might take a dislike to the camera. We then retired to bed, leaving instructions to be called at some dark, ungodly hour.

My head seemed no sooner on the pillow than Ben was standing over me with a bush lamp. I managed to get up, but the others remained like logs breathing heavily under their mosquito nets. I had to fetch the gramophone, put on one of Louis Armstrong's loudest, and place it between their beds before they showed any signs of life. By the time we had breakfasted and got out the guns, a little knot of hunters had collected outside the house. We were far up the side of the mountain before dawn began to light up the sky.

From then on the world began to take on a very grim appearance, at least to us. Though I had imagined that we were going up a mountain to look for a gorilla, apparently the hunter who was leading us, and whose face I had always suspected, had other ideas. He seemed bent on showing us how many mountains there were in Assumbo and how straight and tall and fine they were. First we marched up the road by which we had descended into this country and when we got to the very summit where the tall forest ended, the hunter suddenly plunged to the left among the dense undergrowth. We followed, only to be confronted by his heels. Then began a perpendicular ascent, which he and the other Assumbos tackled at a steady four miles an hour, in fact at the same speed that they would a stretch of perfectly level ground. We scrambled up behind them as best we could, taking hold of anything we could lay our hands, our feet, or even our teeth and chins on to gain a hold.

Soon we were buried deep in a more or less solid mass of intricately woven and interwoven creepers covered with long moss and branches festooned with lichens like old men's beards.

But we went on up for ever into the cold mists at the same hectic rate. Perspiration broke out all over me, saturating my clothes from within as the dripping vegetation was doing from without. This was no ordinary sweat—it was icy cold.

Then matters got even worse. The plexus of wiry creepers descended in one great mass to the very ground, bringing even the hunters up sharp. We fell on our stomachs and began squirming forward. Progress was naturally rather slow, because all these creepers in this part of the forest were armed with long thorns. At last the hunter in front of me beckoned and pointed out some small plants about six inches tall. These looked like tiny saplings having a woody stem with only about half a dozen large leaves. Some of these leaves he showed me had semicircular pieces bitten neatly out of them.

"Gorilla!" he said, pointing to his mouth and making his jaws work as if eating. Then we were all brought to a halt.

The ground fell away before us. We were at the top at last. The chief hunter informed us that it was at this spot that he first saw the gorilla. He pointed forward with his finger and we wriggled cautiously onward. Before us lay a solid wall of undergrowth into which we cautiously thrust our way.

Suddenly there was a crash almost at my elbow, the foliage parted, and a great expanse of silvery hair flashed by in the same direction that we were moving. All my nerves gave one great lurch. I fumbled hysterically for the camera. Then I glanced round, but Ben was well out of reach, firmly caught up in a mass of creepers, with the gun so tied up that I could not possibly get hold of it for action. At that instant there was a shout from the hunter further to the right, and, stepping forward, I fell headlong.

The ground dropped almost perpendicularly and so did I. Right before me I just caught a glimpse of a colossal black and white object, then it disappeared behind some leaves and emitted the most fearsome gurgling grunts. I sprawled among the undergrowth.

When I scrambled out, I found myself on the edge of a small banana plantation choked with other low growth. Beside me stood all the hunters, and lying in their midst was an enormous swollen corpse. It was a huge male gorilla, now belching up the gases formed by the decomposition of the food in its dead belly.

Apparently the hunter's chance shot of the night before had found its mark and the animal had died where it stood feeding on the top of the bank. As we advanced, one of us must have released a creeper that held it up, and it had fallen down under its own weight, flattening the undergrowth and emitting those blood-thirsty gurgling sounds as it rolled over and over, the gases pouring out of its mouth.

Men left at once for the village and we settled ourselves down to await their return. During this time we had ample opportunity of examining our prize. A really large male gorilla in the flesh is a thing that very few have the good fortune to encounter, and still fewer the chance to handle in perfect comfort. Such sights come only once in a lifetime, a thing that we fully realized and appreciated as we stood there gazing at this sad old man of the mountains.

I shall never quite forget the emotions that this sight conjured up inside me. I had always been taught to think of the gorilla as the very essence of savagery and terror, and now there lay this hoary old vegetarian, his immense arms folded over his great pot belly, all the fire gone from his wrinkled black face, his soft brown eyes wide open beneath their long straight lashes and filled with an in-

finite sorrow. Into his whole demeanour I could not help but read
the tragedy of his race, driven from the plains up into the mountains countless centuries ago by more active ape-like creatures—perhaps even our own forebears; chevied hither and thither by the ever-
encroaching hordes of hairless shouting little men, his young ones
snatched by leopards, his feeding grounds restricted by farms and
paths and native huntsmen. All around him was a changing world
against which he bellowed his defiance to the end, rushing forward
to meet the bits of lead and gravel blasted at him by his puny rival.

At last the Munchis came and the sad old man was lashed to two
young trees and borne away by thirty staggering, chanting humans;
away from the silence of the mists, away from his last tangled
stronghold; and yet not quite the last of the giants and not quite un-
mourned.

To complete the story of this gorilla would fill a whole book.
The journey down from the mountain where he died to the village,
which we estimated was no less than four thousand feet below, took
seven hours. As far as we could ascertain by a process of weighing
—first the gorilla against men, then the men individually against
stones, and finally the stones against our scales—this old male was
more than a quarter of a ton in weight, probably between six and
seven hundredweight. Thirty very strong men had been employed
to get him down to the village and a path had to be cut every foot
of the way through extremely dense vegetation.

When the procession arrived at the house, awful problems instantly arose. There were six "parties" claiming rights over the
corpse: ourselves; the chief, who owns a communal share in everything; the hunter, who killed the animal; the villagers, who wanted
the flesh for food and ju-ju; the Munchis, who had done all the
work carrying the corpse down; and, finally, I allowed the request
of our staff for some meat. The first move was my purchase of all
but the chief's rights from the hunter for the sum of one pound
sterling, three quarters to be paid in shillings and the remainder in
large pennies with holes in them. This did not, however, give me

sole claim to the whole animal. The bargain was sealed only when a clear understanding was given that I might do the skinning and sectioning at my own time and to my liking. In return I promised to leave three-quarters of the meat by weight for distribution among the villagers, giving the chief first choice from the whole and allowing the hunter to select small portions of various organs for purposes of ju-ju.

The first thing to be done with a dead animal is to measure it, so that if ever one requires to stuff and mount it, the skin, which is necessarily stretched during the process of drying, may be shrunk down to the right proportions again. Our findings upon the gorilla were rather staggering. The arm-span, from the tip of the third finger on one hand along the arm, across the chest, and thence along the other arm to the tip of the third finger, measured nine feet, two inches. I frankly did not believe this when it was reported to me as I held a palaver with the chief. I therefore had it repeated under my own eyes and it was undeniably so. We photographed it as proof. The ear was only two inches long, but the face, from the crown to the point of the chin, measured over thirteen inches—more than a foot! While the distance from the top of the head to the caudal appendage was just over four feet, a great deal larger than the same span in any man, the legs were proportionately short. Yet they measured more than two feet, which can be verified from the skeleton we brought back. Male gorillas can then stand over six feet if they wish, or are able to straighten their legs. Many specialists will dispute this statement; all I can ask them to do is to pay a visit to the British Museum, inspect the skeleton for themselves, and then go home and lay out their own largest male example. They will receive a rude shock.

Next in order came a systematic search for any external parasites. There were only a few very minute ticks that proved to belong to a quite unknown type. The length of time the animal had been dead had undoubtedly given ample opportunity for others to take leave of their host.

We then began skinning. This proved to be a great work, and as many people as could crowd round the body applied themselves to the job. One man was employed solely to keep sharpening the knives. The limbs were severed at the elbow and knee joints, to be carried away with the skin and dealt with later at leisure, when decomposition had been checked around the belly area of the skin where it had already set in. I was then left with the mountainous corpse, but being anxious to take this opportunity of performing a detailed dissection, I had to prevent a number of people from plunging in and cutting out their share of the bargain themselves.

Chief Ekumaw's authority came in useful here; the raucous crowd that waited around was kept off, although the hunter prowled about at my elbow with a murderous-looking knife and a glazed expression that defies description but was really quite unearthly. There were many interesting points in the internal anatomy, but no parasites, which surprised me in a vegetable feeder.

At last I was finished, and announced that the hunter might take what he required. He literally dived into the corpse and cut away feverishly. I have never seen a man truly "possessed" before or since. It was quite uncanny; he seemed insensible to all else around him. His knowledge of anatomy was remarkable; with amazing deftness he selected pieces of the muscular covering of the eye-ridges, flesh from the armpits and groins, the whole heart, a part of the small intestine, the tip of the left lung, some abdominal muscles, and the pancreas. I tried to fool him by offering the left lobe of the liver for the last named, which was exactly the same in colour, but he was not having any of it, and after glaring at me as if I were only fit for a ritual ju-ju murder, he carried the pancreas off. As soon as his job was done, he seemed to collapse and had to be almost carried away. His subsequent behaviour was outlined to me by Ekumaw.

I quote from the diary: "A medicine is made (the recipe for which is bought) out of various vegetable products and kept in a pot surrounded by a small fence of sticks in the man's compound. Some of this is taken and rubbed on the man's gun before he goes out hunting, in order that he may find animals and shoot them dead when he fires. If he is successful, he takes, as this man did, small portions from certain organs of the animal and, cooking them together with a fowl, places half in the ju-ju pot in his compound and eats the other half. Palm-wine is brought and divided likewise. Thus by each successful hunt the potency of the man's ju-ju grows and his aim becomes more accurate." There may be more truth in this than the incredulous might suppose.

When the meat was all cleared from the bones, it formed a waist-high pile in the compound. The chief selected a rump steak and the whole of the remainder of the intestine. This apparently makes a very fine dish—the distant origin, I should imagine, of the American Negro's chitterlings (the small intestine of the pig)—but it is also most extremely powerful ju-ju and the prerogative of the religious head of the tribe. It is medicine in the true sense, being an antidote for the common African complaint "tiger-for-belly," which means a belly ache!

Altogether, twenty men worked for thirty-six hours on that corpse before it was properly preserved. The skeleton had to be picked and scrubbed, the skin cleaned of all fat—a tough job in itself—then stretched on a frame and dried over a slow fire for three days, and, lastly, the hands and feet had to be skinned out to the tip of the last joint. This was the worst of all, not because it took place in the early hours after a strenuous day, but because the tough skin on the palms and soles is bound rigidly to the bone and flesh beneath by a maze of ligaments as strong as wire.

It may sound disappointing to announce that we never shot a gorilla ourselves, yet this is actually very satisfactory from two points of view. First, they are, I am pleased to say, rigidly protected by law; and secondly, it implies that we were never called upon to shoot in self-defence one of these proud sub-human ancestors of ours. The natives do not hunt these animals and do, I believe, in all honesty, shoot them only in self-protection. Farther to the west in Ikom, Nigerian territory, I think this is not the case, because of the number of skulls offered for sale and in ju-ju houses, and also because of the objectionable proclivities of the local peoples, a despicable tribe known as the Bokis, or their relatives, of whom Africa ought to be ashamed. They are despicable because they sell all their women to the coast towns and spend all their money on sun-glasses and sola-topees.

The people of Assumbo believe gorillas to be another race of man, and not an animal at all. The chimpanzee is, on the other hand, a great monkey to them and only aping man. They are an honest people and not given to imaginative story-telling, as we had good cause to find out later, and as they probably see more gorillas and know more of their habits than does any other group of human beings in the world, I think their opinions should at least be listened to. They affirm that there is no case in their records or memory of gorillas trying to carry off women, which would be the first thing that they would pretend gorillas did if they wished to confirm their statement that these apes are really men. I myself, as a zoologist, a naturalist, and an ordinary sane person, am in absolute agreement with the Assumbos, though doubtless my opinion is not of the least consequence.

Seeing these creatures in life, listening to their calls and talk, and examining them both alive and dead alongside chimpanzees and men, I can only regard them and treat them as a retrograde form of human or, at the least, sub-human life. They not only have hands, faces, and, to a certain extent, feet like our own, but they use them in exactly the same manner that we do. Their speech contains as many different sounds and types of sounds as any human language. They have constructive ability, shown in building platforms, using sticks, and sorting out objects, that is on a par with that of some adult humans. Furthermore, they bear strong family likenesses and equally well-marked interfamily differences. The natives of these mountains live alongside the gorillas and know all the families by sight, so that they can tell you more or less in which district one will meet certain parties, what they will look like, and how many of them there will be.

Scientists have been at great pains to define a number of different races of gorillas. There are undoubtedly two, the mountain and the plains forms, the latter being really distinct and confined to a small area in the east. I have seen in Assumbo a greater variety of colour, shape, and size among the gorillas within a small area than all that displayed by the numerous so-called sub-races described from all over Africa where the gorilla is met with. Individual gorillas vary and show family resemblances just like men. One family may have bright-red crests on their heads, even the very young, another may be almost entirely silvery-grey in colour, and others almost jet-black. Of course, there are, apart from these, certain colours that go with age, notably grey hair, as among men.

We spent a great deal of time hunting gorillas with our friend Afa. George once actually got right among a large party, listened to them belching, was bawled at by the old male, and saw them beating their chests with their clenched fists. I inspected several of their "nests," which are really great platforms raised a few feet off the ground and constructed for use during the night's rest when on the move from one feeding ground to another. These were formed by bending saplings inwards and placing on top of this springy mattress a mass of leafy branches torn from the surrounding trees. Among these I counted more than two dozen complete knots made in the creepers and saplings to keep them down. They were mostly "grannies," but there were three real "reef" knots (one of which I cut out and kept) which had undoubtedly resulted only by chance. The size of some of the branches torn and ripped to make these platforms was quite staggering and bore testimony to the terrific strength of these creatures.

The natives have many tales about the habits of gorillas. They assert that they will conceal themselves if surprised feeding near a path, and, as the train of people passes, the big male will dart out, grab the last man by the thigh, take one great bite out of his leg, and then bolt. I was certainly introduced to two men with useless legs from which a large chunk had been removed. One assured me that this had occurred not a mile from Tinta village. Usually, they told us, the man died as a result, presumably of blood poisoning.

That the male gorilla will attack on sight, or rather as soon as he knows that he has been seen, is an undoubted fact, at least in Assumbo, though of course this may not necessarily be the case elsewhere. When he does so, he stands erect and gathers the branches in his arms before him to screen himself. Is there anything but a human that would do this?

There is another fact that may perhaps also serve to clear up an argument. The great length of the gorilla's arms has been somewhat of a mystery. Though they are indeed useful as levers to pull down trees and even to be used for walking on all fours, a trip to Assumbo would soon demonstrate another use that probably exceeds all others. To walk about this precipitous country one needs not only a pair of legs to keep erect, but also a pair of arms, and very long ones at that. The gorilla's arms are exactly the right size to enable him to walk straight up a steep bank and still use his hands as an accessory pair of feet. I have with my own eyes seen one descend a bank backwards with the aid of his arms, just as a man has to do in this perpendicular country.

Other facts about the attack of the gorilla are open to considerable doubt, as the following story will demonstrate.

Late one night a sub-chief came to announce that he had a man, recently come from Ikom to his territory, which bordered both that place and Tinta, who had a baby gorilla for sale. This man was brought in and proved to be a tall, very black individual who spoke quite a lot of pidgin-English. This, combined with his appearance and the direction from which he had come, made me at once suspicious. He was not actually a Boki—no one of that tribe would take the trouble or have the guts to travel so far—but he still "smelt" of that part of the world. He carried a little black mite with big brown eyes who sucked her thumb quietly while regarding us all in interested silence. I determined at once that I must have this baby gorilla, whose whole demeanour was far more childlike than that of any human baby I had ever seen, except in educational films.

We began bargaining. I was not disposed to give more for this baby than I had for the whole male gorilla. Although she was worth more to us, it would not have appeared proper to the friendly Assumbos. The owner could not appreciate this. When asked why he placed such a high price on this animal, he related the following tale in pidgin-English:

"I was walking through the forest on a hunt, when I heard gorilla. I advanced cautiously and saw a party consisting of a male and a female who was holding this baby. I stalked them and fired a shot at the mother. This penetrated her posterior regions and she dropped her baby to hold the wounded part. I then ran forward, but the male, who had been stalking me, suddenly charged. I had not had time to reload my gun and was therefore defenceless, so I handed the weapon to him. He took it and broke it into small pieces over his knee. I (plucky little fellow that I am) meanwhile ran on and picked up the baby. I have brought it to you and want to get money to replace my gun."

"Ben!" I called out. "Fetch Ety'i at once."

There was an awkward pause during which time the doughty hunter stood by grinning and well pleased that I was so impressed by his tale of daring and skill. Then Ety'i, the court messenger, came running in.

"Ety'i," I said, "you fit take this man, who is a foreigner in this country, for put him in jail in Mamfe for shooting protected animals, until the district officer do come back?"

"Yes, I fit plenty," replied Ety'i, although we knew that this was extremely doubtful.

I turned to the hunter—so-called. He had become rather a different person.

"I go pay the chief of Oliti eight shilling for bringing you here," I said, "from which he will pay the man in his tribe who sold you the goila [pidgin-English for gorilla] six shilling. Here is two shilling for your own trouble and to pay for your food in this foreign

country. Now GO for your own country one time!" And, believe
me, he went.

The old chief of Oliti and I then settled down to a good laugh and
a long gossip about beef and ancestors.

It was not until several months later that I came across this same
story in an old magazine, and then I made more inquiries as to
hunters' exploits with gorillas. All those I questioned, who were
doubtful hunters in the first place, and who lived in the low forests,
told me with great solemnity the tale of how they once captured a
baby "goila" alive. It was always the same tale.

It was a very peculiar and extremely unlucky thing that we never
came across chimpanzees in their native haunts. Many times we
penetrated places where they were known to abound, and we even
lived in such country for weeks at a time, yet they never made an
appearance. On several occasions I heard loud, chimp-like noises,
but one can never be sure of the origin of any sound in the deep
forest.

This lack was, however, made up to us by our pet chimps, of
which we had many. Two young ones in particular stayed with us
almost throughout the trip, and had not gentle and lovable little
"Mary" died from a chill, both would have returned with us and
still be sharing my home now if they could have braved the English
winter.

Mary came to us one rainy evening on the shoulder of a very
dirty Hausa trader from the north who had bought her to sell to
Europeans at the coast. She cost me two pounds, but I could not
possibly resist her. She was dirty, her hair matted and straggling
over her face so that she looked more like an old woman than ever.
I noted something even more pathetic. The terminal joints of nearly
all her toes and several of her fingers were swollen up like marbles.
In these I knew jigger-fleas had taken up their residence, and the
pain must have been excruciating.

As soon as she became mine, I carried her to the back of the house, dumped her into a bath of soapy water, and gave her a good scrub all over. While at first she screamed worse than a child, by the time she was enveloped in a bath towel being dried, she was cooing and muttering contentedly—the most human behaviour. I then set to work operating on one toe at a time. As I advanced with scalpels and tweezers, screams burst forth afresh, but after the first gash, at which Mary winced, there was absolute silence except for tiny baby noises of contentment, while she watched operations with as much interest as anybody. She fully understood that we were relieving the pain which she must have been suffering for weeks.

The jigger-fleas are a parasitic species picked up from the dust around human habitations. They enter beneath the nail, where they proceed to grow into fleshy white bags of considerable size, forming painful, small boils which continue to increase in virulence until the whole of the interior of the last joint may become merely a hollow bag of pus. One of Mary's toes had reached this stage. When I cut away the rotten skin, all the liquid ran out and left the bone standing up white and completely naked. I had to amputate this and fold the skin over the next joint. This was extremely painful, but she only whimpered, and when I had finished and bandaged them all up, she quite voluntarily put her arms round my neck and hugged and kissed me and refused to let go.

The rest of the evening she sat up in an old armchair, wrapped in a blanket, watching the work going on on the skinning tables.

"The Oaf" arrived in a wooden box some three weeks later. He received his name the moment we looked at him; of all the dumb, idiot faces I have ever seen, his beat the lot. He remained a bad-tempered fool to the end. As the box was opened, I put my hand in and petted him, being used to Mary's gentleness. The native owners were scandalized and advised me not to touch him again, as he was extremely spiteful and bit everything he saw. Once I had learnt to fear him, the Oaf felt it as well, and the next time I tried to handle him I got a bad bite. After that I could never touch him.

Young chimps have pink faces like white people's. The Oaf

already had black spots, the forerunners of the adult coloration. He was mean and irascible, worrying Mary all the time till she died (a matter of many months), screaming because he did not like his food, and generally being a nuisance. Only once was he funny, and then quite unconsciously.

When we went on trek to a new camp, the livestock travelled in their cages on the heads of carriers. On this occasion there were so many that the chimps had to go in a large cage with the live fowls which we had to carry for food. During the journey I heard a con-stant caterwauling from the fowls farther along the line, and arriv-ing at a river where the carriers were held up, I spotted the Oaf busily plucking the fowls alive. The poor creatures were almost naked and looked altogether ridiculous. The stupid chimp retained his perfectly blank expression.

These chimps played happily about the house or camp until the arrival of the baby gorilla. They could never make her out. She seemed to them so like themselves and yet they felt some difference. They would walk up to her, peer into her little wrinkled black face, and then run away screaming.

When Mary was let out of her cage, she would promptly set off with great determination towards me wherever I was sitting at work. As she saw me and drew near, she would let out a scream that mounted into a crescendo while she ran faster and faster towards me, and only subsided to a little soft conversation when she had climbed onto my lap and was happily seated there examining the various objects before me.

There could not have been two more contrary characters than Mary and the Oaf; and yet this was not exceptional, for every chimp has its own individual distinctive character just as humans have. There are good ones and bad ones; kind and gentle ones like Mary, and evil treacherous ones. If one wishes to keep a chimp, one must study its character exactly as one would that of a child of about seven years of age, and train it accordingly. They can learn to act consistently, as well as any human being, but their keen little minds tire readily and concentration wilts after three minutes except in certain peculiar females with a nervy disposition who can study a problem for many minutes together and are most persistent in their efforts to fulfil their desires.

The calls and greetings of the chimps were always the first sounds to meet our ears as we approached camp.

━━━

11

Life of the Grass and of the
Mountain Forests (Monkeys and Frogs)

"WELL, Duke, I'm afraid there's nothing else for it. If the A.D.O. comes by here on his way back to Mamfe, you will have to take the opportunity and go back with him. If he doesn't, you must be carried to Bamenda."

"Wouldn't it be better to go back to Mamfe?"

"With three dozen suppurating sores on your legs, you can't walk much. Besides, I don't want you to exhaust yourself on the way back and then be told when you get there that you are suffering from tubercular ulcers, like the only other man who ever came to this country."

"No . . . I suppose you're right, but it is a blasted nuisance having to leave here just as things are getting going."

"Listen," I said, "I am going to be quite frank with you. George and I cannot go on bathing your legs with permanganate of potash every two hours for the rest of our lives, and we have work to get done in these mountains before we spend any more of other people's money. Besides, if you want confirmation of impending tragedy, just listen to that ghostly wailing outside; you know what has happened each time we have heard that noise before. I may be stupidly superstitious, but you must admit its effects seem to be uncanny."

We fell into a gloomy silence waiting for the next unearthly wail. As it came clear and solitary through the still night air, our spirits plunged into the very depths.

Of all the weird, uncanny, and unearthly sounds, this soul-pene-trating whistle that comes out of the night among these lonely mountains is the surest drive to insanity. Starting as a tiny sound, it gradually swells into a dismal wail on the same pitch and then abruptly dies away. Then, after a period of horrible silence lasting exactly fifty seconds, it comes again. Its carrying power is prodi-gious, and every time that we heard it something went very wrong. It wailed like a soul in torture all night before the Duke got seriously ill. It moaned and sighed when I was down with fever. It mounted in a crescendo in tune with our own sorrow as we left this strange country among its mountain fastnesses with the wind moaning through the grass and the lightning playing about its peaks.

That night there were many tormented souls scattered about the gigantic valley, all declaring their dreadful loneliness in their own area and their own time. We knew that our little party was about to separate, perhaps for many months, but that was not the only gloomy problem that beset us.

"Confound those wailing things!" I spluttered out. "We must find out what creature causes them. I'm sure that it's not a mammal, though I don't know why, and I am very sure it is far from super-natural."

"Let's go and look," suggested the practical George.

"We will."

But we didn't, at least not that night. Instead, we went to bed and lay listening to the dismal warnings.

Next day the Duke left in a sort of hammock suspended from the heads of four burly Africans, and George and I were left among the friendly Assumbos and their waving grass. Having partaken of an alfresco breakfast, I advanced to the back of the house and shouted: "Hi, everybody get going, we go walker for mountains. Bring gun, plenty bottle, and field glasses."

George and I grinned at each other. We even stood up and solemnly shook hands, a little custom we indulged in when life suddenly took a turn for the better. The whole expedition breathed again; we all felt like small boys coming out of the headmaster's study after a beating, all misery relegated to the past. This was no reflection on the poor Duke—Lord knows it was not his fault—but the effort required to nurse him, combined with the fact that we had as a result been closely confined to the house for nearly two weeks, had depressed us all to such an extent that his departure, sad as it was, came almost as a relief.

We were soon on our way along a small trail that wriggled up the side of the valley. The whole lot of us had turned out, even the household staff, the little mud house that was our home having been turned over to the tender mercies of Ibi, headman of our little band of Munchi carriers, for a thorough spring cleaning. Women from the village of Tinta were also being sent by the chief to patch some holes in the wall that had resulted from a too vigorous shifting of furniture combined with the internal activities of white ants.

The sun shone in a cloudless sky as we plunged into a veritable forest of gigantic grass twice our height. Everybody disappeared like beetles into a sponge; we could hear one another's scramblings and call to one another, but remained altogether cut off.

When we had ascended about a thousand feet and could look down upon the village and our house as if they were figures on an ordnance map, somebody let out a startled yell. I shouted for enlightenment; a cry of "snake" came back. We then concentrated on Eméré and found him belabouring an ugly yellow and black fellow. After this we went more warily, and as a result saw several others, but we soon came out of the tall grass onto the summit of a spur where ordinary waist-high grass began. We were right among the mountains now; on all sides the same thing met our gaze: grass, endless grass, rolling away like thick felt over the gently moulded inclines and depressions.

I called to the others and, deploying, we began to advance up a long, gentle slope. Before long a number of small antelopes sprang up in front of us and went bounding away over the tall grass, taking flying leaps first to right and then to left. Whether these were the duiker (*Cephalophus rufilatus*) in somewhat unusual surroundings or a species of gazelle that we never obtained I am not sure; they certainly resembled the former in size and coloration, being a bright, reddish orange, with white undersides.

When we reached the summit of this incline, we came upon an area dotted with small orchard-like trees. This is a crazy part of the world where forests grow above the grass, though by all known laws of nature they should be confined to lower levels. Some say that all this grass is due to fires' having destroyed the forests; but this is absurd, because tropical jungle won't burn. Others even go so far as to attribute the burning to human agency. This theory need not detain us. The probable cause is the absence of soil combined with the tilt of the land. As we advanced through this exalted orchard, we were taken unawares by a large troop of monkeys who set up a great racket and went streaking away in front of us, running in the manner of dogs.

By their long legs, all of about equal length, and their sandy rufous colouring we knew them to be a gathering of patas monkeys (*Erythrocebus patas*), a common species outside the forests. Our pet Sanga was of this breed.

This cheerful little fellow lived around the house for many months, behaving exactly as any dog would do. When he was tied up, his chief pastime, apart from repeatedly uttering long-drawn-out, twittering, high-pitched calls, was a kind of dance. First he leant forward against the cord which was attached round his waist and which was so short it supported him. Then he bounced his fore-paws alternately on the ground and in the air, holding them neatly together. His hind legs remained immobile and on the ground. When he was free, he would gallop round and round the camp, only stopping to catch grasshoppers and locusts or to take a flying leap into our midst, often landing on treasured objects and sending them scattering. On the march, he was led by Omezi and he trotted along as well behaved as any dog.

As the chattering and calling of the patas monkeys died away in the distance, other calls came to our ears closer at hand. We presently came upon a troop of quite different monkeys. These were pale grey in colour with a white face-fringe, and they all took to

the trees on seeing us, carrying handfuls of small roots that they
had been grubbing out of the loose soil. These were the common
African grivet monkey (*Cercopithecus æthiops*) that fills the cages
of zoos to the exclusion of most else. They are sturdy animals easily
adaptable to other climatic conditions than those of the land of
their upbringing.

These monkeys were so bold that we were able to approach
within a few feet of some and take a considerable footage of film.
They seemed to be more interested in the clicking of the camera
motor than they were frightened by it; some of the pictures show
them inclining their heads to this side and that with the most
puzzled expression on their faces.

Beyond the patch of orchard growth was a small pocket in a
miniature level plateau. This was choked with tall lush growth.
After a picnic lunch I went with the shotgun to investigate this.
Upon entering the marsh part, something suddenly leapt up in my
path, and as I parted the tall grass I saw two beautiful heads with
lyre-shaped horns and great lustrous eyes poised above the vegetation. They remained for only an instant, then vanished without a
sound. I saw the tall grasses waving as they passed along. Making
my way back to the others, I gave orders to surround the little
marsh, but though we did so in the shortest possible time and
though all the surrounding country was more or less open, the animals had completely disappeared.

I presume they must have carried right on when I disturbed them
and retreated over the near-by hills. The larger buck and antelopes
are common features of the fauna of East Africa, but in this part of
the west they, like many other animals, are rarer and much better
hidden, so that one has to spend a great deal of time tracking them
down. To come across them is the exception, not the rule, and on
the very summit of the bare mountains it was a genuine surprise.

After this we managed to get lost very successfully. Having
crossed over into another great natural arena, we decided to try a
short cut over the mountains in a direction that we judged should
lead us home. When we arrived at the top of the divide, however,

we saw before us an endless panorama of other valleys and ridges. We therefore veered to the left and kept going, but after a couple more hours' wading through the waist-high grass we were getting a bit tired and were still only half-way to a ridge we had selected as the next point from which to get our bearings. Next we discovered that there were a number of deep defiles and ravines cutting across our path. Into these we plunged.

Now these appeared from above to be quite small copses, but as soon as one plunged in among their matted, tangled growth, the ground was found to drop almost straight down to crystal-clear streams that descended between large boulders in a series of small waterfalls alternating with still pools. The vegetation was in some places absolutely solid and we had to form a line and cut our way through. This is ideal gorilla country; in fact, viewing it from within, one felt that not only might a whole troop of gorillas appear without being a surprise, but one almost expected to run into one or two dinosaurs contentedly browsing on the exotic cacti and other primeval herbage.

Emerging from one ravine, we found ourselves on a large, gently sloping area covered with small clumps of very short grass and a great number of small green plants, rather like lettuces, dispersed evenly about so that one almost imagined they had been planted in rows. While we were discussing these oddities, a startling noise somewhere between a grunt, a cough, and a bark came from above us, and, looking up, we saw some animal seated on a prominent boulder high upon the face of a scree. Before we had time to get out the glasses, this creature let out further coughs which were answered from somewhere ahead of us, and a huge troop of baboons came scampering up the slope grunting, barking, and generally complaining at being disturbed during their evening meal.

They were wise enough to keep out of range, because, had they not done so, they would have received a positive barrage from us. You see, we were emboldened by our numbers and our assortment of defensive weapons. The old sentry went on barking until all were past him and fast disappearing among the loose boulders.

Then he got up and came leisurely down the slope towards us. When just beyond the range of our guns, he turned to the right and took up his position on a new vantage point. From then on he never took his eyes off us and we were compelled to pass along beneath him.

When we reached the other side of the open ground, we came across the place where the troop had been feeding. All the little lettuce-like plants had been torn up, their leaves strewn about, and their tuberous roots bitten clean off. Beyond this point we had to climb a little to get round a deep gully. Here we were immediately beneath the baboons, and the sentry had also moved along keeping pace with us a little further up. He must have thought that we were opening an attack, because he let out a yell and went bounding off to move the others. They heard his warning, however, and a headlong flight began, which released a number of boulders from the loose scree. These came hurtling down upon us, bouncing over the ground like a line of miniature cavalry. Some stopped short, others passed uncomfortably close between us.

I am sure that most people would have vowed that the baboons had thrown them down. There are many reports of their doing so!

By this time daylight was on the wane and we were still not in sight of the Tinta valley, but the going was much easier and we were more or less sure that only one further ridge separated us from it. We were just discussing this when out of the stillness of the evening came that dreadful crescendo whistle.

We immediately forgot all about Tinta and its geographical position and decided to track down this phantom once and for all. Calling a halt, we dumped everything, then stood waiting for the noise to be repeated. There was a long pause, but at last it came once more. There followed a heated discussion as to which direction it had come from. All the Africans except Faugi and Gong-gong thought it had come from the valley below, George wouldn't be tricked into any pronouncement at all, and I was as sure that it had come from everywhere at once as I was that it had come from anywhere in particular. As both Faugi and Gong-gong hailed from grassland countries, however, I was disposed to listen to their theory. They pronounced that it had come from somewhere at the head of a long narrow valley ascending the mountain to our right. When the sound came a third time, both George and I were disposed to accept their theory, but we thought that they were exaggerating considerably in saying that it had originated so far away.

We left the others behind and started off towards the sound, pausing every now and then to listen. It never seemed to get any louder or any softer, yet it came through the rarefied air clear and melancholy. Slowly we wended our way through little patches of mountain forest, up grassy slopes higher and higher, but still the sound continued, though now there was no doubt about the direction from which it came. When the valley narrowed to a ravine, the sound became gradually more piercing and as we still ascended, its volume increased to an extent that I had never believed possible; in fact, I have never met a louder sound caused by an animal. The whole air literally reverberated each time that it swelled forth. It might have been a really powerful fog-horn. Then we reached the sharp col at the top of the ravine and stood among great tufts of grass with the sound rattling our ear drums.

I turned to Faugi to ask him to what they attributed this noise in his own mountainous country, as he had told me that it was heard there also. In the pause between the half-minute wails, he replied laughingly that they considered it to be dissatisfied ancestral ghosts but that nobody really knew what caused it. His imparting this information seemed, however, to annoy the sound and I began to wonder if, after all, it could be an anguished and disembodied village senator. The sound ceased abruptly and we were left standing foolishly about.

But I was not to be put off even by the fast-gathering dusk, having got so near the bottom of the mystery. I just sat down like a mule and refused to budge, glaring at anybody who so much as dared to make a sound. The minutes passed. We sat on watching the shadows of the mountains creeping one across the other. It was an utterly remote world possessed of an almost tangible solitude. No wonder certain peoples go to the tops of high places to worship. Communion with the unknown from these fastnesses is not only easy, it becomes automatic.

All at once it happened. From beneath the very next clump of grass to that on which I was sitting that awful whistle began; but as I whisked round, it was cut short before reaching the peak of its crescendo.

"Surround this clump!" I shouted. "Faugi, clear away all the other grass."

We fell on the place and as soon as it was isolated we began hacking away the clump. It was quickly removed, but there was nothing there at all. Every bit of the clump was carefully examined in case there should be some insect lurking in it that might be the perpetrator; there was no sign of a living thing. Then an idea struck George.

"Dig," he said, and we did.

As we scraped away the earth, a hole about the size of a rat's was laid bare. This descended steeply and we had a hard job keeping track of it as we scooped out the earth. At a depth of about two feet, it took a sharp turn. As Faugi plunged in his bush-knife, some blood spurted out. Dropping his tool, he reached down with his hand and extracted a large lizard.

When we had got this out, it uttered a feeble echo of that always gruesome wail and then delivered up the ghost. Its backbone had been severed.

So this was the phantom. No wonder nobody had ever suspected its true origin. Lizards are a silent group except for the geckos, and none other has ever been recorded that makes a noise like a foghorn. Many have been disturbed, annoyed, almost driven mad by this noise in Africa; they will know what to hunt now. It is a large skink (*Lygosoma fernandi*) which inhabits sandy places. Its back is boldly striped longitudinally with black and white or black and cream, the underside is white, and the flanks, side of the head, and rings on the tail are a vivid cherry-red. Natives attribute all kinds of dire potentialities to this animal, saying that its bite is deadly and

WHISTLING SKINK (Lygosoma fernandi)

its tail a ju-ju powerful enough to turn even a chief into a madman.

Although I have been back now from this expedition for nearly four years, the pressure of work entailed in dissecting rather more important animals has not yet given me time to examine this lizard, and find out how it makes its eerie noise.

Overjoyed at our capture, we struggled back to the others in the eerie semi-darkness, and having refound them we at once set out for home. Crossing the ridge at last we came into the Tinta valley, but it remained light enough for us to see that we were still about as far off as we had been at lunch time. We ploughed on through the grass and after about an hour struck a small hunter's trail. This plunged into some "small bush." We were just getting into extreme difficulties, when three local hunters suddenly popped up out of the general darkness. The people of Assumbo were really the most intelligent and helpful of humans!

We fell into line, the hunters leading the way, but it was so dark among the trees that our clothes kept getting caught. The hunters therefore called a halt and began searching about in the bushes. They could not speak any pidgin-English and our knowledge of their language was in its earliest infancy, so we could not ask what they were up to. They eventually found some small rotten logs around the sides of which they searched carefully. All at once I saw some faint greenish lights appear. A few seconds later one of them handed me a whole handful of glowing luminous stuff, which I could see by its own light was a kind of fungus. They then turned over the log, disclosing a number of brighter golden lights. These proved to be luminous centipedes, which they broke in half and entwined in their wiry, spring-like hair.

We then proceeded on our way, guided by the glowing heads of the hunters, and carrying little bits of fungus ourselves to show the way to those coming behind. Arrived at the house, we found that two of the Munchis had taken the liberty of cooking a dinner for us which delighted our hearts but greatly enraged Ayuk, the cook, and was altogether surprising from two ordinary carriers.

I repaired behind the house to have a bath, with a hurricane lamp and several pails of water. These I poured over myself; the soapy water swilled around the hard beaten earth, disappearing down innumerable holes. As I poured away the last bucketful, there was a scuttling in the corner and out shot something long and black.

I fell on it. It was a wailing "phantom" and it had come out of our very house.

This walk over the mountains had, apart from our trip to collect the gorilla, been our first real insight into the life up there. Their solemn loneliness and their utter aloofness had intrigued us. Now that we were no longer confined to the precincts of the house, we were eager to learn more about them. I therefore searched around for a capable hunter who knew the country well and was willing to guide me about in search of zoological mysteries. Luckily I picked on Afa, chiefly because he seemed to bring more unusual animals than any of the others, all of whom were keen to take me for extended hunts after certain animals that were good to eat. This I knew meant the methods of the worthy Eantdudu which, though doubtless a joy to the average sportsman, were little short of a waste of time to us. Afa seemed to be a bit of a naturalist and a particularly intelligent one at that.

We accordingly made a practice of leaving for the hills in the dense clammy mists of early morning with something to drink, a little to eat, and a great deal to smoke. We investigated principally the strip of country through which ran the junction of the tall jungle with the mountain grass. This formed a sort of rampart running from east to west and dividing the forest-clad plains of Mamfe and the Cross River drainage basin from the grassy mountains and valleys to the north, through which the rivers drained away to the great Benue River system which flows into the Niger River far to the north-west. The high deciduous forest and the mountain grass never actually touch. All the way along the crest of this rampart extends a belt of the botanically distinct mountain forest—the home of the gorilla and other strange beasts besides.

As one walks northward from Mamfe itself, one passes across a more or less level basin covered with the forests and inhabited by the animals that have been mentioned in Parts Two and Three. When one enters the foothills of the northern escarpment, a few rather different creatures make their appearance, but as one ascends the southern face of these mountains, a very distinct change takes place, and by the time one enters the mountain forest barrier, one is in another world. Most strange of all, however, is the following fact.

This mountain forest covers the summit of the ridge and extends downward on both the southern and the northern face for some thousand feet (on an average). The animals inhabiting these two faces are quite different. It was Afa who pointed this out to me and proved it by the animals that he led me to on both sides.

On the southern forest side the common monkeys are numerous.

First there are the mona and the putty-nosed monkeys, which range from the lowlands right up to the edge of the mountain forest. Then there is the green and gold monkey (*Cercopithecus pogonias*) that we had seen in the natural forest clearing, and apparently a race of a species delighting in the name of *Cercopithecus erythrotis*, which has an orange nose and tail. In the mountain forest on the southern face, however, were to be found two other monkeys that do not occur elsewhere in this area.

One, the guereza, is that beautiful black fellow with a cape of long white hair which is the source of the "monkey fur" of the furrier. The other is a large animal belonging to the group of monkeys called mangabeys, which are distinguished by having white eyelids. The particular one that is found here is known as *Cercocebus torquatus torquatus!* One we obtained is the largest on record, being more than four feet in length. It is a beautiful animal with smooth grey back, white underside, and a vivid red top-knot and scalp, often to be seen in zoos.

All these monkeys, with the exception of the orange-nosed one, remained on the southern face. The northern face had only two species. The orange-nosed was sometimes met with, and in addition an exceedingly rare type having no popular name but known scientifically as *Cercopithecus preussi*. This is black all over except for a small white waistcoat and a patch of strange orange-tipped hairs covering the lower back.

On our first excursion to these regions we had spent a particularly vigorous morning hauling each other up perpendicular rocky precipices in search of bats and tiny snails. The latter are found only among the rock crevices on the northern side, and they were very difficult to get at—such is the life of a collector! About midday we lay down in the forest near the summit of the ridge to have a smoke, and Afa was showing me how they made a fire without matches.

This had always intrigued me, as I had many times attempted to do so by rubbing various sticks together in the preferred manner, and had always failed to generate more than mild warmth. In a small leather wallet he carried a heavy stone that looked like mag-

BLACK AND WHITE GUEREZA MONKEY (Colobus occidentalis)

netite, and a piece of flinty material, a kind of chert, which he told me was found in the form of large plates embedded in the sandstone of some near-by hills. In a hollow section of a giant grass stem he had some tinder, made by scraping the fluff off the skin of the stem of a palm frond. Some of this he placed in a small wooden crucible neatly bedded round the heavy little stone. He then scratched these with the flint, and as a succession of small sparks was generated, he blew on them gently and the tinder was soon alight. When this was glowing, he put the whole lot into his pipe on top of the tobacco and sucked vigorously. I tried this. It did not seem to spoil the flavour of the tobacco at all.

We were deep in a discussion upon the comparative merits of various tobaccos, when suddenly a long call came from close at hand. Afa extinguished his pipe at once and pinching his nose between his fingers, he began imitating the noise. We then crept forward, answering the calls that now came repeatedly. At the edge of the forest the trees were shaking vigorously; we saw a number of monkeys swinging about. Afa showed me the old male, who had been calling the others in from the grass where this species apparently goes to feed. The animals then started to move off rapidly, but the hunter knew the country too well.

We ran as fast as we could in a quite contrary direction and after several minutes came to rest among some dense foliage near a little gulley. Here we waited in absolute silence for nearly half an hour, but sure enough the monkeys came by, swinging through the trees right over our heads. We obtained one which proved to be the rare black species that I have mentioned. Afa then explained to me that these monkeys, which have a most distinctive clear call note, never go over onto the other face of the hills. From their first position he therefore knew that they must sooner or later travel round the brow of the hill to get home after they had been disturbed—probably by the smell of our tobacco—while feeding on the extreme edge of the forest.

From these mountain forests we unearthed two very remarkable frogs. When clearing away some small trees preparatory to building a small bush shelter, I met face to face a pair of small beige-coloured frogs with their neat, glossy black bellies pressed flat onto a broad twig. I tried to put them into a small glass container but found that the smaller male was holding the female with one immensely long finger of each hand. This third finger was quite four times the length of the others, and these were not short. It was armed with a row of small spines along its inner side. I managed to bottle them in the end.

When I got back to camp, I emptied all my tubes and bottles in order to turn the reptiles and frogs over to George to be dealt with, as that was his department. When all were laid out on the table, the two beige-coloured frogs seemed to have disappeared. A check-up on all the tubes left me short of them only, but with an extra container. As far as I could remember, there should have been only one tube with two specimens in it. So it appeared now, but these two frogs were a dark chocolate-brown, covered with thin white squiggly lines or vermiculations, and pure white below. Then I saw that one of these had immense third fingers. This was most mysterious, but worse was to follow.

We put the frogs in a small cage. After lunch George happened to look at them, and, behold, they were again a delicate, creamy beige. We then tried all manner of experiments with lights and various degrees of heat, and the poor little frogs did their best to keep up with us. They went vivid blue beneath and got covered with black spots surrounded with metallic gold rings; they turned into scintillating rose-milky opals; their backs meanwhile passed through endless phases, brown-grey, pink-spotted, and plain. The whole thing was so fantastic that we gave up trying to record what they did in sheer self-defence.

Later that evening George suddenly gave a whoop of surprise. He was studying the catalogue and had happened to refer back to some earlier entries.

"Give me those frogs, quick," he said in the greatest excitement.

"O.K., but what the devil's the matter?"

"Look at this entry: *Mamfe forests; colour, white below, very dark chocolate-brown above, with wormlike white lines; size, 34 mm*. Isn't that one of the things those frogs did this afternoon?"

"Sounds like it. Let's have a look."

Believe it or not, when we opened the cage, the frogs we saw there were of exactly that description.

The explanation of all this appeared to be that this animal (*Cardioglossa leucomystax*) lives among the dead leaves of the forest floor, but can and does ascend the low trees. Now frogs are cold-blooded creatures and therefore dependent upon the temperature surrounding them. If it gets too hot and dry, their body moisture evaporates away, and the animals shrivel up and die. The conditions are, moreover, very different among the damp leaves on the forest floor, where the heat of decomposition comes from below and the stratum of damp air just above the ground is cold, and among the leaves of trees, where the sunshine comes down hot and dry from above while the evaporation from the pores of the leaves beneath leaves them cool. Conditions are exactly reversed, in fact, and the poor frog has to do something about it. Now it is best to present a dark or black surface to the cold because it absorbs all the heat waves, and a light or white surface to the heat because it reflects them all.

This is just what the frog does, and thereby preserves a more or less even temperature. All the other colours we saw were those through which the animal passes in intermediate conditions, when it is changing from black-and-white to white-and-black, if I may express it that way.

12

Digging for Animals

ASSUMBO was a great place for frogs. Besides being plentiful, they were mostly of types that either did not exist at all or were very rare in the lowland forests. It was in Assumbo, in fact, that I finally rid myself of that rather gloomy feeling which the mention of frogs had always conjured up in me. You probably remember the feelings that welled up within you when asked to recite the dates of the battles of the Wars of the Roses. The frogs of this country were far from dull.

The first marvel appeared with the breakfast a few days after our arrival in Assumbo. It was one of Afa's efforts that went far towards convincing me that he was the man we were looking for as a collector. The morning is never a particularly bright event; even Africans tend to keep their jokes until the sun is warming up. Fried eggs on enamel plates were for us an added infliction on this occasion, and I was therefore highly suspicious of a mysterious package lying beside my tea-cup. It contained something heavy and was neatly wrapped in banana leaves and tied with tough grass stems.

"What is this?" I inquired, pointing to the package and addressing my remark to Gong-gong.

"Hunter-man bring 'em."

"Is it a dash or just something to eat?"

For answer Gong-gong burst with contained laughter and bolted in the direction of the kitchen, whence we heard uncontrolled roars of laughter presently issuing. As it was far too early to deal with such problems, I put on the best face possible and quietly tackled the flabby egg, meanwhile keeping a wary eye on the suspicious package.

Coincident with the second cup of tea I was somewhat shaken upon seeing the package give a small jump towards the marmalade. This caused it to present a new face in my direction and I saw that one of the thin ends was pumping in and out like a small pair of bellows. This decided me. I advanced cautiously upon it with a pair of scissors and at what I thought to be a psychological moment I snipped the grass string. At this it gave another small hop and then remained quiet. George, who suffered from the morning perhaps even more acutely than I did, now seemed to become aware of the little comedy. He poked his end of the package with a knife.

The banana leaves slowly parted and out of their midst was thrust a face—but description fails me. Perhaps you have seen or at least can imagine a dowager duchess declining a Woodbine cigarette! The head was wide, the large mouth tightly pursed, the eyes large and brown, surmounted by pointed structures having the appearance of highly arched eyebrows. This giant toad is known to science as *Bufo superciliaris*. Latin names do mean something.

Our burst of laughter caused the poor animal to withdraw. It accomplished this with the utmost dignity and remained tactfully concealed until the noise had died down. It then swept out in a pompous though obviously premeditated manner, paused for a moment to give a slight hiccup, and paced forward with even tread directly to George's plate. Here it suddenly sat down with a most pathetic, pleading, woebegone expression.

Of all the gentle, sympathetic creatures I have ever met, this enormous, flat, cream-coloured toad was in its way the most human in its demeanour. It was quite impossible to think of it in any other way than as a rather sad old man deserving of every possible sympathy. It was about six inches long and four inches broad, with a big flat head and short though sturdy legs. The whole of its upper surfaces was pale cream in colour, the underside white, and the sides from the tip of the snout to the groins, including the sides of the face and the outer surface of the "eyebrows," a rich blood-red. The legs were banded with creamy white and very deep red tending to black rings on the toes. It was gentle in the extreme, timid, and possessed of one unusual habit. If surprised when solemnly making for bush or otherwise feeling guilty, it would suddenly flop down, pack its legs under itself, and generally make every endeavour to simulate a harmless dead leaf.

It became Pet Number I as soon as we set eyes on it, and soon learnt to be handled without squatting down in terror. It was then granted freedom of the camp, which was quite safe because it required about half an hour to cross the thirty yards that separated our domains from the surrounding bush. Eventually it learnt to walk up our extended trouser legs at meal times, when it took up its position on our laps with its little, intensely human hands resting on the edge of the table awaiting tit-bits. These it would take from our fingers with the utmost gentleness and quietly swallow. If the portions were too large, it would stuff them into its mouth with one or both of its thumbs. Its complete silence made it appear all the more intelligent.

Afa informed us that these animals live in the mountain forest underneath the layer of dead leaves covering the ground. He said that he dug for them.

This was a novel idea and set me thinking.

If friend Afa could dig for beef in the seclusion of the bush, I did not see why we could not do so ourselves on an American plan. Luckily we had the dozen Munchis and some stout spades, and the whole country was open to us. I therefore took the men to a likely spot at the edge of the grass alongside a patch of forest and set them to work removing the surface of the land to a depth of about two feet.

The results were rather surprising. During the digging of the initial ditch a remarkable blind-snake (*Typhlops punctatus*) was brought to light. Thereafter almost every spadeful turned over some fantastic new spider, centipede, lizard, or crab.

After some time Gong-gong arrived from camp to say that my presence was urgently required there, as both tents had collapsed and they were short-handed. I therefore had reluctantly to leave the diggers and hurry back a distance of about three hundred yards round the edge of the patch of forest.

I found the camp in an uproar. The two tents were pitched end to end with a long straight sapling lashed between them from the end of one ridge pole to the opposing end of that of the other tent. Over this was laid an enormous ground-sheet, which was held out on either side by the ends of the two tents and thereby formed a covered connexion between the two, larger in area than either of them. We slept in one tent, worked and lived in the other, and had the skinning table situated in between so that we could move about in all weather inspecting the skinning and supervising the work. The tents were both double, having smaller internal canvas structures with upright walls. The narrow tunnel on either side between the inner and outer tents was lined with gear. The guys having given way all along one side, the whole of this monumental structure had either fallen over enveloping the skinning staff, or sagged to an acute angle in a north-westerly direction.

Those people who were not buried beneath were holding guy-ropes with their hands, teeth, and anything else they could apply. Two friendly hunters who had come to pay a call and do a little business were holding onto the people who were holding the ropes, which were holding the tent. Arriving amid all this complexity, I succeeded only in tripping over one of the last remaining guy-ropes that were doing their jobs unassisted. This gave up the struggle with a resounding twang, the whole structure then subsiding with a muffled groan. We set to work to unearth everybody and everything, and to move the tents.

It soon became obvious that the heavy rains had washed away the soil to such an extent that we were almost down to bedrock. This always occurs when one removes the protective covering of grass and the soil beneath is shallow. Since tent-pegs would not hold at all, we decided to move the whole camp some yards back into the "forest" instead of putting it elsewhere on the grass. This entailed a great deal of cutting and clearing, and revealed a plot of ground sloping at an acute angle, its surface resembling a ploughed field. There was no doubt about it, it would have to be levelled.

We began the back-breaking job with the best will in the world and made very considerable progress. Then suddenly Bassi, who was, so to speak, nearest the ground, being very short of stature, let out a truly African grunt of surprise.

"Master, master, some very funny animal."

Everybody dashed over and found the ground at his feet quite covered with small shiny black wormlike things about three inches long. Some of these broke to pieces under our eyes and the fragments hurriedly went to earth.

When we had eventually gathered up a few intact and put them in a small bottle that had to be hunted out from beneath the pile of tent and other equipment, we saw they were covered with minute circular scales and apparently had no head, both ends of the body being perfectly smooth, rounded stumps. These strange little subterranean animals were totally blind, legless lizards (not snakes) having no popular name, but known as *Melanoseps*. They have been reduced to this lowly estate through taking to a life beneath the soil. They have distant relations that still retain their legs in various degrees of abortiveness—there are the true skinks, which are lizards with very small legs; there are creatures with pathetic little useless points in place of limbs; and others in Asia that have small but fully developed front legs but no back ones at all. *Melanoseps* has arrived at a purely wormlike state and lost its eyes into the bargain.

As we dug on, we unearthed many more of these strange lizards as well as a number of snakes. Then another African exclamation, on the part of Faugi this time, brought us once again into a circle at the double. This time it was a deep hole about two inches in diameter that descended perpendicularly into the ground. Faugi contended that he had heard a loud whistle emanate from this. We were somewhat sceptical, having learnt never to be too sure of ourselves in this amazing country where anything from a full-sized hog to a tiny flea may come out of a hole.

Very carefully we dug around until the hole was isolated in a

HAIRY FROG (Trichobatrachus robustus)

miniature volcano of earth standing in the middle of a large depression. Then gingerly the side was broken away, and we all received a genuine surprise.

Crouching in a small gallery at the very bottom was a large, fat, brick-red frog. As I picked it up, it let out a shrill whistle and struggled violently, planting its large hind feet on my arm and wrist. I felt a sharp pain; before I knew what was up, my whole wrist was covered with small, even, but deep scratches. I passed the animal to Faugi, who held it outstretched while I examined its toes. The pad on the tip of each toe was split beneath by a narrow slit that covered the first joint. From each of these slits emerged a sharp, recurved white claw. These claws were drawn in and out like a cat's, more particularly when the leg was stretched.

This frog was duly bottled and christened the "pad and claw frog," but it was not until we returned to Europe and examined all our collections in detail that an interesting fact concerning it became apparent. We caught several of these frogs; they all turned out to be females. When they were pickled, moreover, they lost their bright brick-red colour and assumed a distinctive colour pattern.

Now in the river that flowed by this camp there was a great deal of a small red water weed growing around the fringes of the smooth little pebbles that covered the bed in certain stiller reaches. Probing among these one day, I was much taken aback to see what I had thought to be three of the pebbles suddenly come to life and leap out of the water, where they resolved themselves into a large frog which sat on a boulder pumping its throat in and out at me. Collaring this audacious personage, I bore him back to camp in triumph. He turned out to be a fine male hairy frog (*Trichobatra-chus robustus*), which only means "hair frog robust." This is a great rarity, in many respects the most extraordinary frog in existence.

It has been known for a number of years. When first brought back from West Africa—by Mr. Bates, of course—it caused a great furore, both scientific and popular, on account of the remarkable "hairs" with which its flanks, rump, and thighs are covered. These "hairs" are not true hairs but filamentous elongations of the skin. Their function aroused a storm of controversy in the scientific world which has raged ever since, though blowing chiefly from America. Our discovery of these two frogs—the "pad and claw" and the "leaping stones"—has, thank goodness, laid the ghost at last and cleared up the mystery.

This matter may be of interest not only for its details but as showing the practical conclusions to which some purely scientific recording and theorizing may give rise.

The crux of the matter is that we discovered that the female of this species—for that is what the pad and claw lady was—is subterranean in habit, whereas the hairy male is purely aquatic. Dissection revealed a great dissimilarity in the structure of the lungs. The female had an ordinary lung; the male had a most extraordinary one. The forepart of his was made up of little sacs like our own and those of other animals, but the hind portion was merely a slender muscular tube. What could be the reason for this?

Now frogs breathe air, and as the male and the female were both about the same average size, they would presumably require about the same amount of it to keep their blood going. The female could do this even in her stuffy burrow, while the male, sunk deep in the water, presumably could not, and he therefore had to devise something else. This he has accomplished not by having a huge lung in which to store lots of reserve air, but by developing the "hairs" which, when their surface is calculated, prove to more than double the area of his skin that is in contact with the water. Frogs, like us, breathe to a certain extent through their skins. His lung is therefore not so important and he has converted it into a sort of adjustable ballast to help him in floating at the surface of the water or in sinking to the bottom to rest. By means of this muscular tube he can pump air into himself, thus becoming more buoyant; by squeezing it out, he can increase his density and so sink to the bottom and rest there without holding himself down. He has grown his "hairs" around the fringes of his fat body and limbs because, when he is squatting among the pebbles, he can with their aid make himself look exactly like a part of the river bed. The "hairs" are reddish in colour, just like the waterweed!

We did not know all this as we held the whistling red frog in the middle of the wrecked camp, yet we were sufficiently interested to forget our real job and set about digging for more. Thus the whole day slipped by until we were disturbed by a peculiar noise that seemed to be gradually approaching the camp. It was indistinct at first, but by the time we had the tents repitched and had collected several other clawed frogs, it seemed to be close at hand.

I went out onto the grass to have a look. There, round the corner of the grass verge, into the little bay where our camp was situated, came the Munchis.

They had dug their way home, uprooting everything in their track to a depth of two feet and a width of about twenty yards. If you want a job done properly get some Obudu Munchis!

There were two things that we had told zoologists in England we would get, though more by way of an abstruse biological joke than in all seriousness. One was a strange tick-like creature named *Podogona*, so rare that all the museums and collections in the world possessed only a handful of specimens. I shall tell you about this later. The other was a wormlike animal related to our newts of ponds and ditches. These animals, named cœcilians or *Gymnophiona*, are, like our newts, amphibia—not reptiles—and are found only in certain tropical and subtropical countries. There are several quite well-known species of these; our joke centered round a not very serious promise to unravel the life-histories of the West African ones, which, like those of all the group, are very interesting and unusual.

When we had re-established our camp on a sound footing and could examine the results of our digging, I became more than ever convinced that this was a method of unearthing the rarest of all objects. There were scores of animals laid out for my inspection, and nearly all seemed to be species and types that we had never seen before. This was very exciting because it seemed to be the door opening to an entirely new world of life which could be got at with ease and in all weather. As a result I went for a prowl around the next morning to find a few likely places for further digging operations.

Just behind the camp the ground dropped abruptly to a depth of a few feet. A small tributary of the main stream which flowed into this hollow drained into the ground, forming a small marsh. I gained an impression that this might be a profitable spot to try, and returned to camp to muster our small army.

The staff had, however, already got the fever and begun their own ditch on the dry ground a little further off. This marked enthusiasm, coupled with the extraordinarily good results they were getting, convinced me that it was better to leave well enough alone. I set to work typing the diary, which had fallen into rather deplorable neglect during the past few days.

Poor George was weltering in a maze of catalogues as a result of the previous day's digging, aggravated by the fact that Bassi had taken Faugi's place as his chief assistant. Faugi had his good points but also a rather too liberal selection of bad ones which George had tolerated as long as he could, merely because he was in charge of the specialized work connected with the reptiles and amphibians. A change had had to be made.

After a time Ben came to me with the announcement that the digging party wanted to know whether it was worth while going below the mould into the subsoil. Having no strong views on the matter, I decided to go and have a look. The scene of operations appeared like a modern battle-field. Great piles of earth and logs rose on all sides, long deep trenches plunged off into the undergrowth in all directions, and great areas denuded of all vegetation and soil to a depth of several feet connected them. On the top of one of the mounds stood an imposing array of bottles, tubes, tins, and nets reminiscent of a chemical laboratory. African enthusiasm once aroused knows no bounds.

I was conducted round by Ben as if I were an engineer being shown the foundations of a new town hall by the foreman of works. This was the spot where that snake was caught, this was where Ayuk bit a rat in the excitement of capture, this place is where the Munchis are still quarrelling over the use of the broken spade! So it went on, but for the life of me I could not decide whether we should try to go deeper into the real soil under the leaf mould.

Mustering all possible labour, I ordered a square plot to be cleared of vegetation and denuded of leaf mould from the edges inwards. As the work proceeded, we carefully collected everything alive that came to our notice. When at a depth of about two feet the subsoil proper was laid bare, we started again from the outside and worked inwards, digging to a depth of a further two feet. Not a living thing appeared.

The obvious conclusion was that it was not worth while, so I gave orders to work laterally. By this time some of the diggers were approaching the steep bank that led down to the small marsh; they wanted to know whether they should continue in that direction. As the bank itself was literally filled with snakes and other animals, this seemed to be the obvious procedure, and everybody disappeared over the edge.

No sooner had they done so, than things took a completely new turn. The ground was covered with matted grass and weeds which were more or less floating on soft mud. As the diggers came to the edge of this, Ben unearthed a long bluish-grey thing like a monstrous worm. It was a cœcilian bearing the name of *Geotrypetes seraphini*, though we did not know this at the time. It was about six inches long, somewhat thicker than a pencil, and possessed of a pair of the smallest eyes imaginable. The nearer we approached to the marsh, the more of these animals we unearthed.

The matted grass was cut along its edge like the crust of a pie; then, instead of digging it out, we simply rolled it back in one immense piece.

The first things we came across were a great number of enormous red mites. These were a gigantic edition of our money-spiders, as large as the small flies that dance around the light in the kitchen. There were thousands of them, which we bottled assiduously. Their vivid scarlet colour contrasted with the sombre grey slime in which they apparently dwelt.

Then I came upon a most amazing find.

Chasing a giant mite under the matted grass roots, I laid bare a small cavern about the size of a man's fist, in which stood a small mound of pyramidal form like a miniature volcano. On the top of this was coiled a very small cœcilian, purple in colour and no larger than an earthworm. As I opened its little home, its flat snake-like head came round towards me and it spat a small blob of water at me with considerable force. This it continued to do while I gathered it up.

It had been tightly coiled up; when removed, it revealed half a dozen crystal-clear and perfectly spherical eggs tied into a knot by tough, slender, horny cords growing out of both opposing ends. These were perched on the top of the mound and were being brooded by their mother. The eggs, of a greater diameter than the

CŒCILIAN OR WORM-NEWT (Idiocranium russelli)

mother herself, contained minute replicas of herself completely
sealed up within. These whizzed round and round when the eggs
were touched.

I called all the others to show them what I had found. I explained
that this was just exactly what we had come to Africa to look for,
and offered a reward for any more of these broods that they could
find, giving instructions that each time one was laid bare, I was to
be called, would record the finder, and take charge of the animals.

Everybody went to work with renewed vigour. Presently there
was a shout from Anongo, the wag of the Munchis, who, poor fellow, had been born with only three fingers and was otherwise de-
formed. He had the most cheerful and happy personality of anybody I have ever met, and was a first-class collector and a tireless
worker. He had come across a brooding mother cœcilian, but when
I came to examine her I found that she was of the larger species
(*Geotrypetes seraphini*) and not of the small, flat-headed one. This
mother was also in a chamber half filled with water and was sitting
on a mound that just raised her out of it. Instead of brooding a
clutch of crystal-clear eggs, the coils of her body were wrapped
round and round a bundle of smaller replicas of herself, all with their

heads pointing towards her tail. This was most puzzling and very exciting to us, because we were in the midst of collecting the very things we had set our hearts on getting.

After this we denuded the whole marsh of its covering, and nearly a dozen broods of the small species with eggs and half a dozen larger ones with babies were collected. Our staff was enriched by many "dashes"; we, by the acquisition of the most priceless zoological specimens.

George knew nothing of our morning's work. When I returned at lunch time, I popped the whole lot out at him at once, brimming over with excitement and fully believing that he would adopt our festive attitude to life.

His only remark was: "Oh, my God, and I thought I was really coming to the end of the cataloguing!"

Subsequent examination, both in camp during the afternoon and later when we returned home to England, revealed a number of most amazing facts about these catches.

The little cœcilians turned out to be an entirely new form of life, never previously suspected. They were totally blind, the bones of the skull having grown right over the eye-sockets. They are the smallest of the whole group ever to be recorded—the largest being three and a half inches in length—and not only a new specific name but even a new genus had to be created to receive them into the general scheme of life. The eggs showed all stages of development from that where the transparent capsule contained a big yellow bag of yolk from the surface of which a primitive embryo grew, to specimens containing almost perfect little cœcilians ready to burst out of the hardened capsule and with all the great yolk-sac absorbed into them. All the changes the egg undergoes during its growth to a completely formed animal could be observed through the glassy cover. We saw that, at one period, proper eyes and long, branching, feathery external gills are developed, both to be completely lost— the latter by absorption—before the little creature breaks through the egg. This is a most amazing and unexpected fact, because the external gills found in several other species of cœcilians are always developed to assist the young animal to live in water during a true larval stage.

The other cœcilian proved equally interesting. Its babies, which had never been seen before, had most remarkable mouths. Their jaws were armed with a double row of hinged teeth on bony pedicles. These teeth were long, slender, and crowned with square, comb-like sets of spikes. The adult simple recurved teeth were just appearing on the inner side of the jaws.

These weird structures, previously known only from more lowly animals like the shark and other fish, naturally led to the question "Why?" Obviously the answer was their food; the question "What food?" prompted us to open their stomachs and see what we could find. In all of them was a strange crinkled yellow stuff. This turned out to be long strands of their own skin, which they must have eaten as all the amphibia do after a moult. Among this a number of minute spherical green algæ (or water weeds) were found; it must be for rasping these off stones that the peculiar teeth are developed.

Having exhausted the marsh of all the wonderful animals it contained, we turned our energies to other types of ground. After a time one more or less exhausts the possibilities of a particular habitat. Although further collecting may reveal some very rare and valuable specimens, one has to pass on to other entirely different kinds. It is always a very difficult job to preserve a sound balance between working too long a time and too short a time in one place. Most collectors make the great mistake of passing over the country too quickly, with the result that they collect over and over again the same common animals. Only the more patient will come by the rarities when a surfeit of the easily obtainable has been taken. We devoted our attention to the driest grassy areas.

We soon found that most of the subterranean life here concentrated round the bases of large boulders and the giant white-ant hills that dotted the countryside. There were a number of new snakes, many spiders, and other small fry; also a peculiar rat with an absurdly short tail and sleek, short, wine-coloured fur. This animal (*Lophuromys*), a swift digger, makes tremendously long straight burrows that lead hundreds of yards before their owners are cornered. There were many exciting moments when new animals were brought to earth. One was especially startling.

The sun shone out of a cloudless sky and we all toiled away at the hard-baked earth round a tall ant-hill. These structures have a number of tunnels about a foot in diameter around their base, giving entrance to an internal chamber.

This chamber is really dome-shaped, so that the whole ant-hill is a hollow cone which is added to on the outside and subtracted from on the inside by the insects as it grows. In the apical roof of this hollow interior is suspended layer upon layer of cells, like floors in a skyscraper, though diminishing in size as one goes upwards. Here the young are reared. In the centre of all, in a gallery formed of concrete-hard earth, lies the queen, who is about two inches long. Most of this two inches is composed of abdomen, white and fleshy, which is nothing else than a factory for making eggs. Her tiny head and thorax with quite ordinary white-ant legs extend from one end of this monstrous body. To it a continuous line of workers comes bearing food which she eats and keeps on eating for months. At the same time other streams of workers constantly enter her royal chamber by small side portals to carry off the streams of eggs that pour from holes in her sides. By the queen's efforts alone the colony grows; all the rest of their united labours are concentrated upon building the incubator for rearing the progeny, and feeding these and themselves.

Beneath the hanging floors there is a space large enough in some cases to contain a coiled-up man. In this, certain rare snakes sometimes take up their abode. We were keen to catch some of these, but owing to their habit of using deep holes leading from this chamber to the soil around the outside of the nest, we had to dig a deep ditch all around. Just as we were completing this, we cut into a dark tunnel about three inches in diameter.

As one way led towards the ant-hill, we started cutting into the earth along its course. After a few minutes, Eméré announced that it led into a chamber in which he saw something moving. I climbed down into the trench to look.

It was an extremely stupid thing to do. No sooner was my head level with the entrance, than I realized this, yet in the foolhardy way that grows upon one with experience I did not withdraw. Instead, I peered into the gloom; before I knew what was up, something brown, woolly, and about the size of my two fists held together, scuttled into the opening. I just caught sight of something gleaming like a rosette of small cold fires, then the animal sprang straight out at me.

As it did so, I felt the most terrifying coldness come over me. In a flash I let out a scream of pure terror and fell sideways into the ditch.

Luckily I moved to the left, for the giant spider just brushed by my right ear so that I felt its loathsome furry coldness as it shot through the air to land beyond the ditch. Had I gone to the right, it would probably have landed in my face; even if its deadly half-inch fangs had not locked in my face and set it swelling like a purple puff-ball, I should quite certainly have died from sheer revulsion and fright. I do not say this in jest at all; I have a loathing for all spiders that amounts to madness and renders me more or less paralytic, just as some people feel about cats, worms, birds, or other forms of life.

I was, in any case, quite paralysed. Had Eméré not hauled me out of the ditch with more than commendable swiftness, I should have been an easy prey to the horror on its return journey. I later found that the giant hairy spiders are regarded in Eméré's country as the personification of the devil, who is a far more terrifying person in their mythology than in our own. Eméré felt as I did about this animal!

While I was recovering at a respectable distance from the ditch, the spider was taking six-foot leaps, first this way and then that, at anybody who approached it. Though all the Africans treated it with respect, they tried to catch it with their bare hands despite their knowing it to be deadly poisonous. It eventually walked back to its hole in that precise and evil way that spiders have, its bloated body slung low among its battery of angular soft-pointed legs.

We drove stakes into the ground behind the hole and gradually dug away the earth while I held a bag-net over the exit. When the animal saw that the game was up, it rushed out into the net. We were amazed to see that it was covered with small replicas of itself about the size of a quarter. The babies clung to their mother in a dense mass and several more dashed out after her. This perhaps was the reason for her furious attack.

When this terrible creature had been drowned, I steeled myself for an examination of her. As soon as I had satisfied myself that she was dead beyond a shadow of doubt, I spread her out in the enamel dish that we used for dissections and other work on the dead specimens. The great legs, fully extended in all directions, covered the bottom of the dish exactly, from front to back and side to side. The dish measured twelve inches by eight inches.

13

The Giant Water Shrew

THERE is a fantastic animal, a veritable living fossil, that inhabits the mountain streams of West Africa. It was first discovered many years ago by the famous traveller and explorer du Chaillu, who had a distinct penchant for the sensational and a more than lively imagination. Since his time, little or nothing has been done towards elucidating the habits of this giant aquatic shrew (*Potamogale velox*), very little material about it has been collected for study, no pictures have ever been taken of it in life, and nobody has been able to add to or subtract from the original descriptions by du Chaillu. This has led to the *Potamogale's* becoming almost a zoological myth.

Since I have already mentioned several animals that were the essential reasons for our going to Africa, I feel that before I do so again and lay myself open to the criticism that we went for nothing in particular but everything in general, I should make clear the exact position as it was before our departure. We intended to make a general survey of all the mammals, reptiles, and amphibians of this country, as well as a collection of all the spiders, centipedes, land snails, and parasitic worms that we came across. In particular, we set ourselves seven special tasks of greater difficulty, as follows:

First, obtaining certain internal organs of the flying squirrel and Demidorff's dwarf lemur; secondly, a collection of leopards' skins and skulls; thirdly, an elucidation of the breeding habits of the cœcilians; material about the *Potamogale*; specimens of the clawed toads; *Podogona*; and, lastly, something concrete concerning a fresh-

GIANT WATER SHREW (Potamogale velox)

water dolphin or small whale that had been reported as inhabiting the great rivers of West Africa.

In the preceding pages we told how we stumbled across three of these; we were successful during our trip in catching all the rest except one. This one was the fresh-water whale; but, as a certain great expert said to me on my return, "It probably doesn't exist anyway," so we may be excused even if we do not excuse ourselves!

The giant water shrew or *Potamogale* was one of the most important to get and the most elusive to find.

Du Chaillu's original description is full of interesting detail as to the animal's habits of pursuing fish in the "limpid" mountain streams and lying in wait for its prey beneath stones at the bottom of the river. Both these things were confirmed by the native inhabitants of the mountain countries that we visited. The Assumbos, and Afa in particular, were not nearly so insistent upon the fish part of the

story; that is to say, they confined their observations upon its natural food to the all-embracing term "beef." This only goes to bear
out their natural honesty, because the whole of du Chaillu's story
and popular belief concerning this animal's habits are as fallacious as
the majority of stories and facts gleaned from natives. This we
learned for ourselves by a slow and somewhat painful process.

The *Potamogale* stands alone in the great scale of wild life. Apart
from a small mouse-like animal from Madagascar named *Geogale,* it
has no relations. It is indeed a living fossil, having a great number of
exceedingly primitive characteristics in its internal anatomy, some
of which are found only in the fossil bones of the first mammals
from rocks of very great geological antiquity. For this reason, perhaps, it is placed in the order of Insectivora, which is a grouping of
all the mammals left over when everything else has been assigned to
its proper and obvious place in the scheme of life.

This animal is about two feet long and has the appearance of an
ordinary otter. Its body is clothed in a short, thick, sleek fur, but the
tail, flattened from side to side like a tadpole's, is covered by the
barest coat of extremely short, sparse hairs. Though these can hardly
be seen, if the hand be passed along the tail towards the body, their
presence may be detected by the resistance that they offer to one's
skin. The head is flattened from above just like that of a dogfish or
shark; like those animals, also, its mouth has accordingly been
pushed onto the underside of the snout. The legs are short and stout,
the ankles being provided with peculiar longitudinal flanges of
tough skin. The eyes are minute.

We knew all this before we went to Africa; besides, we were completely under the influence of the general opinion, namely, that this
animal was confined to streams on the summits of the mountains.

"Ask the chief if he will tell all hunters to bring us any animal
that looks at all like this." I held forward a photographic reproduction of an extremely bad picture purporting to be the *Potamogale*
in life.

I did not expect any real response, because the picture resembled nothing on earth—though I did not know this at the time—and al-though the African is quick at identifying objects shown two-dimensionally in pictures, I was really uncertain whether the animal existed in their country. There are of course peoples, notably in the Orient, who are completely incapable of figuring out pictures and photographs. One Oriental dignitary that I know of, when shown a picture of himself, held it upside down at arm's length, exclaiming: "This is very dangerous! I hope such things will never be brought to our country." I may add that we for our part thoroughly agreed with him and promised that such things should be kept in their rightful places for ever!

Chief Ekumaw's reactions were of an entirely different nature.

"Ah-ha, ah-ha," he said. "Ekoredzaw, n'a quille, uhummo eko-redzaw," which was loosely interpreted as "It is the ekoredzaw, oh, very definitely the ekoredzaw." This was confirmed by no less than fourteen hunters gathered from all parts of Assumbo.

"So they know the beef?" I asked.

"They know 'em plenty," Ety'i assured us. "They do live for all small water."

"The chief think him hunterman fit go catch 'em, bring 'em come?"

"Ah-ha," said everybody, and the palaver forthwith broke up.

This took place a few days after our arrival in Tinta. As a result of the various turmoils caused by the precipitate departure of the Duke, the arrival of gorillas, the death of the chief's brother (whose burial ceremony had been held over for a twelve-month), our ex-haustion after losing ourselves in the mountains, and George's spring cleaning of every detail of our entire equipment, we almost forgot the ekoredzaw. Then one night the clear, still air of the val-ley was suddenly filled with the sound of little drums made of earthenware and beaten with tiny sticks so that they tinkle like bells.

We assumed that some other distant relative of Ekumaw had con-cluded his term of office in purgatory and that his grateful descend-ants were preparing to give him a real boost as he passed by on his way to the land of eternal palm-wine and litigation. I may say this with every emphasis, for the after-life of the Assumbo religion provides a more or less perfect African heaven but no hell whatsoever, only a rather dismal purgatory as a final reminder to the departed, in which the chief irritant is a fairly copious leaven of Europeans!

The drums, however, were heralding the arrival not of a hopeful disembodied ancestor, but of a positively exultant spirit clad in the body of the sub-chief of N'tamele (a neighbouring village). When this was reported to us by a breathless individual from the village, we set to work to prepare a reception, because it was suggested that his arrival had some intimate connexion with ourselves. Ety'i, who had as usual made a belated appearance, informed us that we need not hurry ourselves, since it was very doubtful if the said sub-chief would put in an appearance before next morning. Further inquiry elicited the fact that N'tamele, which showed up on the map as a little less than four miles distant as the crow flies, lay immediately behind the nearest range of mountains, and that a swift walker might cover the distance in eight hours should he be on the trail of his wife's lover. The sub-chief, it seemed, was not thus actuated; besides, he was a very-great-grandfather.

We had therefore to wait patiently, while the drums grew louder and ever more convincing, and the compound filled with interested people who came to "look-see," bringing their beds, families, drums, and dogs with them. It was a stifling night. We were sitting at work in the open. By midnight I was entirely surrounded by a solid phalanx of nude brown humanity that stared in absolute silence and immobility while I dissected rats, measured minute frogs, and filled in catalogues, and that only burst into fits of laudatory cheering when I refilled my fountain-pen. George was similarly hemmed in a few yards distant. Whenever occasion arose, we were able to converse and exchange questions and answers without the slightest interruption, so quiet did the assembled community remain. If a child dared so much as to whimper, it was immediately smothered.

This was all extremely tactful and polite on the part of our only semi-invited guests, but as soon as the pressure of work lessened, the atmosphere became somewhat oppressive. I therefore asked

George if he would mind the gramophone, a mere matter of form, because we both felt the same about it. The entire staff came to life accordingly. The Assumbos looked puzzled, for this was only the second time they had seen Europeans at close quarters; they were as yet unaware of the properties of this holy engine!

There happens to be a group of persons of most undoubted African descent now resident in America who call themselves—or are called by their manager—the Washboard Rhythm Kings, and they make music. Their records were a particular passion with us, one of them in fact being the expedition's national anthem and always employed as an opening number. The opening bars caused a "riot." It immediately became apparent that we were among people with tastes uncannily similar to our own. The whole compound began to rock with a syncopation that must have penetrated to a depth of several feet into the hard laterite below. Banks of drums appeared from beneath cloths—little skin-covered fellows, angular earthenware instruments, and giant hollowed logs. These fell into the rhythm one by one.

The effect was weird, because with that intuitive sense possessed by the African, every drummer knew exactly when the "breaks" were coming, and whole banks of bass drums would drop out precisely on the beat. Cuban rumba music was an equal success; it was not only augmented but a great deal improved by the extemporizations of the Africans. The party gradually became wilder in the truly West African manner. Soon, greatly syncopated gentlemen swathed in half a monkey's skin were rushing to the edge of the compound and letting off excessive charges from Dane-guns. This seemed to us a good idea which our home-grown cabarets have thus far neglected, so we loaded the shotguns and at rhythmically psychological moments let off volleys into outer space. The local populace greatly appreciated it; to expend ammunition in this manner is considered both extremely good form and the very height of hospitality. Our glorious night out—or in—continued with sporadic bursts of exceptionally fine dancing, until we had lost all sense of time and a great deal of reality.

I much regret to have to state that I had for the time quite forgotten the object of our mission to Assumbo. This was probably the
reason for the jolt I received when the climax came. In the midst of
a record entitled "Shootem"—which we were doing with some emphasis—the dawn and an opposing army of drummers appeared
down the valley. Carrying small flares made from pulverized resin-
ous sticks, a band of people was seen advancing up the hill towards us.

All of us became aware of them at about the same time. There was
a lull during which everybody must have gone through much the
same mental processes and arrived at the same conclusion, namely,
that there had been some reason for all this gaiety. A shout went up.

"N'tamele! N'tamele!"

Sure enough it was, and, what is more, nearly the whole of the
male population of that exclusive hamlet. The sub-chief, probably
the ancestor of most of them, was completing the journey in a horizontal position. His wizened person was buried deep in a stratum
of drums. If the night had produced wondrous things, the dawn
wrought a miracle.

The visiting chief was hoisted over the palisade of the compound
and erected like a carven image before Chief Ekumaw and ourselves.
He at once came to life and began shouting with a volume and con-
tinuity altogether unexpected from a man of his apparently advanced age; nor did his palaver abate for twenty minutes, during
which time all of us Tintaites slowly wilted into a perspiring anti-
climax. Ekumaw alone remained standing, his wide brow wrinkled
and his keen eyes riveted on the speaker. Every now and then he
would interject an abrupt "uh-huh," whereupon the raconteur
would retrace his words, presumably giving a more strictly accurate
rendering.

At length he came to an end and there was a dreadful silence. The
scene was remarkable. This particular dawn came balefully yellow,
its hard light slowly flooding the valley and illuminating the undersides of flat blue-black clouds above. Arising out of the darkness
that still shrouded the earth like a black mist stood great rocks and

placid feathery palm-fronds like ply-wood cutouts. Around us the still harder yellow glow of the wood flares illumined a wide circle of perfectly motionless muscled forms, standing like an army of bakelite statues, glistening, smooth, and mysterious, the gleaming yellow rays glancing from every curve of firm muscle and plastic flesh. In their mist stood the tall white-shrouded pillar that was Ekumaw, their chief.

Then Ekumaw spoke with a solemnity that befitted the occasion, because he and all his friendly subjects had taken our interests very much to heart, making our endeavours their own and our strange successes their own.

The chief of N'tamele brought a man who carried an ekoredzaw; he considered both objects of such special importance and material value that he had deemed it advisable to accompany them himself to see that neither escaped.

The excitement and surprise was now on us, because nobody had so much as breathed a word to any member of our household concerning the reason for this dignitary's visit. I simply did not believe that the precious animal could actually be within purchasing distance. I tried to arise from my seat but failed altogether in my eagerness.

"Let me see," I pleaded, holding out my hands in a gesture so pathetic that the witty Africans instantly sensed my internal commotion and burst into roars of laughter. This to them was a complete "give-away," and probably any woman will admit that it is no way in which to begin to make a bargain.

"Here," said N'tamele collectively, "is the man."

Their ranks opened. Almost the smallest human being that I have ever seen standing on two legs unaided was pushed forward. In its (for I don't know to this day whether it was male or female) tiny hands it held a large sack, the other half of which formed a loin-cloth covering its minute haunches. The little toddler advanced upon us, grinning all over and quite unabashed. I had no further need to stand up; our eyes met. With a peal of gloriously unselfconscious laughter, the child fell on its knees, opened a hole in the sack, and began shaking. Everybody cranned forward chattering excitedly.

Slowly, inch by inch, a sleek body was coaxed out into the fantastic light of dawn, until at last there at my feet crouched a real, live *Potamogale* complete with fish tail and pin-point eyes, just as the text-books describe.

The whole of our household let out a yell of delight. They all knew that we had before us the animal we wanted, and not something else, as had so often happened before. They all knew also that I had completely given myself away, and I suspected that they were eager to see how I would get myself out of it. When issuing a demand for some special animal, I had always stated the sum it was worth to us; in the case of the ekoredzaw I was so eager that I had forgotten to do so in the first place. Now the tiny owner was entitled to name the price.

With Ety'i as interpreter I began the palaver by asking how the youthful hunter had come by the beef. I soon observed that this was a somewhat tactless question and therefore hastily switched to further inquiries as to its habits. The youthful owner was then a purely economic factor. One cannot well bargain with a "minor," let alone a "minimus." N'tamele had won the first round.

I deduced the fact that the animals are not uncommon in the waters of N'tamele, also that they are not prized as food and are never hunted for that reason. Everybody assured me that they were neither good nor bad nor any other kind of ju-ju. I proceeded to ask whether the skin is used for anything. Old Ekumaw began to laugh. First he tittered, then he chuckled, then he guffawed. I turned to him with a serious face, but he was too wise and had been presiding over the village council and native court for too long. Nothing would stop him. He had spotted what I was up to. He spoke to Ety'i.

The latter turned to me. "The chief say to you," he said, "go on, ask how much dash for beef."

"All right, ask 'em," I said, turning to watch Ekumaw.

"The little one, he say five shillin'," came the answer.

"Ben," I called, "bring money bag, pencil, and small paper."

"Now, Ety'i, make you ask the chief of N'tamele to tell me all the man who live for the house of this small one. Quick, one time, make 'em."

A tense silence fell while a very quiet conference went on among the interpreter, the N'tamele elders, and Ekumaw. I could see them glowering at me and saying to themselves: "So this white man is a cheat like all the rest. He has lied to us and said that he has nothing to do with the government, yet now he is going to devise some tax on our beef according to the males in our households, just as all the rest do." At last Ety'i was ready. Slowly and reluctantly he recounted the little list using his fingers.

"Are there only five?" I barked at Ekumaw, who winced at the suddenness of it. Ety'i explained in his own language and he nodded emphatically by shaking his head, as was the Assumbo custom.

"Right!" I said. "How much tax man pay for N'tamele?"

"Three shillin' and six penny-penny," Ety'i replied with the utmost despair.

I did a quick calculation on paper, watching Ekumaw all the time with the utmost satisfaction. I arrived at the figure seventeen shillings and six pence. Then I opened the money bag and counted out this amount beneath the flap. I concealed it in my hand.

"Come here." I beckoned to the now shrinking mite.

He was pushed forward with extended hand. Into it I crammed the money, then turned him about and pushed him towards Ekumaw.

There was a pause, during which the child stood speechless with its great eyes opened to their fullest limits, while his chief towered above him in a mental mist of a density unmistakable to all. Then he opened his little hand from sheer terror and a stream of hard coin tinkled to the ground. Everybody gasped. Ekumaw's face was contorted into one awful grimace. His eyes also opened wide and he sat down on a collecting box that was fortunately at his heels. Babel broke loose.

That even a white man—colossal financial imbeciles that they are alleged to be—should give more than he is asked in payment for something that such a person had never before been known to desire, was beyond the comprehension of the African mind. That the sum should be more than three times as great could presage only two things—either a foreign and virulent form of insanity or some form of low cunning previously unsuspected of existing.

Time, the great healer, I assured Ekumaw, would show him that what I now promised was correct. This was to the effect that in future I would pay the equivalent of the yearly poll-tax of any man who brought these beef, adding that I had a ju-ju eye which could travel about and ascertain how many men there were in their respective houses, which was an extremely white lie, because I had a helpful promise from the local court clerk that he would verify statements from the court register.

There was no time for further explanations. I could not be sure that we would live to see another potamogale alive; besides, the animal might escape, or die, or be ju-jued away, so I decided that it must be photographed at once. Since we could not wait until it was light, the animal's natural environment must now be brought to the house and the poor creature coaxed into it.

The palaver was over. I made this clear. Everybody must leave for the village at once. I wanted fish—live, dead, and very dead. The chief of N'tamele must return in the morning. The whole staff must go and dig up a portion of the river bank and bring it back; yes, even the cook's wife must go. I was so unexpectedly peremptory that everybody went at once.

By the time they were back, George and I had the lamps lit, the cameras out, and the precious animal housed on the dining table.

Then came the problem where to set up the river bank. You have probably heard of those huntsmen who bring their animals back alive, and others who show their wives felling sporting rhinoceroses with a rifle little larger than a .22. Perhaps you don't know, but they do all that—at least nearly all that you see on the films—behind can-

teens in movie-lots or on a cactus-bestrewn plateau a few miles behind Hollywood.

We tried every possible corner of the house; we went outside
with our cameras and our river bank and all the staff. We came back
again and lay about looking for "photo-angles." Eventually we
ended up on the dining table; it was the only place at which we
could get the camera properly ranged.

The *Potamogale* was released. It instantly glided in among the
rocks and grass before we had time to focus. Heaved out again at
the risk of our being bitten by its needle-sharp teeth, it steadfastly
presented its posterior to the camera. We coaxed it with live fish,
but it was so scared at their flapping tails that it bolted back into its
cage. Dismayed, we proffered dead and very dead fish. These it
sniffed, then backed sneezing into the grass once more. When full
daylight came, photography become impossible owing to the grey
skies. We still hadn't taken a single shot.

We retired to bed utterly beaten in body and spirit.

About midday I was called to accompany Chukula down the
valley, where he was to lay a new line of traps. Ben came also, for
work was slack. We took guns, cameras, and collecting bottles. A
dreary afternoon was passed standing about while the endless line of
traps was baited, set, and laid.

I sauntered down to the river and began wading along, on the
look-out for frogs. All of a sudden from beneath my feet something
long, dark, and slender shot forward in the water. This thing swam
like a fish, its body curving and recurving.

"Master, master, look—a *Potamogale!*" Ben was off like a torpedo.

I scampered after him as best I could, unfurling the camera as I
went. With a swirl of water the animal shot to the surface, passed
out into the air, and landed with a bang on the mossy verge. Here it
turned about, raised its flat snout at us, and chattered its teeth. I
raised the camera to my chest; the excited shaking of my hand did
the rest.

The result was the first one of the only two good pictures I have ever taken in my life, and I believe the first ever to be taken of the giant water shrew alive.

During the following weeks we spent many hours hunting the elusive ekoredzaw. Though we never killed or captured one ourselves, we acquired sixteen in all, of various ages. We discovered many things about them, as we watched them at play and at work through the field glasses, which were really just as valuable data as their preserved remains.

By examination of their stomach contents we ascertained the fact that they feed exclusively on fresh-water crabs—at least in this part of the country. The terror that a live fish engendered in a *Potamogale* seemed to point to the fact that they do not feed on them here, though, of course, they may do so in other parts of the country, which remark leads to an interesting observation.

Months later, while we were collecting on the low coastal plain of Nigeria at a point where some animals that inhabit the brackish estuaries are found, we came upon the *Potamogale*. The first indication of its presence was a portion of a dried skin brought by a small African boy. As it lacked tail and limbs, I was doubtful whether it was from this animal or from some form of true carnivorous otter. Then a fresh skin with moist blood still on it was brought. This had the tail and hind feet complete. It was a *Potamogale*. These obscure beasts not only carry on their antediluvian existence in the seclusion of mountain fastnesses, but still live and multiply unnoticed on the lowland plains. Perhaps they eat fish there, and du Chaillu got muddled about his topography.

There is one point about which everybody seems to have been confounded, though how anybody could have been deceived by this, I fail to see. It has been said that the ekoredzaw lies beneath stones under the water in wait for its prey and, when it has made its capture, returns there. This an air-breathing mammal cannot do indefinitely. The truth of the matter is that the animal's burrows extend beneath the water level, sometimes, strangely enough, several feet below, and the animal makes its onslaughts from the openings.

It was the sub-aqueous tactics that proved our undoing. The only way in which one could attempt a capture was to wade up and down the streams at night by the light of stick-flares and attempt to hit the swift-swimming creatures on the head. We tried every form of trap, but the water was too deep and the animals have no regular track. One could not shoot them, for the same reasons. After a few weeks of wading about in the cold water up to our waists, we both got disturbingly ill and, as a result, suffered acutely for a long time after. I was painfully reminded of the ekoredzaw at frequent intervals two years later.

There were other mammals in Assumbo that diverted our attention from the giant water shrew. The most numerous group in any part of the world is the rats. Assumbo was no exception. A major part of our work was a survey of the rats of each locality. As there were so many kinds, I adopted a system by which each specimen brought in was examined for eleven routine details, such as colour of fur, general shape, comparative measurements, etc. The most useful points of all, I soon learnt, were the undersides of the feet and forepaws with the arrangement of pads. These appeared to be the most constant features in any species.

When we got to Assumbo, I found that while all the rats that we had come to recognize at sight in the lowlands were represented, their pads in nearly every case were augmented by little accessory tubercles. Even tree rats were present, yet there were practically no trees. This, added to a lot of other data gleaned from the frogs and the local vegetation, convinced us that the whole country had in former times been clothed in dense virgin jungle, but that for some reason this had been totally exterminated, and probably quite recently, because the typical fauna of such growth still lingers on. The country is in fact not true grass country or savanna, as it is loosely termed. Some animals, like the rats, are trying to adapt themselves to the changed conditions by developing new feet suitable to a life among grass stems and upon hard, sun-baked earth.

The great Charles Darwin would have doted upon these prizes,

HYRAX OR CONEY (Procavia ruficeps)

but would have been somewhat confounded by the apparent speed at which evolutionary change is proceeding in these strange uplands.

The nature of these barren mountains interested us more and more as time went on; we took every opportunity of going up to their summits to see for ourselves what might be going to happen next.

On one of these trips in the company of Afa and two other quiet hunters we climbed high up into the bare, rocky summits of a long range on the east side of Tinta valley. There had been bright sunlight as we left the village, but two storms had rolled up, one from the northern plains and the other over the southern lip of the mountains. As we entered the low grass at the higher levels, the clouds descended upon us, hurrying down the slopes in deathly silence and cutting us off from the world, each other, and even our own feet. The hollow silence of a mist is always eerie; the loneliness that now poured around us was quite terrifying. Afa pounded stolidly onwards and upwards among immense boulders.

Without warning, a shrill, piercing cry somewhere between a whistle and a scream reverberated among the sodden wraiths of mists. We all came to a halt. Afa beckoned to me. When I was at his side he made me understand that this noise was caused by a small beef that ran very fast. At first I could not decide what it might be; the fact that it was said to be tailless and have two large front teeth inclined me to believe that it was a hyrax.

"Do they live in hole?" I asked. The hunter said that they did and we began searching for their lairs.

After a time we rounded some tumbled rocks on a very steep incline just in time to catch a glimpse of three little greenish-brown animals galloping over an apparently perpendicular face of smooth rock. They disappeared round the corner; we ran after them at a lower level. They had all disappeared as we entered a small gulley, but a terrific commotion was taking place somewhere out of sight among some clumps of grass higher up. We rushed forward.

Ear-splitting shrieks issued from a small hole. Before we could apply the net, out shot a frenzied hyrax hotly pursued by another. Almost at our feet the pursuer caught the pursued and pitched in with the most ghastly vigour and viciousness. Over and over they went, snarling and shrieking and quite heedless of our presence. We dived at the furies, but in doing so we were unwise in the extreme, because the savage little brutes rounded on us and, baring their glistening teeth, rushed at our legs. The bigger of the two fastened his jaws on Afa's calf and made him bellow like a fog-horn.

We captured this one. As soon as he was safely in the bag, the other, which had been scooting about in the grass trying to get at his quarry, made for the safety of the rocks. This animal, a relative of which is found in Palestine and is referred to in the Bible as the "coney," is mentioned in every text-book, travelogue, and sporting tale as being the most timid and wary of all known mammals. Everybody remarks upon its retiring ways and its uncanny habits in concealing itself.

It may be that all the animals of Assumbo behave in a manner altogether foreign to that of their counterparts elsewhere, but this I find difficult to believe. I am persuaded to think that a considerable percentage of all that is written about the habits of wild animals—particularly those that are not counted as big game—are mere repetitions, copied by one person from a previous writer, and so on backwards to the first raconteur. This originator in many cases seems to have been a native who often either mistook the animal about which he was being questioned or invented habits for it to suit the mood of the inquirer.

Certainly a more bold, bad-tempered, vicious, and unwary animal could not be found than this hyrax (*Procavia ruficeps*). The ones we kept alive were for ever flying at each other's throat or our legs.

These animals are not rodents, though they resemble a rabbit in many respects. They are ungulates, with no nearer relative than the elephants. Like the latter, they have little hoof-nails on the four front and three hind toes. There is a gland on the hyrax's back which has special hairs, supplied with muscles at their roots by which the animal can open them out like a flower. These hairs are yellow, in vivid contrast to the rest of the pelage. The area is opened when the animal is angry or afraid—if ever these furies could be in fear.

Part Five

THE GREAT WATERS

14

Hippos; Giant Ray;
Clawed Toads and a Trip Upstream;
A Crocodile Gets to Work; Manatee

THERE were hippos in the great pool that lay below Mamfe station. During the dry season this great circular basin, into which two rivers flowed but only one flowed out, was covered with large semi-circular sandbanks between which the remains of the Cross River drainage system meandered disconsolately. Upon this clean, smooth, silvery sand one morning appeared a number of large footprints which crossed and recrossed. We climbed down to examine them.

A few days later, by some extraordinary chance there was a lull in the work and we were able to retire to bed at an early hour. This was so unusual that I found it quite impossible to go to sleep. After hours of forlorn sheep-counting and other mental gymnastics, I stole out of the sleeping quarters onto the veranda with the intention of brewing tea. As I rounded the corner of the house, I heard a strange rasping noise. A thin white mist covered the whole ground to a depth of about six feet and this was vividly lit up by an intensely bright moon. The noises continued from several points. I moved about trying to pierce the mist and see what could be their cause.

All at once a stream of mist drifted away. There, almost at the foot of the veranda, appeared the gigantic backside of a hippo. Mist is so very deceptive, that this object appeared much larger and nearer than it really was. If you can picture to yourself an immensely fat man, clad in excessively long, baggy trousers, with the forepart of his body down to his waist pushed through a hole in a white sheet and hidden from view, you will have a pretty accurate image of what I saw. It was a completely ludicrous vision.

The mists rolled silently in again. When they next drifted apart, there were two hippos facing each other, broadside to me. I think I must, from their point of view, have been partly hidden by mist, because one advanced cumbrously straight towards the veranda, then, pausing as if it sensed some obstruction ahead, lowered its great head and sniffed furiously at the bare earth. Finally they lumbered away. It was several weeks before I saw them again on the short grass between the bungalows of the station. On this occasion they were strolling about in the moonlight in a long line as if playing "follow-the-leader."

Yet, believe it or not, with all this warning, with hippo picnic parties round the house, and with footprints on the sands, we were idiots enough to go collecting frogs in a two-seater dugout canoe— but let me explain.

There are many purely aquatic animals of great interest and considerable rarity which we were very keen to collect. It seems that their rarity is not actual, but results from the fact that they are not so commonly seen, being hidden in or about the water. Moreover, the rivers of West Africa are turbulent maelstroms during more than half the year, so that any animals that may be living in them are completely hidden beneath their muddy waters. Among these aquatic animals we suspected that there might be the clawed toads that we had selected as one of our special goals.

The only method of travelling about this country during the rainy season is by boat. These are called "launches"—though why, nobody can rightly say—and are either glorified punts with steam engines or healthy turbine-driven vessels about the size of trawlers. Since Mamfe is several hundred miles from the sea, we were transported there on one of these launches. During the next two months, while we waited for the rains to stop, we were resident near the great rivers. We had never seen any of the animals peculiar to this type of habitat, however, for the reasons that I have mentioned.

When the rains had eventually spent themselves, we moved out into the forests, and so it was that we did not begin a detailed study of the "great waters" until many months later. As a matter of fact, it was a beastly fellow in our employ—a Sobo from the delta of the Niger—who first stimulated us to action. We had constantly grumbled about the quality of the fish that appeared on our bill of fare; he, being a man who "savvied water too much," guaranteed that he would produce finer fish out of the Mamfe Pool than any of the local inhabitants had ever dreamed of as existing. We didn't believe him because we didn't like him, which was on the face of it extremely silly.

What was our surprise then one morning, while we were partaking of an alfresco breakfast on the veranda facing the pool, when we saw a small canoe come paddling round one of the sandbars. On inquiring who it might be, we were told that it was our beastly Sobo employee. Both he and the canoe looked a good deal smaller than a tin tack away at the bottom of the towering cliff-like bank upon which our domains were raised from the river. We got out the powerful field glasses and verified Faugi's statement. It was the Sobo, sure enough, and he had with him in the canoe a large circular fishing net like those the Chinese use over the shallow mud flats at the mouths of the great rivers of their country.

We then spent a most entertaining half-hour. The Sobo manœuvred the canoe with all the water-cunning of a good delta tribesman. It was the first thing we had ever seen him do well. It proved to be the last, because he shortly afterwards resigned his position with us and went to await His Britannic Majesty's pleasure in another place for income-tax evasion, or its African equivalent. At the tip of the sandbar he beached his craft, then waded out into the shallow water. Here he sprinkled something on the water and coiled his net as a seaman would a rope. Then he waited.

Presently little rings began to appear around him. He cast the net so that it opened in mid-air like a gigantic mushroom and fell, a complete circle, into the water. When he hauled it in, it was quite full of fish. The whole household became more than interested in the sudden display of energy and prowess on the part of the beastly Sobo—we all stood in a little knot admiring his success far below.

Our behaviour was so unusual for this early hour that a number of the local inhabitants who were passing by from the village came to "look-see" what it was all about. When we explained, they stayed on. We let them have a look through the field glasses, which greatly intrigued them. They were, however, more than scornful of the Sobo's performance. They not only agreed that he was in every way beastly, but they assured us that he was only catching some fish that seemed to be, in their minds, equivalent to our home-grown minnows.

"Let us show you how to fish," they said. I pointed out that that was exactly what I had been imploring them to do for days past. "Oh," they said, "of course you didn't get any decent fish because you employed only the professional fishermen. They don't know anything about it—how should they? They are only fishermen, and fishermen don't know anything. Everybody knows that," meaning everybody except white men.

So when the beastly Sobo arrived back at the house, perspiring freely and loaded with fish of all kinds, among which were some really excellent tiger fish that made a delicious supper, he was met by something in the nature of a round horse-laugh.

"All right!" he shouted angrily at them. "You dirty bushmen, you, make you go catch fish. You no fit. You no savvy water for this country. You ——" (The rest censored.)

Whereupon the local people departed by no means in silence.

At about four o'clock that afternoon, however, they were seen approaching the house again in company with a lot of other people. As soon as they were close enough, I hailed them and asked if they had been fishing.

"Yes, some of us have," one replied; "and we done catch the mother of your Sobo-man." They all roared with laughter.

Then we received the most terrific shock that it is conceivably possible for a zoological mind to sustain. The men swarmed onto the back of the veranda staggering under a great weight. This they suddenly dumped on the floor, then stood aside. For several seconds I was literally not at all sure whether I was dreaming or had gone completely off my "chump." I was only certain at first that I was quite assuredly not normal, but as the seconds passed and the thing that lay before me did not turn bright purple or resolve itself into one of my best friends, I began to regain confidence in my eyes. For a long time after that, both George and I were still entirely speechless.

There lay before us a fish in every detail, as far as one could see from a cursory glance, resembling a sting-ray, but of dimensions more suitable to the dinosaurs of old. It was diamond-shaped, like all fish of this class, and measured from the tip of one lateral point to the tip of the other, four feet eight inches; from the snout to the base of the tail, five feet eleven inches; and from the base to the tip of the tail, which had no fin, five feet two inches. Emerging from the upper edge of the tapering whip-like tail near its base was a long, straight, sharp spine or sting, one foot seven inches in length.

The arrival of such a monster, and more especially of a class of fish which, in lamentable ignorance, I had always associated with the oceans and not even inland seas, altogether unhinged my sense of logic. That it was still alive and therefore undoubtedly caught in the Mamfe Pool, as the natives stated, was almost incredible, because this bit of water was nearly three hundred miles from the sea. I therefore had to adjust myself to the idea that such things are true fresh-water animals indigenous to the great rivers of Africa.

Why do not natural history books depict these fish instead of the everlasting crocodile? Why don't they tell us what they do in the dry season and even in the rains? Where do they breed, and has anybody ever found their leathery, purse-like eggs?

We didn't want the brute because we were not collecting fish, but we photographed him alongside sundry natives and inanimate objects and purchased the sting. Though the Africans told us that to be pierced by it meant certain death, this is open to doubt. It is highly probable that if one received a dig in the rump from one while bathing and had the bad fortune to see what was at the other end of it, one would die from sheer fright; as to its toxic qualities, more definite evidence is required. When this sting got really dry it split longitudinally and opened like a star, revealing a clear crystalline plug within. This substance gradually broke up under the damp atmospheric conditions; some of it dropped in water fizzed furiously. I could not find anything that would preserve it among our selection of travelling drugs and chemicals, which was most unfortunate because I should like to have had it analysed to ascertain its exact nature.

This fish disturbed us greatly. We more or less implored the "perpetrators" of it to go back again regularly and try to produce something equally startling on the reptile, amphibian, or mammal line. They promised they would, saying that it was an easy task, since they could bring us crocodiles and snakes and suchlike things. For some time afterwards, however, they did not seem to have much luck. I began chafing.

Now this is where the clawed toads came in. The beastly Sobo went away as I have said, but in his stead we now had Dele. His keenness knew no bounds in certain respects, one of which was frog-hunting. This proclivity of his resulted in our spotting a young clawed toad of a species named *Xenopus tropicalis* among one of his catches. When asked where he caught it, he pointed across the pool to the mouth of the Mainyu Gorge, which debouches into the pool through a canyon less than a hundred feet wide and of an unknown depth. The Germans once tried to take soundings in this canyon, and failed to reach bottom.

Asked how the devil he—a Munchi, who doesn't understand water —managed to get across the river to this point, Dele replied that he "done walker-walker for water," which is a somewhat misleading pidgin-English term. Further painful questioning elicited the fact that the Sobo had thoughtfully hired a small two-seater canoe for an outrageous sum but failed to inform us either that we were henceforth liable or that we had use of the liability. Dele, by some African

means unknown to us and incomprehensible even to the staff, had
discovered both this fact and the abandoned canoe.

Thus it came about that we set out to inspect the Mainyu Gorge
for the first time.

We both prided ourselves on being more than normally handy
with a boat. George is one of the very few Britons who can sail with
certainty in the northern Mediterranean—no mean feat—and I had
my own reasons for being bumptious about boats. Our combined
efforts in, upon, and sometimes under the two-seater dugout canoe
were nevertheless little short of a fiasco.

I still stick to it that the basis of the trouble was that this craft took
a turn for the worse amidships, that is to say, to port if regarded from
down aft, or to starboard if one looked at her from the region of the
bows. The exact situation of forward in relation to aft was another
debatable point, which neither ourselves nor the owner could settle.
The means of propulsion was two paddles, one of extremely light
wood with short, straight stem and long, pointed blade, the other
long, crooked-handled, circular-bladed, and of a density somewhere between that of cast-iron and lead. Paddling on one side, one
revolved in an ever-diminishing circle, on the other, one set out
upon an entirely unpredictable course like Professor Einstein's light
near a great star.

By the time we had discovered these astonishing facts we were in
mid-stream with nearly as much water inside the outfit as there was
immediately outside it. George therefore had to give up propulsion
in favour of expulsion. With the first hatful of water that went over-
board the shotgun slipped down into the bilges, and I found myself
in sole control, with every prospect of continuing so for some time.
What followed was a nightmare, but by using both paddles alternately, the heavy one for the concave and the light one for the con-
vex side of the canoe, I eventually reached the mouth of the gorge.

Here we landed on some sheets of waterworn rock that hung
over the surface of the water. In them were countless pot-holes on
an average two feet in diameter, of great depth, and filled with stag-

nant water left by the receding floods at the beginning of the dry season. Many, with only small openings to the surface, were spherical below and so large that they had broken through to their neighbours. In these we captured a number of the precious clawed toads.

These are not toads but members of a group of very lowly amphibians coming somewhere very near the base of the frogs' genetic tree. Unlike all other frogs and toads, they have hard black conical claws capping their toes. They are completely aquatic, spending their entire lives in the water.

We were so pleased with our discovery that we made a systematic search of all the pot-holes. In those nearest the river the toads mostly escaped by passing through from one chamber to another, finally emerging underneath the rock and leaping into the racing current. This was very strange, for how any frog could survive in this mill-race we failed to understand. We decided to investigate, and clambered back into the canoe.

Pulling ourselves along the edge of the gorge, we crept in under the shelving rocks. Here the frogs were thick about us, all swimming against the tearing current. As soon as we made a lunge at them, they simply stopped swimming and were whisked away under the overhanging ledges. By following them we slowly worked our way further into the gorge.

In the end we found ourselves in a predicament that might be described as being firmly wedged among the horns of several dilemmas. By paddling with all our might we could just counteract the current, though meantime the boat was making water at a speed hitherto unheard of. To stop paddling meant being projected under the shelving rocks at a speed of about twenty knots, while to delay baling meant a constant increase in the weight of our craft and eventual submersion. We were broadside onto a large cave in the wall of the canyon, when without any warning there was a positive eruption, and we were right in the middle of a crowd of extremely startled hippos intermingled with a few apparently hysterical crocodiles.

They did not charge the boat or try to drag us from it, as they should respectively have done in a well-regulated travelogue; they remained concealed in the semi-darkness of the cave, emitting the most blood-curdling snorts, growls, and rasps. Did we shoot them between the eyes in best story-book manner? No, sir! We paddled— oh, boy, did we paddle!—despite current and rising internal tides. Round one small bend and we were in a strong backwash, so that George could bale while I fairly hacked at the water. In a few minutes we had landed on a tiny spit of sand that somehow found a place to squat under the towering walls of the canyon.

We sat down exhausted and fumbled for cigarettes, but the matches had gone. This was an absolute bombshell— I knew that I had brought some. We rested in the deepest gloom, then began to make the best of our plight by searching among some broad-leafed plants that clung to the sand in patches, hoping to unearth some frogs.

At first we found nothing, but at the farther end we came upon some small pools of still water between the sand and the rocks. Poking a stick into one, I was amazed to see a number of stones at the bottom drift mysteriously away into the deeper parts. Hailing George, I demonstrated this phenomenon again. We set to work to scoop in the depths of the brown-stained water with the collecting net. After a time we fished out two amazing creatures.

It was obvious they were tortoises of some sort, though they had speckled leathery backs in place of hard shells, slender pointed snouts, flippers with claws, and they were quite flat from top to bottom like circular pancakes.

"Turtles," said George.

"No, tortoises," said I.

"Funny tortoises," said he.

"Water tortoises."

"That is, turtles."

"No, turtles live in the sea and are quite different."

"They're not different from these."

"Not much, but these are tortoises."

"They don't look like real tortoises."

"No, they're water tortoises."

"Why not river turtles?"

"Because they're not."

"Well, then, let them be mock turtles," George said with an air of finality.

And so it remained for the rest of the trip, lest the harmless water terrapin (*Trionyx triunguis*) cause a dissension leading to civil war.

This seemed to exhaust the wild life of the sand spit. As we were still cursing the absence of matches and totally ignoring the whole question of the gorge, we proceeded sullenly upstream as best we could. The going was not so bad, because the canoe was now kept dry within and we were almost through the gorge. Our next stop was on a long strip of sand covered with delicate little wading birds of several kinds. Most of them took to flight, uttering plaintive sandpiper cries. Only the rather pompous wattled plover (*Anomalophrys superciliosus*) remained. These birds are about the size of a green plover with a large wide head and two long bright-yellow wattles depending from the corners of their bills. They were so bold that we landed and lay down among them.

The scene here was of such staggering beauty as to be almost beyond description. The narrow river passed through the billowing jungle in a straight line as if it were a man-made canal. Its banks were smooth grey rock, immediately above which lay a gently sloping sandy beach. As this approached the trees, lush bright-green herbs grew in great profusion. Above the sky was a smooth intense blue nothingness. As we lay on this island sandbank looking upstream, the whole world seemed perfectly regimented into straight belts—to the right, dark-green trees, chartreuse herbs, golden sand, grey rocks; in the centre, brown water; and on the left, the same thing reversed as if it were an imprint.

I have already tried to express the sensations that these vistas of purely natural beauty conjure up in one. Perhaps this is a vain task, because there may be many, if not a majority, of people who would feel nothing when confronted with a mass of tropical jungle under a blazing sun. Its beauty could not, I believe, be denied, even by those who have suffered most at the hands of the demon tropics; still, that beauty, like an ultra-sophisticated woman, has a strong air of danger and allure. Such painted glory is apt to have a very surprising effect upon members of the Nordic race. They may often be heard comparing women's red-lacquered finger nails to the bloody talons of a bird of prey; similarly, the tropical jungles are to some a sort of nightmare green hell. This is very extraordinary, since it cannot be due to a distaste for artificiality, or for wild nature, or even for bright colours. In fact, however much one may dislike it as an excuse or a reason, it can be simply explained as the outcome of the intense hidden erotic perspective possessed by this strange race which construes these things in such a way when others would merely regard them as colourful, gay, and beautiful.

One could, I suppose, regard this unbridled riot of growth and colour as something terrifying, though I do not see how it could be regarded as more fearful than the continuous multiplication and drabness of our industrial districts. One is to me the very apex to which life can reach, the other the very depth to which it can sink. Man alone seems capable of digging these depths, and therefore I consider him a creation of the mythical devil, though I know full well that my opinion is of no consequence.

Alone in the unspoiled eternal jungle, one merely becomes another animal of only comparative efficiency and almost incredible ugliness. The little wading birds with their feathers arranged in perfect order and cleanliness, the zooming insects performing feats of aeronautics beyond our powers of comprehension, the spotless sands, and the trees breathing silently through a million verdant pores are our rightful background. Our sweaty social strivings will raise us to the level of super-ants, whereupon we will go underground for fear of being preyed upon by winged birds and crawling reptiles, in the guise of airplanes and tanks.

Lest the theorizing of our silly minds should become so intense as to cause total annihilation, we bestirred our still sillier bodies and crossed to the sandy beach on the left of the river. Here we set to work searching among the water weeds for other mock turtles and the like.

We found none, but George unearthed a water snake (*Natrix ferox*) which made off towards the main stream with its slippery head raised above the surface. This creature gave us a few nasty moments, because, once in its liquid element, it displayed remarkable agility and a vile temper. Cutting off its retreat, we tried to scoop it out with a net, but it avoided us and took to terra firma once more. We pursued it into the low broad-leafed herbage.

It entered a small gully up which we beat with great show of bravado. Then we lost it and became a great deal more circumspect in our movements, because a snake hidden beneath a continuous bed of leaves is a positive menace. George went to the left, I to the right.

Just as he yelled that he had the reptile, something broke cover at my feet. I raised the gun. All I could see was a line of greatly disturbed leaves in the wake of the animal's departure. When the cause of the "going" came to rest after a few yards, I advanced cautiously, being greatly interested to know what it might be. All at once there was a scuffle; the thing started up again, described a small circle, and came hurtling back straight at me with unbelievable speed. I fired both barrels at the movement, but, as I could not see it, missed. The thing came on and passed within a foot of me.

Dropping the gun, I took off my hat and hurled it after the flying form. It found its mark. All motion came to rest except that of two boxes of matches, which were projected to a great distance through the air. I suddenly remembered having hidden them under my hat to prevent their getting wet. I went after one of them with an eagerness that would have had to be seen to be believed. In doing so, I stumbled across my hat. Under it lay a little spotted antelope. I had not missed.

This beautiful little semi-aquatic antelope (*Hyemoschus aquaticus*) is hardly bigger than a rabbit, with little delicate feet no thicker than your finger. The whole body is striped longitudinally with lines of small white spots on a reddish-brown background. The

WATER CHEVROTAIN (Hyemoschus aquaticus)

animal is rare. Later on we had two of them alive and noticed that they ate any insects that came within their reach. This seems to be a very strange thing for a member of the antelope family to do, but animals take to the strangest habits when in captivity and kept from their natural food. Certain natives make a specialty of hunting these animals and other small antelopes with crossbows just as were used in the early Middle Ages, loaded with minute arrows no bigger than a pencil, whose points had been dipped in a vegetable poison extracted from a certain creeper. This plant is common, growing upon the trees in the high jungle. Its great strands fall down to the ground; if one be slashed through, a stream of milky juice pours out as fast as milk out of a jug.

And so we dived back into the gorge fully emboldened by clouds of cigarette smoke and our catches. We went so fast that we had no time to see hippopotamuses, crocodiles, or frogs. The canoe, as I have said, had a shape of its own. Now it took an entirely original course. We could not paddle it anything like fast enough to keep steerage way. We were hurtled towards the walls of the canyon, we were sucked bodily into the cave where the hippos had been, spun like a top, and shot out again. Eventually we emerged into Mamfe Pool stern first, or at least with the end which we had selected as stern first.

Perhaps you may have observed another moral in this tale. When you can neither advance nor retreat, keep moving.

"Holy cat-fish, where's that crocodile? Ben! Faugi! Bassi! Eméré! *Hi*, all of you, where's the crocodile?"

Sounds of feet running, and the whole of our small army streamed up onto the veranda.

"Where is the crocodile?" I asked, indicating the open door of the cage that had housed a four-foot example during the past week.

"Go on, find him quick. George, George! Where is the other master?"

"He done go for bush."

"Which bush? Make you go fetch 'em, one time."

Then began the most eager search I have ever witnessed. We were all armed with loops of rope and nets of various descriptions. We were all actuated by a desire both to recapture an escaped treasure and to avoid losing a few toes or fingers by inadvertently picking up a savage reptile in place of an innocent wooden object. This one would not be likely to do, save for the fact that it was rapidly approaching sundown and the house was quite filled with an assortment of objects that might be mistaken for almost anything in the dark.

"Master, the other master do come."

"Hi, George, the croc has got loose."

"Master, master."

"Coming."

We bolted round the house. There lay an overturned cage with its wire netting ripped and torn as if a bomb had exploded within it. Splinters of wood and earth lay around. In the midst of all this, a tangled mass heaved and writhed.

We all formed a ring round the combatants. The crocodile had apparently torn open the cage in which was housed a five-foot monitor lizard (*Varanus niloticus*), dragged the animal out, and set upon it. There seemed to be no motive for this strange crime; the *Varanus* is an eater of small animals, insects and the like, the crocodile is a carnivore on a larger scale, but not likely to attack such a prey without serious provocation. There may have been some morsel in the *Varanus's* cage attractive to both animals, but by the time we got there, all trace of it and most else had gone.

The two animals gripped each other by the snout, the lower jaw of the lizard in the crocodile's mouth, the upper jaw of the latter being likewise held by the *Varanus*. Neither would let go and neither could make much impression upon the armour-plating of the other. Meantime they writhed and twisted like belts of steel come to life and possessed with a thousand devils each.

"Grab a tail," said I, having no intention of doing so myself.

"Wait a bit, till I get the movie camera," said George.

On his return, we all made a dive for the croc's tail with a noose of rope. When eventually we got it firmly caught, we threw the other end over a beam and hoisted away. Up came the crocodile until he was a helpless long thing suspended upside down. But he never let go of his adversary. He clung to the lizard's snout and the latter clung to him.

In the end both of them were clean off the ground, firmly joined in a long string; no amount of beating, prodding, or even "warming" with tapers would make them let go. We had to lower them again with half a dozen people pulling on each tail as in a tug of war. Even then their writhings carried the whole party over the edge of the veranda, to continue the struggle in the dust beside the house.

Only when we had piled a mountain of canvas bags filled with

traps, stones, and other weighty things on the back of both combatants could we get close enough to prise open their mouths with
the ever-handy trapper's friends.

Both these ferocious denizens of African waters are now greatly
disjointed white skeletons in a European museum.

The great waters form a network over the whole of tropical
Africa. They are the highways of commerce, the boundaries of
man and animals alike, and the home of a strange life of their own.

Near Mamfe we pursued monitor lizards down slopes at top
speed, only to see them take a flying nose-dive into some still stream.
Far away in the forest we bathed in pools at the base of crystal-
clear waterfalls from which the local inhabitants of the near-by village forthwith extracted crocodiles of such size that we could only
keep the skull to show that they had once existed. Whenever one
camped near a river, peculiar rats, snakes, and frogs began to appear in the daily bag. They came from the river.

There were two other animals in the rivers that we wanted. One
we knew existed in considerable numbers. The other was more in
the nature of a myth. We decided to make a special trip in search of
them. In doing so we made the acquaintance of a third animal which
we could have easily overlooked on account of its size, had it not
been for the fact that it is the real lord and master of the whole
country and of every man's destiny.

We piled all our gear into four immense dugout canoes and set
out at four o'clock one afternoon in face of the incredulity and
warnings of the whole populace. But it had to happen thus, because
I won't get up and do things before breakfast; and unless one did,
one could not possibly get off before tea-time. Besides, I will not
miss my tea either, so willy nilly we had to leave with only two
hours of daylight to travel thirty-five miles. The paddlers—ten to
each boat—disliked the whole proceeding so much that they struck
after half an hour, demanding a fabulous sum to take us to the
near-by very uninviting shore. We prepared to compose ourselves,
remarking that we should in any case be carried down to Calabar

in the end by the current, provided we slept long enough. Thereafter the Africans paddled with an energy, a goodwill, and a torrent of laughter that only such people could muster.

When we arrived at Ekuri, all we could see was the dim reflections of some fifty naked blacknesses by the light of the solitary bush-lamp.

There was no rest house or other accommodation, and it was too late to pitch the tent, so we went to sleep among great piles of yams and cacao in a native storehouse.

We awoke to another day amid a crowd of interested spectators of all ages and sexes. Dimly through the mosquito netting I saw them—a solid wall of humanity blocking out the rays of the early morning sun. I bawled at the top of my voice for succour. Ben came at the double from behind a pile of cacao.

"Make all this man go away," I commanded in lordly fashion.

"They no agree, master."

I began to foam at the mouth and fight with yards of netting in a frenzy of rage to get at the intruders. Then it struck me that we were after all occupying the local stock exchange, which, unlike its European counterparts, opens its door at sunrise.

"What do they want?" I asked. "Must they move cacao today?"

"No, they want to see you shave," came the surprising reply.

"Ah-ha," said I, leaping into full view, for my face was adorned with a magnificent black imperial. This they did not know because I had arrived under cover of darkness.

"Oh, aha!" A dismal wail went up from all around.

"Master, they want to know if the other masters will shave."

At that moment George and the Duke appeared like two great flying foxes blinking in the sunlight and wrapped round with sheets to hide their nakedness, as bats are with their wings. This finished our audience, because George wore a quite superb Vandyke in a glowing auburn shade and the Duke's entire face was clothed in a wind-swept growth ranging in colour from red to blond with flecks of very dark brown, all of which curved mysteriously from right to left, ending in a remarkable point below the left ear.

Despite this bad beginning and subsequent extremely rough treatment at the hands of our Munchis, who had to parade up and down in front of the house all morning to keep the audience away by force, the entire village fell in with our plans with an astounding vigour. All including the smallest "went to bush" in search of beef; one very old lady actually "went to earth" in search of tortoise, where she promptly got stuck with her nether regions wildly oscillating in plain air. Willing hands dragged her out.

The chief came to call. He had been a policeman in a far, far country before his father died and he had been recalled to guide his flock. He was a horrible man—even more beastly than our long unlamented Sobo—who made the mistake of entering our abode with a fantastic European hat on his head. I can abide anything but a Homburg manufactured in Japan on the head of an African. Worn in our house, it was a breach of etiquette and gave me my opportunity. I refused to notice him until he removed it. His subjects saw the point; they forthwith removed the hat and their chief along with it. After that we got along with the business more easily.

A very long man was unearthed by somebody who said he owned a canoe and "savvied plenty water plenty." We went into secret conference. The result was that we set out in a handy little canoe of admirable construction. It seated four at a pinch, but as there were three of us, the hunter's assistant could not come. A great palaver ensued, because the satellite was the "engines," which should be situated aft while the hunter sat for'ard. I suggested that we should be alternate "engines," adding that we savvied every possible kind of water. Nobody agreed, but we pushed off.

As "engines," my instructions were to paddle in the direction indicated by the hunter's arm-waving, which much resembled the gyrations of a policeman on traffic duty. The first flap indicated that we were to breast the full current and head upstream. I thenceforth perspired for half an hour in hopeless imitation of a Redskin, pressing the paddle against the bulwarks and pinching my fingers at every second stroke. However, we slowly progressed in a vague north-easterly direction. We then dived into a wide side-creek.

Here the hunter unwrapped a canvas contraption and proceeded to piece together a venomous-looking harpoon, which he balanced on his right shoulder. This was his last move for the next four hours. We paddled alternately in a state bordering on dementia.

Late in the afternoon our leader began waving his arms like a windmill. As I was at that moment "engines," I set the boat into a violent spin. There seemed to be no concrete reason for this sudden activity, yet, intent upon preserving Britain's sovereignty over the waves—of whatever nature they might be—I pinched my fingers again and again in a valiant effort to keep pace with our leader's directions.

We rounded a verdant corner in bottom gear. I was just about to pull her into the straight with the blade of the paddle when I observed something small alight on my forearm. Looking closer, I received a nasty shock. The thing was mosquito-shaped and banded black and white. No further investigation was required to realize that this was *Stegomyia*, carrier of the dread yellow fever.

This disease is not only deadly, as everybody knows, but contagious, infectious, and incurable. Only on the rarest of occasions does anybody recover from it. An American institution which tackled the problem in Central America, to which place the deadly disease had been introduced from West Africa by the Negroes taken there, has now turned its attention to Africa. Specimens of blood are taken from all and sundry of the native inhabitants and sent to America for analysis. From the district where we were they have so far failed to find a single one that is free from endemic yellow fever. This means that any *Stegomyia* mosquito biting any member of the local populace and subsequently settling on you may, and doubtless will, produce the first case of epidemic yellow fever.

I did not go through all this when I saw the little death-speck on my arm. I knew it, and it flashed through my mind. As the mosquito raised its tiny head to puncture me with its lance, I hit out. I think I arrived first, but at the same instant something pricked my neck. I swiped that way, and when I looked at my finger, it was covered with blood and the squashed remains of another zebra devil.

Everybody turned round to see what I was up to except the hunter.

"Look out," I said, "stegomyia," and made a swipe at the Duke's forehead.

He lunged sideways. There was a pause. I just caught sight of the hunter's amazed face; then like a spinning top of extravagant design the canoe turned turtle. There was hardly any splash.

When I appeared above water, I took one look, then slowly began to sink again through sheer surprise. Besides the intrepid hunter's and my two noble colleagues' bobbing heads, there were some dozen other dark faces with Old Bill moustaches of prodigious dimensions. As I rose and fell in my own gentle swell, these curious personages, disappearing and reappearing here and there, stared in sullen silence. One was accompanied by a diminutive replica of its grotesque self—an infant with monstrous moustaches.

Just as I was beginning to remember crocodiles, the hunter reached the bank towing the canoe. I scrambled after him, still clutching the paddle. We all got ashore without incident, though several items of equipment remained permanently in the depths. The strange faces went away below as soon as we showed ourselves *in toto*. The hunter's beloved harpoon was tied to the canoe and, when hauled up, brought a large clot of water weed to the surface with it. We re-embarked in moisture and silence, and set off back to the village with Britannia's proud ensign now sadly bedraggled.

When we landed, we looked quite dry and normal, but the hunter's tongue soon saturated us again in the eyes of the populace. Worst of all, the horrible chief appeared, as we thought, to leer.

Here I was wrong. He announced in solemn terms that a fine manatee lay on the beach, if we cared to see and perhaps purchase it. This was a final degradation, in which the hunter was included, because it was to harpoon these very animals that we had set out, and it had been they that we had caused to rise to the surface of their liquid abodes to investigate our quixotic behaviour.

What had actually occurred was as follows. The chief, in great

MANATEE OR RIVER-COW (*Manatus senegalensis*)

pique at his forcible removal from our temporary abode, had given
his own secret orders for a small creek leading off the big river to
be fenced off by stakes driven into the muddy bottom. In this a gap
had been left and into its waters a great pile of fresh leaves of the
cacao yam had been thrown. Next morning, when the fenced-off
portion was quite filled with poor helpless manatees come to feed
on their favourite food, the horrible chief had the stockade closed
and the largest harpooned neatly under the right flipper so that the
sharp head just penetrated the heart.

This is illegal, which the chief had forgotten, as the animals are
protected. We therefore drove a bargain. The whole animal then
being ours, we foolishly tried to eat a portion of the liver. Perhaps
we discovered the origin of the native sandal!

This is not an animal that can be skinned. We wanted the skeleton, however, which is no small thing. The animal being a female

—at least as far as one hundred and nine people could make out—
I theorized that there must be a uterus somewhere. But the underside of a manatee is somewhat misleading, so I set to work with a
long knife by the light of two lamps, as it was now dark.

Now the manatee (*Manatus senegalensis*) is a strange animal belonging to a minute group of large herbivorous animals that have
taken to a purely aquatic life. They have no near relatives at all.
The nearest is perhaps the elephant, though scientists have probably
changed their opinion about this during the last week. There is a
relative living in Australia and the Orient called the dugong (*Hali-
core dugong*), and there used to be a larger representative of the
group in the sea off Alaska called Steller's sea-cow. This is now totally extinct, owing to the efforts of our own species.

The manatee has no hind legs at all, is shaped like a seal, but has a
peculiar circular, fan-shaped tail arranged horizontally. It is said to
be the origin of the mermaid fable, because its head looks human
and it has a habit of standing erect in the water. The females have
well-developed breasts and clasp their young with their foreflippers.
This speaks slenderly for the ancient mariners' choice of feminine
beauty, apart from the fact that one can hardly credit that our
extremely-great-grandmothers grew moustaches.

I eventually got out the uterus, which is zoologically unique and
quite amazing.

This animal took three whole days to prepare. Ten men worked
continuously, cutting mountains of flesh off the skeleton, boiling
the bones, scraping them and drying them in a specially constructed
hut over a slow fire.

We somehow never went out harpooning again. Because we
didn't, the Africans said we should never obtain the fish-beef with a
fin. This we presumed to be the little fresh-water whale that we
longed to see, but I am not certain that the locals didn't make their
description—if not the whole animal—to tally with the inquiries of
our staff.

They were quite right, nevertheless. We never saw it.

Part Six

ALL OVER THE PLACE

15

Bats

EVERYBODY is at least vaguely aware of the existence of bats. Even the town dweller may, if he care to, notice their little phantom forms flitting around the houses. Believe it or not, there are bats sleeping in the Albert Memorial in Kensington Gardens every day of the year. Still, probably less than one person in every five hundred thousand could describe accurately what any bat really looks like.

In Africa, as in other tropical countries where bats are even more numerous, it is much the same. These strange creatures are one of the most diverse and numerically predominant groups of animals in existence, yet they live around and among us like ghosts, unnoticed and unknown.

What is the reason, or what are the reasons?

This was a question that we asked ourselves as soon as we got to Africa. The answer was fairly simple—bats fly by night. But it is how and where they fly that are the vital points; these lead us into a number of problems that have so far been confined to the realms of pure science. Nevertheless, they proved to be so interesting to us, as we investigated each problem in turn, that I feel our troubles may be shared with you.

Scientists divide the bats into two classes—the *Megacheiroptera* and the *Microcheiroptera*—which only mean the "large bats" and the "small bats." The former are vegetarians, the latter mostly carnivorous, eating insects or sucking blood. We soon discovered, however, that from the point of view of the collector this division was not quite satisfactory. The habits of the two groups overlap somewhat.

We noticed, in fact, that the bats fell into the following two classes: those that fly in the open air away from trees and obstructions when they first appear every evening and, secondly, those that do not. Nearly all the large frugivorous bats belong to the first class, almost all the small insectivorous ones to the second; but, still from the point of view of the collector, there is another vast difference between them. The first can be shot, the second cannot, except in unusual circumstances.

When the sun begins to set, the first group of bats leaves its hideouts and soars into the air. They ascend to a very great height, moreover, primarily because the insects are still flying in the warm upper atmosphere or, in the case of fruit bats, because they have to travel some distance to their feeding grounds. Also, this first lot of bats descends towards the earth only by degrees, and all the time it is getting darker every second. By the time they are within gun-shot range, it is far too dark to sight them; they are an almost impossible target at the best of times.

The second type of bat—those that do not fly in the open—has even more aggravating habits. As dusk comes rapidly in this country of forests, woods, and endless vegetation, deep shadows are cast across the whole landscape, so that little patches of ever-extending night mottle the whole countryside. The bats—all the small ones— emerge as soon as these shadows are black enough, and content themselves with flashing back and forth from the gloomy depths of one patch of forest to another, always keeping in the darkest shadows in their flight.

Both groups are therefore from the outset well out of range of any designing human. These facts we quickly appreciated. Had we realized that our troubles were really only just beginning, I believe we should have given up the attempt to collect these animals right away. In our ignorance, we believed that we would be able to shoot them none the less, and also eventually discover them in their retreats during the daylight hours. In both these things we had made serious miscalculations.

Nobody seems to appreciate just what a bat's flight consists of. Practically all birds behave in the air in much the same manner as an airplane, or at least as a helicopter, but a bat—words fail me entirely! To support the body in the air during flight the wings, which are formed, as everybody knows, by the elongated fingers with a thin membrane stretched between them, are moved up and down and, what is more important, backwards and forwards. The wing is, in fact, used exactly like a hand clawing at the air to gain a grip. Since this hand is a multitude of joints bent in a score of different directions, and because the whole animal is constructed to facilitate the capture of minute, swift-flying insects, the so-called flight becomes a jumble of the most fantastic motions imaginable. Flight consists of a series of collapses, jerks, spurts, headlong drops, side-slips, and indiscriminate tumbles that defy description, all known laws of dynamics, and the swiftest aim with a gun.

The species that fly in the open air are not such bad offenders in this respect as those that do not, but apart from the fruit bats, which have a steadier flight, they are nevertheless best described as tortured animated springs let loose in the clear air.

Now if you will just consider the following facts, you may be able to appreciate the difficulties that we were up against. The body of a bat may be taken as, on an average, about one-fifteenth of the area of the whole animal when the wings are fully extended. The flight of some species is so swift that when they are proceeding in a straight line—which is rare—they cannot be photographed with an ordinary film-camera. There is no given direction for a bat's flight —it depends solely on the spatio-temporal relation of the next insect! Lastly, the animal is either at the very limit of gun range or makes its appearance only for a second in a deep shadow among dense vegetation. I may add that a bat frequently closes its wings entirely in mid-air during flight to increase the speed of its descent upon a crisp mouthful.

Will you place yourself on a plot of rough ground covered with fallen trees, ant-hills, and tangled ground creepers, and imagine yourself gazing up into the rapidly darkening sky (a thing you have already been doing for twenty minutes, to the discomfort of your neck)? Suddenly a tiny flitting thing skids out of the invisible beyond and you imagine it is within the range of your gun, now that the latter seems to weigh half a ton. You stumble backwards trying to take aim at the dot above. First it is to your right side, now above you, then to the front, now right behind. At last you are roughly covering it with your sight—then suddenly something happens, in a flash it has become only one-fifteenth its former size. You blaze away—or perhaps you don't—only to see the wretched creature streak off in the least expected direction just slowly enough for the eye to follow. Disgusted with this encounter, you repair to the adjacent forest and take up your position in a silent narrow glade.

An endless stream of small flashes is projected out of the trees from one side to the other. You raise your gun, determined to fire at the very next to appear. At first they are too quick for you. Since it is almost dark, you determine to press the trigger as soon as one flies by your aim. Not one comes out. The stream has ceased, but presently commences again in the opposite direction, the vanguard passing between your legs and between your nose and the end of the gun. Exasperated, you wheel about, but as you do so the whole ground bursts into eddies of practically invisible flitting forms. You fire at random but there is nothing there.

It is now so dark that you light your torch, affix it to your forehead, and stand with your gun to your shoulder facing down the beam of light which is cast into the glade. Bats rocket from everywhere. All at once a flopping, fluttering entity appears, coming straight down the beam of the bright light. Overjoyed at this unexpected chance, you try to take aim, but the bat is now here, now there, and always advancing directly at you.

You fire. Bang! Out of the smoke appears the bat. With a sideslip it skids past the muzzle of your gun and is gone over your left shoulder.

I ask you—what are you to do with tangible ghosts?

Our base camp at Mamfe was housed in a structure known locally as a rest house. These abodes are thoughtfully provided by the government at all the "stations" and in most of the more important villages on the main forest pathways between them. They vary greatly in size, shape, and development. The most primitive are little better or even worse than the meanest local native houses; the best, in big towns where many white officials and traders are domiciled, are truly palatial dwellings with verandas, gardens, ice-boxes, and electric light. The village rest houses are mere mud and wattle structures built on the native plan. The worst station rest houses are glorified editions of these, but the better ones are stone-built structures with "pan" (corrugated-iron) roofs.

Mamfe provided just such a one. It consisted of two square rooms, each with two doors and two windows, built on a raised concrete platform which formed a veranda all round. A conical tin roof covered the whole. The underside of the roof over the veranda was neatly covered in with match-boarding brought at great expense from Europe; the rooms were similarly roofed, though here the boarding was horizontal, so that a small "un-get-at-able" attic was sealed above to catch the dust, the dead rats, and the heat.

We slept and bathed in one room, worked in another, and fed on the veranda on the leeward side. Simple though perfect domestic arrangements that should content the most élite.

A few days after our arrival at Mamfe, George and I were contentedly browsing on platefuls of rice and chicken with groundnuts, and gazing out at the night between the cascade of miniature waterfalls streaming from the pan roof above. It wasn't raining; it was pouring as it can do only in the tropics. It was, to be precise, the seventy-third hour that the elements had been giving vent to their pent-up emotions in this unmistakable manner. We were so pleased to have reached our destination and got unpacked without a single loss, that not even all this water could dispel our satisfaction.

The rice stowed neatly away in its appointed place, we leant back preparatory to a period of groaning. Then we noticed that several bats were silently flitting round the veranda in the angle formed by the match-board lining to the roof and the outside walls of the central living rooms. A multitude of insects had congregated there, attracted by the bright light.

We watched these bats flying round and round the house with such regularity that we could time their exact appearance round the corner. There were about half a dozen of them. This seemed to be a direct challenge which we groaningly accepted despite the rice and groundnuts.

Butterfly nets were lashed to long light poles and raised up to the angle of the roof. The bats continued to circle round and round the house. We waited half-way along a wall facing the corner around which they appeared. As they flashed by above us, we endeavoured to pop the net up at the psychological moment. Though some practice was required before we could judge their speed, soon we were very near the mark.

It then became apparent that the bats could slip through between the rim of the net (which was circular) and the roof-wall angle. We therefore lowered the nets and constructed angles in their rims to coincide with the corner of the roof. Assured of a capture, we again raised the nets.

Now the bats flew straight at the net, partly entered the mouth, then backslid out again; by a couple of deft stallings, like an airplane in an air-pocket, they squirmed round the bottom edge of the net and proceeded on their way round the house. It was obvious that whatever we put in their path they would be able to avoid with comparative ease. Exasperated, I loaded a shotgun, seated myself by the dinner table, and, to the great amazement of the kitchen staff and the detriment of the government's valuable roofing, fired both barrels at the further corner of the roof as soon as I saw a bat appear. Perhaps it is unnecessary to mention that I did not hit the bat, but blew an eight-inch hole clean through the match-boarding.

Two bats, however, were close enough to be thoroughly dazed by my performance. These were scooped into the nets as they fluttered amazedly about above us. Our first two bats were brought to earth, where they promptly fixed their needle-sharp teeth on my and George's fingers respectively.

Since we were guests of the government, we could not continue blowing the roof of the rest house away, a square foot at a time. It therefore became imperative to devise some other method of capturing our nightly visitors. This led to most interesting discoveries.

I had heard that bats had some marvellous mechanism by which they find their way through the air, and more particularly those parts that are cluttered up with obstructions. All the microcheiroptera have minute eyes, some even are totally blind, their eyes being reduced to pin-point dimensions and covered by skin. The ones we captured at our first attempt (*Hipposideros caffer* and *Nycteris arge*) had the smallest black beads totally concealed in the thick fur. Bats have been released in a confined space across and throughout which up to four hundred piano wires were stretched at all angles. The bats continued to fly indefinitely among them without ever so much as touching a wire with their wing tips either in bright light or in total darkness, even when what eyes they had were completely sealed over. By what method is this performed?

If a bat is caught, look at its face. This will probably give you quite a shock, but it is nevertheless worth an inspection. Bats' faces vary enormously, probably more so than any other animals'; few of them are straightforward visages and many are beyond the wildest nightmares of a deranged liver or fancies of the grotesque. The nose is often developed into a whole series of leaf-like structures one on top of another, and there are wrinkles, folds, and feelers of naked skin. One bat we found had a fleshy crucifix surrounded by a dozen complicated leaves spreading from its nose all over its face.

No less remarkable than the endless variety of noses are the extremes to which the ears go. These are, in the first place, often immense in proportion to the animal—I know one bat whose ears are very much larger than the whole animal itself. Inside the main ear there may be another pinna or false ear of almost any form. Some are exact replicas of the big ear, and the whole thing may be multiplied so that there appears to be a series of ears of diminishing size, one within the other. The eyes, as I have mentioned, are negligible quantities.

Those peculiar people who take an interest in bats have debated for many years as to whether these wonderful structures are the means by which the bat directs itself through the maze of piano wires or natural obstructions to its aerial passage. They seem to have decided that not only are the nose-leaves and ears the centre of a kind of super-tactile sensitivity but that the wing-membranes also serve this purpose. This sixth sense must in some way be connected with a power of touch so acute that the animal can feel objects before it actually comes in contact with them. This is not nearly so strange as it seems, if we do not judge all senses by our own, which are feebly developed to say the least. It is possible that in the case of the bats this sense is effected by minute increases in air pressure, or responds to electro-magnetic waves propagated by matter.

George and I had debated these interesting facts from every angle during the days that followed our first captures, having had such clear proof of their potentialities. As I lay in bed at night, the problem assumed gigantic proportions, until one night when, just after the light had been extinguished, I was galvanized into action by a material example of my mental speculations.

From within my mosquito net I saw a phantom form flutter momentarily across the rectangle of moonlight cast by the window opposite my bed. There was definitely a bat in the room. We held a rapid conference in the dark. The torch was unearthed and lighted, and disclosed not one but half a dozen bats flying round the room. As soon as the light came on, they streamed out of the window. This gave us the idea.

The bright paraffin lamp was set blazing near the window. Long pieces of string were attached to both doors. Members of the staff were crowded into the room, the window was closed, and the light extinguished. We then sat patiently in the dark; sure enough, bats began to enter almost at once, presumably in search of the insects that had been attracted by the light. We pulled the strings, which closed the doors with a bang. We were now sealed up with the bats. The lamp was relighted and our troubles began.

The room was approximately twenty feet square and fourteen feet high. There were five of us, all supplied with nets, and four bats. After twenty minutes, we had caught only one, although all four followed each other round and round the room in a wide figure eight, never deviating from their course except to avoid our nets, which feat they accomplished with maddening regularity. The whole business made one feel quite impotent. People have given me glowing accounts of capturing bats in butterfly nets over ponds or around a house in the open air; they must either be blatant liars or have operated in some other part of the world, because the average West African bat seems to be something of a flying ace.

These bats provided us with golden opportunities for observing the way in which they can avoid almost any object while on the wing. When we had at last captured them all, which was only accomplished by their becoming tired and hanging to the wall upside down, we tried the experiment of sealing over their eyes with tiny pieces of adhesive tape. This had not the least effect on their efficiency, but when we folded one of the ears downwards and attached its tip to the face, they all behaved in a most ludicrous and far from competent manner. The right ear caused them to gyrate in an anti-clockwise or left-handed direction with ever-increasing velocity, so that they eventually went into a violent spin in mid-air and slowly descended to earth like a whirling helicopter. The sealing of the left ear had an exactly contrary effect. Moreover, when the ears were released, the effects were still apparent for some time.

Other experiments affecting the nose-leaves and parts of the ears had very strange results, all of which seemed to prove conclusively that these organs are the centre of their balance- and direction-finding mechanism and that they function quite involuntarily. If the right ear be sealed, one would have supposed that the constant pressure on it would have been construed by the bat's nervous system as implying that an obstruction lay constantly to its right front. The animal would therefore keep veering to the left, exactly what we observed the little animals to do.

One evening lingers in my memory as being the first which I consciously realized was dry as opposed to wet. We had been in Africa for more than two months, during which time it had rained every day and often during the whole day. There had been weeks together without sunshine, so that animals skinned and stuffed had remained limp and damp as on the day when they were first prepared. It had been a most trying time. We had waited patiently for the rains to cease so that we could move out into the uncharted forests under canvas. We had so far been contenting ourselves with a detailed investigation of the commoner animals and those that have survived or taken up their abode among the semi-cultivated land and secondary forest around the settlements of man.

Sitting at work on the veranda facing the clearing of Mamfe station, I had an uninterrupted view of a great expanse of sky to the west. The sun began to set, flaming like a furnace behind a false skyline of dense, black clouds whose pillars and towers stood motionless, like a monstrous, shadowy mirage of New York's stately skyline. Above, the air was crystal-clear and depthless. Towards the disappearing day it remained delicately blue between great horizontal zones of pale, soft gold. As it towered above, the blue melted to glowing heliotrope, lilac, violet, and thence, to the east, into the indigos and the mysteries of the oncoming tropical night.

Work under these conditions was impossible and sacrilegious. The Africans, who had already discovered this, had melted away into the twilight without permission and without a sound. I followed suit and drifted out across the soft green grass, gazing up into the immensity of the sky with that hopeless yearning that all mortals feel when confronted with the immense calm of the evening heavens. I found Ben perched on a termites' nest facing the setting sun, his chocolate skin burnished with the reflection of the flaming glory. He just sat and stared and I was happy.

Here was an example of that much scorned type—the white man's African servant—who had, in addition, been subjected to the indignity and stifling stupor of a mission school. And yet, although he was born of a race that we are incessantly told can only be lazy or sensuous when not asleep, here he was sitting quietly enraptured by a sight that must after all have been as commonplace to him as a blaze of electric signs is to us.

"T'ick-ehn, it's very fine" was all he said. Then very mysteriously he spoke in his own language, enlarging upon the beauty of the scene, as I later discovered. I could almost feel a European "used to managing natives" at my elbow, whispering: "Damn it, boy, what infernal insolence!"

Under the dome of the sky we sat together in silence, watching and mentally recording the ever-changing flush of colours. The air was still except for a very distant drum throbbing in unison with the blood coursing through our veins, and an occasional croak issuing from a near-by, frog-infested ditch.

Yet, was that all? Every now and then I felt rather than heard an infinitesimally faint noise. Slowly these indescribable sounds became more pronounced until I could ascertain that they came from the sky above. Looking up, I could see nothing. Every so often, and ever more plainly now, rang out a faint, high-pitched "tit-trrrr." Then, all at once, Ben looked up and pointed out a black speck, fluttering and tumbling hither and thither. Bats!

As the night came on, the air became filled with "tit-trrrrs." The busy little animals circled slowly towards the earth. It was not until several days later that we obtained our first specimens of these bats, and then we received a great surprise.

They were large, powerfully built animals with relatively small wings, simple, rather pig-like faces, and almost naked bodies. The whole skin glistened with a pungent-smelling oil, while the flesh, which was dense and excessively heavy, oozed a similar substance for hours after death. Most strange of all were pocket-like pouches under the chin and directed forwards. On the skin at the back of these pouches (that is to say, on the throat) a nipple connected with a gland was situated and, clinging to this, we found on several occasions a peculiar parasitic fly which has no wings.

These bats (*Saccolaimus peli*) belonged to that aggravating class that flies in the open air. They were the first we encountered.

After several weeks' intensive trapping around the camp, we appeared to have more or less cleared up or frightened away all the animals. Trap lines were thus being moved to another locality, because, with that particular method of collecting, a practice known as "completing a circle" is employed. This means that one selects a circle and works inwards from it to the camp, so that all animals, to get away, must either pass through the ring of traps, or congregate in the end around the camp. When the traps reach the borders of the camp, a final swarm of animals appears. After they are collected or have escaped, the whole area is played out.

With a view to selecting a new ground I left camp for a day's outing by myself, in order to cover a wide area and quietly investigate its possibilities to the best of my knowledge and ability. These days alone were most profitable, as we had discovered, not because we wanted in any way to be away from each other, but because the absence of conversation and freedom to wander wherever the spirit moved one brought to one's notice an extraordinary number of new facts and phenomena.

On this particular occasion I set out towards a large "lake" of grass that had been reported to me as existing to the south-east of the camp. I chose this as a starting point, since I was rather keen not to get lost in the forest again as I had done only a short time before. Entering the dense forest beyond this open grass area, I was rather surprised to find that the ground descended very abruptly. Before I had gone far, I saw at a distance below me the glimmer of sun reflected from water. By some exigencies of local geological structure, the Mainyu River that we knew so well elsewhere had got twisted up into a knot and meandered off into the jungle, to appear here flowing in an exactly contrary direction to its main course. This we discovered later by following it downstream. I at once decided that this was to be our future happy hunting ground and the site of our next camp.

The whole structure of this gorge will one day prove of the greatest interest to geologists. It is a natural model of the great Rift Valley of East Africa. Following a subsidence or a great release of pressure, the land surface has simply collapsed along a central line now occupied by the river. The "country" rock, as it is called, has fractured all along into gargantuan cubes which, with the general subsidence, have shifted about so that they may be likened to the lumps of sugar in a bowl. Between them and under them are almost endless narrow clefts and passages leading into the side of the gorge, along its face, and out again into the open air.

The whole area was covered with dense forest. As I began exploring the level, sandy floors of the street-like passageways between the great chunks of rock, the light became fainter and fainter. There was practically no bare rock at all, every inch of its surface where there was any light being covered with smooth, soft, bright-green moss. The place was like a buried city, silent, mysterious, and eerie.

Turning an abrupt corner, I came upon a wide sunken arena overhung by a tall cliff. In the very dim light under this natural arch I saw an endless stream of bats passing to and fro from the mouth of a cave at one end to a monstrous horizontal crack at the other. The whole roof of this archway was a dense mass of sleeping bats, suspended upside down in serried ranks. The ground below was covered to a depth of more than a foot with their excrement, which had disintegrated under the influence of the weather and resulted in a mass of broken remains of uncountable millions of insects.

In this stratum of bat guano, I found a number of peculiar insects and a small bright-red millepede that I have never seen anywhere else.

By a mere fluke I had a torch in my collecting bag; with its aid I entered the cave. Though the mouth was just wide enough to permit my squeezing through, it expanded somewhat within and rose to a great height above. On both walls, as far as the light of the torch penetrated, bats were hanging or crawling about. The air was literally filled with them. The floor here was covered with guano to such a depth that I could not reach the earth below even by digging with a trapper's friend!

I was so amazed at the whole place and its denizens that I forgot all time and scrambled onwards into the depths, following the endless streams of bats that hurried along and round the corners just as busy traffic does in the streets of a great city.

Turning a corner, I was confronted by a blank wall. The bats were all passing upwards and disappearing over the top of a miniature cliff. I clambered up with some difficulty, to find that I was on top of one of the great blocks of rock. The next one above it was held away by a third block's edge far to the right. This left a horizontal gallery that stretched far ahead, beyond which I could see a large chamber. Into this I eventually emerged complete with gun and all other equipment, after a few uncomfortable minutes of wriggling through, all the time obsessed with that ridiculous but persistent impression that the roof would suddenly cave in and pin me in a not quite dead condition where nobody would ever in any circumstances find me.

The place I now found myself in was much larger than any that I had previously passed through. It was nearly the size of one whole block and almost exactly cubic in shape. The air was as dry as a desert sandstorm; whether it was due to this or the pungent smell of the bats I do not know, but my lips became hard and cracked in a surprisingly short time and my eyes began to water. The roof was altogether free from resting bats, but on the walls were what I at first supposed to be a great number of them. Some being very low down, I put down my collecting bag and gun, and advanced with the torch and a net only, to try to effect a capture.

As I approached the side, however, these things that I had supposed to be bats vanished as if by magic. One minute they were there; the next they were gone. By the time that I was close enough to the rock face to be able to see what they were, had they still been there, there was not one in sight. This was most perplexing.

Deciding that the light must disturb them, if they were not mere shadows, I put out the torch and crept forward to another wall. When I judged that I was close enough, I suddenly flashed on the torch again. A perfectly horrible vision met my eyes. The whole wall was covered with enormous whip-scorpions, crouching and leering at me. Only for a second did they remain, then, like a flash, they all shot out and away in all directions, disappearing into paper-thick crevices with a loathsome rustle.

Their behaviour and appearance are, as I have remarked before, revolting in the extreme, but they were of such unusual size and colour that for the sake of science I steeled myself to a systematic hunt with all the low cunning of a cave man in search of food. Eventually I captured a few after many misses, once being subjected to the nerve-shattering odiousness of having one of them scuttle over my bare arm in escaping from the net.

After this experience I deemed science had sufficient material to gloat over, and I devoted my attention to an examination of the ground for other invertebrates. The bats were entering by the same route as I had done. After crossing the gallery diagonally, they disappeared through one of three vertical fissures, though most of them streamed into and out of the left-hand one, which was the widest. Across the floor below the line of their flight stretched a ridge of their droppings, showing that they excrete while on the wing. Elsewhere the floor was covered with silver sand and spotlessly clean. Only in one corner of the room, remote from the bat highway, was there a pile of small, pellet-like dung.

Examining this, I at once noticed that it was not composed of the crushed remains of insects as was that of the other bats. It resembled more the droppings of a rabbit, although there seemed to be a few small bones projecting from it. This prompted me to search the ceiling above to ascertain where this might be descending from. All I could see, however, was a small cleft above; so, taking the shotgun, I managed by degrees to lever myself up the sharp angle of the corner and eventually peered over the brink into the cleft.

As I switched on the torch, I went cold all over and felt as if my skin were wrinkling up everywhere preparatory to splitting and falling off in one piece. The only alternative to looking into the crevice a second time was falling down backwards. Therefore, after summoning up courage, I switched on the torch again and took a second look. The result was just as bad.

In the mouth of the hole not eighteen inches from my face, four large greenish-yellow eyes stared unblinkingly at me. They were so large that I thought involuntarily of some dead human thing, but the face that projected in front of them soon dispelled this impression. That face is indescribable, and I resort to a detailed reproduction of it alongside. In addition there were clammy groping fingers all muddled up with endless flaps of wrinkled naked skin. I pushed in the net and made a random scoop; then I slipped and crashed to the bottom of the cave.

The gun, luckily, fell in the soft sand, and I retained hold of the net in which a huge hammer-headed bat (*Hypsignathus monstrosus*) was struggling. My left leg was emitting piercing pains and both wrists were quite numbed. There followed an awful period during which I tried to kill the bat in the net and nursed my leg and arms, making, I am afraid, a great deal of noise about it. At last I got the animal under control and chloroformed in the "killer," and then set about gathering together the wreckage. When I came to the gun, my wrists were still numb, but being anxious to make sure that there was no sand choking the barrel, I foolishly tried to open the breech. I am not exactly certain what happened; anyway, both barrels went off almost at once and the gun shot partly out of my hand.

At the same moment the light went out.

There was a period of tremendous echoing, then the whole of this eerie subterranean world seemed to give way, starting with a gentle "swussssh" and culminating in a rattling roar. Things fell down on all sides; choking dust filled the air; while I groped for the torch, hundreds of bats wheeled around my head screaming and twittering.

HAMMER-HEADED BAT (Hypsignathus monstrosus)

The torch would not light; for some maddening reason it was not forming a proper contact. I had to sit down and take the batteries out in the dark. I pulled out the metal strips on the ends and procured a flash of light by holding on the screw cap at the back of the container. In my excitement I could not for the life of me get this screw onto the thread. Finally I had to light a match, but before I could see anything, the flame went greenish-blue and quickly died. Other matches did the same.

I had just discovered that they burnt better at a higher level when, with an awful crash, a shower of earth cascaded down from my right side and covered my feet and most of my equipment, which was lying on the floor. There was a wild scramble to retrieve all my possessions and move to a bit of clearer ground, but every time I bent down, the match went out. There was obviously some gas or lack of gas that killed a flame near the floor. I therefore concentrated on fixing the torch. At long last it lit up.

It was less use than a car headlight in a dense mist, because the air was filled with clouds of billowing dust from which a very much startled bat periodically emerged. Groping forward, festooned with gun, collecting bag, net, and torch, I tried to locate the wall with the cleft through which I had gained an entrance, but I soon lost my sense of direction. Then I stumbled across the ridge of bats' dung. This I followed up until it disappeared under a great scree of fine dry earth which was still being added to from above. After further fumbling I found the cleft; the dust was so dense that I could not see more than a few feet into it. This was, however, quite sufficient really to disturb me.

The cleft was choked with earth and rubble. Slowly it dawned on me that the percussion of the shots had released all kinds of pent-up things and perhaps even shifted the roof, as I had imagined might happen through natural causes.

By this time the dust had begun to clear considerably and the rumblings and droppings had ceased. I trekked back to the other side of the cave and tried each of the three exits. The largest, upon which I based my hopes, narrowed quickly, then plunged downward into a low, uninviting crevice. One of the others was too narrow to permit the passage of my head, while the third, although very small, seemed to continue endlessly. Its floor descended rapidly, however, and I soon discovered that the air was very bad a few feet down—matches hardly lit at all. I had therefore to return to the central cave from which I felt almost certain there were no other exits. As the dust was by now less thick, I determined to go all round and make certain.

There proved to be a hopeful-looking chimney in one corner, but try as I would, my left leg steadfastly refused to assist me to climb! This was rendered even more exasperating by the fact that a piece of burning paper thrown upwards to its mouth was instantly sucked up out of sight never to return, which all went to show that the passage had some connexion with the outer world. Burning bits of note-book were then applied to the three exits. In one the flame promptly went out, in another it just wilted, and only in the narrowest one did it sail away into the distance, burning merrily. Such a result might, of course, have been predicted!

It then struck me that the choked entrance might not be all choked, so, scrambling along the ledge formed by the long horizontal mouth of this, I peered among the piles of earth that now clogged it, pushing small pieces of burning paper into any gaps or hole that remained. About two-thirds of the way down to the right the paper left my hand and blew straight into my face. I could feel a small draught. The hole was very low and descended towards the right, whereas the part of this gigantic crack through which I had come further up had distinctly sloped upwards out of the square chamber. There was fresh air coming in, so, provided it was not too small, it seemed the only feasible exit. I accordingly packed everything into the collecting bag, including the stock of the gun, wrapped the gun-barrel in the muslin bag of the net to prevent its getting scratched, crammed my felt hat onto my head for the same reason, and, holding the torch in my right hand, committed myself to the depths and the will of Allah.

Progress was slow and at one period extremely painful, for the ceiling—being the flat underside of a giant tilted cube—gradually descended until there was room for me to squeeze through only with the greatest difficulty. This effort I had to make, because I could reach for and feel the angular edge of the ceiling cube just beyond. This edge was as sharp as the angle on a small pack of cigarettes, though the block of rock above must have weighed thousands of tons. Through this slit I must get, and it was a struggle in no way made easier by having a now more or less useless left leg and also having to get the collecting bag over my head in order to push it through before me. How I envied those beastly *Amblypygi!*

Once through, I found myself in a long wide corridor again immaculately carpeted with silver sand. Having by now lost all sense of direction, I set off to the left, where I was soon involved in a tumbled mass of immense angular boulders. To climb over them was a little more than I felt prepared to attempt, so I dived in and tried to find a way through. This led me into a tunnel that smelt

HORSESHOE-NOSED BAT (Hipposideros sandersoni)

strongly and vaguely familiar. Before I had time to think what the cause of it could be, a rasping grunt echoed out from its depths; realizing at once that I had walked voluntarily into a leopard's private quarters, I lost absolutely no time at all in passing back through those boulders as if I were a sandworm brought up to perform such feats. The only course now was to try the other way, as I had no desire to meet a leopard, and even less to fire at one with a shotgun in the depths of the earth, considering what had occurred after the last cannonade.

The other end was a perfectly smooth blank wall. I began to feel rather desperate, a thing one should not do in well-regulated adventures. The feeling was nevertheless sufficiently insistent to call for a cigarette. How I thanked everything, not least myself, that I had cigarettes!

While seated on the sand smoking, feeling sorry for myself, and recounting a lot of things I should like to have done, I played my torch hither and thither over the opposite wall. It was only after a long time that it dawned on me that I was gazing at great patches of green moss. Even after this it was a long time, during which I re-packed my equipment, bandaged a knee, and smoked another ciga-rette, before my idiot brain put two and two together and arrived at the simple fact that green moss meant sunlight. Then all at once this fact penetrated my silly head and I realized that I had never yet looked at the roof. I flashed my torch upwards and saw a line of green branches dangling down into the cleft. During my subterranean meanderings night had come— I was actually standing in the open air.

Putting the gun together and loading it against a chance en-counter with the inhabitant of the boulders, I advanced on his do-main. After some exertion I managed to climb up over the boulders to arrive among the roots of the trees near the bottom of the gorge.

Two hours later I was back in camp, sore, temporarily crippled, and very thirsty.

I have mentioned so far our introduction to five West African bats. We collected during our stay around Mamfe no less than twenty-five species, though most of these were represented by only one or two specimens.

Whenever we smoked trees in the high forest, the first things to come out were bats. They emerged around the summit, fluttering about and trying to regain an entrance, until they decided it was too warm and rocketed off into the surrounding forest. When we did eventually reach some of these with the guns, they turned out to be of three species, two of which were closely allied to the two species we had caught in the rest house at Mamfe. The third (*Hip-posideros cyclops*) was something entirely new.

This was a stout animal of moderate dimensions covered with

thick, long, rather woolly hair of brindled silver-grey and dark brownish-grey colour. The eyes, set in a most saturnine face, were large for a bat, the nose-leaf was a flat, more or less simple circle, and the lips were rather taut, so that the sharp teeth were visible. But the ears gave the whole face a very startling appearance. Almost as long as the body, they tapered to fine points, besides being corrugated throughout their length.

We kept alive several of these that had fallen upon the wire netting dazed by the smoke. During the day they hung upside down as all good bats should; in the evening they began to stir and climbed down the side of the cage. They then walked about the floor on their wings, supported by the fingers, pointing backwards and upwards. When they prepared to take to the air either from the ground or the side of the cage, they thrust their heads forward and flapped their great ears just as if they were an accessory pair of wings. The arms then took up the motion in rhythm and the animal was on the wing.

These bats, which slept in trees by day, came to us with greater ease than any of the others, provided they were within the range of the gun. As almost every tree housed a few, we gradually accumulated quite a number.

One of the two species that we obtained in the Mamfe rest house (*Hipposideros caffer*) was small and grey in colour, with small, rather pointed ears. Another variety of this species made up the swarms that inhabited the caves in the Mainyu Gorge, and another variety came from hollow trees in the forest. When staying at Ikom further down the river, we again converted the house into a bat trap and obtained another variety of this common type. This was an exceptionally beautiful little animal having bluish-black wing- and tail-membranes and ears. The fur covering the rest of the body was long, silky, and of a rich reddish-orange colour. This is the only bat I have ever handled that emitted a long-drawn-out whistle, a noise to which I can find no reference in any literature upon the subject.

There was still another form of this bat that we met with in a rather odd manner.

Mamfe Division, which has an area almost exactly equal to that of the whole island of Jamaica, has only one road. This is about twenty miles in length and extends from the station towards the east, where it terminates at a fine steel bridge of three spans which abuts at its farther end onto a solid wall of virgin jungle without so much as a native path leading from it. This road and bridge were constructed by the public works department as the commencement of a projected trade route to carry motor traffic from the hinterland of Bamenda down to the British ports of southern Nigeria. The financial depression, yellow fever, which accounted for a dozen Europeans, and the fact that a score of large rivers flowing from north to south were overlooked when drawing up plans, killed the project, which had, in any case, been started in the middle. Its main use, therefore, is that two Ford trucks, and occasionally the remains of an Austin-7 that have been brought up the river on a "launch" during the rainy season, can be employed for the first day's trek to the east of Mamfe. This was the one direction in which we never had cause to go, so our acquaintance with it was confined to strolls in the evening and an occasional joy ride in the Ford truck with the hospitable district commissioner.

We had noticed that this man-made canyon through the forest was a great place for bats. Towards dusk they appeared either flying high in the air, as they must do all over the forest, although they cannot be seen elsewhere, or darting back and forth from the shadow of the trees on one side of the road to that of the trees on the other. Closer investigation disclosed the fact that bats came out along this road in the evening at a much earlier hour than elsewhere. The apparent reason for this was the presence of a number of large drains or culverts running under the road at intervals. The bats used these as a dark passage between the gloom of the trees on both sides of the road.

Having ascertained this fact, we laid plans for catching them. As we had been away working very hard in the less accessible parts of the forest for some time, and the birthday of one of our number was approaching, we reckoned that there was ample excuse for a little harmless frivolity. Into this scheme the only other two European inhabitants of Mamfe (at that time) entered heartily. We organized a fancy-dress bat shoot.

After tea the Ford truck came to the door of the district officer's house. The party foregathered in the most amazing assortment of improvised fancy dress: "le sportsman très gallique"; "the Yankee in the tropics"; a valiant edition of General Göring clad to chase the Polish boar; and a "not-very-sporting English squire." The African truck-driver wore a sky-blue cap and a shirt, so that we were not quite certain whether he was entering into the spirit of the thing, being simply chic according to local custom, or behaving in a manner that called for reprimand on the grounds of incivility. The only truly normal members of the party were our five skinners, who came in their ordinary uniforms of grey shirts and white shorts, bearing guns and nets.

The party set out for the road some three miles into the forest and there deployed, taking up positions over the various drains. Quite soon the bats began to appear. A fusillade was let loose, but the tiny animals are so swift that one saw only a vague flash as they shot across the space separating the entrance to the culverts from the neighbouring wall of the forest. Nobody secured a direct hit, but Mr. Gorges, the district officer, who was an extremely good shot, on two occasions aimed sufficiently close to upset the bats' sense of direction. As animals fluttered around in a circle, Bassi, who was stationed at one end of his drain, dived in with a net and made a capture of the first. On the second occasion, however, the bat managed to flutter into the drain and Bassi went in after it. As he did so, a perfect flight of bats came out of the other end, and I joined Mr. Gorges in an attempt to pot them. This we continued to do quite merrily until all of a sudden Bassi's nut-brown head appeared amid the flying targets. By some fluke we were not firing at that instant. He had crawled right through the drain.

This gave us a new idea. We climbed down into the ditch and lay in position to look down the drains. As soon as a number of bats had entered from the other end, flown towards us, and sensed our presence, we fired a shot. We never once hit a bat, but they were so bewildered by the percussion of the shot that they came to rest on the roof of the drain and we sent the Africans in to collect them alive.

This resulted in the capture of a great number of bats which turned out to be this other variety of *Hipposideros caffer*. They were all some shade of brown and much smaller than the types we had collected elsewhere.

This method of collecting was indeed child's play compared to the highly technical skill and great patience which George devoted to the shooting of another species. These were the smallest bats I have ever seen; in actual bulk they must be the smallest of all mammals, despite the claims of the pygmy squirrel (*Nannosciurus*) to that distinction. The trunk of this animal when skinned was about the size of a bumble bee and a good deal smaller than the last joint of a small woman's little finger.

As I have already mentioned, George, when in the deep forest, adopted the method of sitting in concealment and waiting for the passing of the animals. When thus employed one evening, he noticed far up in the sky above the trees some very small bats flying about in a manner quite unknown among these animals, so that at first he mistook them for swallows. Deciding that he must discover what they were, with more than praiseworthy ambition he set himself the task of shooting some, a problem which I should have judged quite hopeless. However, he eventually found a place where the ground rose sufficiently for him to gain a clear view over some trees. There he patiently waited for several evenings until one of the bats happened to fly low enough to be within gun-shot range. By this painstaking method he obtained two specimens of this extremely rare species (*Glauconycteris beatrix*).

These animals were dark steel-grey in colour with long slender wings and simple noses like a dog's.

Another bat, *Rhinolophus landeri*, which we collected and which also proves to be very rare, was represented by four specimens. When living with the friendly peoples of the northern mountains we had a kind of working contract with the hunter named Afa, as I have already mentioned. One day I asked him for bats, indicating my wishes by exhibiting a stuffed specimen.

"Ah," he said in his own language, "I know where one sleeps."

This was such an astonishing remark that I was not sure that my rather sketchy knowledge of the language combined with the interpreter were not letting me down. However, Afa disappeared and did not return until just before dusk. When he did so, he extracted a live bat from his gun-powder wallet. It was this species, covered in silky grey hair, with a tuft of red bristles in each armpit, and bearing a small fleshy crucifix on its nose.

Apparently he had walked, or rather climbed, about nine miles to a tiny cave which I afterwards visited, where he had seen this animal hanging asleep some days previously when sheltering there from a storm.

Two other rare species, one new to science, came to us quite by chance. They could not be distinguished apart by colour and size alone, both being bluish-grey and small. Only their nose-leaves and ears showed them to be quite different. One, a new species of *Hipposideros*, was shot by the district officer in his house; the other, named *Rhinolophus alcyone*, landed at my feet after I had shot at a squirrel in a tree near a plantation. One pellet had passed right through the head. I had never seen this bat before.

Just before returning home, we paid a visit to N'ko, a large village lower down the Cross River. Here we met with extraordinary hospitality at the hands of the local inhabitants. They had never seen more than one white man at a time before, never heard a gramophone, and, I believe, never imagined that such a thing as a bug-hunter existed, especially attended by nearly forty retainers, to which number our staff of skinners, trappers, collectors, and household servants had by that time swelled.

When we announced that we required local animal life and

would pay for it, the whole populace disappeared into the neighbouring bush and was soon returning in an endless stream bearing every imaginable kind of animal.

Later that evening a tribal dance was organized for our entertainment. In the headdresses of the various ju-ju figures I spotted the dried remains of a species of bat that I did not know. I inquired of the chief whether he could procure for me some live specimens of this animal. He seemed morose. After some effort I discovered that the animal was regarded with considerable veneration from the point of view of a fertility ju-ju. A monetary contribution to the privy purse, however, combined with the fact, soon observed by the chief, that I had almost as virulent a dislike of Christians as he had, prompted him to dispatch a number of small boys into the jungle.

They returned some time later with handfuls of fluttering little bats (a species of the genus known as *Eptesicus*), among which was an albino. I subsequently stumbled upon the "mine" from which these bats had been obtained. It was a small ju-ju tabernacle not more than two hundred yards behind the hut where we were living. Under the eaves of the tabernacle countless bats were sleeping, covering the altar with their guano, which had been cleared away except within an area that had an outline representing a gigantic bat with outstretched wings.

The frugivorous bats or megacheiroptera are mostly larger animals, some in the Oriental region having a wing span exceeding four feet. We obtained eight species of this group, four of which were, however, of very small size. They do not have nose-leaves and their ears are usually simple, like those of other animals. Their heads, nevertheless, show an amazing variety of form; one was exactly like a calf's, another like a mastiff's, and the hammer-headed bat's more like a horse's than anything one could imagine.

In the mountains of Assumbo we pitched a camp on one occasion in a little tongue of grass that descended into a patch of mountain forest. This was Camp III, from which we carried out most of our investigations upon the wild life of these weird grass-covered mountains. It was a desolate place miles from anywhere in the clear still air, raised far above the teeming life of the tropical forests, and completely cut off from the rest of the world. As far as the eye could see, long grass waved in the sighing wind as shimmering flushes crossed and recrossed it like surf on a wide beach. Our little encampment nestled in a hollow backed by the peculiar tangled trees found at this altitude, through which rippled and tinkled a broad, crystal-clear brook.

There were only two ways of penetrating this mountain forest: first, by following strange little paths made by large buck, or, secondly, by wading along the beds of rivers and streams. We passed by both these ways, though usually along the main stream in the evening.

This was a somewhat difficult feat as I will endeavour to explain. The clear water swirled along a bed, now deep and narrow, now wide and shallow, but everywhere strewn and piled with boulders both great and small. Only occasionally were there deep, still pools between perpendicular rock walls where the cold water lay oily and brown. There were endless rapids where cascades gushed between boulders the size of a house, and beyond them great, wide, boulder-strewn fields where the water all but disappeared, being subdivided into a hundred thousand tiny trickles. This made a passage down the bed of the little river rather difficult. Nevertheless, it remained the lesser evil, because the banks were both impenetrable masses of vegetation. Even those who know the tropical forests and mangroves of the great tropical deltas would be confounded by the true mountain forest. It is a growth found nowhere else but on elevated areas in the equatorial regions.

It seems that in these regions there is a constant battle between the trees and the high altitude for mastery. The altitude usually wins, and the trees are replaced by grass, giant heather, or some other growth. Occasionally the reverse is the result, and then the trees make up for lost ground. They grow in all directions—upward, outward, and downward—into one solid, tangled, matted conglomeration. A man might force his way through a gorse bush but never through this African plexus. It was impossible to follow the river along its banks.

During the first few days at this camp, I had been employed throughout the twenty-four hours in and around the camp. The ground was uneven; tornadoes blew up; houses for the staff took an excessive time to construct in the absence of sufficient straight bush-sticks; hunters kept calling; I nursed a bad foot; and all the time the "office" work piled up. The Duke had been sent back to the base camp, as I have told above, his legs covered with festering, two-inch sores, called "tropical ulcers." A skinner and one of the household staff had had to go with him to minister to his wants, not to mention half a dozen of the Munchi carriers—backbone of our little empire.

We were short-staffed, overloaded with work, unable to obtain food, and in the throes of pitching a new camp. I therefore had little time to inspect the countryside.

Perhaps George was more efficient with his half of the work on hand, or perhaps it was because his department was the frogs and reptiles, expeditions to collect which we were naturally unable to organize at this juncture; at any rate, he alone was able to get away during the first few evenings and inspect the neighbourhood with a gun.

He came back with ever more remarkable accounts of what he had seen, including details about some fruit bats that sounded like fish stories. As soon as our house was in order, I put myself in George's hands and he conducted me to the bed of the river which I had not previously seen.

It was a peculiar evening. The sky was neither overcast nor clear. The sun shone somewhere to the west behind the mountains, but the sky above did not reflect any of its glory, remaining a pallid, colourless sheet above our heads. The light was bad even before true dusk began to fall.

We entered the archway formed by the trees over the river where it was narrow, and waded downstream for some minutes.

The water here was waist-deep, the boulders no larger than a man's head. Eventually we emerged into the open. The river widened and huge rocks appeared out of its ruffled surface. Upon these George advised we should take up our positions.

No sooner had we done so, than a number of large fruit bats commenced a series of reconnaissance flights from above the trees on either side. One had the impression that they were flying there just out of sight all the time and merely came to peep over and see what we were up to. Near at hand were some singularly inedible-looking trees that proved, however, to be a source of unaccountable attraction to the bats. Into these they slipped from the far side. The first that we knew of their arrival was a noisy lip-smacking and munching noise which drifted down to us. As we remained quiet, others came flying up the fairway over the river to join their kind.

We fired at them, spraying the shot in their paths. One landed on a patch of dry stream bed. When retrieved, it turned out to be a very large specimen of the hammer-headed bat, the species that I had previously encountered sleeping in the caves by the Mainyu River. A second one was quite different. This animal would probably have been termed a flying fox, though its fur was thin and like polished brass, stiff and shining. A third fell in the water almost at my feet.

Leaving my gun on the rock, I stepped down to try to catch it before it drifted into the main current and was carried away. I stepped on something hard and firm, but before I knew where I was, this thing suddenly came to life and lunged forward. I was flung sideways into the main stream. Here the water, though quiet, was deep and very swift under the surface. Since there could not have been crocodiles in this river, all I could think was that I had trodden on a tortoise. Swept forward by the current, I was soon involved in the rapids among great boulders. The bat disappeared. I had to concentrate on half swimming, half floundering back to my perch.

Suddenly George let out a shout: "Look out!" and I looked.

Then I let out a shout also and instantly bobbed down under the water, because, coming straight at me only a few feet above the water was a black thing the size of an eagle. I had only a glimpse of its face, yet that was quite sufficient, for its lower jaw hung open and bore a semicircle of pointed white teeth set about their own width apart from each other.

When I emerged, it was gone. George was facing the other way blazing off his second barrel. I arrived dripping on my rock and we looked at each other.

"Will it come back?" we chorused.

And just before it became too dark to see, it came again, hurtling back down the river, its teeth chattering, the air "shss-shssing" as it was cleft by the great, black, dracula-like wings. We were both off our guard, my gun was unloaded, and the brute made straight for George. He ducked. The animal soared over him and was at once swallowed up in the night.

We scrambled back into the river and waded home to camp, where we found a number of local hunters waiting with their catches laid out for sale. They had walked miles from their hunting grounds to do business.

"What kind of a bat is it," I asked, "that has wings like this (opening my arms) and is all black?"

"Olitiau!" somebody almost screamed, and there was a hurried conference in the Assumbo tongue.

"Where you see this beef?" one old hunter inquired amid dead silence.

"There," I told the interpreter, pointing to the river.

With one accord the hunters grabbed up their guns and ran out of camp, straight across country towards the village, leaving their hard-earned goods behind them.

Next day the old chief suddenly appeared in camp with the whole village council. He had walked miles from the village capital. He was concerned. Shyly he asked whether we needed to stay just there; wouldn't the hills beyond interest us, he wanted to know.

No, nothing but here exactly would suit us, we explained.

The chief was sad; the elders were uneasy. They went back to the village. We stayed at Camp III, but we never saw the bat again and never received the spoils of any more hunters' trips.

16

Mosquitoes and Other Parasites;
Insect Parasites; Chameleons; Frogs;
Podogona; Birds

YOU have probably wondered why, when speaking of the unusual vermin that are found around Mamfe station, I omitted to mention certain rather "obvious" creatures that are essentially verminous. People who know the tropics well may have spotted several.

The only adequate reason that I can offer is that the list of vermin could be extended almost indefinitely and fill a whole book. The ones that have been mentioned were chosen because they have for the most part taken up their abode in such surroundings as are a direct result of man's deforestation and other activities, or have actually been introduced into the country by him. The others, perhaps more verminous in some cases, are animals indigenous to the country, so that clearing away the trees merely lays them bare. These animals are apt to pop up anywhere as soon as one makes a little pool of sunlight in the great ocean of greenery. They are the "local" counterparts of the creatures you met in the opening chapters.

Most outstanding of all is the mosquito. This is misleading because the mosquito "isn't": one should say "mosquitoes are." There are many different kinds. In England we call some kinds gnats, but unfortunately not always the same kinds. An old lady in Yorkshire has a different idea of a gnat from a young Cornishman's. In Norway within the Arctic Circle they have mosquitoes (or gnats, as you will) that any self-respecting Englishman would count as daddy-long-legs. They bite in proportion.

In Africa there are three types or genera that matter out of a considerable host of such two-winged flies. These are: *Culex*, harmless as far as we know from the present state of our information, but a magnificent biter; *Anopheles*, a small speckled chap that stands on his head and exchanges malarial parasites for a liberal quota of your blood; and, lastly, *Stegomyia*—striped like a zebra—the dread carrier of the annihilating yellow-fever virus.

Mamfe was liberally supplied with all three. Every African had endemic yellow fever. The year before we arrived, a *Stegomyia* hopped from one of the Africans to a white man who had not got it and the result was that everybody in the station (except the doctor, a man who was already ill, and another who wasn't actually there) died within a week. In addition, several hundred natives were swept away by "malaria with jaundice," which is only a cautious way of saying yellow fever. We met a few *Stegomyia* and their breeding ground was traced to an old tin lying on the roof of a near-by house.

It is useless to mention *Anopheles*. There it is; it bites everybody as soon as he goes to the coast; everybody gets malaria. We were no exceptions. *Culex* is always around in various forms but one place stands out in my memory.

Obubra is the station capital of the division of that name which lies next to Mamfe but is in Nigeria. Its bungalows are dotted about a low flat hill standing alone in the middle of an immense swamp through which the Cross River meanders. When we were there for a few days there was a full moon. Looking out of the house at night, one would have supposed there to be a dense, white ground mist about one foot in depth. This was mosquitoes. Luckily they were all *Culex*, because they bit so furiously and so continuously that even our African staff came to us for an advance on their wages with which to purchase mosquito netting.

There are, however, more interesting and even more nasty insects than mosquitoes. If you have ever stood in a forest glade in England or America or any other country for that matter, you may have seen orange-coloured flies stationary in mid-air, like helicopters, their wings vibrating with incredible speed. These hover-flies are often of a genus named *Chrysops* which has some relatives in Africa that are blood-sucking in habits. These horrors often have minute parasitic worms in their heads which escape onto one's flesh at the moment when the fly punctures one's skin. It then bores its own hole and after a series of gruesome expeditions into one's organs, growing all the time, it produces various forms of loathsome disease. The worm is a *Filaria* of some sort, which gets stuck in one's lymphatic ducts, producing elephantiasis, or creates a painful lump on the back of the hand—Calabar swelling—which recurs at irregular intervals. There is another *Filaria* which arrives in the same way and disports itself by passing across one's eye between the transparent skin (conjunctiva) that covers it and the cornea below.

Afa came to us one morning in Assumbo and announced that he had "breeze for eye." He need not have told us, because there was a great blister within which the thread-like worm could be seen crinkled back and forth. As we did not carry surgical instruments, we had to make the best of it and be quick about it.

We sterilized the slenderest of our skinning scalpels and a pair of forceps. We then burned a piece of rubber and dipped a sharpened match stick in the melted latex. Seizing Afa's face, the eyeball was slit, whereupon a lot of liquid fell out so that we thought we had opened the entire eye. It was a nasty moment, during which we very seriously doubted our knowledge of human anatomy. However, the fluid cleared away exposing the worm. This adhered to the rubber and we began winding as slowly as our shaking hands would allow us. At first, worm came from both directions, but soon only that emerging from the outside of the eye was attached to both the stick and poor Afa. My knowledge of tropical medicine did not include the length of a *Filaria* and I was therefore quite amazed at what came out, but despite this and the extreme fragility of the parasite, it came out whole—an examination under a powerful lens showed two unbroken ends. Afa never moved during the whole operation. In a few days he appeared to be quite all right—at least sufficiently so to shoot a monkey.

Let us turn from these unpleasantnesses, which can be augmented by any text-book on tropical medicine, and revert to the horrors of the insect world pure and simple.

Almost every house of any standing in this part of Africa has the underside of its roof adorned with a number of little papery bags suspended on little, very slender cords about two inches in length. As one sits within the house, one is occasionally disturbed by the low hum of a passing insect of grotesque appearance. This is a type of wasp, metallic blue or black and gold in colour, with a tiny, spherical abdomen joined to the thorax and head by a long, slender portion no thicker than a pin. Some of these are the owners of the suspended bags.

Others are the builders of small compact fortifications that cling to the walls and corners. These are made of an earthy substance manufactured by the insects which is as hard as concrete. If you observe these wasp-like creatures carefully as they pass by you on their business, you will notice that on their return journeys they often carry trailing bundles. Capture the creature and you will find that it is transporting an apparently dead spider clasped in its long legs. If you then climb aloft, chisel the nest off the wall, and open it, you will discover a number of lozenge-shaped cells, some completely sealed up, others filled with their grim contents but still open, and others only partly built.

These cells are filled with spiders, in a remarkable state of suspended animation, and wasps' eggs, and are eventually sealed up. This horrid food is thus stored for the young wasp hopeful, which gobbles it up, grows in exact proportion, and then pupates.

We collected the nests because these wasps are the finest spider collectors in the world. From them we got hundreds of spiders, including species that had never been seen before. Some seemed to recover partially when released from their death-cells, but all were as perfectly preserved as if they had been in a refrigerator. Is this fluid that the wasps inject into their victims the answer to our quest for "suspended animation"?

There was a small cage which I had constructed from the remains of a packing case and some wire netting. It was my pride.

One day a man brought a chameleon in a gloomy brown mood, which was forthwith placed in the cage. Being the first chameleon that we had seen in Africa, we subjected it to a number of uncomfortable experiments with a view to discovering whether or not it would react as such animals are supposed to do and turn through a variety of colours. Apart from a few peevish green spots, however, it refused to produce anything startling in the way of colour change. This was so disappointing that we lost interest in the beast.

The animal was forgotten until one day the cage door was found open and the animal gone. Apart from George's delivering a lecture to the staff on carelessness, we did nothing more about it.

The cage subsequently housed in succession various rats, a giant spider, and a small snake. These were gradually added to the collections, then the cage stood empty for several days. While strolling through the high forest with Bassi, we met proceeding towards us along a small path a very remarkable little animal. It was pale beige in colour, shaped like a chameleon, but graced with the smallest of tails and bearing an expression of the most exaggerated disdain due to a small, squashy, upturned "horn" on the end of its nose.

The animal was placed in the empty cage. By the time tea was over, it too had disappeared. This, we considered, was a bit too much. We carried the cage to the edge of the veranda and perched it on a table in order the better to conduct a search. At first we could find no living thing at all, but on turning the leaves and sticks out onto the table you can picture our surprise when out walked, not the disdainful one, but the original chameleon. This was now a vivid apple-green in colour and excessively thin, not only through lack of food, but also because it had made itself so in order the better to avoid detection.

We then scoured the cage in search of the small fellow and eventually found him wedged between the end of the boards which formed the roof, and some of the side ones which had come loose.

This all seems to be a most practical demonstration of the habits of chameleons. Everybody knows that they change their colour to harmonize with their surroundings, but nobody knows how extremely difficult it is to induce them to do this. They do alter their general tone and even their pattern to conform with whatever they may be seated upon, yet I am of the opinion that the greater part of their change is due to internal alterations of tone more akin to our emotions and feelings. These may be induced by such physical forces as heat, moisture, and light, but also by mere temper, boredom, fright, or depression. Swift flushes of anger are a common feature of the colour change of the octopus, which is in every way more adept at altering his hue than any chameleon. Most change is slow among reptiles; the quickest is due to internal emotions.

The chameleon which had returned from the limbo of departed spirits was an example of the commonest species in the locality, *Chameleon cristatus*. Its subsequent behaviour reduced us to a state of incoherence. First it tried to pretend that it was still missing. It clung to a small twig and, whenever we looked at it, switched round to the opposite side and deflated itself, becoming so thin that only its protuberant eyes were visible on either side of its slender concealment. Having finally realized that it had been detected, it stalked out at high speed and proceeded towards the open table. Here it slowed down, the epitome of all cautiousness. Instead of walking, it would tentatively put forth its right foot and its left hand and, when just about to place them on the ground, hurriedly withdraw them. This it would repeat several times in quick succession before taking the plunge and accomplishing a step. The result was that the whole animal swayed forwards and backwards, though remaining always parallel to and at the same height from the table. It might have been attempting the Viennese waltz except for the turn.

To add to the animal's general air of extreme suspicion, it kept rolling its eyeballs about so that sometimes it was watching George

THREE-HORNED CHAMELEON (Chameleon oweni)

ahead of it with one eye, and myself behind it with the other at the same time. This it could do because the eyes are covered with skin except for a tiny opening at the summit.

We took this strange creature out to the string on which the skulls were hung to dry. The place was, as I said before, a buzzing mass of flies and therefore a positive chameleon paradise.

"Little Alfred," as we named him, seemed to be of the same opinion. He simply sat and shot flies with his prodigious tongue until he was so swollen that—I regret to have to state—he delivered up his little ghost, which doubtless passed on to the limbo of even more fly-blown profusion.

The smaller nozzled chameleon (*Rhampholeon spectrum*) then held our attention. He was a creature of more sedate habits, in fact he preserved his expression and air of exalted disdain whatever we did to him. Moreover, he steadfastly refused to alter his colour beyond a slight lowering of tone under stress of excessive moisture. He is, I fear, an animal of interest to scientists only.

Greater surprises of a chameleon nature appeared later. There arrived a large fellow with two large, slightly upturned horns projecting from its snout. This animal went through a whole series of colour changes—so much so that we were unable to decide at all what his commoner coloration might be. He usually managed to arrange his outfits in wide bands or stripes encircling his body and tail. These were apparently light and dark alternately, but in certain phases, notably the green ones, the lighter patches were reduced to blobs or even spots.

The climax in chameleons came a few weeks later, when George unearthed a three-horned chameleon. This was even more erratic, flying off into pink, brown, or black furies, sulking in buff, yellow, or grey, feigning purity in immaculate white, or turning through a whole series of greens not only in envy but in harmony with sunlight. The horns projected from above each eye and from the tip of the snout.

We thus had chameleons without horns (*Chameleon cristatus*) but adorned with a crest—a lozenge-shaped depression covering the whole top of the head and edged with a line of small raised beads coloured pale blue—with one horn on the snout (*Rhampholeon spectrum*), with two horns (*Chameleon montium*), and with three horns (*Chameleon oweni*). They are all weird, spectre-like animals with vile tempers and strange ways.

A considerable amount of our time in Africa during this expedition was devoted to the collection of frogs, as I have already mentioned. This doubtless sounds quite crazy; you may well ask what on earth might be the use of making such a collection. Everybody who has spent any of his youthful time in the country probably collected tadpoles and watched them grow and subsequently die in a small glass vessel. This may have seemed interesting at the time, but when regarded from a more adult point of view, it becomes associated in the mind with all forms of bug-hunting and is therefore relegated to the activities of old, bearded gentlemen in strange suitings. When thought of apart from such activities, frogs are just slimy creatures that live in ditches, and there the matter ends.

The activities of frog collectors and frog experts have nevertheless resulted in the discovery of many very remarkable facts that have a more than merely incidental economic importance. The full significance of their findings has not yet been sufficiently realized, however, partly because these collectors are one of the lesser groups of practical scientists, but more especially on account of the monopoly held by entomologists in the field of economic zoology. Pestologists—which does mean the people who study pests—are mostly buried deeply in a sea of insects of various kinds or are badly "rat-bitten," as somebody once appropriately remarked. They study animals that are harmful to man and his crops.

Frogs are not harmful; they are very definitely beneficial. This fact has never been realized. A very shrewd observer, Mr. H. B. Cott, who has worked and experimented with the food eaten by frogs and upon the density of frog populations in areas of given size, has propounded some astonishing facts concerning the numbers and bulk of insects eaten by frogs. Analysis of these statistics shows that most if not all the insects that pestologists wish to exterminate are eaten by frogs, provided they are present. Coupling these findings with the results that have emerged from all our voluminous data recorded in the field—which show that the whole countryside is parcelled out among a great variety of frogs, each of which clings to its own particular habitat—one arrives at a remarkable conclusion.

This is that frogs are one of the great natural controls against insect pests. When man comes along and upsets the vegetation of an area—particularly in the tropics—by clearing away trees, draining swamps, etc., he destroys the habitats of many frogs, which therefore become exterminated. Insects which have before been consumed literally by the ton on every acre of land find themselves free from their natural enemies and so multiply to an unprecedented extent.

Take for instance the mosquitoes. They breed and spend the earlier part of their lives in the water. In this water under natural conditions are countless frogs such as the *Rana occipitalis*, which feed upon the mosquito larvæ, more especially in their youth. If the shade necessary to the *Rana occipitalis* be removed, the frogs die out and the mosquitoes get going. As a result, malaria and yellow fever do likewise, unless man goes to the trouble and expense of discovering every little bit of standing water and pouring oil upon it. This may be very clever of him, but if he could devise some way of encouraging his frogs, he need not trouble.

Supposing the tea-planters of India and Ceylon encouraged their local frog populations; imagine the difference in their bushes growing on the slopes around!

Such facts as the above only become apparent when one returns home and can examine all one's collections together in the light of the recorded data. In the field, one is concerned with getting as many frogs of as many different kinds as possible. This, in itself, led us to the discovery of a number of extraordinary things which have a more purely zoological interest.

Connected with grass wherever it occurred—except the peculiar mountain grass—were frogs of a very unusual form. These we called "bullet-frogs" for lack of an inclusive title. Their bodies were spindle-shaped and their hind legs of prodigious length, presumably to aid them in leaping over and through the dense grass stems. They were exceedingly numerous, particularly in the younger stages, when the whole animal is about an inch to two inches in length.

There were grass-fields without soil in the dense forest near Mamfe. Patches of open rock upon these were raised by the heat of the sun's rays at midday to great temperatures. Eggs placed upon them could be fried. In little rills about three inches wide lodged in cracks through these rock slabs these bullet-frogs were breeding. The spawn was in water as hot as normal bath water, the tiny baby frogs hopping about on a rock surface that one could not touch. The mechanism of animals is beyond understanding.

In this respect it is equally impossible to explain the following.

Our twelve Munchi carriers gradually turned into part-time collectors. This occurred because they were always with us and we got to know them all well, and therefore slowly absorbed them into our organization. They became guardians of us all! George had offered considerable sums for more clawed toads. The Munchis had been successful in finding them in large numbers, thereby greatly augmenting their accounts with us. When the price of clawed toads fell to an uneconomic level, the Munchis turned their attention to other frogs in the hope of finding a new market and an outlet for our frozen assets, which to them probably appeared to be unlimited.

In this they were completely successful. They discovered that banana trees housed small tree frogs, which they brought to the harassed George by the handful. One species, of which we received countless examples, delights in the name of *Hyperolius sordidus*. *Sordidus*, mark you!

This animal was obviously named in the first place by some venerable housed in a museum far from Africa and confronted by the frog in a pickled condition. The only other possibility is that he may have been somewhat of a biological humorist and chose a name that was deliberately as far removed from the truth as possible. The frog in a pickled condition is indeed sordid, but in life it surpasses all comprehension and any description. Though its shape is normal enough, the colouring varies so greatly that one cannot really believe one is dealing with only one species until all the intermediary forms are brought in.

The only constant colouring is that of the feet and hands, or rather their under surfaces and inner sides. These are cherry-red, yet even here we found an exception—one female had the vivid cherry replaced by orange. While the commonest type for both sexes was vivid green above and saffron-yellow beneath, one female was metallic blue above and the males varied above from metallic gold, fawn, brown with black markings surrounded by a white line, olive to pinkish mauve, and on the underside from pure white to a variety of mauve mottlings on yellow, brown flecks on white, and brown marblings. Their backs might also be any combination of these colours with brown spots, flecks, and dapples. The whole thing seemed fantastic.

It was not until one day when sitting with a gun waiting for squirrels that I noticed a banana tree in flower and perceived that all the colours found among this *Hyperolius* are present on the tree in about similar proportions. The vivid green is the usual colour of the leaves. The dead leaves are golden, the dried portions various browns. Where the plant is infected with fungi and other plant parasites, it is speckled with brown, spotted or flecked. Lastly, the most outstanding observation was that the flowers are great purple objects with mauvish tips and dark metallic blue petioles. Here, then, are all the colours for the frog to dress itself in if it wishes to adopt a perfect camouflage.

Perhaps the most extraordinary frog of all that we met in the field was a very dingy-looking beast called *Hemisus marmoratum*. Science definitely owes you an apology for the name—it is neuter. This, however, is not all.

Hemisus is small and rotund, with short legs and a sharp-pointed snout. It digs and is in fact completely subterranean. We found it in sluggish streams and still, very muddy ponds, because it was the time of its breeding season. When these frogs were held in the hand, they took fright and, presumably for reasons of protection or merely to show their consternation, blew themselves up to a prodigious extent in comparison with their original size. Once blown, they remained so, deflating only by degrees. The act of deflation seemed to be a great effort.

When we wished to make the animals blow up, we beat them lightly with a small grass stem, to which they responded readily, with the result that in a few days they set to work with vigour at the first touch of the grass.

These frogs are greatly venerated by the local Africans for purposes connected with the fertility ju-ju cult. How they enter into this it was difficult to ascertain, but apparently they are eaten. The effect is supposed to be that their outstanding egg-laying performances are transferred from them to the human recipient.

"Sir, the chief come with other chief."

We were in a new locality and had a new interpreter as the "sir" in place of "master" may indicate. He was a court messenger and we were now in Nigerian territory, where discipline and unsurpassable salutes are the order of the day.

"Show them in," I answered. I wanted to see the chief because I liked him, but I could not help feeling all the time some queer sadness deep down inside. Had it been old Ekumaw, the effect of this announcement would have been very different.

The court messenger had not exaggerated; what is more, there were indeed other chiefs, to the number of approximately a score. We were living in a large native house; in order to get them all in, every available bench and chair had to be produced. They all brought us a "dash," and in order to avoid dissension they had decided upon yams as a suitable present. These were placed on the ground just inside the door. As the names of the donors were called out, the pile rose and rose until it formed a stack of very considerable dimensions. I marked the village of each chief on a map with the aid of a red pencil as far as that was possible, and tried to memorize their faces. And what magnificent faces they were!

When they were all in, the house was entirely filled. There were two doors opposite each other on either side of the house; between these there stretched a passage through the humanity. To one side sat the chiefs in a semicircle with the paramount chief of the district in the centre. Behind them stood their variegated and gorgeously apparelled retainers. On the other, we sat on three sides of a table, myself in the centre, George on my right hand, and the Duke on my left. Behind us and to either side was ranged our personal staff, that is to say, the skinners, who had clad themselves in their best and only remaining clean clothes. In the bare channel between stood the court messenger in his dark-blue uniform with red sash, and facing him a man whose clothes outshone everybody's but my own. His exact function we never determined, but he must have been in the nature of an interpreter from one African language to another.

The door, windows, and every other bit of space were bulging with humanity.

We had been caught unawares by the arrival of all this pomp. George was, as usual, immaculately dressed in Palm Beach trousers and spotless shirt, and the Duke was likewise fully clad, looking brawny and rather English in khaki shirt. I regret to have to state that I was clad in a manner that would most certainly be construed by any builder of our great Empire as in every way detrimental to the prestige of the white man. Such an all-important animal is expected to retain a dignified bearing in all circumstances.

I was clad in a pair of rose-pink artificial silk pyjamas of rather staggering design, which means ultra-bell-bottomed trousers and a top built somewhat like a polo vest. I have remarked that we all wore beards; my hair was, however, so long that I had a béret perched on my head to keep it in place. I had no time to change, because the flood of humanity was upon us before we could move. So there I sat like a glowing April blossom before the penetrating gaze of a score of extremely dignified and conventional African chiefs. I feared the worst.

Silence fell on the assembled company. The court messenger stepped forward to speak.

"The big chief brings greetings," he announced. "All other chief feel the same and hope you like their country."

"Tell the chief and chiefs," I answered, "that we do like his country, and thank them very much indeed for their kind presents."

This was duly interpreted amid murmurs of assent. I always watch the faces of Africans to whom a message of mine is being delivered by an interpreter to see whether the effect is the correct one, though the Negro is the most inscrutable of all races—far more so than any Chinese. On this occasion I was somewhat disturbed to notice that several of the more mask-like faces were staring at me with an intensity that was really quite frightening.

There then followed a palaver of mutual compliments, details of crops, and general agreement between both parties over the vexed question of Christianity, the bane of present-day Africa. The sub-chiefs continued to stare at me in eerie silence. They were then asked by their "King" to make individual comments on the palaver to date. The court messenger turned to one end of the circle and addressed a very old gentleman clad in many yards of batik. There was a pause while the old fellow collected himself, then he spoke to the interpreter.

"The chief say," the court messenger relayed to me, "he think your suit very fine."

He then turned to the next.

"The chief say," came the reply, "the head master's clothes very fine."

The old head chief beamed upon his council. The court messenger turned to the next. This one was ready and burst into a positive tirade in his own tongue. The interpreter began to giggle respectfully. He then turned to me.

"The chief say, why for, man no fit buy cloth in Africa like the master have for him suit? If the white man store by the river buy their palm-oil, why for they only sell bad ugly cloth?"

Economics were a difficult problem, but I was so gratified at the outcome of what I had considered a serious *faux pas*, that I am afraid I let the matter drift on. They one and all admired my rosy pyjamas, each making it an excuse for an ugly attack upon the United Africa Company's methods. It was about economics that they had come to call, moreover.

Eventually we came to the core of the palaver. It appeared that before the depression and before the U.A.C.—as it is called—had gained a monopoly of the West African trade, these people received twelve shillings and sixpence for a drum of raw palm-oil, whereas they are now receiving about ninepence. Though this is not a matter of life and death to them, as it would be to unstable communities like our own, it annoys them greatly. They feel they are being "done."

The head chief pointed out that practically all the ninepence is absorbed by the cost of transporting the commodity to the great river. Had we any ideas, he wanted to know, as to any cheaper way of getting it there? He added that there was a small river near by, which, it had been suggested, might be canalized. The chiefs had come together, he added, to ask us if we could show them what to do and give some idea of the cost.

After explaining that we had come for animals, I mentioned that we were lucky enough to have an engineer in our midst. The Duke took his bow and we arranged to make an expedition to inspect the river if the chief would supply canoes and competent people to record whatever the Duke might say. The trip was to take place next day. With great exchange of compliments, playing of the gramophone, and fingering of my pyjamas they all went away. We were left to proceed with the work.

Next day we pushed the poor Duke off at crack of dawn. He was paddled down the river, found that a lot of rock-blasting and lock-building would be necessary, and returned home by easy stages, doing a little collecting on the way. This was possible because his special department was the invertebrates, which can be found almost everywhere and kept in small tubes and bottles.

He reached home after dark, a weary man, and flopped down at his place at the table. We had a talk about the canal, then dinner arrived. After this we repaired to work again. Complete silence reigned.

Pausing for a moment, I looked across at the handful of little glass tubes that the Duke had produced from his collecting bag and stood on the table. Under the bright lamp the little animals could be seen scrambling about in them. First I looked casually, then I looked harder, and finally my eyes nearly popped out of my head.

"Duke," I said, controlling myself with an effort, "what have you got in that tube?"

"Oh, some small spiders, I think."

"Are you quite sure?"

"Yes, look," he said, tipping the tube towards me so that it rolled across the table. I gave it one more glance.

"Do you realize what is in here?" I asked him.

"No," he replied, but something in my tone must have aroused his suspicion.

"Give me the dish, quick."

"What is it?" George came into the fray.

"This imbecile, this cretin, this Superlative Worm has been harbouring a *Podogona* and doesn't honestly seem to realize it."

They both craned forward as a small leggy creature about the size of one's little finger nail stalked out of the tube into the dish.

It was a *Podogona*.

So ended the last of our quests. After months of unending and untiring search in every kind of soil, in rotten logs, in hollow trees and live trees, in mud and even below the water level of rivers, we had stumbled across the most priceless of all our prizes. A year before, almost to a day, I had been asked to try and find some of these obscure tick-like animals, of which only a handful of specimens were in existence in all the museums and collections of the world. There are a few species known from West Africa and South America, but each species was represented by only one or two specimens. Now we had another.

I gave out a roar, which must have awakened the whole village. At any rate the whole staff came tumbling into the house.

"Look, look!" I yelled, holding the dish aloft. "The new master has found a *Podogona*."

And despite the strange complicated name, everybody knew just what had happened because we had talked of this animal and pored over drawings of it the whole time we had been in Africa.

"Call the Munchis," I said.

"Now listen, everybody, tomorrow you all go with the new master and lie on your stomachs for bush and don't come back until you have all got plenty, plenty of these small beef. All man get dash now and each man more dash tomorrow according to the number of this beef he find. If anybody come back without any he is fired, sacked, OUT!"

Believe me, we got podogona in plenty, five hundred of them. They were living and breeding beneath the leaf mould on a bit of old farmed land. We got the big dark-brown adults and the immature red ones. We found a female carrying a single translucent pink egg and a baby with only three pairs of legs, which showed that it was still in a very early stage of development. We pickled all but twenty which we kept alive in a biscuit tin, though we didn't know what they ate. They arrived back in England and lived there for a year, but still nobody ever discovered what they ate. They were taken to a meeting of the Royal Society; they were introduced to His Grace the Archbishop of Canterbury at a meeting of the trustees of the Natural History Museum; they have been poked and peered at by scientists of all nations; nobody has yet succeeded in cutting a dead one into sections for microscopical investigation. Their skin is so hard that it blunts any known knife. They are indeed stubborn creatures.

Travelling up to London in the train after landing at Plymouth, I had these precious beasts in their dirty tin by my side. The ways of bug-hunters are indeed strange, but full of thrills and peculiar pleasures. We were back again with everything we had set out for, and countless other valuable animals besides.

"Master, man bring beef."

The old familiar call came for the I-don't-know-how-many-thousandth time.

"Ben," I called without even looking up, "bring them in."

The taciturn Ben disappeared without; there was a prolonged palaver. Then he reappeared and announced that neither the man nor the beef "agreed to enter." He added that in his opinion the man was slightly mad and asked whether I would come out to give a ruling on the matter. I went out.

There I found a sulky-looking individual clasping two small bags. He spoke no known language and seemed to be deaf. I made ran-

RED AND BLACK SNAKE

dom signs at him and attempted to take the bags, but he jumped back and made most threatening passes with his hands. We were checkmated.

The court messenger was called. He had been "dashed" as a result of the discovery of the podogona for no other reason than that he happened to appear when I was still in the grip of hilarity and excitement. He came at the double. He apparently understood the dull gentleman and reported to us that he brought two wild and terrible animals.

"Let him show them then, and we go talker-talker price."

He thereupon opened one bag and tipped out a small kitten with bright-blue eyes. I have a partiality for cats and this looked like a very nice one. I stooped down to pick it up.

Before I touched it, luckily, it waltzed about and crouched, snarling, spitting, and baring its teeth at me with a most fearsome expression. The court messenger's observation that it was a wild cat need not have been made. It was a youthful member of a race of cats (*Felis ocreata*) found in these jungles. There is some doubt as to whether they are the descendants of semi-domesticated cats that have gone wild or a true wild race from which the local semi-domesticated cat had originated. We shot two later on, high up in the forest trees. Both these and all others that we saw had pale-blue eyes, whereas the village cats varied as greatly in this respect as our own tame cats. The difference of temperament between the wild and domesticated varieties is most exceptional; I should imagine that the true bush ones are as untamable as our Scottish wild cat.

The cat is supposed to have been tamed in the earliest days of civilization in Egypt. The local wild cat (*Felis ocreata*) of that country by this theory was employed as a rat-catcher, and from there spread all over the world, sometimes intermingling with other wild cats like our Scotch *Felis cattus* and producing new sub-races. It is however quite probable that the domestication of wild cats has taken place independently in several parts of the world at different times. *Felis ocreata* in West Africa is one of them.

Up to this point the man had fooled us. He now tipped out the other bag without further warning. This gave us a real jolt.

On the ground at our feet lay a very striking snake. I mean striking in more senses than one: first, in colour, for it was striped, not transversely, but longitudinally with black and bright vermilion, from the tip of its snout to the extremity of its tail; secondly, it struck in a more literal way squarely and fairly at its owner, who happened to be retrieving his bag. The reptile's long fangs fastened on the man's thumb.

The strange fellow uttered a grunt and jumped back swinging his hand up to throw off the snake, but this was so firmly attached that it left the ground completely and fell over my own and Ben's arms. We both jumped with a yell. The snake fell to the ground. Faugi and Bassi than appeared and formed a ring round it. The snake kept making darts at everybody.

I meanwhile grabbed the man and rushed him inside. I inquired of the court messenger whether the animal was deadly. He replied that it was, but that the man wouldn't die. While I dashed about getting instruments and medicines, I asked him why and he replied: "Because you will see that he doesn't." This was disturbing. Although Africans have an idea that all reptile bites are deadly, the coloration of the snake left little doubt in my mind that it had possibilities, to say the least.

The man meanwhile had been standing silently holding his wrist. I then cut a very considerable piece of his thumb off and rubbed raw permanganate of potash crystals into the wound. This sounds easy enough, but you have no idea how tough the skin on an African's hand can be. With a razor-sharp scalpel I had to dig with all my might. The man never said a word or uttered a sound until his hand had been well squeezed and bandaged. Then he delivered a short peroration in his own strange tongue.

The court messenger turned to me.

"The man want to know if you want the beef," he said. "And if so, how much you go give for each?"

I was so taken aback at his coolness that I consulted the little price book we had compiled as a result of all our purchasing of animals, and named the prices that I was willing to give. The man spoke again very briefly.

"The man say he agree," said the interpreter.

I paid out the money. The man picked it up, put his little bags in his belt, and marched out of the house, leaving the two animals spitting their respective furies on the doorstep.

"Hi, ask him where he's going," I said. "He may die yet from that snake bite."

"The man he go for him country," came the astonishing reply.

Ekuri, on the return journey from the podogona country, was our last stop in the real Africa. From there we passed down river to Calabar and the semi-domesticated and ultra-suburban rankness of the white man's Africa.

That awful morning in Ekuri will never be blotted out of my memory, and I think it will always remain in the minds of some thirty other people, scattered now heaven knows where about this globe.

The dawn was misty, as all African dawns seem to be. I had managed to get away alone. The only sounds were those indescribable and varied noises made by the grey parrots which flew about above the mists on their way to their feeding grounds, whistling, shouting, shrieking, and talking to each other. It was the last African palaver at which I was privileged to be present. The parrots spoke a tongue unknown to me, yet they spoke with a spirit that I knew well and with which I felt completely in unison.

Slowly the mists rose, revealing tall billowing greenery and feathery palms. As the sun penetrated to the earth, all manner of birds and beasts began to stir.

When one is wretchedly miserable and sentimental, everything takes on a symbolic air, but on this occasion I truly believe there was some dreadful design in what I saw.

There stood before me three beautiful palm trees—or rather what remained of three feathery perfections. They were festooned with the spherical pendent nests of the dread weaver birds, who screeched and twittered about them. Almost every shred of green leaf had been stripped from the palms. These busy, active birds in their bright-orange ruffs with their drab, dingy women-folk seemed to me to be symbols. The beautiful verdant trees were, like Africa, stripped and peeled of their green glory by the activities of beastly busy creatures relying on their numbers and building their ugly nests all over the place. Every nest like every other, just like the drab houses and grim workshops of the dull Europeans who have colonized Africa—as they call it—in order the better to raise their unwanted progeny.

As the mists left the ground, other symbols appeared. A number of black and white crows hopped about searching for small food. In them I found a counterpart of such poor souls as ourselves, for I think I may safely include George and the Duke in this simile.

Just as the crows are neither black nor white but resemble crows in shape, so were we neither wholly black nor white in spirit. The poor birds live between the primeval forests and the cleared lands of the colonizer, pleased in some respects at the new and great supply of food brought by the latter, but for ever mourning the disappearance of the former. Our spirits, too, seemed blotched like the crows'; partly realizing the benefits of this infernal civilization, and partly filled with a sorrow amounting almost to misery at the disappearance of the beautiful wild.

I had to tear myself away to go through the awful performance of taking leave of the Munchis. We went down to the little store together in a silent knot. I found them each a shirt and a bale of cloth, because that was what they had chosen as a parting present. We stood before our sealed-up bales and shook hands. Then a sad little line passed out into the forest. I still heard their sobbing when they were out of sight.

The boat came; we piled aboard with all our gear.

We turned in silence to gaze at our last camping ground. As the whistle blew its dismal, solitary wail, a group of white birds rose from the side of the water and planed away across the grass. One tried to land on the remains of our camp table. It missed, as egrets always do. Hurtling against a fence, it closed its wings and remained wobbling drunkenly back and forth. A dazzlingly white bird stood silhouetted against the solemn greenery of the forest.